PROUDHEARTED PIONEERS . . .

From the homestead land rushes of Indian Territory and the struggles for the statehood of Oklahoma, to the eve of World War II, comes this enthralling multi-generational epic of a courageous family who created a bold heritage out of the barren earth.

Whitney Stine, author of the best-selling *Mother Goddam,* the screen biography of Bette Davis, *Fifty Years of Photographing Hollywood: The Hurrell Style,* and, most recently for Pinnacle Books, a dazzling show business saga, *Stardust,* now returns to his roots as he chronicles the fascinating story of the Cherokee Strip and the people who challenged the prairie wilderness that became the great state of Oklahoma. Born in Garber, Oklahoma, in 1930, Stine brings an authenticity to this work that is without peer—a personal tribute from a native son.

Also by Whitney Stine:

Stardust

THE OKLAHOMANS

WHITNEY STINE

PINNACLE BOOKS   LOS ANGELES

This is a work of fiction. All of the main characters and events portrayed in this book are fictional. In some instances, however, the names of real people, without whom no history could be told, have been used to authenticate the storyline.

THE OKLAHOMANS

Copyright © 1980 by Whitney Stine

An original Pinnacle Books edition, published for the first time anywhere.

First printing, August 1980

ISBN: 0-523-40633-9

Cover illustration by Norm Eastman

Printed in the United States of America

PINNACLE BOOKS, INC.
2029 Century Park East
Los Angeles, California 90067

To my family . . .
some of whom lived some of this. . . .

The Oklahomans

PART ONE

The Heritage

1

The Arrangement

A volley of shots rang out over the prairie.

Luke Heron stood upright for one long moment, then with his blond head thrust back at an odd angle, he fell backward and lay sprawling in the thick, red dust. He felt no immediate pain, only a strange and terrifying numbness. His senses sharpened as he looked up into the pale, buttermilk sky, tinged with long, red plumes from the fires that still flared over the range.

It seemed that he could hear the giant, flapping wings of the huge, evil bird that circled lazily above. Time stood still. During the interminable period before his wife, Letty, knelt beside him and took his head in her lap, the last hours came back to him with extraordinary clarity.

He sat easily in the saddle.

The fast cow pony—a newly-purchased roan—tensed under him, sensing the energy emanating from the strong legs that hugged his lean flanks. Horse and rider were one. Luke glanced behind him and smiled at his wife Letty, who was seated in the buckboard with his brother Edward and Edward's wife, Priscilla.

Letty was a beautiful woman, blonde, with pale skin and electric blue eyes that contrasted with Priscilla's dark hair and olive complexion. Luke and Edward's mother, Lavenia, often said that Edward resembled a Viking warrior and was far more handsome than his somewhat wiry brother.

Luke glanced uneasily to either side at the irregular

1

lineup of buggies, carriages, buckboards, covered wagons, traps, sulkies, spring wagons, and the hundreds of lone riders like himself—all gathered in a loose formation along the south border of Indian Territory near Hennessey, eighteen miles below Enid, which lay in the middle of the Cherokee Strip above the Oklahoma Territory.

It was September 16, 1893.

To the right lay the tracks of the Chicago, Rock Island and Pacific Railroad. The cattle cars jammed with hundreds of would-be settlers, and the steaming locomotive also awaited the first cavalry carbine shot that would signal the start of The Run.

Edward, who could manage a team of horses with great dexterity, would follow Luke, who wore a bright red shirt. If one brother failed to stake a claim, they had agreed to equally share the 160-acre government allotment.

Luke looked at his timepiece. The Run was to begin at noon: five minutes more! Suddenly, far down the line, the retort of a pistol was heard and the formation broke. A soldier yelled, "Stop! Stop!"—the official shot was yet to come—but his cries were lost in the terrible din of pounding hooves and creaking vehicles. The cattle car passengers shouted, "Get movin'," "Come on, Iron Horse," and "Let's go!", but to their consternation the train did not move, the engineer having decided to wait for the official shot.

Amid billowing clouds of gray dust, Luke kept pace with the other riders, then shot ahead as the little roan responded to the pressure of his feet in the stirrups.

Barely three miles had been covered when some of the fast Kentucky race horses began to play out, forcing their eager young riders to take land nearby, thereby forfeiting dreams of securing a townsite in Enid.

Horrific accidents were taking place all around. Occasionally, a wagon would bounce off a prairie dog hole and plummet to the ground, accompanied by the tortured whinny of a horse, the sharp cry of a man, the piercing scream of a woman, and once, the pitiful wail of a baby. Carriage wheels crashed into each other as if in combat, and men were thrown headlong over teams

2

of horses, their traps rolling crazily in a jagged line over the flat land.

To the left of Luke, a huge fat man, riding a tiny, exhausted mustang, was thrown clear of the stampede and landed in a clump of wild blackberry canes. Stunned, he stumbled to his feet, his clothing covered with bloody stickers and berry stains and, glancing down at his dead horse, philosophically staked his claim. Luke waved to the man, who waved back.

Luke glanced back several times. Pride swelled through his chest. Edward, Letty, and Priscilla were not far behind. His brother, eyes bright and flashing, was truly in his element: he stood, perfectly balanced, reins firmly in hand, expertly guiding the team. His body was tensed with a supreme, orgasmic excitement. Perhaps, reflected Luke, never again would Edward be in such supreme control of all senses, ready to meet challenges that required split-second timing as he maneuvered the horses in the greatest race of all.

Now that others in The Run were falling behind, Edward slowed down the buckboard, but still kept Luke in sight. They crossed the Chisholm Trail pounded by the hooves of countless head of cattle that made the 1,000-mile run from Texas to Abilene. Their nostrils were filled with the smells of smothering, powdered earth and pulverized cow dung left over from the old cattle drives. The dark, serpentine cloud of choking dust that rose fifty feet in the air would inform the men at the Land Office in Enid that the settlers were approaching en masse.

Up ahead, beside Luke, a woman in a faded calico dress, brunette braids wrapped in a scarf, was strapped side saddle to a small mustang. She wore soft kid boots trimmed with polished boar skin, obviously the work of some foreign bootmaker. The Bohemian woman, handling her horse skillfully, was soon joined by a Negro riding an enormous Appaloosa. The woman's eyes, gleaming lights in a sunburned face, opened her mouth in a triumphant grimace, and dangerously sped ahead of him. Furiously, the Negro bit down hard on a piece of chewing tobacco; an experienced saddle tramp, he

3

had obviously never before been bested by a woman.

Luke figured that Enid must be near, but unlike many of his companions in the race, he was not interested in claiming a townsite. In the back of his mind he saw *his* farm, a wide expanse of prairie, with a creek, a stand of timber, and a slight incline where a house could be built.

Reaching the old stagecoach station that once marked the Skeleton Ranch, Luke knew that it was time to veer off the trail. He started working his way over to the right side, carefully crossing the path of a few stragglers. He came to a slight, rolling hill and galloped down to a creek where he fed and watered the horse. Then he walked up the hill to look at the thundering horde riding past, the dust cloud following them like a plague of locusts. He dared not tarry further, yet he must be sure that Edward had seen him leave the trail. He took off his red shirt and waved it over his head. Half a mile back, he saw the Heron buckboard heading toward him. Bless Letty's sharp navigator-eyes!

He mounted once more, and his gaze swept the horizon where the fire still blazed. The U.S. Cavalry had set fire to the prairie grass so that the settlers could find the sandstone markers that the surveyors had put down. Since it was impossible to ride into the spreading flames, he must choose land farther from the railroad than he wished. Ready transportation of cattle would be the key to the future. Cursing, he pulled the reins of the pony to the right.

Soon, he forded a clear bright stream filled with catfish. Here and there, a settler, having found a sandstone marker that identified each quarter section of land, was staking a claim. Luke continued to follow the creek. A half hour later, he came to a grove of giant oaks that kept company with several hedge-apple trees.

Luke crossed the creek at a low point and rode along a long strip of rich, lush bottom land. No other person was within sight. To the far right, three graceful rolling hills created a scene of tranquility and beauty. He was overcome with a feeling of déjà vu. His eyes teared. He

4

knew this land, now outlined by the fires that licked the horizon. He was home at last.

Hurriedly, he found a marker and dismounted, gently patting the roan's flanks, which were covered with thick, pungent sweat. A grayish foam covered the mouth and lips of the animal that looked as if spread with shaving cream. Laughing, Luke loosened the bridle and slipped the bit from between the horse's yellow teeth. The foam now turned pink.

"Sorry, old fellow," he said, "but you've done your work well." The bit had chafed only an inch of the tender mouth flesh. A bit of salve would soon heal the wound. The roan snorted, shooting froth in all directions as Luke walked him up and down to cool him off. The animal began to shiver in the prairie wind, and Luke covered his back and flanks with an old Confederate army blanket. He tied the reins to a shrub, then with the heel of his boot drove a claim stake into the rich, red earth.

Sighing contentedly, Luke stretched and unloosened his huge steel belt buckle. He paced a quarter mile north from the marker, found the next stone, then tore a bit of cloth from his shirttail to identify his land. Then he paced the rest of the claim, placing two additional bits of red material at the boundaries.

Then he paused, experiencing a rare feeling of complete contentment. Life was good; God was good; the land was good. It was a private moment. He made his way to the top of the small incline where his house would eventually stand. He placed his shirt as far up as he could reach on the oak where his family could not fail to notice the signal.

He was about to pick a ripe wild sand plum, when he turned and stared in utter disbelief at a small canvas tent raised against the sky! He knew at a glance that the invader had set up camp the night before, because there was the remains of a small fire and several cooking vessels were spread about. *A Sooner!*

"Hallo!" Luke cried, his voice sounding hollow and somehow grotesque in the pastoral surroundings. A red-haired man with a beard staggered from the tent, ob-

5

viously having been aroused from a deep slumber. "You're on my property," Luke said evenly.

"Cain't see how that can be," the man replied, steely-eyed. "Seein' as how I was cher furst. I think it's t'other way 'round!" He laughed suddenly. His pale, parched lips opened and a thick squirt of tobacco juice landed squarely at Luke's feet. The stranger's small, pig eyes gleamed out of a freckled, suntanned face. Luke wished that he had a gun, but he and the other settlers in The Run had left their firearms at the registry offices that dotted the borders of the Cherokee Strip.

"I'll give you fifteen minutes to clear your gear off my land," Luke said, keeping his voice low.

"Ain't goin' nowhere except to Enid to register my claim," the man replied with a sneer. "And, even if we both start out now, I'll beat you to the Land Office. I got a fresh horse—your'n is tuckered out."

Luke doubled up his fist and lunged at the stranger, whose reflexes sprang into action. The Winchester, which had been dangling behind his right leg, seemed to have a life of its own. He fired from the waist. Luke clutched his left side in anguish. The man fired again, and again, waiting for him to fall.

As if in slow motion, while Luke was falling backward, the man pumped out his last shot, which struck Luke's belt buckle, ricocheted back, and hit the startled man in the chest. They looked at each other in surprise. As they both fell, Luke managed a grimace that he thought was a smile.

Luke lay on his back in the hot sun, staring at the sky. He had the strange feeling that if he closed his eyes for one moment, all life would go out of his body. He felt numb. As the afternoon wore on, he seemed to be floating a few inches above the hot, red earth. The wispy clouds above, tinged with red from the fires, were propelled along by a high wind. He began to discern shapes—a horseless rider, a cloaked minister, a dancing faun, an unclothed woman. The female form took another shape—the bust widened, the waist thinned, the hips grew more pronounced. Waist-long hair that resembled Letty's when she combed it out at night, flew

6

out in several directions, as the shape in the sky assumed erotic poses: small breasts enlarged, then appeared to be suspended above him. Perhaps, if he concentrated long enough, he could experience, once more, the marvelous feeling of complete release that he often achieved with Letty . . .

Edward expertly maneuvered the buckboard between a phaeton driven by a man wearing a Confederate cap, and a covered wagon with wobbly wheels with a widow at the reins. It was time to leave the other would-be settlers and follow Luke. If he lost him now . . .

"Look!" Letty cried, pointing to the east. A good two miles away, a tiny sliver of red flapped against a tree. "It's Luke's shirt!"

Edward laughed with relief and turned the horses east. In the distance, a covered wagon and a lone horseman were moving swiftly along. "We've got to hurry," Edward exclaimed. "I want the claim next to Luke's."

He urged the tired horses quickly along in soothing monosyllables. He dared not stop to sponge off their foamy mouths. Only the gentle sounds of his voice kept them going. A few hundred yards from the red patch of Luke's shirt, he halted the horses. "This place will do as good as any," he said. "What do you think, Priscilla?"

She looked around with distaste at the dried prairie grass and the feeble stream of water that coursed along the creek bed. Not a wild flower in sight. "It all looks the same to me," she replied wearily. "It's all so depressing!"

Edward gave her a sharp look. "If it's good enough for Luke, it's good enough for us," he reprimanded. "Now, let's find those markers before the others get here!" His eyes anxiously searched the horizon. The covered wagon was no more than a mile away.

He tied the horses to a tree, then ordered, "Fan out and find those markers!" He looked back at the covered wagon, which was approaching quickly, the horses obviously enjoying a second wind. He took a stake from the back of the buckboard and drove it triumphantly into the ground with a ball peen hammer. He unhitched the horses and was cooling them down when the wagon lumbered up the incline.

A tall man in a brown, sweat-stained ten gallon hat with leathery skin to match swung down from the seat, handing the reins to an older man. "Here, Poppa," he drawled. He stretched his legs and flexed his hands. "I'm plumb wore out." He cleared his throat, took a bandanna from his back pocket, and wiped his sooty face. "Bet I look like a nigger with all this dirt," he exclaimed and held out his hand. "Howdy, my name's John Dice." His voice was soft with the twang of Texas. "But everybody calls me Jaundice." His green eyes sparked. "Guess we're gonna be neighbors, 'cause I'm plannin' to take the next piece over. Should be rich soil, with that little crick meanderin' all over the place."

"I'm Edward Heron. That's my wife, Priscilla, coming up the grade, and the lady with the sunbonnet is my sister-in-law, Letty." He saw a rider coming up fast. "If I were you, Jaundice, I wouldn't even stop to water the horses until you've marked off your land."

John Dice looked up. "I see what you mean. Company's comin'!" He paused. "I'll be comin' back this way. Maybe we's can all go into Enid together to register our claims."

"Fine," Edward replied, "but right now I've got to find my brother."

Luke's face was now partially shaded by the chinaberry tree that stood by the stream. His throat was dry with dust; breathing was difficult. If he could only reach the cool water of the creek—but he was paralyzed. His eyes, still wide open, were slightly glazed and he could no longer hear the flapping of the bird's wings or the tiny, hard fruit of the chinaberry tree hitting together in the wind. From the silence, he knew that he had also turned deaf.

Suddenly, Luke sensed a certain presence that was missing before. He smelled the soft odor of tuberoses and relaxed—it was Letty's scent. Her face so winsome, so beautiful, was in his line of vision now. Her golden hair was pulled back from her wide forehead, shadowed

8

by the sunbonnet. He tried to smile. His cracked lips formed the words, I love you.

As she cradled his head in her lap, her tears fell on his numbed face, making huge splashes on his dust-covered skin. "I love you, too, Luke," she answered.

She gazed down at his face; he was staring uncomprehendingly. There was a look of wonder on his face, as if he had been surprised by death.

Edward drew Priscilla to his side. Would he ever forget the sight of Letty holding his dead brother's broken, bleeding body? His eyes brimmed with tears. Their plans of building an empire on the prairie, discussed so long ago back in Minneapolis, would never come about now. Several paces to the right lay the body of the red-haired stranger, a red splash over his heart. Luke had died for his land and, somehow, his memory must be perpetuated.

John Dice swung down from the wagon, shadowed by his sweat-stained ten-gallon hat, his weatherbeaten face furrowed with concern. "See you got bad problems," he said, looking at the two bodies in the red dust. "Do ya know what happened?"

Edward shook his head slowly. "It appears that Luke discovered a claim jumper. There was a fight and he shot Luke."

"Then Luke shot *him*!"

Letty came forward, her face drained of color. "My husband had no weapon, Jaundice."

He turned away. "Well," he muttered under his breath, "the old boy sure'n hell didn't turn the gun on hisself!"

"*What?*"

"Nothin', Miz Heron." He paced back and forth, trying to reconstruct the scene in his mind. He had once been marshal of a small cow town in Texas and knew something about the reactions of lawless men in crisis. He examined the empty chamber of the Winchester, a .22 caliber 1893 model, then paced out the distance from the fallen stranger to Luke's body. "Freak shot," he said at last, "freak shot."

"What do you mean?" Edward asked.

9

John Dice swung around, eyes narrowed. He felt like a lawyer in court. His mind worked logically. He knew what he wanted to say, but where were the words? If he had only been allowed to go to school! "The man shot onct, then afore your brother keeled over," he said slowly, "the bastid—e'cuse me, Miz Heron—pumped off four more shots." The essence of his thoughts were there, but the words were all wrong. Damn!

His mouth worked as he struggled to speak. "There wasn't enough blood for 'im, I reckon!" A dark red color spread over John Dice's face and he clenched his fists until the knuckles were white. His voice was tinged with deep, inner fury. "The bastid pulled the trigger one last time, but his aim was awful bad and the sixth bullet hit Luke's belt buckle and bounced back. As chance would 'ave it, it went straight through the varmint's heart!"

Letty's face was impassive. Now that she knew the story—and she had no doubt that Jaundice's theory was correct in every detail—she was overcome with a terrible weariness. There was a strange kind of retribution about the whole affair. "It was God's way," she said lamely.

Systematically, John Dice went through the stranger's pockets, finding only a twenty dollar gold piece and a faded newspaper clipping. "See what it says," he remarked to Edward, "I cain't read."

Edward read out loud:

DROVER SENTENCED TO FIVE YEARS

Alluding to the unpleasantness that occurred at the Beer Garden just outside Abilene last Friday morning, Jordon Thomas of Austin, Texas, a drover from the old Houghton Ranch in Indian Territory, was apprehended in a drunken condition with a Colt .45. Witnesses, including a Miss Lily Maddoz, of Caldwell, affirmed that Thomas had attacked Albee Tremain, an Abilene storekeeper who . . .

"The newsprint is smeared over the rest of the article," Edward sighed. "Do you suppose this man is Thomas?"

10

"I reckon," John Dice replied stoically, "otherwise, why'd he have this clipping on hisself?" He pursed his chapped lips. "Bet he just got out o' jail and decided to horn in on some free land. With a man like that, why, it'd never occur to 'im to enter The Run fair 'n square." He pushed his ten gallon hat back from his forehead. "We'd better think about gettin' to Enid to register our claims." He turned to Letty. "Miz Heron, are you twenty-one or thereabouts?"

She colored. "I'm twenty-two, Jaundice."

"You can register Luke's claim, then. It's yore property now."

She looked over the claim: to the south, near the marker where a piece of Luke's red shirt still fluttered in the wind, lay a piece of high pebbled ground. "Let's bury him over there," she said and looked down at her blue dress. She had no mourning weeds, nothing to single her out as a widow. Then she remembered the saucy little navy blue Evangeline hat made of Milan straw, decorated with flowers and laces and satin ribbons. Locating the hat in the canvas trunk, slightly crushed between two pairs of high-topped shoes, she patiently removed the frivolous trimmings. She would wear this for Luke. Later, she would mix a pot of black dye to convert her wardrobe into attire befitting a bereaved widow.

When she returned wearing the hat, which looked incongruous with her soft blue dimity dress, John Dice held up his hand. "Miz Heron, the community'll have to have a cemetery sumwhars, so why not cher?"

"God's Acre!" she replied. "As soon as a minister can be located, we'll have him make it holy."

While the men were busy with shovels, Letty removed a large handkerchief with a crocheted border from her handbag, wet it in the stream, then held Luke's head in her lap and gently wiped the dust from his face and the bloodstains from his hand.

The digging yielded up a half dozen arrowheads, finely chiseled and fashioned of some hard, gray stone. They had dug over five feet when Edward's shovel glanced off a hard object, which he uncovered with his hands. It was a very old human skull, neatly cleft in the

11

middle by some sharp object. The mouldy remnants of a beaded headdress fell through his fingers. In the days when the plains were overrun with buffalo, an Indian had met his death, perhaps in the same nefarious way as Luke had. Edward gently covered the skull. That Luke's shattered body should rest beside the remains of a red man mattered not one whit—in death, they were equal.

John Dice gathered a few birch boughs and made a bed at the bottom of the grave, while Edward took a square of canvas and shrouded his brother's body. His skill as a carpenter meant nothing here on the plains where there were no planks, saws, or nails.

They marked the grave with a large stone and recited the Lord's Prayer in unison. Then, as if by some silent agreement, the women strolled down by the stream, while the men half lifted, half dragged the redheaded man to the other grave, well outside the boundaries of God's Acre.

2

Hardship

An enormous crowd was lined up at the Land Office in Enid.

In the midst of hundreds of tents of all sizes and shapes —one with a Post Office sign written in what looked like shoe polish—a group of peddlers had set up displays on the backs of wagons, offering for sale lugs of vegetables and fruits and kitchen staples—all the worse for wear, having also made The Run. Potatoes, Letty noted with dismay, were one dollar each, and one over-ripe brown pineapple, covered with flies, was marked down from ten dollars to eight-fifty! Even white navy beans, obviously old crop, the bane of cowhands the country over, were going for eighty-five cents a pound. Women were lining up in front of an old man in a mackinaw pitching water at 5¢ a cup!

While children played hopscotch and marbles in the dusty road, clusters of men, in attire ranging from celluloid collars to cowboy hats, chaps, and boots, sat on their haunches, swapping stories that must be vulgar, Letty decided, from the raucous laughter that frequently poured out from the group.

"Look around, ladies," Edward exclaimed. "You may never see such a sight again." He glanced at the mushrooming tents. "This is a historic time . . . the beginnings of a town."

"Yep," John Dice agreed. "This mornin', there warn't nothin' cher except a lot of soldiers keepin' the peace over a passel of prairie dogs!"

Dusk was falling as Poppa Dice looked out over the

prairie with wonder: campfires and white tents marked the countryside for miles around. Suddenly, he did not feel so alone nor did his former home in Texas seem so remote. In the spring, Jaundice's wife, Fontine, whom they called Fourteen, would join them about the same time that they would start to break the prairie with Jack Rabbit plows . . .

As night fell on Enid, hundreds of tents and even a few Indian teepees were illuminated by flickering coal-oil lanterns. A man with two barrels of kerosene sold fuel at "fifteen cents a fillup;" a boy in cap and short pants, blowing into a harmonica, was joined by another lad in overalls, who sang in a clear soprano:

From this valley, they say we are going/going back to the fields and bright stars . . .

Valley indeed, thought Edward as he closed the canvas wagon-flap against the cool breeze that had swept down over the prairie after nightfall. At the end of an exhausting day, the campfires had been banked early and most of the settlers were snug in their pallets. By nine o'clock, there was not even the sound of a baby's cry. The horses had been bedded down at the old historic Government Springs, where hospitable settlers had invited Edward and his family to set up the wagon for the night.

Priscilla half sat, half lay on a pile of comforters on the bottom of the wagon, which they had divided into two sleeping areas with a quilt. As she brushed her long black hair with quick strokes, her olive complexion gleamed in the flickering light of the coal-oil lantern, which threw her green eyes into dark shadows. Her long, cotton flannel nightgown, high-necked and long-sleeved, hid the magnificently proportioned body that Edward had tried to take again and again during their courting days. But she had stood firm against his onslaught with surprising tenacity. Very much in love with him, she was not to be possessed until the wedding ring encircled her finger! Now, in the third year of marriage, their bodies still responded as if they were newlyweds.

Looking at her, with the exhaustion of the day behind him, and the shocking murder of his brother still fresh in his mind, Edward was disgusted to discover that he was physically aroused.

Somewhere in the wagon, probably in the collection of foodstuffs, a lone cricket began a night song. On the other side of the partition, Letty listened to the chirping and wondered if the little fellow had traveled all the way from Texas, or had come into crickethood in Indian Territory. Luke, her late husband, would be at her side now if they had not made The Run. She ran her hands over her body. Her stomach was still flat. She had been with child for six weeks, but she had waited to break the news until the claim had been staked. But Luke had died not knowing that she was pregnant. Pent-up emotions surged in her breast. She prayed for the torrent to burst, but the tide of tears was mysteriously held back. Still wide awake, she was attuned to the intimate sounds that filtered through the thin quiet.

Edward blew out the coal-oil lantern and modestly removed his clothing in the darkness, which was not easy in the confines of the wagon. Putting on his nightshirt, he crawled into the pallet; every limb was numbed with weariness, yet he was filled with an exciting tension. He took Priscilla in his arms and adjusted his position so that the rough boards seemed more hospitable to their lean bodies.

Priscilla responded to his kisses, although surprised that he wanted to make love to her with Letty so near. Somewhere close, a baby started to fret but was quickly hushed; Letty could hear the contented gurgling as it sucked from its mother's breast just as clearly as if mother and child were there with her in the wagon. *What would Letty think?*

Priscilla dutifully raised her nightgown to her chin, making her body accessible. They would have to be very quiet. Ordinarily, under the circumstances, she would have whispered no in his ear. But in some strange way, she understood his need, which did not wholly concern passion but something to do with the terrible loss of his brother. As Edward's rough, callused hands caressed her body, which usually responded quickly to his ministrations, she felt nothing—only an inward insensitivity. To get it over quickly, she

15

breathed into his ear, but she could not sigh or utter the other intimate sounds of love that she knew always heightened his desire.

Confined to the close quarters of the pallet, she turned on her side and opened herself to him. She thanked God for the noisy cricket who, at the moment, was joined by the chirping of a soulmate. She tried to emulate quick movements of passion for Edward's sake.

It did not matter now whether she was aroused or not as he began to plunge into her, numbing her solar plexus. She bit her lip as her thighs pulsed with a chafing burn. In a way she understood that he was somehow avenging Luke's death. But, because he was very, very tired, she knew it would take him a long time to achieve relief. She steeled herself for the ordeal ahead.

Letty lay very still, listening to the sounds of the crickets and of her brother-in-law making love to Priscilla. It was the first time she had ever shared such intimacy with other human beings, and she suddenly felt alone and abandoned. With Luke dead, how long would it be before she experienced lovemaking again? She was horrified at the thought. There would never be anyone like Luke, as tender, as aware of her needs and desires, as right for her in every way. Thinking about those intimate moments that would never occur again, she recalled the horror and pain of the afternoon, and her eyes burned with tears.

Underneath the wagon, John Dice adjusted to a new position. The damp, cold ground was as hard as he was at the moment. Aroused by the slight movements of the planks above as Edward made love to Priscilla, he could not sleep. His own body cried out for release; he had been on the trail for twenty days without the comforting embraces of his wife. Picturing the scene taking place in the wagon, he ran his hands over his wide chest. Then he reached lower, and for one long, pleasurably agonizing moment, felt the soft, moist warmth of his wife.

He had always wanted to tell Fourteen how much he loved her, tell her how beautiful her eyes were, how he gravitated to her every movement. But he had never been able to utter these intimate feelings in his heart because of his inability to put his thoughts into words. He was cursed because of his ignorance. If he could only speak about what he felt inside . . .

At last, Priscilla felt Edward's body tense. She waited as long as she dared, then whispered, *"Now!"* He withdrew and spilled his seed on her thigh. They did not yet want a child, and there were only a few days during the month when they could stay with each other until the very end. Panting heavily, he lay next to her; thankfully, the sounds of his quick breathing were covered by the intermittent chirping of the crickets.

Tears ran down Letty's cheeks, wetting the neck of her nightgown. Afraid of crying out in agony, she buried her face deep in the eiderdown pillow. The painful sounds of muffled sobs came through the canvas.

"You must go to her," Edward whispered.

"No," Priscilla whispered back. "She must have privacy." How little men knew about the feelings of women!

Her emotions completely spent, Letty lay staring at the dark shadows, silhouetted by the moon, that played on the canvas covering. Only toward morning, when the sky turned the canvas a deep pink, did she sleep.

By the time John Dice drove the wagon onto the Heron claim, located sixteen miles east of Enid, a long, golden twilight touched the prairie. The landscape, thought Letty, looked like a rich medieval tapestry viewed through a piece of amber-tinted glass. "I've never seen anything so beautiful," she said.

John Dice clicked his tongue. "I seed this ever time after a prairie fire. The smoke gits up in the air and it just stays up yonder. Miz Heron, the sun tries to shine through and it cain't make it . . . It's kind of a . . ." He worked his mouth.

"Reflection?" Priscilla put in quickly. Oh, the man was a dullard!

"Yeh, that's it!" John smiled to himself. She was a bright woman, all right, and she and Edward were perfectly matched. He liked to be in the company of intelligent women, even though he always felt inferior. Fourteen had no formal education, either, yet she was smart in her own way, and she was certainly wonderful between the covers. Thank God, he reflected, it didn't take brains to fuck.

Up ahead, a small crowd of settlers gathered in God's Acre over four mounds of red, freshly dug earth. "What's this, Poppa?" John Dice called as he reined in the team.

His father came forward. "We been busy burying four fellers. Three of 'em got trampled in The Run and one had a heart attack when he staked his claim. Seems word got out that we'd set up a gravey'ard and people begin cartin' in their dead. One of the widders even rounded up a preacher, Reverend Haskell. He's over there now spoutin' verses." He paused. "Git your claimin' done, Edward?"

"No," Edward replied. "People are lined up for city blocks around the Land Office, and the Post Office is about the size of an outhouse."

"Edward!" Priscilla admonished.

"All right." He threw her a sharp look. "Privy."

"That's just as bad!" She turned up her nose, then smiled sweetly at Poppa Dice. "Would you help us down, please?"

He held out his callused hands to support Priscilla and Letty, glancing at their ankles as they descended from the wagon. Although he felt few stirrings below his belt buckle these days, he still admired a well-turned calf. Then he smiled at the thought of a herd of longhorn heifers, and chuckling at his private joke.

"We jest mailed in our papers," John Dice said. "We'll get word as soon as they git through that pile o' claims."

Poppa Dice spoke in a low voice. "The preacher rode in about four o'clock yestidy, according to the widder Barrett. Seems he got confused, thought he was near Enid, and ended up out here after all the land was claimed. Guess he's pretty pore with a horse."

Priscilla smiled weakly. "Let's hope," she said wryly, "that he preaches better than he rides!"

Letty took Edward's arm. "I'd be willing to contribute an acre of ground for the church and the parsonage."

He nodded. "With Luke buried here, it seems fitting, Letty."

Poppa Dice clicked his tongue. "Some of these settlers have been talkin' about formin' a little community. One feller is a blacksmith, another used to own a provision store and says he'll put in for a fourth class postal permit." He paused. "I guess if we got a church 'n a gravey'ard, we got the makin's of a town!"

Letty frowned. "I can't possibly farm this land by myself. Leasing out a few acres for cash might be the answer."

Priscilla threw Edward an icy look. "I don't see why we can't have a town on *our* property, Edward."

"No, Prissy, our claim is too far back," he explained with more patience than he felt. "Eventually a county road will run right along here, because this is the section line. Besides, we've got a lot of timber that has to be cleared and not much open pasture."

As the Heron family joined the other mourners around the graves, an Indian squaw and her small son stood on a nearby hill in the golden dusk. She and a few others of her tribe had been on their way to Osage Country when the news of The Run spread throughout the Territory. In the old days when the Cherokee Nation leased these lands to cattlemen for pasture, Indians passing through had been shot on sight. But, when the government bought the lands from the Cherokee to make way for the white settler, and surveyors swarmed over the area, Indians were once more allowed free entry as long as they had permission.

The old woman's face was creased with the passage of many sun-drenched summers. She had not embraced the white man's religion as most of her tribe had done, although she treated missionaries and Indian agents with deference. But now, as she observed the ceremony below, she clicked her tongue and drew the boy protectively to her side. The Cherokee were foolish, she thought. They had adopted the ways of the white man for over two hundred years and dressed and behaved as he did. They had forgotten their real heritage and had made no use of this hunting ground that the government had given them. She smiled bitterly. They had forgotten how to hunt. The Cherokee were content to stay in the Council House in Tahlequah in their white collars and suits and negotiate endlessly with Washington.

As the sounds of a kind of chant filtered up from below, she turned her ear to the wind to catch the meaning: *shepherd . . . green pasture . . . still waters . . .* She had been told that the Christian priest could lift up the spirits of the dead. She waited patiently, waiting to see the graves open and the souls drift upward. But nothing happened. She clicked her tongue again. Another example of the white man's duplicity!

With the spirits of the dead still in their mounds, she turned back to her people below, then the little group crept along the creek to find the special place where the mass of running rock was to be found. Each person carried an earthenware vessel. They knelt near the bank and dipped up the thick, black mixture that oozed from the ground and filled the pots. They would not be back by this spot again for a very long time, and enough running rock had to be gathered to waterproof the bottoms of many wicker baskets and replenish their supply of curative medicines and be burned to chase away insects from their homes.

Reverend Haskell, a small man with a sparse red mustache that hid his thin mouth none too well, and his wife, Thelma, who was short and round as a butterball, shook hands solemnly with the group. It was strange, indeed, the minister thought, looking at the settlers in their homespun clothes and at their tired animals, that a catastrophe had brought them all together on the lonely prairie. None of the little group knew what the future held; they had assembled, it seemed, on faith alone. He hoped he and his wife hadn't made a mistake coming to this harsh, alien place. Everywhere in the United States a massive economic depression raged, and he wondered if money matters would change in this territory.

If appearance was any indication of wealth, the citizens gathered near the freshly filled-in graves were certainly poor. Rough homespuns, cheap, store-bought calicos, rough twill, homemade shawls, and warm wool jackets. Even the animals tethered under the trees were sorry-looking specimens, and the collection of covered wagons, springboards, and shays, had all seen better days. Had he and his wife made a mistake coming to such an unfriendly, alien land?

Poppa Dice introduced the Herons and his son.

"What is your calling?" Letty asked quietly.

"Methodist," Reverend Haskell replied just as quietly.

"We're Baptists," Priscilla put in quickly, her dark eyes flashing.

"And you, sir?" The minister turned to Poppa Dice, who exchanged glances with his son.

"Nothin' much, Rev. We allays go wherever it's handy—'bout twice a year—Easter 'n Christmas. John's missus is a Dunkard. I s'pose you, being out here in the middle of nowhere, ain't gonna be strick to Methodist ways."

The Reverend smiled tightly. "I believe, of course, in Wesleyan principles, but I do think that a nondenominational approach would be best. I'll build a church and parsonage if I can barter some land."

Letty nodded. "It's already been decided," she said kindly, pressing his arm. "I'll be pleased to give you space beside God's Acre."

He looked at her in wonder. "I'd be much obliged." His eyes were suspiciously bright. "I'd be much obliged indeed." He turned to the group. "Before we disperse, let's all recite the Lord's Prayer."

As the familiar words echoed over the claim, the three widows drew closer together. All wore borrowed dark hats and veils—there had been no time to hunt through trunks and packing crates for their own things after the remains of their husbands had been sewn into the canvas sacks ready for burial.

Leona Barrett, whose auburn hair matched her temperament, was already pondering her future. Before she had met Lawrence, at thirty, she had owned a millinery shop in Detroit. She had banked the money from the sale of her business, and she knew that her husband, who had died of a heart attack, had a five hundred dol-

21

lar insurance policy in her name. She was not one to look at the past or grieve unduly. She knew that her modern views would make little headway among women of her age group. Yet she had never met a man with whom she did not feel equal.

The second widow, Mary Darth, smothered a sob with her handkerchief. She was not as delicate, however, as her five foot three, ninety-eight pound frame would indicate. Having been raised in a family of twelve, she was certain to find employment as a hired girl.

Liza Galbraith, the third widow, was a tall, buxom blonde of nineteen. Married only ten days, she felt lost and abandoned. She could not think of the future because she could not think about the present.

Reverend Haskell intoned the last lines of the prayer, wondering if it were proper to give church sanction to the burials when the deaths had not been legally certified. He was already learning that here on the prairie, certain formalities had to be overlooked. As the chorus of "amens" resounded over the prairie, he glanced up into the sky, drew in his breath sharply, and cried, "Look!"

Across the heavens stretched a startling cloud formation, highlighted by the glow of sunset. "A sign," he exclaimed breathlessly. "A sign!"

Above them was the exquisite silhouette of a divine being, wings unfolded, head surrounded with a halo and garments flowing to the horizon.

"If that ain't a perfect sight!" Poppa Dice cried, awe-struck.

Letty stepped forward dramatically. "If a town is to spring up here, let's call it Angel."

3

The Burgeoning

The sky was still dark at eight o'clock in the morning.

A dust storm that had rolled out of the west during the night swirled over the charred soil left in the wake of the cavalry torches. The prairie was covered with a dark, menacing haze.

Leona Barrett carried a pail of water to the tent, where she regarded Mary and Liza with a steely eye. "I was awake most of the night thinking," she announced quietly, "and I think I've come up with a solution to all of our problems. We can't become wards of the community and we have nowhere to go. So we've all got to be willing to make an investment."

Liza's eyes filled with tears. "Frank had a hundred dollars on him when he got trampled in The Run—all the money we had in the world. When I found his body, he had been robbed. I've got exactly seventy-five cents in my pocketbook!"

"Don't jump to conclusions, ladies." Leona went on patiently. "When I speak about an 'investment,' I'm not referring to money. I mean *time.*"

"Time"? they chorused.

Leona smiled softly. "It's difficult to think now, but there is no point in sitting back, playing 'ladies in distress.' That sort of behavior went out with the Civil War."

Mary leaned forward. "What *are* you talking about?"

Leona took a deep breath and patted her auburn pompadour. "My husband died claiming our one

23

hundred and sixty acres and I'm going to build a house on that land. I've got a bit of money put away, some jewelry that my grandmother left, and Lawrence's insurance policy."

"But what has all this to do with us?" Liza wailed.

"Just this!" Leona plunged on. "No one hereabouts is going to have much loose change for a couple of years, but there will be visitors in and out of the Territory, land speculators, cattlemen, and so on—all of these people would welcome a home-cooked meal." She lifted the tent flap and looked out at the swirling, black dust, so heavy that the sun was unable to penetrate it, then turned back to the other women. "I'm offering jobs to both of you."

"You're going to open a cafe?" Mary asked incredulously.

"Wash out your ears, young lady," Leona snapped. "Must I repeat everything? Food will be served in my home. You see," she went on earnestly, "that's the whole point. It's going to be *years* before these people are going to have decent places to live. No one will be able to afford nice furniture and trappings until the crops are in and harvested and maybe not even then. My house will be tastefully furnished. There will be Oriental carpets and Nottingham lace curtains at the windows." She was fired with enthusiasm. "I've got a beautiful setting for twelve in Spode and I just might invest in a Graphophone that I can play when I'm not at the harpsichord."

Mary laughed. "Serving cowhands on Spode?"

Leona threw up her hands. "Yes, if they have the price of a fifty-cent dinner! I'm not proud. If an occasional cowboy comes by who'd be more comfortable in the kitchen—fine!"

Liza tapped her foot impatiently. "We are going to do all of this without the help of menfolk?"

"Menfolk!" Leona cried. "Great day in the morning! Why on earth will we need menfolk? We're all healthy and in full command of our senses. A bit of ingenuity and elbow grease, and our routine is established." She placed her hands on her hips and looked

24

from one pale face to the other. "What do you say, ladies? Are you going to come in with me or not?"

"Oh, yes, yes," Mary said, eyes sparkling.

Liza sighed. "Anything would be better than going back home and doing laundry for my brothers and sisters." She smiled. "And who knows, perhaps a young man will come along . . ."

Leona looked skyward, counted to ten, then, temper under control, raised the tent flap once more. Miraculously, the dust was clearing. Good—maybe they could get something done after all. She turned. "I suggest that we go through our wardrobes and select the dresses to be dyed black. As soon as it's clear outside, I'll build a fire and put a big kettle on to boil. Mary, would you gather a few walnuts for the dye?" She paused. "Liza, would you ask Mrs. Heron to go through her trunks? By this time tomorrow, we'll all be appropriately attired in black."

John Dice stood back and proudly surveyed his work. He had dug a 16x20 foot hole between two small hills located near the creek and placed beams of blackjack timber over the top. "When we git the front planks in and an isinglass window, we'll have a dugout that'll last all winter. It ain't gonna be fancy, but there'll be space for a couple of beds, a potbellied stove and a table, with a partition between."

John Dice waved as Edward and Priscilla, who were making their way up the slight incline, came into sight. "Mornin'," he said, tipping his hat. "It's gonna be finished today or my name ain't Jaundice. How's the well comin'?"

"I'm down about fifteen feet," Edward replied, "and there's a good deal of moisture. Another five feet should do it. Reverend Haskell cemented the widows' well yesterday. He found water at twenty feet." He examined the dugout. "I've got to start mine tomorrow, but it will have to be bigger. I want to give Letty a room by herself."

John Dice squinted into the sun. "How's she doin'? Bearin' up?"

Edward nodded. "Surprisingly well. She's been doing

most of the cooking, which isn't easy. It takes practically all day to prepare meals over a campfire. We've ordered a few necessities like a cook stove from Sears & Roebuck in Chicago, but Lord only knows when they'll reach Enid."

Poppa Dice nodded. "I've got to pick up some lumber, but I dread the trip. The widows went in yesterday." He leaned forward conspiratorily. "I heard Mrs. Barrett is going to bring a whole crew out cher and build a twelve-room clapboard house. Her husband must've left her pretty well fixed."

Priscilla smiled wryly. "Twelve rooms is surely a mansion!" She glanced at Edward. "We must be going. We've got our work cut out for us."

They retraced their steps down the incline. Out of earshot of the Dices, Priscilla turned to her husband. "If you think that I'm going to live in a dugout, you've got another think coming. Maybe it's all right for those white trash Texans, but it's not all right for me! Cooped up in little more than a cave—have you lost your reason, Edward?"

"Look, Prissy, it's autumn. We'll have frost in another month. I'll build us a dugout for the winter. In summer, I'll get to work on your clapboard."

"But if Leona Barrett . . ."

He threw her a long look. "She has money. I've got to save what we have. We need all kinds of equipment and furnishings and seed for crops next spring. I'll build the house myself, with maybe one hired man. We can't afford a whole crew. Construction work is going to cost an arm and a leg."

Priscilla turned away angrily. "For certain, I am *not* going to live like a pig!" She paused. "I'll simply go back to Minneapolis."

He felt his temper rising. "A clapboard is out of the question," he said, keeping his voice low and quiet, "but maybe I can manage a sod house. At least it'll be free-standing and have doors and windows and a roof. Would that satisfy you?"

"Satisfy me?" she replied bitterly. "Oh, Edward, why are you always willing to settle for second best? If Luke was alive . . ."

"Let's not discuss Luke!" he replied angrily. "You've always resented the fact that he had more talent, was a go-getter. You've always compared him to me. Now he's dead, Prissy, but I'm still here!"

She knew that she had gone too far. She took his arm tenderly. "Now, calm down," she said softly. "Is it so strange that I want a decent house?" She paused. "After all, we have Letty to think about . . . and the baby!"

The next day, Edward struck water at twenty feet. He placed stones around the bubbling spring, then went over to the Dice claim. "I need some advice," he said to Poppa Dice. The big man pushed his ten-gallon hat back on his snowy white head and grinned. "I'm a thinkin' that the Missus don't cotton to livin' in a dugout. Right?"

Edward smiled slowly. "She has her heart set on clapboard, but I think she'll settle for a sod house right now. I'm a good carpenter, but I don't know the first thing about building a soddie."

"Hellfire, nothin' to it." Poppa Dice laughed. "You jest git one o' them sixteen-inch sod plows that'll turn up the ground about five or six inches. There's plenty o' buffalo grass hereabouts and that's the best kind. You cut up the sod pieces in strips a yard or so long, and jest lay 'em on top of one another like they was brick. Slosh a little water between 'em and you got pretty good cement. Then add lumber or boughs or whatever over the top for a roof, with more strips of sod on top o' that. Set in yore windows and doors out of wood and glass and you got a first-rate house. Me and Jaundice'll help. We'll have it up in no time atall. I reckon for a two-room place, you'll use up about an acre or so of buffalo grass. And next spring you'll have a place all set for a garden where you took out that sod."

"Well, I'll certainly be much obliged," Edward said.

"Hellfire. Helpin' each other out is what neighborin's all about!"

Leona Barrett stood on the newly painted porch that surrounded the house on three sides and surveyed her land. She was very proud of what she had accomplished in the short span of three months. Time, of course, had been of the essence—time and money. Men and material had miraculously appeared when she flashed a pocketbook full of greenbacks. She had been fortunate to have found a contractor who commandeered—for an extra fee—one of the twelve carloads of lumber that had been brought surreptitiously into Enid before The Run.

She glanced down at her hands devoid of jewelry. The ruby bracelet had paid for the dining room and the fireplace, the tiny sapphire dinner ring for the two bedrooms on the lower floor, her engagement ring—she went down the list in her mind. And, wonder of wonders, she still had Lawrence's insurance policy to collect!

Returning from her reveries, she almost ran into an Indian woman dressed in deerskin, and a boy in overalls incongrously wearing a turban of white toweling too big for his head standing beside the back door. She looked around quickly, expecting to see a whole tribe in feathered headdresses massing in the background. Seven-thirty in the morning—what a time to come calling! She nodded pleasantly, opened the screen door and bade them enter, quickly checking again to be sure that other tribal members were not lurking under the cottonwoods. All was clear.

Signalling the boy to remain where he was, the woman followed Leona into the kitchen, went immediately to the bubbling kettle on the stove, and wrinkled her nose appreciatively. The stew, which had only been in the pot for three hours, could not possibly be done yet, Leona knew, but the broth should be delicious. She filled a bowl with the fragrant liquid and handed it to the woman, who made signs that she would serve the boy first. When she reappeared, Leona filled another bowl. The woman sipped the broth with much smacking of lips.

Leona saw Mary and Liza watching the performance from the corner. She was furious. Had they expected the squaw to be carrying scalps around her waist and

28

brandishing a tomahawk? The women began to breathe easier, sensing that the woman was well-intentioned.

Leona opened the sliding door into the parlor and motioned for the woman to enter, indicating a chair, but the woman went immediately to the mantel and ran her fingers over the Waterbury clock, feeling the small bronze ram's heads that graced each side of the metal casing. As if in response to her touch, the clock intoned seven thirty-five. The woman stood back, smiling, then spoke in a singsong voice that sounded not unlike the chiming of the clock. "Come—long—way—with—boy son." Her dark face grew serious as she searched for the right English words.

"Sit down," Leona said graciously.

The woman smiled uncertainly and sat down gingerly on the Morris chair. "Son—" She held up two hands in front of her face and flexed the fingers twice.

Leona smiled. "Your son is twenty years old?" Actually, she thought, he looked no more than fifteen.

"Twen-tee," the woman repeated. "Name—Born-Before-Sunrise." She paused. "Good trapper—strong—brave." She lowered her eyes for a long moment, then, still not looking up, continued. "My people—laugh—at son." Her head dropped farther until all that Leona could see was the sleek black hair that smelled faintly of grease. "Big Snow year." She held up ten fingers to indicate the passage of years. "Enemy men of—bad tribe, Ke-so-be-ta . . ."

She clutched her fingers together in anger and despair, and her voice deepened with the pain of remembrance. "Ke-so-be-ta catch—son . . ." She placed her palms together beside her face. "Sleep under tree." The woman paused a moment and went on in a very low voice. "Ke-so-be-ta bring knife . . ." She looked up and Leona knew there were not enough words in the English language to describe what had happened.

The woman held up her right hand as if holding a knife, and made the quick, unmistakable gestures of disemboweling an animal. Her eyes filled with the terror she had felt so long ago, then her features grew hard and her temples throbbed. "Born-Before-Sunrise—hurt like—animal." She brought her hands up before her face in a hopeless gesture. "No babies . . ."

Leona leaned forward to be sure that she had understood the woman. She spoke slowly. "What you are saying is . . . your son is . . . no *man* now?"

The woman lowered her head once more, nodding vehemently. "Squaw boy."

Leona drew in her breath sharply. So it was true, the raiding Indians had emasculated the boy! She shuddered, and for a moment thought she would become ill.

The woman arose, waved her hands around the room and announced, "Take son," then grabbed the clock off the mantel and was out the door before Leona could collect her wits.

Finally, she rushed after her, calling: "No, no! Come back, come back!" If there was one thing in God's world she did not need, it was a star boarder, and an Indian at that!

When Leona reached the back door, the woman was nowhere to be seen, but the boy still stood on the stoop, the empty soup bowl in his hands. He looked into her face and smiled brightly, showing perfect white teeth. "My white name is Sam, Lady," he said in fluent English.

Fontine's train from Dallas was twenty-eight minutes late.

John Dice snapped his fingers impatiently and shifted his position in the covered wagon. The horses were skittish; their hooves danced in the mud. Next to him, the stage driver walked up and down, chomping on a large piece of tobacco, waiting to take the passengers to Enid, three miles to the south. Carriages, wagons, and traps were lined up at the depot, all covered over with a fine mist. At last a cry went up from the crowd as the old locomotive finally chugged into the station. Passengers disembarked immediately, like sardines spilling out of a can.

John Dice waited, his heart in his mouth. Where was that woman? Typically, she would be the last person off the train. Finally he saw her, pausing on the steps, anxiously looking for their wagon. He waved his ten-gallon hat. Fontine saw him and waved back. She seemed tinier than he had remembered. She looked very frail in the lavender-flowered dress; the dark blue shawl accentuated her thin shoulders. She had purchased a new hat, he saw, and the wide brim threw her white face and pale blonde hair into shadow. She carried a huge gladstone bag.

He tied the reins, jumped down from the wagon, and took her in his arms, holding her frail body tightly against him. How he loved her! She was as precious as the exquisite china shepherdess in the museum in Santone. He wanted to say that he had missed her, that he had been so lonely without her, that time had been his enemy. Instead, he said slowly, "Sure a sight for sore eyes, you are!"

She held him at arm's length and looked up into his tanned face. "I'm struck dumb, I am, Jaundice, seein' yore looking so—so—*manly!*" She giggled and pressed his hand.

His breath came in little gasps. Oh, if he could take her to the hotel right now, how the bed springs would jiggle! He looked up at the dark sky. "We best be goin', honey. We got a long way to go and the trail is pretty muddy in spots."

Soon they were out on the open prairie, leaving the scattered lantern-lights of Enid far behind. Now that they were in the country, Jaundice became shy. His wife's warm presence next to him, plus the insistent jogging of the wagon, caused him to rise stiffly in his trousers. He could hardly wait to get home . . .

She ran her hands over his stomach and down between his legs, and he started. "Stop that, Fourteen! You're actin' like one of them whore-girls."

She modestly folded her hands into her lap. "Nobody can see us! 'Sides, how'd you know what the likes of them do?" she chided. "When we got married you tole me I was yore first."

"Never you mind," he replied. "Just never you mind." All the same, he wished that things between women and men were different, because he loved the feeling of her hands down there.

They had only gone four miles, he judged, when the

31

sky darkened and the rain started again. The wind picked up, driving the rain into their faces and whipping the canvas wagon top to and fro. The horses, blinders firmly in place, jogged steadily ahead, flanks quivering as rivulets of water ran down their sleek coats.

"We're a gonna get soppin' wet!" Fontine cried.

"Let's pull over," John replied stoically, and turned toward a clump of cottonwood trees. A clap of thunder rolled over the heavens and jagged streaks of white lightning flashed along the horizon. Dusk was falling fast. "I'm afraid we're in for it, honey, these damn storms can be something fierce. I was hopin' the worst was past, but looks like it'll last 'til dawn." He examined the terrain with a practiced eye. "It seems ta me, there's a dugout hereabouts."

"Well, we can't just drop in on people!" Fontine said, "it wouldn't be proper!"

"No, no. An old dugout that hasn't been used in years. This here territory used to be overrun with grazing cattle. The cowhands put up barbed wire and made dugouts to sleep in. But, all that had to be torn down when the government bought the land from the Cherokee. Anyway, as I was sayin', all of 'em didn't do it, and here and there, you'll still see a dugout from the old days." He saw a shadow under the trees. "Yep," he announced happily, "we're in luck. There she is. And look, there's even an old lean-to for the horses. Praise God."

He jumped out of the wagon, lighted a coal-oil lantern, and unhitched the team from the single tree. He led the horses to the shelter and fetched oats from the saddlebag.

"You take better care of them roans than you do me!" she cried petulantly when he returned to the wagon. She shivered in her heavy dress, which was so damp he could see her corset stays.

He laughed. "I must say sometimes they're shore better com'any!"

"If that's the way you feel about it, Jaundice, you can jest take your bedroll and sleep with 'em!"

"Aw, honey, you know I'm only joshin'."

"In that case," she giggled, her eyes very blue in the lantern light, "let's just josh into the shelter!"

Once inside the dugout, she crinkled up her nose. "Smells like a hen house!" she exclaimed, looking around the small, damp room, revealed in the light from the flickering lantern. Suddenly, she was afraid, not of the dugout itself, or Jaundice, but of the loneliness and isolation of the prairie. Their life in Santone had been relatively peaceful, and family ties had bound them all together. Everyone knew where they belonged. She and Jaundice had grown up together in the country, their childhoods entertwined. They had gone to the same one room school for half a year, then when their families had taken over a small ranch in joint tenancy, they had worked in the fields with the other laborers. Now they had struck out by themselves, and she did not know whether she had the courage to live in the Territory . . .

"Penny for yore thoughts!" John laughed.

She roused herself from her reverie. "Ain't worth nothin'! Just thinkin'." Then she turned swiftly to him. "Put the bedrolls over there in the corner, and the quilts on top . . ." She was suddenly a housewife again. Gone was the little girl in the gingham dress and the blonde pigtails.

They undressed down to their underwear, and she crawled into the bedding. He knelt down beside her and kissed her neck. She giggled. "Jaundice, you know what that does to me!"

He grinned, "Whad'ya think I'm a doin' it for?"

She was immediately warm. She kissed his rough cheek. She knew that he had shaved that morning, but now his beard tickled her neck. "While you're up, Jaundice, blow the lantern out."

He laughed. "Wouldn't it be fun to do it when we can see ever'thing?"

"Jaundice!"

"Oh, all right. But I can't see nothin' wrong with nakid flesh!"

"Keep a civil tongue, Jaundice!" Fontine exclaimed, holding her hands modestly over the Egyptian cotton vest that hugged her body.

He sighed. As long as he lived, he would never understand women. Just once in his lifetime, he would like to make love when he could see what he was doing. Feeling was all well and good, but to see as well as feel, well, that would be something else again!

She opened her arms to him in the darkness and enclosed him in a tight embrace, and he began to kiss her soft, warm lips. "I love you, Fourteen," he muttered, "I love you like the very devil." He pressed against her and she received him all at once.

After a while, the storm subsided. Jaundice knew he must speak. "Fourteen. . . ." he began, groping for the proper words. "You're still in love, ain't ya?"

She nodded and he felt her head move against his cheek.

"You know we ain't got any money, don't you?"

Again he felt her head move.

"The crops ain't what we'd all hoped. It's gonna be a bad year."

"I know all that," she replied quietly. "It's nothin' new to me. When have we ever had enough?"

"I know I ain't always done right by you." He held her close. "Times have been agin us, but we'll prosper. We're young and our life is afore us . . ."

"What you gettin' at, Jaundice?" she asked slowly.

"Poppa and me did the best we could, comin' up here just 'afore winter set in last year."

Suddenly she knew what he was going to say. "You didn't . . . get me a house built . . . did'ja, Jaundice?"

"A proper dugout ain't bad."

She could not hold back the tears. He held her close until the torrent subsided, knowing somehow that she was crying, not only because of their present circumstances, but for all that they had left in Santone: the small, white two-room house, the friendly neighbors who shared food and water, and the warmth of a roaring fire in winter.

At last, she said in a little voice, "I'm real sorry about breakin' down, Jaundice. You know I ain't no cry baby. We come up here and we're gonna stay. Whatever you fixed for me, will be just fine." She

34

paused, her determination returning. "And, if I get to carryin' on the way I did just now, you got my full permission to slap me silly!"

He laughed at her earnestness. "I'd hardly do that to my honey," he chuckled. "But, as time goes on, things'll be better, 'cause you'll make it so . . ." He paused. "Now, let's get some shut eye. The sun'll be up afore we know it!"

She cuddled up against him. "Let's not go to sleep so soon." She giggled. "I want to behave like one of them—whore-girls."

This time, he did not stop her as she felt between his legs. With each little gasp from Fontine, he made slow and patient love to her—as he had so often dreamed during all the months of their separation. He took great delight in her body, taking care to give her twice as much pleasure as he received himself.

Later, when he lay sleeping beside her, she looked up through the hole in the ceiling. Were the heavens clearing? Could she really see a few stars? The rain had stopped, although she could still hear the trickle of prairie mud down the side of the dugout. Yes, it *was* lighter outside now. She looked up contentedly at the round yellow disk that suddenly flooded the room with pale light. Down south, it was called a Texas moon.

Sam changed the bed in the small back room that had become his bailiwick, then climbed between the cool, sweet-smelling sheets. The coal oil lamp on his bedside table cast shadows over the few school books that he had brought on the journey, and threw his white turban into bright base relief. He was proud of his headgear, which his ancestors had worn so proudly. It was his one link with the past.

He thought of his mother, the plain Cherokee woman who had given him life. His affection for her was undiminished, yet he could think of her dispassionately. She had been reared in the old ways, resisting the encroachment of the white man, yet after that terrible time of the marauders, she had taken him to the white couple who had sent him to school and kept him as their own.

He wondered what it would have been like, had his

father lived—that proud man who had fought for the Confederacy and who had taken his mother while in a drunken state. Though Sam knew all of these things, he never once felt inferior—except in that way that was most important to all men.

He pulled back the sheets and looked at his thin frame. His body had been robbed of the necessary fluids that would give him complete growth, and knowing that there would always be a softness to his bones, he had exercised his muscles so that his arms and legs would be hard and strong.

When he had finished school, proud of his standing in class, his foster parents had turned him back once more to his poor mother, who had heard of the white women who had no men. So they made the long, difficult journey from the reservation to the widows'.

He sighed once for that small, mutilated boy that he knew so well, and again for his mother, whom he instinctively knew that he would never see again. Then, he covered himself, and blew out the coal-oil lamp.

It came to him there in that lonely, darkened room, that the best part of his life lay ahead. Under the protection of this woman, Leona Barrett, he was embarking upon a long journey, and he would thrive. He would work for her as he had never worked for anyone before.

When she had kindly asked what furnishings would be required for his room, he had requested no paintings or other decoration. Especially, he had told her, he did not need a mirror . . .

4

Settler's Fever

The rain had ceased during the night.

Now, at eight o'clock in the morning, bright sunlight flooded the prairie, causing vapors to rise in the glen. Although it was the first week in February, the weather was almost springlike.

Letty made her way through the small wooded section of Edward's claim. She especially loved the meadow with its pungent smell of leaves turning to mulch. She paused under a bare maple tree and, filled with inner joy, surveyed the land before her. She hugged her abdomen, feeling the small form within, and smiled secretly.

She sat on a rotting log, basking in the sun. How wonderful it was to be free of a corset, with only a snug vest and a loose petticoat between her skin and her dress! She got up slowly and walked a few steps into the shaded glen where the mists clouded the view. What a strange, otherworldly atmosphere—a place lost in time.

Startled at the sharp sound of a breaking twig, she turned to find Sam on his knees, his house apron full of mushrooms. He looked up with a slight, formal smile, his white oversized turban slightly askew.

"Good morning, lady. This is the last of the mushrooms. But with the sudden change in the weather, I knew we'd have enough for supper."

"How can you tell the good ones from the bad?"

"It is very simple," he shrugged. "Most mushrooms are edible, but few are tasty. First, it is helpful to know under what trees the good ones grow. The poisonous ones are fond of pine and spruce, some even like aspen. As a general rule, the red, pink, and orange ones should be avoided. The best are the shaggy-mane, I think, or maybe the inky-cap." He looked up expectantly. "Would you like some, lady?"

Letty shook her head.

"Very good for an expectant mother! When is the baby due?"

It was strange to be talking to a boy she barely knew about her pregnancy, but he had such a gentle manner. "It will be an April Fool baby if Dr. Burgen's calculations are correct."

He smiled, showing his snow-white teeth. "The doctor is coming from Enid to help you?"

Letty frowned. "I hardly think that's possible, it's so far. I've been looking for a midwife . . ." She broke off, suddenly embarrassed, and turned away.

"I have had such experience, lady."

"You *have*?"

He nodded. "I have brought forth many babies. When I lived on the reservation, I helped my mother."

"Isn't this a strange occupation—for a boy?" she blurted. "I mean . . ." Her face went beet red.

"I know what you mean, lady," he replied gently, "but I am not like other men." He got up quickly, his apron filled to overflowing with mushrooms. "I must leave now," he said. "If you are going to have an April Fool's baby, I will have birthed two women by then. Perhaps they will recommend me."

Letty was still flustered. She had not meant to insult the boy. Somehow she trusted him. She smiled and held out her hand. "We'll talk again soon."

He shook her hand formally without dropping a single mushroom. "Goodbye, lady," he nodded and went through the wood silently on his moccasined feet.

There was something pure and innocent about Sam, she thought—something spiritual. She squared her shoulders and walked back into the sun, smiling to herself, appreciating the strange mood of the morning.

On her way back to the sod house, Letty heard the pounding of hammers, carried by the prairie wind over

38

the strip of land that separated the Heron claim from God's Acre. With the farmers toiling from early morning to the late in the afternoon, the church would be finished for Easter services.

Letty and Priscilla pressed the spring flowers firmly into the foot of Luke's grave, then went into the church. Few of the settlers had arrived when they knelt to pray.

Letty asked that she be given strength for the baby's delivery, which was imminent.

Priscilla asked to be able to keep her temper when Edward behaved like a child and Letty annoyed her. She asked for the community to grow quickly so that she would have more friends. She asked that the next six months pass soon, so that she could discard her mourning costume. She missed the Saturday night socials, the spelling bees, and the quilting parties, but most of all, she missed the admiring glances of Edward's friends when she wore a particularly pretty dress.

When Bella and Torgo Chenovick came in and genuflected to the bare pulpit, Priscilla stiffened. They did not belong in church! They were *Catholic*.

Bella prayed: Hail Mary, full of grace, the Lord is with thee . . . She hoped that the next year, she and Torgo would feel less like outcasts. It was not that the community of Angel ignored them; indeed, the men always tipped their hats to her, and the women nodded cordially and exchanged pleasantries with her at the General Store, but she and Torgo had yet to be invited to a single dugout during their six months in the Territory. Next year, when the barn was finished, they might hold a dance on a Saturday night and invite all their neighbors. Torgo was a good violinist, although he had not practiced lately, and she could make the smallest tambourine in the world sound like a small set of drums. Her feet ached to perform the steps of the Schottische . . .

Torgo prayed, fingering his beads. The rosary was made of pure crystal and silver, a precious keepsake given to him by his mother on the eve of his departure from Prague. He moved his toe gingerly; in the stocking

39

of his right shoe, he could feel the five dollar gold piece placed there in the event of sickness or other catastrophe. He had worked for seven years to accumulate money for passage on the ship . . .

He looked up briefly at the pulpit, and in his mind's eye saw the old, hand-carved sanctuary at home. He and Bella had debated long and hard about coming to this place, but the nearest Catholic church in Perry was a day's travel. It was a mortal sin, they knew, to attend the services of another religious sect, yet it was also a mortal sin *not* to go to Mass, and they finally concluded that the former was a lesser sin. How could it be wrong for everyone to come together to worship the same God, especially since he and Bella repeated the words of the Mass to themselves?

Of course, he and Bella did not take communion. Besides not being blessed by a priest, the crackers, he suspected, were stale, and obviously the grape juice had been greatly watered. One Sunday when the weather was good, they would take the long trip into Perry, spend the night in the wagon, attend Mass, go to confession—a rather long one—and take proper communion.

Torgo saw the widows, Leona Barrett, Mary Darth and Liza Galbraith, enter the church and sit in their customary pew on the right side. He admired them because they had banded together to make something out of their lives. And the full-blooded Indian, Sam, was a good boy who taught him how to track game on the prairie and through the woods.

Leona Barrett smoothed the wrinkles from her black moire dress ordered by catalogue from Chicago, becoming so involved in this little ritual that she forgot to pray.

Mary Darth prayed that customers would line up each day for dinner, because more customers meant her profits would grow. Already she had seven dollars under her mattress . . . money for transportation when she could no longer bear the Territory.

Liza Galbraith prayed to be less restless, less nervous, yes, even less lonely. Even with her household duties, there were times when she was so homesick that she had to go to her room to cry. She felt unfulfilled. She missed the attentions of a man . . . a secret feeling that she could confide in no one, not even Leona.

Sam looked at his hands, fragile but strong, and wondered what he could pray for? There were some things the Lord could do—like bringing prosperity—and there were some things the Lord could not do—like making him whole again . . .

Fontine came in last, face flushed. Every Sunday, sharp words were exchanged between Jaundice and Poppa about attending church. She would not give up; sooner or later, as with everything else, she would wear them down. She would pray that—Suddenly, she felt faint, and the breakfast of eggs and grits churned in her stomach. She had heard about morning sickness, and she knew that she was two weeks past her natural time. Oh, dear God, she prayed, let it be just a touch of the complaint, please don't let me be pregnant . . . not until the cement block house is finished . . .

Reverend Haskell looked out over the little group and counted the members of the congregation that were missing. Where were the Stevenses, the Blocks, the Walpoles, and most of the men? He sighed. The collection plate would be bare today! Still, he should not complain—the community had come together and built his two-room house and the church. Even if the men did not come to worship regularly, they would sometimes share their game with him, knowing that being a man of God, he could kill no living thing. He opened his hymnal. "Please turn to page forty-six," he said, "and we'll sing, 'To Him From Whom All Blessings Flow.'"

Rain beat down incessantly on the roof of the sod house. Letty awakened as the first pain shot up through her solar plexus. It was a small twinge, yet enough to set her teeth on edge. She could hear Edward snoring in the next room; Priscilla, ill with a cold, was sleeping on a pallet before the fireplace. Turning over on her side, Letty felt another twinge. She did not want to be like Aunt Bertha Schreiber, who had kept her household in turmoil for three days, screaming at imagined pain, then

41

had the baby in three minutes on the back porch with a mess of greens in her apron. No, she was positive . . .

Letty got up very slowly and went to the hearth. "Prissy," she said, resting her hand on her sister-in-law's arm.

Priscilla opened her eyes, wide awake immediately. "I'll get Edward!" she said. "Better lay back down, Letty."

A moment later, Edward came into the room, adjusting his suspenders. "Are the pains bad?"

Letty shook her head. "They've barely just begun."

"Still, I best go for Sam." He put on his mackinaw. "Wouldn't you know it would be raining pitchforks and nigger babies?"

Priscilla stirred the fire angrily. "I still think we should have brought in a midwife," she said.

Edward pulled an oilcloth cap down over his ears. "Will you please stop harping about that, Prissy? It's been settled months ago. Now you be civil to Sam, do you hear?"

"I'll try."

Edward pulled her around. "You'll do more than try!" he said sternly. "You know damn well there isn't anyone else who can midwife around here. Getting Doc Burgen in Enid is out of the question." He slammed the door so hard that a few beetles fell out of the flour sacks nailed to the ceiling.

Priscilla held up her skirts as the little army dispersed in all directions. Letty was perspiring heavily.

"I'll get a cold wash cloth," Priscilla said. "Mama always said not to worry until the pains were five minutes apart."

Letty smiled wanly. "I'm just uncomfortable."

Priscilla placed the cool cloth on her forehead. "Would you like for me to read to you?"

"Yes, that would be nice." Letty gritted her teeth. The pains were very severe, and although Priscilla had an eighth grade education, she read badly. "On second thought, Prissy, maybe you could tell me again exactly how you met Edward. I don't believe I ever got it straight."

Priscilla was still angry at her husband. "Instead,

why don't I tell you about the time Grandma Larson killed all the chickens by giving them the wrong medicine drops in their water?"

Oh, God, Letty thought, not that again! Aloud she said, "Why I think that would be fun." As Priscilla launched into the long story, she tried to count the pains. Sam had told her that the usual birth brought an average of two hundred and eight pains. Indian women believed that any less was not considered womanly. "Prissy, would you change the cloth, please?"

"Certainly." She returned a moment later. "Now, where was I?"

Letty only listened with half an ear. Where were Edward and Sam? The pains were deep and sharp now, and she had to grip her hands to keep from crying out. She had lost count of the pains. Was it one hundred and thirty or thirty-one?

Suddenly, in the midst of a spasm, she heard the door open, and Sam's calm, smiling face was looking down at her. She had never realized before how handsome he was. He took her hand, and she felt the softness and gentle strength in his fingers; his palms were cool and comforting. He grinned. "You're going to have a March baby after all, lady," he said lightly. "No April fool!"

She smiled crookedly, remembering that day in the woods. It all came back to her, the slippery green moss, the musty autumn leaves turning to mulch, the crackling of dried walnuts underfoot . . .

"I have something soothing for you to drink," he said. "It's a little bitter. Do not trouble yourself," he reassured her with a laugh, "it is not a poison cup!"

She sipped the strange herb brew, then sank back down on the pillows, her body relaxing. Sam's face was still very close to her—so close that she would smell his fresh, sweet breath. "I must now prepare you, lady." He patted her hand and went into the other room. "Sir," he said politely, "I need your shaving bowl and many newspapers. Also, please put on a kettle of water to boil." He washed his hands with lye soap, then tied a large Mother Hubbard apron around his waist. He went to Letty. "How do you feel?"

43

"Better, much better."

She felt the covers being laid back and his cool, expert hands on her body, then smelled the sharp, stinging fragrance of Edward's shaving cream. It always comforted her that he used the same brand as her father. When she was a little girl in Minneapolis, she would watch her father shave and trim his mustaches at the kitchen wash basin. She could see him now: twelve feet tall, he looked, peering into the mirror, the straight-edged razor gleaming as he dextrously scraped off his beard. Sometimes, if he was in a playful mood, he would smear a bit of the white lather on her chin. She loved its lemony odor.

"Press my hand," Sam was saying, "with each pain. I must look at the watch." He lay the timepiece in the light of the coal oil lantern and massaged her hips lightly under the covers. When the water broke, he was ready with newspapers. He took her hands again. The pains were now four minutes apart.

The pain came and went—one moment Letty was very warm, the next moment, very cold. Miraculously, she could look at herself with complete objectivity through a strange, sweet haze.

"I'll be back in a moment," Sam whispered. He went into the other room and washed his hands again, lathering the strong suds over his delicate fingers, paying special attention to his close-cropped nails. "It's going to be an easy birth," he reassured Edward and Priscilla. "The medicine I gave her was very strong. She will not feel much pain, and later will remember almost nothing."

Priscilla leaned forward, impressed with his efficiency. "I've always heard women describe how awful it was until the baby came. What did you give her? She hasn't even whimpered!"

"A recipe of my people," he said simply, his high-pitched voice a peculiar counterpoint to the bubbling water on the stove and the raindrops hitting the isinglass windows. He did not tell her that one ingredient of the brew was obtained by distilling the black, sulphurous running rock that seeped out of the bank of the creek.

44

Letty opened her eyes with difficulty; the room—and even Sam's face—was hazy. The contractions were coming in quick succession now. "Breathe very deeply," Sam said quietly, "take as much air into your lungs as possible, hold for a moment and then expell all at once. I will help you, lady, by counting: one, two, three, *in*; one, two, three, *out*; one, two, three, *in* ... ."

She was consumed with a burning sensation, as if her womb was on fire. "My—my—my God!" she cried.

"Now *push!*" he urged. His authoritative voice, which still somehow reminded her of a woman's, gave her confidence. "Push!"

She bore down, holding her breath. The burning sensation increased. She felt his cool hands on her inner thighs. Then the burning ceased and she felt herself go limp. There was an interminable pause, then she heard a sharp, wailing cry. She smiled crookedly, and the room went out of focus again.

From the depths of a comforting, soothing mist, every muscle in her body relaxed, she felt a little form being thrust into the crook of her right arm. "Here is Luke, Jr." Sam said triumphantly. With superhuman effort, she opened her eyes. A tiny red face covered with fragrant oil was framed by a pale blue blanket.

Tears gathered in Letty's eyes. She could hardly form words, her tongue was so thick. "Is—he—all right? Fingers—toes?"

He laughed out loud. "Perfect in every way." He took her hand. "Just like his mother."

Sam came out of Letty's room with a bundle of newspapers. "It is a healthy boy. Nine pounds, I judge. There were no complications," he smiled wearily, "but if you do not mind, I would like to sleep for the rest of the night by the fireplace."

Priscilla stood up, her face drained of color. "I'd like to see her," she said.

Sam shook his head. "She is exhausted."

"But if the baby cries?"

He smiled. "She will know what to do." He thrust the newspapers toward Edward. "The placenta should be burned," he said quietly.

* * *

The Heron household slept until six o'clock. Priscilla was boiling coffee when Sam arose. "Good morning," he said pleasantly, "may I help you?"

She looked at the boy. "A man's place is not in the kitchen," she replied, "but thank you anyway."

Edward came out of the bedroom, rubbing his eyes. "I'll look in on the livestock and be back in a few minutes," he said. Then they heard the treble cry of the baby. Sam excused himself and went to Letty's side. "Good morning," he said. "You look very beautiful, lady."

It was true—all the pain and anxiety had slipped away from her face, and the baby at her breast gurgled happily. She smiled, "I remember so little. Was I difficult for you?"

He shook his head. "It was an easy birth." He took her hand. "You must get up and walk around the room after breakfast," he said quietly, "and in three days you will be up and around."

She pressed his hand. "Thank you, *doctor*."

He waved his hands in front of his face, an Indian gesture. "No, lady, I am only a helper."

She grinned. "Thank you, helper."

After a breakfast of oatmeal, baked eggs, and side meat, Sam turned to Edward and Priscilla. "She must walk today for about five minutes, but she will need support."

Priscilla's face drained of color. "Are you out of your mind, boy? She must stay in bed three weeks."

He shook his head slowly. "No, lady, she must get up today. The tissues of the body grow together with women who stay down so long."

Priscilla straightened her spine, then returned to her pots and pans. Her resentment of the Indian boy returned. Imagine, ordering Letty up when the baby was only hours old! When she had her first baby, she would send for Doctor Burgen in Enid, even if it meant putting the old coot up for a week. No red Indian would touch *her*!

5

The Blessing

Thirteen people came for dinner at The Widows on the Sunday after Labor Day.

Sam had roasted a small pig in a pit in the back yard, and Leona could have kissed him when he brought the magnificently browned meat into the dining room with a little ceremonial bow. There was a pause, and then everyone let out their breaths in a spontaneous "ahhh!"

The pig's ears had been trimmed with pinking shears, enormous red cherries held its eyelids open, and a large red apple rested in its jaws. Sam had skillfully performed the carving in the kitchen, dextrously fitting the generous slices together, much like a jigsaw puzzle. Rich brown gravy glistened over the crusty skin and ran down in little rivulets over the meat onto the huge Spode serving dish. Accompanying the pork were candied sweet potatoes, dried maize cooked in milk, fried green tomatoes and cabbage, eggplant pudding, green pickle catsup, and cracklin' bread. Parson's spice cake would be rewarmed in the oven before being served with cups of steaming coffee in the parlor.

The only stranger in the group was a Mr. Reginald Savor, a Kentuckian on his way to visit relatives in Garber. The gold studs in his shirt sleeves, the diamond stickpin in his cravat, and the silver signet ring on his little finger proclaimed his weath. He spoke about politics in Washington, D.C., which none of the others understood. He had extraordinarily good manners, but Reverend Haskell noticed that his fastidious ways did not prevent him from having a third helping of the roast

47

pig! After dinner and cake, he announced with gusto, "One of the best meals I've ever eaten," and finished his coffee with a flourish of his serviette. "May I smoke?"

Leona nodded. "Ladies, shall we go into the solarium?" She led the way to the middle bedroom, a bright room with chintz curtains and potted plants. While the ladies exchanged recipes and gossiped, she peeked into the parlor, but only the Reverend was still there, reading the Bible in the corner. The other men were outside looking over the Kentuckian's new fringed surrey.

Sam called her into the kitchen. "Mr. Savor suggested a game of Faro. Is it proper on Sunday?"

Leona shrugged. "I see nothing wrong with a game, but I suggest the men wait until the Reverend and his wife leave, which should be soon." Her eyes glittered. "Sam, is Faro like Old Maid?"

He doubled up with laughter. "It is played for legal tender," he said when he had quieted down. "I suggest that since we are in the business of earning money, that we take a portion of the winnings, and charge them for supper, too!"

"But it's barely one o'clock now."

"Knowing how games like this progress, they will probably be here well into the night."

She pursued her lips. "Perhaps I should say no. I don't like gambling, but if this rich man has money to throw away . . . after all, we are providing a service." Her voice had grown with her conviction. "Sam, go down into the cellar and get some hard cider. Then take the lace tablecloth off the dining room table. Bring some additional ashtrays. What should our percentage be?"

"I believe," he replied with a tight smile, "that ten per cent of the take is usual."

"Now," she admonished, "I will not tolerate disorderliness or drunkenness. It will be up to you to keep the peace. Do you understand, Sam?"

He made a slight bow, a new twinkle in his dark eyes. "Yes, lady," he said as he disappeared down the cellar stairs.

She called down after him. "Sam, I don't have a deck of cards!"

He paused at the bottom of the stairs and looked up. "Mr. Savor has the cards, which are not like an ordinary deck. There is a little metal box from which the cards are removed."

"Then it's not like poker?"

He smiled. "It is not at all like poker, lady."

The Reverend, his wife, and two other couples left at 1:30, freeing the Kentuckian and the other men for their game.

At two minutes past midnight, Leona closed the account book with a snap and looked up triumphantly. "We took in three-fifty on dinner," she said, "a dollar-sixty for supper and twenty-four glasses of hard cider at five cents each—that's a dollar-twenty for a total of six dollars and thirty cents."

"How much did we make from the Faro?" Mary asked.

"Nine-sixty." Leona clicked her tongue happily. "Ladies," she said with a raised eyebrow, "I think we're in the wrong business!"

Fontine surveyed the spring wagon loaded with lumber. "Where did you get that from, Poppa Dice?"

He scratched his head. "Darndest thing, Fourteen. I was a goin' around the square in Enid, pretty as you please, and this fella is sittin' there on top of a load of sugar pine, and he's a cryin' like all get out—real tears—and he tells me his poppa died in Hennessey and there was no money to bury 'im." He paused and grinned. "I got this here stack for five dollar! It's only third grade and got a lot o' holes in it, but it'll sure be good enough for a barn, I reckon." He looked around expectantly. "Where's Jaundice?"

"In hot water!" Fontine cried and, flouncing her skirts as best she could in her expanded condition, disappeared in the dugout, where her husband was washing his face. "This is a fine kettle of fish! Do you know what your poppa done?"

"He's old enough to take care o' hisself."

49

"That crazy old man bought a wagonload full of lumber. Me, seven months gone and livin' in a dugout, and he's gonna build a *barn*!"

"Yore soundin' more and more like Prissy Heron." John Dice waved his hand. "Now, jest settle down and let me look the situation over." He returned a few minutes later. "Poppa's right. A bargain it was, but it ain't fit for a puttin' in studdin', honey. As it is, we'll have to use a little brain thinkin' to make it work."

She burst into tears and threw herself on the bed. "I hate bein' pore," she sobbed. "If we'd stayed home where we belong . . ."

"This here's home," he reminded her gently, "there ain't nothin' left back there. This is all we got." He lay down beside her on the bed and took her in his arms. "Honey, times'll improve. I know it's turrible at furst, but the wheat crop was good this year, and soon's we git a hunnard dollars together, you'll have that house, I promise. With me farmin' both Letty Heron's claim and part o' the widders', next year'll be good, you'll see." He hugged her close and started to unbutton her dress.

"Don't you dare do what yure thinkin' 'bout doin'," she cried. "Poppa Dice'll be in any minute, and besides, it's *daylight* out!"

"Poppa's busy unloadin' the lumber. 'Sides, honey, we gotta do it while we can. Sam says it'll harm the baby after the seventh month, even if we lay down like he tole us, on our sides."

His hands were playing a touch game on her back and she was beginning to feel warm. "Well, all right, Jaundice, but I don't want you gittin' the idea that you can have it any time o' the day. Mama always said that a man who'd make love to his wife in the afternoon would jest as soon rob a bank!"

"Yure motha never was much good a prophesyin'," he said, and then they had no need to talk.

The next morning Fontine paid a call at the sod house. "Miz Heron, can I borrow an egg? Our hen didn't lay yesterday."

"Here, take a half dozen. My hens have been outdoing themselves. Would you like a cup of coffee?"

50

"Thanks, but no thanks, I gotta git a cake ready. It's Jaundice's birthday."

"Then take a pan of these Sally Lunns."

"I will! Bread don't do too good in my old stove, cooks all around the sides, but not in the middle!"

"How about all of you coming over for dinner tomorrow? We'll have plenty. Edward is hiring a couple of farm boys to help put up the barn, and we'll celebrate Jaundice's twenty-third birthday in style."

"*You're* gettin' a barn?" Fontine asked.

"It's quite unexpected. Edward had the strangest experience in Enid. A man sold him an entire wagon full of lumber for five dollars! It was quite a loss to the man, but he needed the money to bury his father."

Fontine set down the pan of rolls and the sack of eggs on the kitchen table. "Miz Heron, I think you and me got bamboozled."

"I don't understand."

"Seems as though Poppa Dice run into the same man!" She leaned forward, her face pinched. "I think our menfolk got together. They want barns wors'n we want decent living quarters." She began to fume. "The devil take them! Bastids, that's what they are, bastids!" She picked up the rolls and the sack of eggs and slammed the door of the sod house.

Priscilla did not approve of women using swear words, but she had to agree with Fontine Dice. There were ways of dealing with men like Edward Heron. A plan began to form in her mind and she smiled secretly to herself.

Three days later, the barn was finished. "It's not what I really want," Edward said to Priscilla, "but it will shelter the animals. The tack room will be fine for my woodworking tools. I'll put in a coal-oil stove and be able to work out there all winter. I've got a table and four chairs to make for Stevens and the widows want a bedroom suite, and a fellow near Garber wants to give his wife a library table for their anniversary."

Priscilla nodded coldly. "That sounds fine, Edward, just fine."

That night Letty gave little Luke his eight o'clock feeding, then excused herself. She was weary and had

51

decided to retire an hour earlier than usual. At eight-thirty, Edward took Priscilla's hand. "Let's go to bed," he said, the gleam in his eye betraying his thoughts.

Priscilla smiled brightly. "All right!" He blew out the light and they undressed in the darkness, then lay side by side. "Good night, dear," she said gently, and turned over on her side.

He ran his hand along her thigh, but she did not respond. "Don't you feel well?" he whispered, his voice heavy with desire.

"I feel wonderful, Edward," she replied softly. "Why do you ask?"

His fingers increased their intimate exploration. "I thought . . ."

"I've been thinking too, dear," she murmured back, not wanting to awaken the baby or Letty, "that we must have a little talk."

His hands, making tiny circles over her buttocks, crept up to her breasts, which he knew were tremendously excitable. "Can't we talk later?"

"You want to make love to me?"

He sighed. Leave it to Prissy to be maddening at the oddest times. "Isn't it apparent?" he replied crossly.

"It must also be apparent that I want a decent place to live. When you give me the positive date that the clapboard will be started, then we will resume our husband and wife relationship. Until then, I'll cook, wash clothes, and attend to household duties, but you can't have your way with me."

There was a long pause. "I hate blackmail," he said tersely, and turned away from her.

For the next ten days, Priscilla was the model wife. Each meal was prepared superbly, the sod house was kept spotless, even Edward's work shirts were starched and beautifully ironed. But at night, they lay beside each other like strangers.

On the eleventh day, Edward came in for dinner, washed his hands at the basin, then sat down and folded his hands. He prayed as usual: "Lord, we offer up a prayer of thanks for this meal and for our loved ones gathered here." Then he added, "We thank thee for the four additional orders that came in this morning from Mr. MacAlister in Enid, and we look forward to starting the clapboard on July 15, 1895, right after the wheat harvest."

That night, after the lights were out, Priscilla lay in Edward's arms a long time after making love. "Oh, Edward," she whispered, "isn't it wonderful—our being together like this?"

"Why, yes, of course," he answered.

"Oh," she cuddled up against him, "I love you so much, I can't tell you." She ran her fingers over his chest, entwining the mat of hair around her fingers. "I love you—all of you."

"Even the strawberry birthmark on my thigh?" He knew she hated to look at the angry red welt.

"Yes," she giggled, "even that! But especially *this*." She touched his flesh, which had remained turgid.

He smiled in the darkness. She was being so open, so vulnerable. He had never before seen her in such a loving mood. He decided to take advantage of the moment and test home ground. He moved over her again.

"Oh, Edward, you're *wonderful*!" She churned and thrashed under him with such enjoyment he thought surely she had been secretly studying a marriage manual. He had never experienced anything quite like it and he reveled in making her gasp again and again.

Afterward, she snuggled in his arms and would not allow him to go to sleep until he had made love to her for a third time.

Six weeks later, she was hanging clothes on the line in back of the house when she suddenly felt faint. She sat down quickly by the petunia patch, gradually regaining her equilibrium, but she had no sooner stood up and reached for the clothespins in her apron than she was suddenly violently ill in a bed of wild white violets. Had the breakfast bacon been tainted? she wondered. She finished hanging up the clothes, went back into the kitchen and was sipping a cup of cocoa when Letty came in, her apron full of darned socks. "What's wrong Prissy? You're white as a sheet."

"My corset must be too tight. Would you loosen it

53

for me, please?" She slipped out of the house dress, and Letty loosened the stays. "Oh, that feels *divine*."

Letty looked at her suspiciously, "Have you been sick to your stomach?"

"Why, yes, just now, outside. I think it was the bacon, although I carefully scraped off the mold."

Letty smiled softly. "I don't think it was the bacon at all, Prissy. I'll bet you dollars to doughnuts you're pregnant!"

6

The Gift

*Poppa Dice rode the spring wagon to The Widows'
front door. "Miz Barrett," he cried out, "I'm back from
Enid!"*

Leona was on the porch in an instant, face beaming.
He found her a handsome woman in the red and white
Mother Hubbard she wore over her black dress. He
handed her the manifest. "Ever'thing came in on the
train."

"Including the Japanned Plunge Bath?"

"Yep." He jerked his thumb behind him. "That box
that looks like a coffin. Can't wait to set it up for ya."
The only place that he had ever seen a bathtub was in
the Sears & Roebuck catalogue.

"After you finish bringing in the merchandise,"
Leona replied, "of course you'll stay for supper. Sam
caught some hogfish which I'll sauté in Indian meal
with a bit of butter." She paused, and then added:
"*Blancmange* for dessert."

Poppa Dice leaned forward. "Ma'am?"

She laughed. "Cornstarch pudding."

He nodded. He lived in a truly wonderful new world,
peopled with rich widows who ordered Japanned
plunges all the way from Chicago and talked French!
At home, the family bathed in galvanized wash tubs in
the kitchen every Saturday night and French was something that men did with women other than their wives.
Hellfire! Even the Widow Barrett, at her age, was
looking good to him! He pushed his unclean thoughts
away and jumped down from the wagon.

"After supper," Poppa Dice said, "I'll have to go

55

after Jaundice to help me lift out the plunge. Oh, by the way, Miz Barrett, see that big crate over there? It wasn't on your order, but the station master said to bring it along anyways. Came in a couple o' days ago!"

"You don't suppose they sent two Japanned tubs by mistake, do you?"

"Search me," Poppa Dice scratched his head. "Why don't you look on the label?"

She glanced at him, momentarily forgetting that he could not read. She examined the crate. "It's from an R. Savor in Lexington, Kentucky!"

Poppa pried off the lid with a crowbar and peered inside. His eyes lit up. "Aged in wood, the best kind. But what will you do with a barrel of whiskey, you bein' temperance?"

Leona smiled softly. "Our customers aren't, Poppa Dice! This is really a twenty-five gallon money bank!" She picked up an envelope that had been attached to the barrel. "Listen to this," Leona exclaimed:

To the Widows:

In deep appreciation to three of the loveliest ladies I have ever met. May this bring you even greater prosperity.

Most sincerely,
Reginald Savor

P.S. I will be returning to the Territory next spring, with a gift for Mrs. Darth.

Leona turned to Poppa Dice. "How many gills to a gallon?"

"I may be dumb and ignorant, but I can figger! Let's see, there's eight gills to a quart and four ounces to a gill . . ." He paused, his mind working. "You've got a hundred quarts of bourbon, or eight hundred gills, or," he announced triumphantly, "*thirty-two hundred ounces*!"

"How much can we charge for an ounce?"

He laughed, showing his tobacco-stained teeth. "The saloons in Enid, or so I've heard, git a nickel a shot."

"This gift, then, is worth roughly a hundred-and-sixty dollars!" Leona smiled, patted her auburn pompadour, and tapped the bung hole of the barrel, which reeked faintly, but affluently, of whiskey. "I think," she said softly, "our fortunes are improving."

The snow swirled gently out of a milk-white sky, adding a new layer of white powder to the four-foot drifts alongside the barn. John Dice shoveled a path from the dugout to the new barn and the silo where the grain was stored. He checked on the livestock at two-hour intervals. The manure he hayforked over a snow bank steamed in the cold, attracting a small flock of blackbirds that had tarried too long to go south.

At the Heron claim, the new apprentices kept the wood stove in the tack room supplied with logs. "We've got to keep the temperature up to sixty degrees, men," Edward cautioned, "otherwise, the varnish on the headboards will bubble." He surveyed the room with pride. Four finished bedroom sets were wrapped in brown paper tarps and two dining room sets were near completion. Jake Stevens, the journeyman, was gluing legs on an extension table. While neighboring farmers were idle, Edward's employees toiled as usual.

He was very tired, what with supervising the men, helping Letty, and taking care of Priscilla, who was still in bed after the birth of Mitchell. Doc Burgen had spent thirty hours at the farm, bitterly complaining about cancelled appointments at his office in Enid. He had read a medical book most of the time while Priscilla suffered with labor. Edward had said nothing about Sam, who surely could have eased her pain. But the baby was born round and pink and very beautiful.

Leona Barrett finished crocheting the last pineapple square for the bedspread, and Liza and Mary tatted edges on the lace lambrequins that would eventually hang over the curtains in the parlor.

Sam was polishing shoes in the pantry. He sighed with boredom. They had been snowed in for four days. His only trips outside had been to empty the chamber pots each morning and evening. "I think I'll go out and

57

track some game," he said finally, unable to stand the tedium any longer.

"See if you can catch some quail," Leona replied, not taking her eyes away from her fancy work. "I'll cook them dry for supper with a little yellow mustard."

He put on his fleece-lined coat and went outside. Within minutes he had picked up the tracks of a cottontail, easily identifiable by the occasional imprint in the snow from the animal's tail as it rested briefly. Sam liked the cold because he and nature were one. The cold could only kill, he knew, if you did not respect it . . .

He broke a hole in the frozen creek with a stone so that the wild animals could drink, then headed toward the barren, ice-covered oak tree that shaded the driveway in summer. Then he saw a strange mound near the base of the tree that had not been there the night before. He peered at the strange shape. He knew that bears and moose frequently burrowed down in a snow drift to wait out a storm, but his was not bear or moose country.

He approached the mound silently, then, as gently as a butterfly lands on a flower, brushed away some of the powdered snow. A blue serge overcoat covered the form, which he dug out of the snow. The man—in his middle twenties, he judged—was still breathing. It would take two men to lift him. As swiftly as a wild deer, Sam ran to John Dice's claim.

For two days, the man lay motionless in Leona's upstairs guest bedroom. Liza and Mary had taken turns rubbing his frostbitten feet with snow until the circulation was restored. He was a handsome lad, with dark brown hair and a short beard, and his big frame was too large for the three-quarter bed. At last, on the third day, he opened his eyes and looked about the room with wonder. Liza, who had been reading at bedside, introduced herself. "You're quite safe and warm," she said encouragingly. "And, if I were you, I wouldn't worry about a thing."

His face creased in confusion. "The last thing I remember was the cold air burning my lungs," he said feverishly. "It was dark and my horse had played out back on the trail, and the snow was coming down thicker and thicker. I thought to myself how foolish it was to start out when the weather was so bad. I thought about all the wrong things I'd done and then it was warm and . . ."

She smiled and patted his head. "What's your name?"

"Fennel. Louis Fennel. I'm a teacher from Covington."

"Well, Louis Fennel from Covington, just lie still. I'll get some hot broth."

"My face is clammy. May I have a wash cloth?"

"I'll do better than that. I think a warm sponge bath—"

"No . . . thank you!" he said, red-faced, panic creeping into his voice.

She laughed. "I'll send up Sam, our Indian helper."

After two bowls of chicken soup, Louis Fennel felt better, but he still could not turn over in bed. Even sipping the soup was tiring. Sam knelt by his bedside and trimmed his beard. He knew, more than the man did, how close death had come: exposure was often fatal to the soft white man. But even tough drovers perished in snow storms because they did not use common sense. The man's exhaustion would gradually disappear, Sam knew, and on the fifth day, he would be up and around again.

Sam turned up the coal-oil stove in the bedroom, and when the air was warm, folded up the quilts and pulled back the damp sheets The man's long flannel underwear was ringed with perspiration stains. Sam deftly unbuttoned the front and slipped off the sleeves, then gently lifted his legs and pulled off the underwear. Using castile soap and warm water, he cleansed the man's pale, freckled skin with a soft cloth and dried him with a furry towel.

It was strange, Sam reflected, seeing the genitals of a white man: the thick root curled over the thigh and the egg-shaped testicles lay snug in their sac. He did not touch the man in that private place. He thought of his own childlike member and the ugly scars underneath.

When he finished washing the legs and feet, he clothed him in a set of clean gray flannel underwear that Jaundice had provided. Then he changed the sheets, rolling the man gently from side to side.

"I feel so refreshed," Louis Fennel murmured. "Thank you, so much. I . . ." He drifted off to sleep in mid-sentence.

Liza sat beside the bed and finished the last lambrequin. She gazed solemnly at the man. He was breathing easier now and had stopped perspiring. How handsome he was, and how—*masculine*—was that the word? She wished that she had been able to bathe him, to touch his body . . . She dropped her hands in her lap in dismay. What was she thinking about? Horror-stricken, her temples pounding, she went to the window and looked over the snowy landscape, illuminated by a blue moon. A fear started somewhere in her breast. Was she so depraved that the first man that came along . . . What would her mother think? What would her husband think? She fingered the lace curtain nervously. But Mother was in Duluth and John was dead. She quickly left the room without another glance at Louis Fennel, and rushed down the stairs two at a time. In the kitchen, she nervously poured a mug of coffee from the pot on the back of the stove and took a quick sip, burning her mouth. In sudden fury, she threw the mug against the pantry wall.

Leona called from the solarium. "What broke?"

Liza nursed her lip, composed herself, and replied calmly, "I wanted some coffee before bedtime. Sorry I broke a mug."

Leona's voice was tinged with relief. "Thank God it wasn't the Spode!"

Liza picked up the pieces of glass with shaking fingers, then, very much under control, went back upstairs, removed her garments and crawled into bed next to Louis Fennel. . . .

He was warm for the first time in what seemed like many days. Dreamily, he reached out his arms and encircled the column of warmth beside him. Suddenly, fully awake, he opened his eyes. The room was lighted by a pink sky glow, and he was holding a warm, naked form. Now that his eyes were growing accustomed to the room, he recognized the profile of his angel of mercy, Liza. But, what was she doing stretched out next to him in bed? He was very tired now—his body ached and his mind refused to dwell on what was happening. He was only conscious of a wonderful glow that suffused his entire being. He felt as if he would never be cold again.

When Fennel awakened again, the house was silent, the stillness of the room broken only by the slight fluttering that emanated from the coal-oil heater. His mind was clear and he was in full command of his senses. Liza still lay in his arms, but she had turned away from him in her sleep. His arm was carelessly thrown over her breasts. Suddenly, the comforter was too heavy, the blankets too warm. He gently peeled back the sheets. "Liza," he murmured, "Liza . . ." She turned in his arms and kissed him on the lips, and he responded with fervor.

Although he was twenty-two years old, he had never lain with a woman. He had spooned on several occasions with several different girls during hayrides or in a buggy, with the reins tied up and the horses following their instincts home, but he had never thought of himself as a ladies' man. He was too shy, he felt, to be attractive to members of the opposite sex. Yet Liza had obviously thought him a Lothario.

Eyes closed, he experimented with kissing, and she was as inventive as he. It was obvious from the way that she moved in his arms that she was also inexperienced, and since she clearly expected him to lead the way, she followed his every move. If he ran his fingers along her back, she shivered and returned the touch. If he held her tightly, she responded likewise, and when he touched the inside of her mouth with his tongue, she kissed him deeply. As if he had made the gesture dozens of times before, he moved over her, seemingly guided by a stronger force.

Liza lay under him, reveling in the pressure of his body. She loved his strength and his guidance as he made love to her. As he pressed, she found herself opening slowly, like a flower revealing itself in the warm sun. During their two weeks of marriage, she and her husband had only been together twice, and she had been terribly frightened both times. A burly, muscular man, he had fumbled and was seemingly more helpless than she. The experiences had been over very quickly, and he had left her uncaring. . . . Now, as Louis Fennel moved over her, she shivered and writhed and shook under him. This feeling of warmth, once ebbing, and then suddenly returning . . . was the most glorious she had ever known.

As a rapturous, tingling warmth spread out in ever increasing circles over his groin, Fennel knew that if he moved in a certain position, she would reach up for him and cling to him so that he would stay with her even more. Then he could pause and take a deep breath, and begin the motions of love all over again. It seemed that she was not only one woman, but two or three . . . and that she was continually renewing herself. At last, when he knew that the final energy was draining from his body, he had one moment of regret at its passing. And when the spasms subsided, he was not prepared for the gentle, relaxed aftermath. Liza felt his body grow limp from exhaustion. His eyes closed. She waited a moment to be sure that he was safe, to be sure that he was asleep, then she, too, closed her eyes against the morning sun.

Leona regarded Liza quizzically over a steaming cup of coffee. While the girl was bright-eyed and flushed, there was a new air of confidence about her as she took hot water from the kettle on the cook stove to wash the morning dishes.

Louis Fennel had gone back to Covington but had returned twice for dinner, and each time Liza and he had gone for a long afternoon walk through the snowy woods. Although they tried valiantly to hide their feelings, their growing affection could mean only one thing: they had spoken, however silently, for each other.

Liza would be the first widow to break up the triumvirate and, Leona reflected, there were certainly worse things than having a school teacher for a husband! In a way, she envied them their youth, and their exuberance as they strode down the back path toward the cotton-woods was very touching. Oh, to be in love again!

When the snow melted and turned the prairie into a sheet of ice, no one ventured forth; even Sam stayed indoors in the intense cold. Louis Fennel had promised to come for dinner on Thursday, but even John Dice's plowed field was slick with frost, and the section roads impassable. A week later, a warming trend came to a thankful Territory, and a few dinner customers arrived every midday that week.

Liza had become a walking ghost, moving like a wraith through the house. Although she performed daily tasks as meticulously as before, there was a kind of quiet desperation in the way that she watered the plants in the solarium, set the table so precisely for supper, or added new flour to the starter after punching down the bread before going to bed. Leona and Mary did not bother to converse with her, knowing that she, was aware of nothing but longing.

One morning, Liza came downstairs in an olive green traveling dress and matching hat and veil. "I'd like Sam to take me to Covington," she announced without looking at Leona.

Leona nodded. It would do no good to point out that a woman did not chase a man or leave herself open to ridicule. The fact that Liza had taken off her widow's weeds was significant enough.

Covington was not far—perhaps eight miles over hard, red shale prairie, but the town was older than Angel. The schoolhouse was the largest building, and there were three or four cement block houses and a few clap-boards besides the general store and blacksmith shop.

Sam stopped by the livery stable to feed the horses, and Liza went into the general store. A tall, gaunt woman in widow's weeds was standing behind the cash box. "Hello," she said pleasantly. "You must be new around here. I haven't seen you before. I'm Grace Riley."

Liza smiled wanly. "I'm Liza Galbraith, from Angel, and I'm here to inquire of the whereabouts of Louis Fennel, the schoolteacher."

63

The woman's face fell. "Oh, you haven't heard?" She sighed. "It was such a pity, him being so young and talented. We all thought he had such a good future. Personally, I felt he'd prob'ly go to Gutherie next year and try out for a principal's job."

Liza steadied herself against the coffee grinder. "What happened?" she whispered.

"He got stuck in a snow storm three weeks ago near Angel." Mrs. Riley paused. "Could you be the young lady who nursed him?"

Liza nodded, her body numb.

"He came back full of cheer after that last trip over and seemed all right, then a day or so later had a relapse. He complained of chest pains and took to his bed. He seemed to be improving, then he turned real bad. The weather was fierce out. His pa had the telegrapher at the railroad station send a wire to the doctor in Perry—the line ain't supposed to be used for personal business—but the boy was worse off. The doctor came on the afternoon train, but pneumonia had set in and the next morning, Louis just slipped away." She paused. "Say, would you like to visit the family? They just live in the second house."

Liza turned. "No, thank you, Mrs. . . . Riley . . ." Outside, she walked slowly to the livery stable and climbed into the carriage. Ten minutes later, Sam came out of the privy at the rear of the property and found her sitting in the back seat, immobile as a statute.

Edward had secretly worked on the plans for the clapboard all winter. Besides a parlor, dining room, kitchen and pantry on the lower floor, he included a bedroom and sitting room-nursery for Letty. Upstairs were to be four bedrooms off a central hall. He had painstakingly carved the balustrade, using a wheel-spoke design. Decorative stained glass had been ordered for fan-shaped windows over the front and side doors, and he had included a second closet off the master bedroom, where a plunge tub could be conveniently installed. Because cash was still scarce, he did not add any special features to the interior, planning instead to

64

add such luxuries when time and money was more plentiful.

By doing most of the work himself, with the help of two farmboy apprentices and the services of a finish carpenter for three weeks, he was able to complete the house for approximately six hundred dollars, only a small fortune. He envied Leona Barrett, whose ample-sized house cost twice as much, but Lord only knew how much she had spent in furnishings. But Priscilla would have to wait for furniture, most of which he would construct in the shop when business slowed. Truthfully, he looked forward to making love to Priscilla in privacy without worrying about Letty being a few feet away, although he was sure by now that she was as familiar with his bed technique as was his wife.

Fontine raised up from the vegetable patch, and awkwardly massaged her back. She removed the large straw hat and wiped her perspiring face with her calico apron. For early June it was very hot. The rows of string beans curling upward on sticks made a pleasant sight indeed; they loved warm weather. The peas, tomatoes, and squash were progressing equally well. Little Emma, aged one, slept in her cradle at the end of the garden, sheltered by the mulberry tree.

Fontine had worked hard in Texas, but never with the dedication with which she worked here on the claim. She tried not to complain, even though tired all the time. She was up at four to start the cooking and baking; Jaundice and Poppa Dice stayed in bed until six.

Wearily she picked up a small tin can half full of coal oil and moved over to the potato patch. She picked the hated black-and-yellow-striped potato bugs from the leaves and dropped them into the Certain Death Can. 1896 was a bad year for insects in general and potato bugs in particular. It seemed that she had sent thousands on their way to heaven. She raised up and stretched her back again. Did bugs go to heaven? She could see a black swarm flying in a huge formation landing on enormous potato leaves. Wasn't everyone supposed to do what they liked best in heaven? In that

65

case, she thought wickedly, there would certainly be a great many *beds!* Then she blushed at the mental picture. Had the sun gotten to her? It was time to take a rest!

She walked to the fence that Poppa Dice had erected to keep wild animals out of the garden, unlatched the gate, and picked up Emma, who was still sleeping. On her way back to the dugout, she saw Letty and Priscilla approaching, wheeling little Luke and Mitchell behind them in a miniature spring wagon. "Aft'noon," she said pleasantly, "what's the occasion?"

"Oh, nothing," Letty said, "except giving the boys some air."

"Sit a spell," Fontine said, waving to a log that Poppa Dice had dragged up. Emma began to fret, and she opened her shirtwaist and held the baby to her breast.

Priscilla fanned herself with her apron. All the mothers she knew modestly covered the nursing head of their babies with a handkerchief. "My, it's hot. I'm not used to so much humidity," she said, trying not to let Fontine's lack of propriety bother her.

"It's tornado weather."

"How can you tell?" Priscilla asked. "It looks so clear."

"Can't say, but listen to the stillness. There ain't a leaf turnin'."

They all listened intently. "I see what you mean," Letty answered. "There *is* a difference."

"You goin' over to the Bohunks tonight?" Fontine asked, taking off her straw hat and shaking her long blonde curls down to her shoulder, taking care not to disturb Emma. "It's Saturday."

"I'll leave it up to Edward and Prissy," Letty answered.

Priscilla sniffed. "We haven't been anywhere all winter, and only once to Enid this spring. I hope Edward will want to go. He's dead tired after a full day in the shop."

Fontine smiled softly. "Jaundice is too. Plowing's hard on him, and Poppa Dice is not far behind, but *I'd* love to go . . . that Bohunk food is supposed to be real good!" She smacked her lips. "They don't cook like anybody else."

The dessert table was decorated in green and red crepe paper. Bella Chenovich reviewed the pastry and smiled widely. She had been crimping dough for three days and the fillings—apricot, plum and prune—were the last of supplies that she and Torgo had shipped down from Wichita. She looked down at her ample figure, clothed in her "good calling" native dress of white silk embroidered with multicolored flowers and overspread with a white lace apron. She adjusted her starched white lace cap. Torgo, in a red shirt and black satin vest, was tuning his violin. "Hurry up," she exclaimed in Bohemian, "I think I hear the first carriage!" She peered out of the huge barn door. "It's Reverend Haskell and his wife. The Virgin Mary! Never thought they'd come! Torgo, play something, but not too spicy."

Torgo started the "Beautiful Blue Danube Waltz." Couples gathered on the pounded earth floor, and as the violin soared, the men whirled the ladies to and fro with great ease while Bella shook her tambourine vigorously in accompaniment. The next dance was the "Laughing Polka," followed by a Schottische, "Little Irish Queen." When everyone hung back, Bella stepped forward. "The steps are simple," she said, placing her right foot forward. "Watch carefully!" She demonstrated the quick-step. John Dice and Fontine were the first on the floor. They picked up the movement quickly and others joined in, awkwardly at first and then more gracefully as they mastered the steps. There was a great deal of laughter and frivolity.

Between dances, the men gathered around the hard cider punch bowl, while the women hovered near the lemonade stand. "We may not be able to dance because we've got to look after the babies," Priscilla said, eying the dessert table, "but there's nothing in the rule book that prohibits us from eating! Oh, Letty, I've just *got* to sample those little cookies."

Letty leaned forward. "Prissy! Everyone will think we didn't have supper. You've got to wait."

67

"I suppose so!" she replied peevishly, turning her back on the table. "I'll try to think of something peaceful, but my stomach is absolutely growling."

"Oh, look, Prissy, there's Sam in his white turban!"

"You don't suppose the widows were invited too?" Priscilla hissed behind her fan.

"I imagine everyone in the community of Angel was invited. What is that dance, Bella?"

"A Schottische. It's lively!" She looked over the gathering. "Everyone seems to be here but Poppa Dice."

"He's been plowing all day," Fontine explained, "and he's tuckered out. But he was a high stepper back in Santone!"

Bella laughed, conjuring up the picture of Poppa Dice on the dance floor with a beautiful girl young enough to be his granddaughter.

Between dances, the men discussed the wheat crop that was due to be harvested by the independent threshers, and the exploits of the infamous Dick Yeager and his outlaw gang, some of whom, it was rumored, were in the Territory from time to time.

The women discussed the Gibson Girl profile illustrated in women's magazines, recipes, complicated birthings—including twins by breech—and how the Pullman railroad strike was delaying the arrival of relatives from Chicago.

At nine-thirty, Bella and Torgo brought in a wash tub half filled with freshly boiled coffee and presided behind the dessert table as couples lined up for refreshment. Then Torgo stood up and plucked the strings of his violin for attention. "The wind is rising," he announced. "I do not wish to make anyone uneasy, but the clouds are coming in fast."

The men rose hastily and the women gathered their wraps and collected children sleeping in the tack room next door; all were used to sudden electrical storms. They hoped to reach their farms by the time the rain started.

The procession of traps, carriages, and surreys, each one lighted by a coal-oil lantern, progressed rapidly up the new county road that separated the section line. Edward turned off at Angel, and as he passed the general

68

store and the post office, the first huge raindrops splattered out of the dark sky.

"Hurry up, Edward," Priscilla cried. "If this dress shrinks any more, I won't be able to get out of it!"

He spoke softly to the horses, which pranced nervously at the sound of a far-off clap of thunder. "I'll get down and lead them," he said. "If there's lightning, they'll likely bolt. Give me your shawls, girls!"

He climbed down from the wagon, handing the reins to Priscilla, and draped a shawl over each horse's head. "Come on," he coaxed in a low, melodious voice, "It's just a little way. Then you can have some nice fresh oats." A flash of lightning rent the sky and the rising wind threw raindrops against the horses' flanks.

By the time they reached home, the wind was a rising gale. Edward put the horses in the barn and checked on the other animals, who were oblivious to the downpour outside, then secured the bar on the barn door. He fought the wind to the cellar, but could not raise the door. He called out, but his voice was hurled back into the wind. He was drenched to the skin now, and the cold rain lashed his face like sharp needle points as he pounded his fists against the cellar door.

Just as Edward felt someone hitting the door from the inside, a bold flash of lightning crashed into the oak near God's Acre, splitting the tree neatly in two. "My God in heaven!" he shouted, expecting the tree to burst into flame, but the branches only smouldered: it was a scene out of hell. The door was finally flung open by Priscilla. Edward scrambled into the small cellar and the door was slammed shut by the wind. He looked at Little Luke and Mitchell, quiet on a comforter on the floor. "Babies who'd sleep through this," he smiled, shaking his head, "would sleep through *anything*."

At four-thirty in the morning, the storm subsided. When Edward looked out, the sky was clearing and stars were shining through the clean, filtered air. The moon, full and round and bright, came out as they removed their damp and aching bodies from the cellar.

Reaching the house, they found a small form cowering against the door, dripping wet and obviously in a state of shock. "What is it?" Letty asked, drawing back.

Edward laughed out loud. "A wild turkey!"

Priscilla clicked her tongue appreciatively. "It's a long time until Thanksgiving," she said, "but this year we're going to celebrate in high style. Let's dry the poor thing out." She squeezed Edward's hand. "Tomorrow you can build him a pen and we'll fatten him up."

"Let this be a lesson to all of us," Letty said. "Out of all chaos comes some good!" She sneezed suddenly.

"Yes," Priscilla's voice rose, bell-like, her pent-up emotions released, "and that's nothing to sneeze at!"

Wet, tired, and out of sorts, they all laughed. Then Edward yawned. "Let's all retire. I see no reason why we can't all sleep in. It's been a long night."

As if in agreement, Little Luke opened his eyes, gurgled appreciatively, and answered a call of nature. It was, Edward thought, a suitable comment on the progress of the night.

The Faro game lasted until five o'clock in the morning.

Mary Darth could not sleep. When she closed her eyes, silver dollars and five dollar gold pieces danced before her eyelids. The banker from Enid, the lawyer from Dallas, and the rich Kentuckian, who was visiting relatives in Garber again, had started the game immediately after supper. Mary knew the stakes would be very high because the bourbon was flowing freely. She dressed, tiptoed down the stairs, and went through the solarium to the kitchen, where she put on fresh water for coffee.

Reginald Savor, whose face was very flushed, could hold his liquor. He chomped on his cigar and selected the last card in the Faro box. He had kept count and knew the last card, the figure of the pharaoh, would give him the game. The lawyer, dressed nattily in a gray suit, set off by a red polka dot cravat, was so drunk that he could hardly sit. He held his cards immobile, like a wooden figure, in stiff, unbending, arthritic fingers. The banker, a fat, heavy man with jowls covered with muttonchop whiskers, was only slightly more sober. Sam, who never drank, yawned discreetly behind his fist, and

70

when the Kentuckian displayed the last card, he nodded. "That is the game, gentlemen."

The lawyer blinked, carefully placed his cards on the table, and reached for his wallet. He counted out the bills, his face expressionless.

The banker nervously searched his pockets and finally extracted a roll of bills from his coat pocket. He laboriously selected three bills; the large diamond on his left hand flashed obscenely as he threw the money on the table.

Reginald Savor rose and casually shoved the bills into his coat pocket. At that moment, Mary Darth brought in the coffee, and the Kentuckian followed her back to the kitchen.

He was very calm; the hearty cordiality displayed earlier was gone. "This has been a good night for The Widows," he said evenly, taking her hand, "and it can be even more prosperous for you, Mary. The money I won tonight is yours—if you will be good to me."

Mary removed her hand from his, her face flaming. He was so matter-of-fact, speaking to her as if she were an object instead of a woman. "Mr. Savor, I think you'd better leave." She had never been so embarrassed in her life.

He regarded her. "I'm a lonely man far from home, and you're a lonely woman stuck out here in the country," he said gently. "What harm is there for us to have a bit of fun?"

Fun? she thought. She had never considered the relationship between men and women *fun*. That was duty and forebearance. She had loved her husband, of course, but she could not in all honesty say that she had enjoyed bedtimes with him. The money in the Kentuckian's pocket would be payment for a performed duty. Why should she feel guilty when she would not enjoy the performance?

He took her silence as refusal, and pressed on in a matter-of-fact voice, "I am old enough to be your father, Mary Darth, but I'm very taken with you. I've thought about you often in my travels. Please be kind to me." If he had pleaded, if he had bent down on one knee and looked up at her with a beseeching expression

71

on his face, she would have called out for Sam. But it was obviously to be a businesslike relationship. She thought about the money.

She smiled. "We must be very quiet," she replied, "so as not to disturb the others." She took Savor's hand and led him through the hall into the solarium and up the stairs to her room.

Strangely, she was not afraid as she undressed in the dark and lay down on the counterpane. In the moonlight, his large form seemed like a comforting shadow. He kissed her cheek. His long sideburns tickled her neck and she almost giggled. She was surprised at her calm composure. Her mind went back to her husband as she placed herself in an accommodating position. He kissed her temples, her eyelids, her mouth, and she found the experience strangely detached.

He began to make love to her, gently, as if she were a very fragile china doll. As he held her loosely, she began to think about a green, warm meadow. The sun was shining dimly through patches of clouds, casting large shadows over the grasses below.

At long last, when she felt the breath rise in his throat, she moved against him once, then again. The wind was moving the leaves of the sycamore trees in the meadow, and a lark started a tentative song.

"You were wonderful," he said, his voice low and melodious.

She felt nothing, only the warmth fading as their bodies parted. The room was filled with moonshadows. While he rested, she got up and methodically put on her clothes, then patted his shoulder and whispered, "How about a cup of coffee?"

Leona had taken a pan of cinnamon rolls out of the oven and was dribbling a mixture of milk and powered sugar over the swirls of fragrant bread when Mary entered. "Good morning," she said, not looking up from her task.

"Where are the men?" Mary Darth asked.

"The lawyer is sleeping on the sofa in the parlor," Leona replied. "He passed out on the dining room table. Sam won't be back until late. He took the banker to Enid. Where is Mr. Savor?"

Mary paused, then replied quietly, "Upstairs."

Leona added several drops of hot water to the icing, which had become a sticky white mass. "He's a very nice gentleman," she said carefully. "Didn't you find him so?

Mary reached into the pocket of her dress and lay a stack of bills on the kitchen table. "He's a very rich man," she said sharply, "and I'm tired of not having any money of my own."

Leona drew in her breath. "There is forty dollars here."

"After all," Mary replied defensively, "he's a lonely man far away from home, and I am a lonely woman stuck out here in the country."

Leona picked up the bills and put four dollars in the cookie jar in the cupboard. She knew the future of The Widows had changed; they were in a different business now. "Why don't you let him sleep late?" she asked, calmly placing the tray of rolls on the window sill. "He must be exhausted." She paused. "I understand Faro is a very debilitating game."

Poppa Dice poured the red cement mixture into the wooden molds, then sat down with a sigh. "I'm not used to such manual labor," he said. "Don't mind plowin' and such, although that wears me out too, but this liftin' and all is hard on your old pa."

John Dice threw a handful of small pebbles in the five gallon can, then added water and red sand. "Take it easy, Poppa Dice, we want ya around a while longer."

"We gotta git this house finished 'fore bad weather comes or Fourteen'll skin us alive."

"To hell with Fourteen!"

"What's that you said?" She was coming up the path, a pail of water in each hand.

"God dammit, I told you not to carry water!" John Dice cried, taking the pails from her. "With you carryin' the baby and all! What would happen to Emma if you hurt yourself or had a miscarriage? Why don't you git over there and start puttin' up pickle relish with the Heron women? There's kraut to make and—"

"All they talk about is how much money Edward's makin' off the furniture and sewin' up them Gibson Girl outfits from patterns! I wanna stay here and see what's goin' on. After all," she added, "it's *my* house!"

"Yes," Poppa Dice exclaimed, checking the moulds, "but unless you git off'n yure tail, young lady, there won't be a glass jar of anythin' to eat in the middle o' winter!"

"Poppa's right," John Dice agreed. "Now, *git!*"

Fontine sighed as if the weight of the world rested on her thin shoulders. "I guess I asked for that." She laughed suddenly and looked very appealing. "Jaundice, you've got my permission to slap me silly if I start actin' up again!"

"Oh, afore you go," John Dice called, "how'd you like to have a mansard roof on the house?"

"How's that?"

"Oh, you've seen 'em here 'n there. They're kinda propped up at the ends." In his mind's eye, he saw the roof, with four corners sloping upward at a sharp angle and then rising up again to form the apex. "It's a bulky roof that don't look bulky," he finished lamely.

"Maybe we could have a couple of gables stickin' out, too," Poppa Dice said. "Would you like that, Fontine? It'd give you some light in the attic."

John Dice shook his head. "She don't want no gables! Besides bein' almost impossible to make without a professional carpenter, the birds always use 'em for a toilet!"

"Birds or no birds, let's have gables!" Fontine cried. "How elegant they'd be, with rolled glass windows. I'll make curtains—"

"Hellfire, woman, the next thing you'll be wantin' is a three-hole privy!" Poppa Dice laughed. "Now, let's git cleaned up. I'm treatin' ever'body to dinner at The Widders."

Fontine's face froze. "Indeed, you're not! Respectable people don't go over there anymore, you know that! The way they been actin' lately . . ." Her blonde sausage curls under the bandanna quivered with indignation.

74

Poppa Dice waved his forefinger at her. "No one's ever proved that they're carryin' on!"

"No?" she cried. "Well, no one's ever proved they're *not* carryin' on, either. Ya can't tell me that them carriages is comin' in all hours of the day and night just for people to git a bite to eat! And, ever'one knows Leona serves likker."

"Ain't it better for a man to go over to her place for a drink of booze than to go into Enid for a real toot at them saloons? I ain't never seen anyone staggerin' out o' The Widders. And, they don't stand for any roughhouse either! Them card games are run fa'r and square . . ." In the heat of the moment, he knew that he had said too much.

"What card games, Poppa Dice?" Fontine's eyes blazed.

"Don't rightly know," he replied in a subdued voice.

"Now, Fourteen," John Dice interjected, "there's nothing wrong with a little poker onct in a while with them men comin' in on the train at Enid with cash in their pockets." He caught Poppa Dice's warning look, too late.

"The train?" Fontine gasped. "Men are comin' in on the train? And then way over here to Angel?"

"A few, I reckon . . ." John answered feebly.

"And, I suppose yore gonna tell me next that they make that long trip to git a glass of booze and a game of poker, when they can stay at home base and do the same thing? Those widder women are carryin' on, I just know it!"

Poppa Dice threw down his leveling stick. "Woman, so what if they are! What has this got to do with you?"

"To think that we're livin' right next to a . . ." She colored and stopped just short of saying the word. "And with them goin' to church ever' Sunday and all. No wonder Leona Barrett can put in a five-dollar gold piece in the collection plate! It's plain old brib'ry. I suppose the parson's in on it too!"

John Dice spat on the ground. "Fourteen, take that back!"

She looked at him sheepishly. "Well, maybe he ain't,

but he sure as heck don't object to usin' tainted money!"

Poppa Dice sighed heavily and looked toward the half finished cement block house. "Now, about that roof . . ." He glanced at her out of the corner of his eye. "As long as we're gonna rustle up one gable, might as well have two."

Her mood changed instantly. "Oh, that's really puttin' on the dog, ain't it?" She paused. "Of course, Leona Barrett has *three* gables . . ."

Poppa Dice frowned. "All right, Fourteen. You'll get four, but don't you be tryin' for five!"

She laughed. "People will be blowin' it all over the Territory that Fontine Dice has one more gable than anybody else!" She sang all the way back to the dug-out, the widows forgotten in the sweet ecstasy of the moment.

Edward washed his hands at the pump, then took a sip of water from the dipper in the five gallon can. "Prissy, Poppa Dice dressed a couple of squirrels for us. He says the trick is to catch them just before hibernation, when they're plump and juicy. They're not much good in the spring, according to him, because they've been living off their own fat all winter."

"Squirrels always remind me of cat." Priscilla looked at the skinned creatures, which were nice and pink. "I wonder how you cook them?"

Edward raised his eyebrows. "Fontine says to put a few slices of bacon over them, a bit of salt, some pepper and a pinch of nutmeg, and roast with the lid off. They're supposed to taste exactly like fresh pork."

"Fresh pork, eh?" Priscilla's salivary glands started to work, although breakfast had scarcely been finished. "Oh, I'm so tired of salted meats and canned sausage. What I would give for a nice piece of shoat." Her eyes gleamed. "I'd take a whole hindquarter and simmer it in a pot, then roast it so the flavors would ripen, and serve it on a bed of candied sweet potatoes!"

She looked out over the claim, tears gathering in her eyes. The sun shining over the plowed acreage was certainly a beautiful sight, and nothing was so refreshing as the smell of freshly-turned fields. "Edward, I'll go knock down a few pecans." She looked at him dreamily. "I'll make pralines tonight after supper."

She went down by the meadow and suddenly wished she were back in Minneapolis. Tonight was Saturday, and there would be a dance at the Odd Fellows Hall, the girls attired in their prettiest dresses. She could hear the waltz music in her mind, and she began to move over the dried prairie grass at the foot of the cottonwoods. If the baby was a girl, she would name her Charlotte. . . .

Edward scratched his head as he watched her dance slowly across the turf, which was probably, he reflected, a tiled parquet floor to Prissy. She was like a young girl again. If pregnancy affected her this way, he would have to see that they had a lot of babies!

7

The Arrival

It was raining in Wichita.

Lavenia Heron brushed a speck of dust from her new
green Cheviot traveling suit and adjusted her bolero
sleeves, which were trimmed in new soutache braid. She
was the smartest-dressed woman in the railway car. She
peeped a bit, observing her Gibson Girl profile in the
window glass; her green hat, of a nobby textured milan
straw, trimmed with coils of black ribbons, added the
final touch of elegance. She sniffed at the other ladies
in old-fashioned serge with flannel petticoats—which,
of course, did not rustle the way that her taffeta-lined
skirt did—and sighed happily.

It was a rare and exciting experience to travel alone.
Although she had celebrated her fifty-first birthday the
week before, in Minneapolis, she looked—and felt—no
more than forty. Admiring glances from men, which
she did not acknowledge, told her that she was still attractive. Her complexion was unmarred by deep lines,
and her hair was only faintly tinged with gray.

The train was scheduled for an hour's stopover in
Wichita. The passengers embarked at Union Station
through the comfort of an enclosed gate that led directly into the modern depot. Lavenia was extremely
conscious of the loud rustle of her petticoats as she hurried to the luncheon counter. While the food on the
train was quite good, she had not cared much for the
weak coffee. The water, served along with the meals,
had been stronger!

Sipping hot, strong coffee, she observed the crowd, a

78

delicious experience. She loved the atmosphere of the huge station with its white tiled parquet floors and L-shaped magazine stand, but most of all, she loved being part of an obviously affluent group.

When departure time was announced, before joining the queue at Gate 3, she went to the magazine stand to purchase a copy of the *Ladies' Home Journal*. Reaching for the magazine, she accidentally brushed the hand of a young man who was similarly reaching for the *Police Gazette*. She drew back. "I'm *so* sorry," she said, blushing.

He smiled and tipped his hat. It was then that she noticed his uncanny resemblance to Luke—he had the same blond hair coloring, the same nose and mouth, except his jaw was more prominent, and he was a trifle taller.

If Luke had been fortunate enough to have a twin brother, this man. . . . She pushed the thought away. How absurd. What was she thinking about? She paused a moment to calm her racing heart, and her eyes filled with tears, which she brushed away with her gloves. You are a silly woman, Lavenia Heron, she admonished herself sternly before joining the queue at the gate.

Lavenia settled herself in the seat and opened the magazine. When she glanced up, her heart skipped a beat. The young man opposite was reading a copy of the *Police Gazette*. The conductor came by at that moment to take tickets, and when the young man saw her, he smiled. "We meet again."

"So we do." She could look at him now without seeing Luke.

He inclined his head. "My name is Bosley Trenton, ma'am."

"I'm Lavenia Heron, and I'm stopping at Enid."

"Then we have a long way to go. I, too, am leaving the train there."

From that point on, conversation flowed. He was a geologist, she learned, employed by the United States government. When the first call for luncheon was announced, Bosley Trenton rose and extended his arm. "Would you sit with me, ma'am?"

79

Lavenia smiled and accepted his invitation with pleasure. Over small portions of fresh perch in cream sauce, they came to know more about each other. "I think it would be very interesting to be a geologist," Lavenia said firmly, "but I'm afraid it wouldn't lend itself to the feminine mind."

He laughed out loud. "No more than a man baking a chocolate fudge cake!" He paused. "Actually, ma'am, I'm going to be dealing with a substance that looks and feels very much like flour. It's called gypsum. I'm to do some borings in the Gyp Hills in Indian Territory. Washington wants to know if the deposits are sufficient to be mined commercially." He leaned forward earnestly. "The catch to it—and I've always found that there is a catch when the government gets involved—is that outside of making plaster of paris, a use for gypsum has yet to be found! But, I'm going to be very dutiful, because I'm being paid rather well." He paused thoughtfully. "To be on one's own during these times is important."

Lavenia nodded vigorously. "Which is exactly the reason why I'm journeying alone. My husband—may his soul rest in eternal peace—would have had a heart attack at the thought of me going anywhere alone. He died of pneumonia twenty years ago, and of course, women in those days stayed sequestered in their own society. One didn't even go shopping by one's self." She paused a moment and looked at him with wonder. "You know, Mr. Trenton, you resemble my late son so much—it's really quite startling. Were there any Herons in your family? Or Burkes or Hipples?"

He shook his head. "My mother's name was Tartery, and she came from Scotland. My father was British."

Lavenia sighed. "It is only wishful thinking, I suppose. Still, it gives me a turn every time I look at you. . . ."

He leaned forward. "If you like—I understand about these things, ma'am—I'll be pleased to sit in another seat."

"Oh, no, please don't! In fact, I like to look at you!"

He was so polite, so gentlemanly, so handsome, and

she thought: *Oh, God, if I was only thirty years younger!*

The porter helped Lavenia down the train steps, and she surveyed the platform for familiar faces. Someone touched her arm, and she whirled around and into Edward's embrace. "Momma!" he exclaimed.

She held him at arm's length. "You've changed, son," she said soberly. "You've grown up!"

"But, Momma," he laughed, "I was grown up when I left Minneapolis!"

She patted his arm. He was taller and bigger than she had remembered, and there was a look about his face—had it widened?—that made her think of her late husband, and there were deep furrows between his eyes. Edward would never again be compared to a sleek Viking warrior. The dewy look that the family had cherished was gone. She said, "Edward, I would like you to meet Bosley Trenton. Isn't he the spitting image of Luke?"

Edward held out his hand. The man certainly had the same light coloring as his brother, but he could not really say that the resemblance was very great. "How do you do, sir."

Bosley smiled. "According to your mother, Mr. Heron, you're a cross between Grover Cleveland and Thomas A. Edison!"

Edward laughed. "Don't believe everything you hear, Mr. Trenton! Mother is inclined to look at her children through very heavy isinglass. By the way, I have my carriage. Could I drop you anywhere? I don't suppose you know the Territory very well, but we live in the country near Angel, which is close to the towns of Bloomer and Garber."

"Thank you, but I'll just walk up to the Donley Hotel. I'm here to do some work for the government."

"He's a geologist!" Lavenia added.

"Oh?" Edward replied. "Too bad you're employed. Some people in our community would have use for you. Some of our land won't grow a thing. We suspect it's alkali."

Bosley shook his head. "That's interesting. I'm going to be working in the Gyp Hills, testing for gypsym, which is sort of an antidote for alkali." He paused. "I don't start work for a week. . . ."

"I have a suggestion, then, Mr. Trenton—why don't you come home with us? We have a large house with plenty of room. We'd be happy if you'd be our guest. Our community isn't rich, but our farmers would pay for whatever tests are necessary. It's next to impossible to find a geologist."

Lavenia turned to him. "Oh, please do come!"

Bosley grinned. "You don't know anything about me, ma'am. I might turn out to have a six-shooter in my pocket and there might even be a price on my head."

Lavenia laughed. "We'll take that chance!"

Edward held out his hand. "Then it's settled. I'll pick up your luggage."

It was dark long before they reached Angel. Priscilla hung the coal-oil lantern outside as a homing beacon for Edward, then stoked the fire in the cook stove, punched down the bread for morning rolls, and checked the stew in the oven.

Letty was setting the table when she heard the carriage in the yard. "It's eight o'clock, Prissy. We'll be eating fashionably late tonight!"

Priscilla took off her apron and smoothed her dress over the corset. "Come on, Letty, this is a moment I don't relish. I hope Mother Heron's disposition has improved."

They went out on the back porch a bit apprehensively. Lavenia gave a little cry and gathered Priscilla into her arms, then Letty. "It's so good to see you both, my birds!" she trilled.

Birds, indeed, thought Letty—gingham birds, while Mother Heron was dressed like a parrot in the bottle-green suit.

Lavenia opened the screen door. "I'd like to introduce Bosley Trenton."

Letty drew in her breath. For a moment she thought Luke was standing on the porch, and the resemblance was heightened further when Edward moved up beside him. It was like the old days—two brothers again.

Priscilla was also taken aback by the illusion. "Do come in," she said in a shaky voice. "Dinner is ready to be put on the table."

"Mr. Trenton is going to stay with us for a few days," Edward said, "and do a bit of surveying."

"He's a geologist," Lavenia put in proudly, and led the procession into the kitchen.

"If I had known that we were having company," Priscilla said under her breath, "I would have had a fire going in the parlor, Mother Heron. The nights are nippy."

"I can't wait to see Luke Jr. and Mitchell. Ah, grandsons!" Lavenia cried. "And where is the new baby, Betsy?"

Letty took her arm. "I've just managed to get Luke down, and Mitchell has a bout of the croup."

"And," Priscilla said, "Betsy is due for a feeding in half an hour. At least you'll get to see her tonight."

The beef stew and crusty hot rolls were followed by coffee and sandplum pie, which was served in the parlor. Then the women left to wash the dishes while Edward and Bosley continued to talk.

"It was," observed Lavenia later, "just like the old days." In a way, she had her boys back with her again.

To Letty, however, deep in the eiderdown feather bed, meeting Bosley Trenton had been a disturbing experience. He was a great deal like Luke—except he did not have Luke's appeal. Yes, she thought, that was the word—*appeal*. He certainly resembled Luke physically, but no inner spark flashed between them. She was not even sure she liked him.

She turned over on her side and fell asleep almost immediately, and dreamed that she was riding horseback behind Luke. For some reason, she was not riding side saddle and could feel the saddle horn pressing against her abdomen. She tried to catch up with him, but his horse shot ahead, and she screamed: "*Luke! Luke, wait for me!*" He appeared not to hear her and soon disappeared over a slight incline. She dug her spurs into the horse's flanks, but instead of galloping ahead, he slowed down. "Luke!" she cried. She could see his silhouette by the widows' oak tree. The rider

83

turned around—it was not Luke at all, but Bosley. In her disappointment, she quickly reined in her horse, who stumbled over a prairie dog hole. She fell heavily, impaling herself on the saddle horn.

Letty awakened and sat bolt upright in bed. Perspiration had soaked her nightgown and she was gasping. Her solar plexus throbbed with a pain that gradually diminished. Looking at the full autumn moon that threw the bed into a patch of pale yellow light, she suddenly felt foolish. It was the first time since Luke's death that she had dreamed about him. Yet even in the dream he was unattainable. The only reality was feeling the saddle horn plunged deep within her. She felt weak with a peculiar physical release that was new to her. She changed nightgowns and washed her face in the china basin on the night stand, thinking of Bosley in the room next door, stretched out on a bed that was too small for his big frame. It was as if she had—what penny novels called—"known him carnally." She shuddered at the thought. Although his resemblance to Luke was startling in the extreme, she had no wish to know him—carnally or any other way.

"What do you think of Angel, Momma?" Edward asked the next morning as they came out of the general store. Lavenia regarded the dirt street, minus sidewalks, the blacksmith shop, the livery stable, the church in the distance and a small office building that was being constructed out of scrap lumber. She sniffed. "When I think you left home for *this*, son, I could just cry!"

He patted her arm. "You should have been with us when we staked the claim. There was nothing here but prairie. We've come a long way in just three and a half years!"

"And how much have you made in profits?"

"A neighbor puts in wheat for me on a share basis, but what has surprised me is that I make more from building furniture than I do from the crops. Some settlers have already left, especially townspeople. We farmers do better because we raise our own fruits and vegetables. Tomorrow, I'm going to butcher a hog that I've been fattening up with corn."

She shook her head. "I don't know how you manage. After all, you're a city boy."

"*Was* a city boy," he grinned. "You know, Momma, I've never felt better than out here in the middle of nowhere. There's a good deal to be thankful for. . . ."

"And Priscilla?"

He paused a long moment. "She's doing fine. It takes time for a woman to. . . ."

"To what?"

"Well, to come around. I thought she'd adjust better when I built her the clapboard. I thought the happiest day of her life would be when she moved out of the soddy, yet all she's done is complain that the house isn't fixed up fancy enough."

"And Letty?"

"She never complains, Momma. Living with us can't be easy for her and Little Luke, yet she is always cheerful and works harder than Prissy does, I swear, and she's wonderful with Mitchell and Betsy."

"She's a good woman," Lavenia conceded, then said, "Why don't you go back on home, son? I want to stop by Luke's grave."

"Do you know the way back?"

She smiled. "It's only a mile. Time I got my exercise. Besides, the trees are turning." Most of all, she loved the maples, that deep shade of red and orange caused by the first frost. "I'll be reminded of home."

8

The Surprise

It was Saturday night at The Widows.

Sam lighted the kindling wood in the stove in the washhouse. Then he laboriously carried water from the well to the fifteen-gallon can on top of the stove. The big container would be filled three times during the evening for the bathers—mostly hired farm hands who had brought along a fresh change of clothing.

Audrey, the new cook, a big Irish woman who had worked briefly for a madam in Gutherie, placed her hands on wide hips and surveyed the huge kettle of chicken and noodles. "I've got enough food for fifteen," she said, "but, Miss Barrett, if we have a few more show up than expected, they may end up with middling and hen fruits." She patted her iron gray hair under a white bandanna. "If it turns cold, we may have a lot left over."

"I doubt it," Leona laughed. "I've seen them trudge on foot through a snowstorm on a Saturday night, male instincts being what they are!"

Audrey glanced out the window at a man on a mustang, riding over the incline. His frame was so large that he dwarfed the pony. "First customer, and it's only three o'clock," Audrey muttered. "Looks like a cowhand."

Leona sighed. "Is it Liza's turn?"

"Yep. Remember, Mary took the last one at one A.M."

Sam took the reins of the pony and looked up at the big grizzled man, whose long, tawny red hair under the sweat-stained stetson looked as if it had not been combed for a week. His weather-browned face was covered with a reddish growth of beard.

"Is this The Widders, boy?" he asked, showing an array of brownish teeth.

"Yes, sir. I'll feed your horse, mister," Sam replied. "The washhouse is over there. You will find cold water in the barrel and hot water on the stove, plenty of towels on the hanger, and a bottle of witch hazel. Want me to scrub your back?"

The man looked at him suspiciously. "I don't want no bath," he retorted. "All I want is a piece of tail meat."

Sam nodded. "To obtain the one, you must have the other."

The man surveyed the house and grounds with an appreciative eye and nodded. "All right," he said gruffly and made his way to the washhouse.

Sam debated on whether to unsaddle the horse. The man seemed to be in a hurry. He led the animal into a barn stall and tied the reins, put out fresh hay, and retraced his steps to the washhouse. "We have chicken and noodles for supper," he called through the door, "and apple pie for dessert."

"I already et," the man called back.

"You'll find a razor on the shelf under the mirror. If you do not have supper, your bill will be two twenty-five; if you do, you will owe fifty cents more."

There was only a snort for a reply.

When the man came up the steps to the back porch fifteen minutes later, Leona looked at him with approval. His hair was combed back from his forehead, his face was shaved and shining, and even his finger-nails were clean.

"I'm Leona Barrett," she said graciously.

He smiled pleasantly. "Name's Nelson," he replied and shook her hand. As she led him into the parlor, Audrey nodded her head. I *know* that man, she said to herself, but she could not place him—the red hair confused her. Partial to redheaded men, she could remember most of them she met in the course of a work day. She was sure that the man—or his twin brother—had visited Madam's place in Gutherie. . . .

Liza sat demurely on the Turkish sofa reading the latest edition of the *Woman's Home Companion*. Leona made the introductions, then took a seat by the front window and resumed her needlework.

Liza smiled and indicated the stairs. Nelson followed meekly. He was so tall that his head almost touched the chandelier over the stairs. He started to undress before he reached the room. Liza excused herself and undressed in the closet. Most men who made the long journey over the prairie by horse preferred a more leisurely introduction to lovemaking, but if he was in a hurry. . . .

While Nelson was removing his long suit of underwear, she pulled down the counterpane and climbed between the cool sheets. She observed him in the mirror and was amused to see him place his wallet in his shoe. How extraordinary! Regular clientele knew there was nothing to fear from the widows and did not bother to hide their valuables. His small, wary eyes took in every piece of furniture in the room at a glance. In his midtwenties, he did not have an ounce of extra weight on his big frame.

A regular patron of whorehouses, Nelson had never before encountered anything quite as strange as The Widows. The woman, the sheet outlining her young body, was young and exciting. It was like looking at another man's wife—a thought that aroused him further. He was used to painted women with dyed hair in the houses in Gutherie and Enid, lying on scarlet bedspreads or musty sheets. But this could be his mother's house, it was so spotless. There was something about bedding a woman in an antiseptically clean room that was extraordinarily moving—especially after sleeping on the prairie with only a horse blanket for protection. He had also enjoyed the bath, a luxury seldom available on the trail.

Instead of climbing over her as was his wont, he lay down beside her and opened his arms. She enclosed his big shoulders in a loose embrace while he kissed her tentatively. Her lips were very soft and yielding, and he knew instinctively that she liked him. He had planned to ride as far as Pond Creek before nightfall, but, he reflected, there was no actual hurry—especially when so toothsome a delight as Liza lay beside him.

He kissed her again and felt her excited response. How unusual. Most whores brazenly exposed themselves, using words only heard in a cowtown saloon to urge him on; when it was over a few minutes later, he always felt a mixture of sadness and guilt. But, he knew today was no ordinary day when he placed his tough, callused hands on her shoulders and heard himself saying: "I'm sorry. I didn't mean to be so rough."

She giggled and snuggled close to him. Cradling her in his arms, he thought about the first woman that he had ever possessed—in his awkwardness and discomfiture, the performance was concluded prematurely. Of course, he was experienced now, and even though it had been a long time since he had bedded down with a woman, he was still in command. Between kisses, he nibbled her ears, which sent a small series of shocks through her body. How willing she was, how expectant of him! A shiver ran through his big frame.

Adroitly he moved so that he was looking down into her beautiful dark eyes. He must be careful not to hurt this creature trembling beneath his touch. She did not anticipate his movements, which he found delightful. Obviously she knew much about the acts of love, yet never once did she give any indication that this was not her first time. Only when he gently pressed against her did she move up to meet him, enclosing him fully. He sighed and paused a moment as a warm, luxurious feeling stole over him. Oh, to be able to stay this way forever! Oh, to be so sweetly imprisoned until the last dawn of the last day!

Finally, he began to move very slowly. As he sighed again and again, the soft tinkling sounds of a harpsichord wafted up from below. The tune, which he did not recognize, was not a music hall number, but rather a soothing accompaniment to his slow movements. This was truly a house of treasures, both of the spirit and of the flesh. Liza was very warm and her breath was coming in small gasps. He had forgotten the joy of giving pleasure instead of taking it!

"You're won-der-ful, Liza," he found himself saying,

complimenting her as he would his wife. When his climax came, it was sweeter than all the climaxes that he had ever experienced before. There was a gentle, sustained feeling of relief—not a temple-pounding, harsh relaxation of muscles, but rather a soft and mellow outpouring. He sighed softly and dozed.

Leona Barrett closed the lid of the harpsichord with a snap, went into the kitchen and poured a large portion of hard cider into a china mug. A moment later, she heard the stranger's tread on the stairs, then the sound of his boots in the hallway. He was more subdued than she had expected, but she was glad he was leaving, because another man—a regular client—was in the wash house and another was waiting outside, drinking a glass of whiskey. She handed Nelson the cider.

"Thanks," he grinned, and downed the liquid in one gulp. He placed two silver dollars and a twenty-five-cent piece on the kitchen table and strode out of the kitchen without a backward glance.

Audrey watched him as he swung his long legs over the back of the mustang, then she hit her palms together. "Now I remember who he is!" she cried, her cheeks coloring. "What threw me off was his red hair. Now it all comes back to me. He used to dye his hair black. Madam was furious because she had to throw away the pillow case. That pyrogallic acid in the dye wouldn't wash out!" She paused, eyes glittering. "Do you know you've been entertaining an outlaw? That was Dick Yeager!"

"Oh, my God! I hope Liza's all right," Leona cried. "What if he killed her!" She picked up her skirts and ran into the hallway and took the stairs two at a time. Dick Yeager, she had heard, had murdered at least fifteen men.

She rushed into Liza's room, half expecting the bedspread to be covered with blood and Liza lying on the floor with her throat cut. She breathed a sigh of relief, Liza was standing at the window, stretching her hands toward the ceiling and yawning.

"Thank God, you're all right. That man was Dick Yeager!"

Liza turned; her face was soft and relaxed. "All the

90

same, he was gentle and satisfying," she replied slowly. "He's a good man inside. You know very well, Leona, a man can't hide what he is in bed. Who knows what led him to his occupation? What led us into ours?" She poured water into the bedside basin and began to wash her face and hands. "By the way, Leona, what were you playing on the harpsichord? It seemed appropriate somehow."

Leona Barrett smiled quizzically. "A classical piece. I believe it's called 'Sheep May Safely Graze'. . . . "

On Thursday, Edward took Bosley on an inspection tour of the Heron claims. As they rode over the combined half-section of land, Bosley shook his head in wonder. "After being cooped up in that train for days and sleeping in those cramped quarters, it's a joy to see land this beautiful. You have everything here—pasture and farm land, a creek, timber, and even hills to relieve the bleakness of the prairie. Do you know how fortunate you are?"

Edward nodded. "But I don't see very much of it— I'm in the tack room from sunup to sunset. But I do try to take Priscilla riding in the carriage on Sundays; our pastor is one of the most boring men alive." He paused. "I'm used to the place, Bosley, I don't see it with your eyes." They rode on in silence for a half a mile or so, each absorbed with his own thoughts. In the few days that Bosley had stayed with them, the men had become friends.

That night after dinner, Bosley said to Letty, "Don't you get lonely out here in the middle of nowhere?"

"Why—no, not really. There's a great deal of work to do. . . . "

"You don't miss civilization?"

Letty smiled crookedly. "We are *quite* civilized, Mr. Trenton," she replied wryly. "I realize we may not seem so to someone like yourself who travels so much, but we observe the amenities."

He had started off badly. He laughed, trying to regain lost ground. "Going about the country is a bore, actually." He paused. Now he sounded like a prig. "I'm rather drawn to the peaceful life. I would not mind settling down here in Angel," he said wistfully.

She wiped the table oilcloth carefully, concentrating on removing nonexistent soil. "I don't know if such a small community could support a geologist," she said quietly, without looking up. ____

He had offended her somehow. This was not one of his better days, and she was also making it very difficult. He finished the coffee and set the cup on the table just as Lavenia swept into the room. He brightened and turned on the charm. "I'm sorry I won't have your companionship on my journey to the Gyp Hills," he said. "How long do you plan to be in Angel?"

She looked at him with glowing eyes. "I'll be leaving before the first snow. Do come visit me when travels take you up Minneapolis way."

"I'll do that."

At that moment Little Luke came in from the yard. "Uncle Bos. A caterpillar. Come take a peek!" The boy looked up at him with wide eyes, and held out his hand. For a four-year-old, he looked quite grown up as he frowned, squinting up at the big man.

"Yes, of course." Bosley looked helplessly from Letty to Lavenia.

When they had left, Lavenia sighed. "Isn't he wonderful, Letty?"

"I don't know that he is very wonderful, Mother, but Little Luke has surely taken to him. He called him 'uncle,' did you notice?"

Lavenia nodded. "I think it's rather sweet."

Letty hung the wash cloth over the side of the sink and smoothed her apron. "Mother," she said slowly, "I think Bosley Trenton would like to court me. . . ."

"He'd make a very good husband, Letty. You've got to realize that Little Luke needs a father. And then, too, how many eligible males are there in Angel?"

"You wouldn't mind, then?"

Lavenia glanced heavenward. "Why should I mind, Letty? Don't ask permission. You have your own life to live."

"I know that, Mother Heron. But every time I look at Bosley, I see Luke. . . ."

Lavenia's eyes sparkled. "It's like having him back with us again, isn't it?"

Letty turned away. Luke was Luke and Bosley was Bosley. She did not know whether she could tolerate an exact replica. Still, after a while, perhaps the two men would meld together in her mind. She was sorely tempted, but could she love him the way she had loved Luke?

Bosley entered and deposited the caterpillar in a Mason fruit jar. He smiled. "Little Luke's going-away present. I could hardly refuse, could I? I'll turn the critter loose once I'm out of sight." He paused. "Now I must go. It's a long ride into Enid and I'm expected to stop in Garber and Brekenridge and pick up some other soil samples as well, which means I won't get into the town until late." He turned to Lavenia. "May I write to you, dear lady?"

"Of course, please do." She beamed.

"And may I also write to you, Mrs. Heron?"

"If you like." She still could not look at him.

"Thank you. Now, I'll say goodbye to Edward." He held out his hand.

When he had gone, Lavenia took Letty's arm. "Give him a chance, my dear." Her eyes grew misty. "He's perfect in so many ways."

"All right, Mother Heron," Letty replied slowly. "I'll keep an open mind, I promise." But inside, she felt a twinge of nervousness. While Bosley Trenton was working in the Gyp Hills, she would have time to think. . . .

The wheat crop of 1898 was plentiful: forty bushels to the acre at 84¢ a bushel. Edward took his share of the profits and turned the old sod house into a furniture showroom. He also sent a request to Lavenia in Minneapolis to send the trunks in the attic that contained his father's furniture designs, and paid an art instructor in Enid for elaborate sketches that depicted his new line of sideboards, buffets, extension tables, bookcases, roll-top desks, bedroom suites, and four-poster bedsteads. Lastly, he ordered a case of beveled mirrors from Germany.

When the Reverend and Mrs. Haskell inquired about a rattan rocking chair, he also laid in a small supply of odd reed furniture—the fashion rage of the moment—

93

and increased his apprentices to four to take care of an order for eight buffets from Gutherie.

Priscilla, with Mitchell by the hand, surveyed the tack room skeptically. Edward was working alongside the journeyman woodcarver; a load of quarter-sawed oak lumber was stocked in the corner. "I hope you're satisfied now, Edward Heron," she said heatedly, "all the money we have in the world is tied up here—including the wheat money, cash laid away for our burial and the ninety dollars we were going to spend for longhorn heifers."

He looked at her quizzically, then added the finishing touch to the final coat of shellac on Bella Chenovick's chiffonier. He replaced the paintbrush in the can of turpentine, wiped his hands on his new Black Crook overalls, then sat down at the grindstone and sharpened a knife. "Prissy," he said quietly, "if I'm to accept orders from as far away as Perry and Blackwell, I've got to be able to schedule enough time and materials. As it is, I'm low on tools. We can't scrimp now." He spoke quietly so that the other men could not hear. "You've got your clapboard, nicely furnished, a new privy, a couple of chicken coops and this summer you'll get a gazebo, so I don't understand what you're complaining about."

"You never know when another depression will come, either!" she retorted.

"You weren't worried about a depression, Prissy," he whispered savagely, "when you brought Doc Burgen from Enid to bring the baby into the world!"

"Oh, shut up!" she cried, and flounced out the door.

Edward placed the carving knife carefully on the table and followed her across the yard into the kitchen. He took her shoulder and turned her around in one movement. "Listen," he said angrily, "don't *ever* do that to me again!"

"What do you mean?" Her eyes were wide, innocent, uncaring.

"Embarrass me in front of my employees. In fact, I'd rather you didn't come into the tack room at all."

She drew herself up stiffly. "It's all the same to me, but don't expect any special favors!"

He knew what she meant. "I don't know why I married you," he said simply.

Letty stood by the window in the barn. She had heard the words exchanged between Priscilla and Edward and waited until he returned before she opened the door to the tack room. She wore a blue calico dress that exactly matched her eyes. "Prissy doesn't understand the word 'expansion,' Edward," she said quietly, handing him an envelope.

"I don't know why you and she get along so well. You're absolutely opposite in temperament."

She smiled indulgently. "She moved next door to me when I was five." She smiled crookedly. "We *do* get on each other's nerves once in a while, but we understand each other."

"I wish I understood her!" Edward unfolded a set of ornate scroll designs.

"Don't forget the envelope," she said.

"What's in it?"

"Sixty dollars I don't need."

"What for?"

"Tools."

"I can wait until I get Mrs. Stevens' money for her bedstead. Keep it."

"I've saved it from the rental stores in Angel. You know, Edward, if the town expands much more, I may have a decent income after all." She paused. "Well, I must go back to the house. Mrs. Chenovick brought over three bushels of peaches for preserves."

He watched her stride up the path, the blue dress swirling around her ankles. Sometimes, he reflected, a man could marry the wrong woman. How much more pleasant life would be if he had married Letty instead of Priscilla!

In early July, 1898, a tall stranger knocked on the front door. Priscilla knew it was a stranger because friends always came to the back door. "Yes?" she asked through the screen.

"My name is Methers, ma'am," he replied, taking off his hat, revealing long, brown, wavy hair that exactly matched his muttonchop whiskers. "I'm with the Rock Island Railroad. Is Mr. Heron home?"

"I'm afraid not. He's gone to Enid for lumber." She looked at him quizzically, debating whether or not to let him in; he might be a rapist. But if he was, she thought, he was a distinguished-looking rapist.

As if reading her mind, he smiled gallantly. "Could we sit under the trees and speak a bit?"

They sat at the log table over which he had placed a survey map of Indian Territory. He traced his finger along a line. "Oh, I see *two* Heron claims here! Are you Letty Heron?"

She shook her head.

"Then it is Letty Heron that I must see."

"She's at the well, but will be back shortly. Could I be of service?"

"As you may know, we are running some spur lines out from Enid—one through Garber to Billings, and one through Angel to Perry. We'll be passing over Letty Heron's claim."

"Did I hear my name mentioned?" Letty asked, setting the bucket of water on the stoop.

"This is Mr. Methers of the Rock Island." Priscilla smiled tightly. "Apparently the railroad is going to run right across your property."

"Really?" She flushed with pleasure at the prospect.

"Yes," Methers replied. "Now, would you like a pond or an underpass?"

"Pardon?"

"Well," he explained patiently, "we can't offer any remuneration because the government's already given us a right-of-way. But we'll build an underpass or dig a pond. It's up to you."

Letty shrugged her shoulders. "I don't need a pond because of the creek, but if I ever decide to raise livestock, an underpass would be handy.

"Would you sign, please?" He made notes on a tablet, then produced a yellow document. He paused. "Would you be a witness?" he asked Priscilla. She added her name with a flourish, then disappeared into the house.

96

"When do you expect to lay down the tracks?" Letty asked.

"We'll start in Enid in a month or so, as soon as I'm able to see all the settlers."

"Could I see the map, please?"

"Certainly."

She looked closely at the heavy lines that stretched out from Enid in two prongs. "I see you're also going through the Dice and Barrett claims."

"Is that the *widow* Barrett?"

"Yes."

He tipped his hat, a glint of undisguised fervor in his eyes. "Thank you, that's all I need to know." His step was quite jaunty as he mounted the roan and headed out over the prairie in the general direction of The Widows.

Letty picked up the pail of water and went into the kitchen. "Oh, Prissy!" she exclaimed. "Think what a railroad will mean to Angel. Growth beyond our wildest imagination!"

Priscilla turned from the ironing board and placed a sad iron on end. "For some, I guess," she said, her mouth turned down, "but not all! As usual you're in the catbird seat."

"And just what is meant by that?"

Priscilla placed her hands on her hips "What do you think I mean?" she demanded. "If the town does grow, it can only grow on *your* land! You'll end up a very rich old woman!"

"If the town spreads out, we all prosper," Letty said evenly, determined not to lose her temper.

"That's a matter of opinion!" Priscilla's face was flushed and her dark curls were quivering. "From the beginning, you've always had advantages, Letty Heron! Even when we were schoolgirls, your folks always treated you special. Butter wouldn't melt in your mouth! Then you had the good sense to marry Luke, and he was lucky enough to pick a claim with a good running creek, and then he died and you gave the community a God's Acre—knowing full well that a town would spring up around a cemetery! Luke even gave you an heir to carry on the sainted name of Heron!"

Her eyes were blazing. "Now you've got rent from all the merchants," she wailed, "and to top it off, the railroad is going through your claim! You've always been treated like a queen." Her eyes narrowed. "But the worst part is that Edward and I have to put up with you and your brat!"

Letty was beyond anger, suspended somewhere between mortification and grief. "One issue can be solved immediately," she said quietly, her heart filled with panic. " 'My brat' and I will pack our things. . . ." She managed to leave the room before the wracking sobs hit her. She stumbled into her sitting room and slammed the door, awakening the child, who was sleeping on the little half bed. She took him in her arms. She would ask Poppa Dice to take her to a hotel in Enid. Now that the end had come, she felt a certain heaviness leave her body. She felt free.

Letty dried her tears on her apron and went into the bedroom, where she opened her steamer trunk; wafts of mustiness hit her nostrils, bringing back memories. Trunks always held a certain benign fragrance that spoke of journeys on trains, trips in spring wagons, shays jostling over windswept prairie roads.

Methodically, she began to pack. Her finances were in good order. The wheat money lay in the bank untouched, the rental property brought in good dividends, and she did not owe a single penny to anyone. She would visit the same contractor in Enid who had built The Widows. By Christmas, surely, she would be in her own home—a step she should have taken years ago. She counted out and placed on the bureau the thirty dollars' "house money" that she gave Edward every month.

There was a tentative knock on the sitting room door. "Yes?" she answered, fully in control now. "Come in."

Priscilla stood in the doorway. It seemed that she had aged in the last few minutes. Her face was gray and ashen, her eyes wide and stricken. "Oh, Letty!" she cried, her mouth working. "What have I done to you? I'd rather cut off my right hand than hurt you! I'm a mean and stupid woman!" The tears started. "Can you forgive me?" Then she went on in a rush. "I didn't mean anything I said, truly I didn't! It's just that I've been under such a strain lately, with us so far behind financially and all our money going out for help and supplies . . . And, when the railroad man came knocking on the door, it just seemed the last straw—as if God was against us somehow. . . ." She ran into Letty's arms. "Oh, please forgive me, please accept my apologies. . . ."

Letty looked down at the dark head. "I forgive you, Prissy," she said gently, all anger gone. "And I understand how you feel." She paused. "One thing you left out just a moment ago. You forgot about *my* feelings. I still grieve for Luke, you know. . . ." She paused again. "Now, here's a handkerchief," she spoke as if talking to a child. "Dry your tears."

Priscilla did as she was told. "I'm so ashamed, Letty. Edward would *kill me* if he knew. You do forgive me, don't you?" she beseeched, her eyes red-rimmed.

"I forgive you," Letty said quietly, "but all the same, I'll be moving."

There was a silence.

"But, I need your friendship," Priscilla exclaimed. "I wouldn't know how to navigate without you. You're part of our lives—a very necessary part!"

Letty smiled crookedly. "I think not, Prissy. It's time you and Edward had privacy, and Little Luke and me, too."

At that moment they heard the journeyman shout, *"Fire!" Fire!"* They rushed out into the yard and saw tongues of flame shooting out of the barn door.

"Don't try to stop it, men!" Edward cried. "Just get those bedsteads out while I free the animals."

Before Letty or Priscilla could move, the apprentices had carried out the furniture and Edward had led Marigold the cow and the horses into the clearing. Belatedly, Letty picked up the pail of water and ran toward the barn. Edward grabbed the pail and doused the burning window, but the heat was so intense that the water seemed a mere thimbleful.

"What can we do?" Priscilla screamed.

Edward took her hand. "Watch it burn," he said. "There's no fire-fighting equipment in Angel. It's useless to bring water from the well. Just be glad that we saved the animals and the finished pieces. . . ." His face was stoic as he watched the roof cave in on the precious lumber. He was thankful that the surrounding terrain was still damp from the previous night's rain.

"At least," Priscilla said, "it wasn't the house. . . ."

In five minutes the whole structure had collapsed; only a mass of glowing embers, heavy with the smell of burned resin, remained. Edward sighed. "It wasn't built right anyway," he said, "makeshift from the beginning." He looked over at the sod house, which contained his precious designs, and the finished pieces awaiting pick-up. He smiled sadly at Letty. "You can have an interest in the Heron Furniture Company," he said plaintively, "if you'll lend me the money to build a new barn. . . ."

In her mind's eyes, Letty could see the house that she had wanted to build so desperately fade into smoke. She glanced sideways at Priscilla who appeared as if she were going to burst into tears again. "I'll do better than that, Edward," she said. "Do you know the lot next to the general store? That would be a good location for your new store, with the railroad coming through. . . ."

He looked at her in amazement. "The railroad?"

"Of course, you don't know!" She smiled meaningfully at Priscilla. "So much has happened this morning." She paused. "The Rock Island representative was here a while ago. The railroad is building two spur lines, one through Garber and the other through Angel!"

Edward shouted: "Whoopee! That means prosperity. I *must* have a store in town, then." He looked from the smouldering remains of the barn to the sod house. "It'll have to be big enough to have a showroom in front and a big workroom and shop in the back." His voice rose enthusiastically. "We'll also build a second story—rooms for the workers." Letty had not seen him so excited since he had stood up for Luke and her in the First Baptist Church in Minneapolis. He took Letty's hand. "Welcome, partner!"

Letty shook her head until her curls danced. "No, Edward, I don't belong in the furniture business. But I will loan you the money to build at simple interest rates."

Poppa Dice galloped into view, his horse sweating and frothing at the mouth. He reined up in front of the barn. "Come as soon as I seed the smoke," he exclaimed.

"Thanks," Edward said, "but it all happened so quick there was no hope of putting out the fire."

"How did it start?" Poppa Dice asked.

"Search me," Edward replied, "but I think the five-gallon can of naptha caught fire somehow. The lid was open—I'd been cleaning my tools—and it was next to a bale of hay. . . ."

"Thank God you saved the animals!"

Edward smiled wanly. "Old Marigold was so scared, I bet her milk is soured!"

They all laughed, and their laughter increased as the very pregnant Fontine, in her wide straw hat, appeared headed down the incline, riding side-saddle on Violet, the mule.

9

The Showdown

Mary Darth looked at the ceiling.

The Kentuckian labored over her, perspiration dripping down his heavy jowls and onto her neck. She shivered involuntarily, and he, thinking she was approaching a climax, increased his pace.

She smiled to herself. He was really a dear man. Among the regular customers, he was her favorite, but he was never able to make her feel anything but cozy and warm. Back in Chicago, she had heard other women exult over the way their husbands made love to them, indicating pleasure with great rolling of the eye and hushed voices. But, truthfully, she never felt *anything*.

Finally, with a great sigh, he finished and lay breathing heavily beside her. She gathered him in her arms tenderly, mainly because she knew it was expected and that a large tip was in the offing.

She roused from her reverie when he kissed her ear. "Mary," he said quietly, "you know that I've been coming up to see my relatives quite often lately."

"Yes," she replied, "and I'm glad."

"You *are*?"

"Yes, of course. It's always a pleasure to see you," she said, but did not add: and your greenbacks as well!

"Well, frankly," he said after a pause, "I've been coming up here to the territory mostly to see you. My old aunt is quite senile and on this visit she didn't recognize me. I've got to hire a nurse." He paused. "I was

102

hoping this time you might consent to return to Louisville with me."

"But," she replied incredulously, when she found her voice, "how would this be possible?" Thoughts were darting in and out of her mind with the speed of a firefly flashing its lamp. "I live here at The Widows."

"You could come back home—as my wife!" His great, soulful eyes were looking at her with a strange look of desire and compassion. "Say yes, Mary Darth, say yes."

She arose and moved to the window, the white peignoir that he had brought on this last trip flowing around her legs. She turned, her face very soft. "Reggie, you know that I can't," she replied quietly. "I—I am a businesswoman." She knew that her statement sounded ridiculous in the bedroom with the sunlight pouring through the dotted swiss curtains, making an oblong pattern over his huge naked frame on the bed. "I'm not wife material—that much should be obvious to you."

"If I didn't think you were, I would not have asked you to marry me," he replied simply. "I understand your position. After all, I was one of your guests at dinner that first day. I've been coming here for six years. I know you, Mary Darth!"

"Oh, no, Reggie, you don't know me—really!" She sighed. "I'm a far different person than you realize." She paused, gathering her words together most carefully. What would she do in the aristocratic world of Louisville society? She was not the gregarious hostess type. And he would give her a small allowance that permitted him to go to bed with her whenever he liked. She would not approve of that. She liked her freedom. "I'm very happy here, and I mean that," she said. "Reggie, you are my favorite. . . ." She was going to say "client," but changed her mind. "You are my favorite—man."

He smiled sadly. "What you are saying is that you don't love me. But how many married people today are in love? I'll provide you with a nice house. . . ."

"Reggie, you don't know me— but more than that, *I don't know you!*"

He turned over in bed to look at her, leaning on his elbow. "Do you know how many times I've been in this house during the last six years? Twenty times! The first times I came either to eat or play Faro—only because of you. I have sat at your table, we have conversed for hours on end. We have been as intimate as two people can be. How can you say that we don't know each other?"

She gestured helplessly. "Oh, Reggie, that doesn't mean we *know* each other."

He smiled quietly. "I think it does." His voice was strained. "Did it ever occur to you there may be little else to divulge?"

She could not stay in the room a moment longer. With head held high, she went into the hall, a sickening feeling inside growing stronger and stronger. What if he were right? What if they both were essentially very boring, uninteresting people? What if they had been brought together purely by loneliness? Should she grasp what might be her last chance for wealth? He was kind to her, loved her, was happy to be near her . . . but was that enough? Did she have the right to expect more, when she knew she could never feel anything inside for a man?

Mary gathered up her courage. She had an answer, and the answer was yes; she went over the exact wording that she would use. But when she returned to the bedroom, he had turned over on his back and was sleeping peacefully. She lowered the window shade, then dressed in the half light that illuminated the room. She was hungry and it was almost time for supper.

When he came downstairs an hour later, she had changed her mind. She knew she could not marry him.

Edward read the letter with satisfaction:

Washington, D.C.
August 18, 1899

Dear Priscilla and Edward Heron:

I have been thinking about my friends in the community of Angel a good deal this past week. I have

104

turned in my report on the Gyp Hills and have another short assignment in the Glass Mountains.

I would like very much to attend the fifth annual Cherokee Strip celebration in Enid on the 16th of September.

If it is permissible, I should like to take the train to Angel on the 18th of September and visit for a few hours. If this is not convenient, I will be staying at the Donley Hotel in Enid from the 14th to the morning of the 18th. Please write me there and mark the letter "hold for arrival."

I trust this letter finds both of you, as well as Letty, in the best of health.

Your friend,
Bosley Adams Trenton

"I didn't know his middle name was Adams," Edward said, laying the letter aside.

Priscilla smiled tightly. "I'm afraid there are a number of things that you do not know about Mr. Trenton, Edward."

"Just what do you mean by that, Prissy?"

She shrugged. "Don't think that he's coming here solely to see us, Edward! Don't you realize that he's crazy about Letty?"

Four weeks later, Priscilla piled meringue on a lemon pie. "If this runs, I'm going to commit suicide."

"Yes," Letty laughed, "all we need is a soggy crust when we've got company coming."

"I don't really think of Mr. Trenton as company," Priscilla replied. "He's really like a member of the family."

"That's a matter of opinion!" Letty said slowly.

"What's 'a matter of opinion'?" a deep voice asked from the back porch. Bosley Trenton was casually leaning against the door frame, looking more than ever like Luke.

Letty drew in her breath sharply and laughed nervously. "We were just talking 'women talk.'" She colored.

Priscilla came forward. "Good to see you, Mr. Trenton." She shook his hand rather tentatively, embarrassed that he had caught her in her Mother Hubbard.

He came forward and held out his hand to Letty. "Aren't you going to greet me, Letty Heron?"

"Of course." She shook his hand much more strongly than she felt. Suddenly she was back in Minneapolis with Luke and they were in the kitchen together and she could feel his breath on her cheek. Her eyes filled with tears and she turned away. "Excuse me," she said and ran from the room.

"What's wrong?" Bosley asked, dumbstruck. "What did I say?"

"She'll be back in a moment," Priscilla said softly. "Didn't you hear Little Luke calling?"

After dinner, while the men talked politics in the parlor, the women washed dishes, then while Priscilla punched down the dough for the morning rolls, Letty wiped her hands on her apron. "I'm going on up to bed, Prissy. If anything is said about my absence, you can say I have a headache."

Upstairs, with the soft, downy comforter over her body, she examined her mixed feelings about Bosley Trenton. He had written her three letters since his last visit, and she had dutifully replied to each in the formalized manner she had learned in school. Yet even with the exchange of correspondence, she did not know the man any better than when he had been brought home by Lavenia Heron. Was she attributing Luke's character traits to him? She did not know.

"Let's ride over to those cottonwoods, Bos," Edward said. "Since I don't farm any more, I don't get out in these parts, and those trees on Letty's claim look strange."

Skirting Jaundice's newly plowed fields, they followed the path down to the creek, dismounted, and tied up their horses on a low-hanging sycamore branch. Then they walked along the trickle of water that meandered along the pebbled bed. "I hope these trees aren't infected. Do you know anything about fungus, Bos?"

He laughed. "I'm a geologist, not a botanist." He knelt by a tree and examined the exposed roots from which the soil had washed away. He rubbed a sticky, discolored leaf between his fingers and smelled the pungent aroma of pitch. He frowned and looked over the edge of the stream at the brown, fetid grasses that rimmed its edge. "How long has the creek been polluted?" he asked.

Edward raised his eyebrows. "Didn't know it was."

"You don't use this for watering, then?"

"No, the stock are fed from our well."

"I see." Bosley followed the creek for a few moments, knowing what he would find. Upstream was a small, ugly, black fissure that spoiled a smooth bank of red sandstone, worn down by time into a small pile of particles. He knelt down and plunged his forefinger into the mass. As a final test, he brought a jagged piece of shale up to his nose. He knew the odor of hydrocarbon. His heart leaped up into his throat, certain that Edward could see it pulsing there. He carefully controlled his face, keeping his excitement inside.

But until he had made a few observations and gathered samples for laboratory work, he would remain quiet. The petroleum deposit might not be very great and, truthfully, further research would have to be done. He regained his ground, looked up at Edward. "I guess the stream has been this way for hundreds of years," he said casually. "It's some mineral deposit or other. I wouldn't worry about it because I don't think it'll get any worse." He climbed back on his horse. "I'd like to examine more of the terrain around here."

"Why don't you stop by The Widows?"

"Won't you come with me?"

Edward smiled. "No, but I'll ride part of the way. I've got all I can take care of at home!"

They rode on in silence, each enjoying the peaceful countryside, covered in dappled sunlight that threw long shadows from the large, white clouds above. Reaching the oak tree, they veered to the right until the back porch of the house was in view. Five clotheslines of sheets and pillow cases flapped in the slight prairie wind. Bosley grinned. "Looks like business is good."

Edward nodded. "Apparently. But no matter what they say, Leona Barrett is a fine woman and she runs her place of business with an iron hand. The houses on Two Street in Enid can't hold a candle to The Widows . . . or so I've heard. Prissy and the other women of the community are dead set against the place, of course." He reined in his horse. "Now, I'll go on home. You follow when you're ready."

"Who is that boy?" Bosley pointed to Sam, who had come out on the back porch.

"Boy? Sam is as old as we are—twenty-seven, I think. He's a full-blooded Cherokee, smart as a whip." He felt the stubble of his beard and rubbed his jaw thoughtfully. "Sad story. When he was just a little boy, some marauding Indians swooped down on his father's house in the middle of the night, set fire to the place, killed his dad, raped his mother, and cut the boy's balls off."

Bosley felt the hairs on the back of his head rise up. "My God, Edward, it makes me sick to my stomach! Imagine being mutilated like that!" He shook his head angrily. "What's he got to look forward to? No wife, no children, and I suppose no sexual inclination. Is he a sissy?"

Edward shook his head. "Not that I know of. He's a kind, gentle man, very expert at baby doctoring. In fact, he brought Little Luke into the world, and a lot of other babies in the Territory, too." He sighed. "Except Betsy. Prissy and Sam don't get along. We had to bring old Doc Burgen out from Enid for a whole day, and that cost a fortune. He's an old fuddy duddy and Prissy had a bad time." He drew in his breath sharply. "I'd better get back. See you around suppertime."

Leona, Mary, and Liza sat in the parlor, each absorbed in needlework, while a wax cylinder of the intermezzo from *Cavaleria Rusticana* played on the Graphophone machine. It was this tranquil scene that greeted Bosley Trenton when he knocked on the front door. Leona bade him enter, he introduced himself, and Audrey brought a large glass of hard cider.

As pleasantries were exchanged, his eyes wandered from woman to woman. Mary was a picture in white dimity, her high lace collar and long cuffs could have easily belonged to a Sunday School teacher, while Liza's pale pink dress, a cameo at the neck, and Leona's pale green cotton swiss were the epitome of decorum. It was as if he had stumbled into a very proper boarding school. Since he was not expected, it was not as if they had dressed especially for him. He noticed that the women were not even wearing rice powder; their cheeks glowed with healthy, natural color.

"What brings you into the area, Mr. Trenton?" Leona asked, patting her auburn pompadour. He did not appear to be a customer, but some men were rather shy. He was obviously a gentleman from the way he was dressed—he had a well tailored look, yet his frock coat obviously had been purchased from a ready-made shop. No tailor worth his salt would allow stitches that large on a lapel!

"Some of the farmers have been having water problems," he was saying. "And since I'm a geologist and in the neighborhood, I thought I'd check on the underground tables." He paused and looked at her in an innocent, matter-of-fact way. "Have there been any reports of hitting salt water when wells were dug for sweet water?" he asked casually.

She shrugged. "I haven't heard of any such cases. Of course, we don't get around socially very much."

He kept a straight face. "Is that so, ma'am?" The Widows were probably, he thought, three of the best-informed women in the Territory. Information obviously filtered in constantly from their clients. If they missed the usual female community maneuvers, such as quilting bees and church suppers, they still did not suffer for lack of gossip. It was common knowledge that men were far more interested than women in talking tête-à-tête.

"It's a rather lonely life out here without women friends," Leona added.

Bosley nodded sympathetically. "But you are fortunate in a way, ma'am. The outside world is not uncomplicated. The simple life, as we used to know it, is a passing parade. Nothing is easy any more—which brings me to the point of my visit."

"This isn't a purely social call?"

He grew a bit red in the temples. "I'd like permission

109

to crawl down the water well outside to check the underground formations."

Leona shrugged. "What do you hope to find?"

"To see if the drought of a few years ago depleted the tables." This statement, of course, was pure hogwash, but he was taking a chance that she knew nothing about how petroleum was found.

Her face bore no sign of understanding, and as the aroma of roasted chicken wafted into the parlor, she said: "Would you stay for a fifty-cent supper?"

He rose and held out his hand. "No, thank you, I am expected at the Herons. Priscilla has baked a gooseberry pie." He wrinkled up his nose. "It's my least favorite, but I must pretend to be the grateful guest." He placed a silver dollar on the tray in the vestibule as he left.

Bosley took off his frock coat and climbed laboriously down into the well on the wooden ladder used for cleaning the cement sides. When his eyes grew accustomed to the darkness, he saw that the rock formations were all straight strata, no curves. He sighed and shook his head.

An hour later, he lowered himself into the well on Letty's claim, holding a lighted lantern aloft. His heart pounded. He found here what he had expected to find at The Widows. Although the earth opening was only thirty feet deep, there was a very slight curve that resembled a house with a peaked roof of shingles pointing upward. At his feet, a red shale deposit was separated from a few feet of glacial clay near the surface by a composition of hard rock. He could see the beginnings of a very slight underground inverted dish, which usually contained hydrocarbon—petroleum—or other mineral deposits. He had a great deal of homework to do. . . .

Obviously there were oil-bearing sands in the area—otherwise there would have been no pitch seepage in Letty's creek—and now he knew there was an anticline. He reflected a moment. This was one time when he had to play his cards carefully. He had come to the Territory to seek his fortune, which was not going to be from his meager stipend from Uncle Sam. But the possibility

110

of a petroleum deposit entrapped under a wide area could mean wealth to Letty Heron. He would say nothing about his petroleum theories for the moment, but would begin to look at the woman with new eyes. He would use all of his wiles. Once they were married. . . .

After he made his Glass Mountain report to Washington, he would stop by Pittsburgh to have the Heron soil and pitch samples analyzed by experienced petroleum chemists. Then he would know how to proceed. . . .

The afternoon was hot and humid for October.

Sam found Poppa Dice in the back forty and waved from the edge of the field. The old man finished plowing the row leading up to Sam and wiped his forehead with a red bandanna. "Aft'noon," he said.

"Here." Sam held out a Mason fruit jar filled with lemonade. "My lady thought you might like a cool drink." He paused, then confided, "It's got artificial ice in it!"

Poppa Dice took a long drink, puckered his lips, then removed his straw hat. He looked long and hard at Sam's face, which was bruised and swollen. "What happened, boy?"

Sam looked away, his dark eyes troubled. "That lawyer from Enid got drunk last night and when I tried to get him to take a nap, he insisted on starting a new game of Faro. He lost fifteen dollars, then picked a fight with Mr. Barrow from over at Covington. He ended up by beating me in the face." Sam hung his white turbaned head. "I was no match for him."

"The sonofabitch!" Poppa Dice cried.

"This is our sixth year, and the first time we've had an altercation." Sam nursed his black eye. "My lady wonders if you could come by this afternoon?"

Poppa Dice looked up at the sun. "It'll be 'bout six-thirty, I reckon." He paused. "I won't be cleaned up or nothin'."

Sam smiled slightly. "She only wants to *talk* to you, sir!"

Poppa Dice replaced his hat. "That's jest 'bout all I can do anymore—talk, that is!"

After the day's plowing was finished, Poppa Dice came up the slight incline by the cottonwoods to The Widows' back door. Inside he heard the Graphophone playing "And Her Golden Hair Was Hanging Down Her Back," one of his favorites. It sounded as if the barbershop quartet was actually singing in the parlor! Leona came out on the stoop. "Got a full house," she said, which was her way of apologizing for not asking him into the kitchen.

He looked down at his dust-covered overalls. "I ain't fit to meet the undertaker!" He paused. "What's on yore mind?"

She bade him sit with her on the stoop. "I've got a problem, Poppa Dice, and I hope you have an answer." She looked him straight in the eye. "Sam's a wonderful lad, but we're getting clientele that are getting too much for him to handle. He told you about the fight?"

Poppa Dice nodded. "That man should have been horse-whipped!"

"He stood a good foot over the boy." She paused and fluttered her hands, hoping that the feminine gesture would appeal to the man. "It's getting down to this: I need someone who understands the ways of the Territory, to run the games with an iron hand. We're getting the railroad men in now, and they can be rough, especially when they've been on the grape. I know the last time that I spoke with you, you were complaining about your back and how hard the field work was getting to be."

Poppa Dice nodded. "I tole Jaundice the other day that after I git the plowing done in this section, he's gonna hafta take on another hired hand. I'm sixty-seven years old. The times are upon me."

Leona smiled. "I'm offering you a job, Poppa Dice, running my games. It's not hard physically, but . . ."

He grinned and thrust his chest out. "Well, Miz Barrett, I'm as pleased as punch. And, I may not know much, but by damn, I can do cipherin'. You can give me a hunnerd figures in a column and I can figger right."

"I know you can, Poppa Dice." She took his big, calloused hand. "If I was a man, I could run the games myself, but the men wouldn't act natural with me around." She paused. "And, besides, I've got all I can handle upstairs." She looked out over the prairie, which had turned golden in the long dusk. "When will you be finished with the bottom land?"

"Next Tuesday or Wednesday, I reckon."

"You'd be free to start work on Friday evening?"

He nodded, then looked down at his overalls. "You know I ain't got no proper duds."

"Here I am giving you details, and I haven't spoken about the important things!" she exclaimed. "Now, part of the bargain is that I buy your clothes. And, of course, you get ten per cent of the gaming profits besides. Is this satisfactory?"

"More 'n fair, I'd say." He stood up and held out his hand. "I'm much obliged, Miz Barrett, I truly am."

"I'll tell Mr. Baker at the general store to outfit you—three suits, some white shirts and shoes with spats. There's a new style necktie that I want you to wear. It's called a Teck scarf, very elegant." Her eyes glittered. "Our gentleman friend, Reginald Savor, from Kentucky says it's the latest style." She paused before going into the house. "Good luck. I hope that Jaundice and Fontine won't put up too much fuss."

He grinned. "Jaundice'll keep out of it, but there'll be all hell to pay with Fourteen. She'll rant and rave, then I'll threaten to leave for good—but knowin' her, she'll cry and feel better, and I'll git my way, same as usual. Goodnight, Miz Barrett." He tipped his straw hat.

"Goodnight, Poppa Dice."

His step was lighter as he headed for the cement block house. It was almost dark now, with only an orange-pink glow at the horizon. He started to hum and then to sing: *Oh, and her golden hair was hanging down her back. . . ."*

10

Happenstance

Sulphur fumes stung Bosley's eyes as he got off the train at the depot in Beaumont, Texas.

The Crosby House, a frameboard landmark, was situated a stone's throw from a clapboard building identified by a sign as the Armbuster Texas Oil Company. Although it was only a little after six in the morning, the two long galleries of the hotel were teeming with land speculators, promoters, residents, and tourists who had flocked into the community to see the six spouting oil wells on Spindletop hill. The first Lucus gusher had come in three months before, on January 10, 1901. What the newcomers saw, however, were not six spouting oil wells, which had been turned into pumpers, but a beehive of activity as dozens of new wells were being spudded every day.

Bosley eased himself between two men in coveralls at the bar and ordered a shot of whiskey, which came with a glass of murky water. He had never before taken liquor for breakfast, but this town, crowded with men in a high humor, some of them intoxicated, made time accelerate, and it seemed to be suppertime.

The water chaser identified Bosley as a tenderfoot to the bartender, who always pigeon-holed his customers into two categories—men who worked outdoors and men who worked indoors. He had only recently become an indoor man, having suffered a leg injury on the rig. He grinned at the well-dressed customer, who was trying so hard to be casual. Accustomed to the rough roustabouts, the slick promoters, and the shifty-eyed

114

land speculators who bought and sold mineral rights on the hill to other shifty-eyed land speculators, he had misgivings about the man in front of him. "What brings ya to Beaumont, suh?" he drawled.

Bosley upturned the shot glass, held the whiskey in his mouth, swallowed hastily, then took a sip of water. He made a face. "Just stranded here between trains."

The barkeep snorted. With six trains a day coming in from Houston, and oil men obtaining thirty-day tickets to be certain of a seat in the day coach, he doubted that the stranger was telling the truth. Could he be an undercover man for the hated Standard Oil Company, which was rumored to be trying to get a toehold in the independent area?

Sensing the man's skepticism, Bosley held out his hand in a friendly gesture. "I'm Michael Brandon," he said cordially. "I'm a journalist for the *New York Times.*" He had decided that if he were going to fabricate a background, he might as well employ the name of America's most famous newspaper.

The barkeep sighed with relief, and smiled. The town was overflowing with newspapermen, and everyone knew they were a little crazy.

"Is Mr. Armbuster around?" Bosley asked.

"No, suh. What do ya want to see him fer?" The barkeep served a customer, then returned. "He's small potatoes. Go see Patillo Higgins, who first had an inkling they'd be oil hereabouts . . . or old Capt'n Lucus, who brought in the first well at a hundred thousand barrels at day. Old Armbuster is a Johnny-come-lately." He almost added, *and a sonofabitch besides,* but he was afraid of being quoted around Beaumont, and Armbuster was a tough hombre.

Bosley nodded, thanked the barkeep and made his way through a rabble of boomers and oil hustlers, some of whom had climbed on the saloon tables and were hawking leases. He heard shouts of fifty, eighty, and a hundred thousand dollars. Money was being discussed as if men were buying peanuts instead of minute tracks of land that just might be situated over a dome of petroleum.

When he tried to check into the Crosby, the clerk

115

laughed in his face. "Men are sleeping two in a bed in eight hour shifts, suh, and ah suggest iffen ya want breakfast, ya best line up in front like everybody else, or you won't get victuals til noon. We got forty thousand new folk in town!"

Bosley shook his head, which was reeling slightly from the early intake of whiskey, and made his way out into the street. He had never before seen anything quite like the scene that greeted his eyes. As far as he could see down Crockett Street, hundreds of men of all sizes and descriptions were milling about willy-nilly. A few women, looking lost and forlorn, were jostled to and fro by the crowd.

A few carriages were pulled up before the various saloons, most of which ran brothels on the second floor. The ladies of the demi-monde were plying their trade more openly, and it was scarcely eight o'clock in the morning! What would the street look like after dark?

The swarthy driver of an old stagecoach, which had been in use for twenty years or so, Bosley judged, stood on the cab, and shouted: "Git in. Git in. Only five dollars for a trip to the hill. Come see the Guffey geyser shoot oil a hundred feet in the air! Git in. Git in!"

Bosley held up his five-dollar bill, which was snapped up by the man's fingers. He climbed into the coach along with several other passengers, and a moment later was juggling from side to side as the horses trod stoically through the deep mud.

The noise was deafening as they came into the spudding area. Derricks were going up every few feet, storage tanks were being constructed, boilers placed into operation, and what looked like hundreds of men were jobbing every tract. Only the McFaddin tract was devoid of activity and when the passengers leaned out the windows and took in the view, everyone understood why. A giant fire had charred the ground, and the stench from the remains of dead animals mixed with the gas and sulphur fumes from Spindletop Heights was almost overpowering. As the carriage moved on, the sun was obscured by a fine mist of black crude oil that stubbornly adhered to hair and mustaches and turned complexions gray in an instant.

"Let's git back to town!" one of the men said, brushing beads of oil from his eyelashes as he gazed sorrowfully at his once pale gray frockcoat.

The driver snorted. "Hell, we haven't even reached the geyser yet," he exclaimed, hitting the flanks of the horses lightly with the reins as the animals struggled in the mud and gumbo. He glanced back at his charges and shouted: "You ain't got yore money's worth yet!"

"To hell with the money, let's git out o' here," another man yelled, "if anyone throws down a cigar, we'll all be incinerated!"

Bosley looked awestruck at the derricks peopled with drillers and pipers. Ants, he thought, the men looked like ants, crawling over the huge wooden frames. It was as if every man's life depended upon whether oil was struck or not.

"There she is!" The driver crowed triumphantly, and all eyes turned to the right. A silence permeated the inside of the stagecoach. Black gold was shooting up fifty feet over the crown block of the derrick, and turning into mist at the top. A sudden shift of the wind brought a heavy spray over the area, causing the horses to whinny in terror. The driver cleared his throat and wiped the oil out of his eyes with a red bandanna that was turning black. If he wanted to make two more runs up the hill this day, he better take his passengers back to Crockett Street. "Satisfied, men? You've seen it all!" He paused, then said casually, "That'll be another five bucks for the ride back."

A little man with a red face sputtered: "Why in the hell didn't you tell us it was ten dollars round trip in the first place?"

The driver smiled wryly, "Either pay up or walk back!"

The little man opened the door of the carriage, took one look at the black mud and gumbo, and slammed the door. He fished for his wallet. "Highway robbery!" he announced in a flat voice. "You're a blackguard, sir!"

The driver opened the door carefully, took the little man by the lapels, and pulled him out of the coach, into the ankle-deep mud. "No one calls me names," he said quietly. "Now crawl back!" He kicked the little man in the rear and watched him lose his balance and fall into the dark sticky mess. He collected the fares without further comment, climbed back to his seat, turned the team around, and headed down the road to Beaumont. The ride back to town was silent.

The driver deposited his passengers in front of the Crosby and a few moments later, they were lined up in front of the bar. "Damndest thing I ever saw," one of the men said. "Makes your flesh crawl, don't it?"

The barkeep laughed. "I take it, you all liked yore ten-buck ride?"

"That man's a fourflusher!"

"Everyone's a fourflusher in Beaumont," the barkeep replied laconically, pouring Bosley a shot of whiskey. "Did ya git your story?" he asked, eyes twinkling.

Bosley upturned the whiskey, not bothering with the water chaser. "Yes. Now, I need to know a little more about drilling techniques. Anyone around who can help me? I want to flesh out the article."

The barkeep surveyed the room. "Yeh, there's Larry Steele over there in the corner with the red shirt. He's a superintendent for Armbuster. He's just learning rotary drilling. He's a cable tool specialist. Why not meander over?"

Larry Steele was a man of thirty-five, with sandy-colored hair and a sunburned complexion that was peeling, leaving his face with large red splotches. He was also half drunk and belligerent, but when he heard the magic name of the *New York Times,* he positively beamed. Bosley held his breath and pushed his chair back to escape a barrage of fetid breath that even whiskey could not purify.

"Hell, yes, I'll answer your questions. Whaddaya want to know?" Steele squinted and poured another drink out of the bottle before him.

"Just need a little background so that when I get into the story, I'll use the right terms," Bosley said, trying to judge just how much Steele had had to drink.

The man puckered his lips and sucked on his teeth. "You ever been in the oil fields before?"

Bosley shook his head. "I know a little about rock formations, that's all."

"Then, I'll make it real simple like." Steele grinned. "We use a method of drilling developed back there in Pennsylvania called cable tool." He took a swig from his glass and waited for the warmth to settle in his stomach. "You start by building a wooden rig—you've seen 'em by the hundreds—derricks. It's gotta be up pretty high, eighty-five feet or so, because it's gotta support a two thousand-pound string of tools about sixty feet long. That still leaves about twenty-five up there to play with. You hang those tools by a cable under a big pulley, which is raised and lowered regular by a hammer with a fishtail bit with strokes of between three and four feet right down in the rock." He looked up and grinned. "Am I going too fast for ya?"

Bosley shook his head and continued to scribble on his foolscap tablet.

The man continued. "So that the hole won't be filling up all the time, pipes are lowered into the well, one after the other, all threaded together." He paused. "Now, that ain't all of it by a long shot, but that kinda gives you an idea of how it's done." He took another pull from his glass, grimaced, and looked up expectantly.

"How many men does it take to run a derrick?"

Steele laughed. "You mean 'work a rig'? First of all, of course, there's the jarhead—he's the fella who does the actual drilling. Next comes the tool dresser—he's got the most interesting job on the rig, to my way of thinking." He paused. "I started out as a tool dresser myself, 'cause my old man was a blacksmith." He paused. "You see, Mr. Brandon, when the bit—or the 'fish' as we call it—is hammered down in the well, it sometimes is bent out of shape if it hits some real hard rock. In fact, it gets bent so crooked, it won't come out of the hole. That's when the tool dresser shows his talent. He's got a kind of flat pan filled with soft paraffin which he lowers into the well. It's hammered down real strong. When he brings it to the surface, an impression of the bent fish is imbedded in it! He selects a tool that

119

will fit around that bit down there, and he goes 'fishing,' and after a while he hooks the tool around it and brings it up." Steele stopped and looked at Bosley to be sure he was understood. "Then he works his bellows—big sons of bitches, six feet long—and fires up his forge. He gets that damn fish red hot and pounds it back in shape, with a fourteen-pound sledge hammer. He's got to have muscle, I tell you! Then, the drilling starts all over again. Got it?"

Bosley nodded, took a drink, and replenished Steele's glass.

"There's usually a couple of other fellows around called roughnecks. One of 'em is in charge of the bull wheel, which is used to operate the block and tackle on the top of the rig. The other one runs the mail pouch, that's what we call the steam engine, that provides power for the jarhead." He paused and spit a heavy stream of tobacco into a spittoon six feet away. "Got it?"

Bosley allowed that he understood. "What happens when you hit oil?"

Steele threw his head back and laughed, showing all of his rotted teeth. "First of all, you don't usually hit it right away. Sometimes you run into fresh water—most usually, you hit gas. Salt water is a good sign, 'cause it's right there with the petroleum oft times."

At that moment, a woman in an orange dress approached, carrying a notepad. "Afternoon, Mr. Steele," she said softly, and Bosley saw that her face was painted. She looked like a kewpie doll at a carnival.

"Hiya, Glory," Steele said. "Ya got any free time tonight?"

Glory giggled and examined her notebook. "Fifteen minutes at nine forty-five."

He nodded. "Put me down." He extracted a twenty-dollar bill from his wallet. "Here. If I get too drunk and can't make it, remember you owe me one." He laughed.

"Oh, yeah?" Glory exclaimed, patting her bosom. "If you ain't there, you're out of luck, mistah!" Then she moved on to the next table.

"Fine body and a good screw." Steele said, and hi-coughed. "Say, are you hungry?"

120

Bosley admitted that he had not eaten since the night before in Houston.

"Well, a friend of mine has a soup kitchen on her front porch. No use standin' in line in front of a cafe. Say, you got a place to bed down?

"No? Well, for thirty dollars, she'll let you sleep in her front bedroom. It's a small bed, but at least you won't have to share it with some dirty, snoring sonofabitch! Come on!"

Bosley was awakened the next morning at nine-thirty by a knock on the door. He pulled on his clothes, as the landlady let in two men in business suits. "Are you Mike Brandon?" they chorused.

Bosley stifled a yawn; his head ached dreadfully. Was that the name he had made up the day before? He nodded numbly.

"Mr. Armbuster wants to see you," one of the men said.

"I'll shave," Bosley replied, trying to keep his voice casual. So he was going to meet the great man himself!

"Just come along."

Bosley dressed hurriedly and was escorted over to the Crosby and ushered into a suite on the top floor. A tall, emaciated, gray-haired man sat at a desk in the far corner of the room. Behind him stood Steele, freshly shaved and quite sober.

The gray-haired man rose and looked at him coldly. "I've just checked with *The New York Times*. They have no Michael Brandon in their employ. Just who in the hell are you?"

Bosley was never very good at lying. He thought very quickly. "I'm a geologist, Mr. Armbuster," he replied truthfully, "trying to find out about oil-drilling techniques." He smiled nervously. "You see, I believe that the horseless carriage is going to catch on all over the country, and there's going to be a need for fuel. . . ."

Armbuster waved a thin hand. "Well, why didn't you come to me in the first place, instead of asking a lot of fool questions in a saloon?" He squinted; his small eyes almost disappeared in his gaunt face. "Why give out a cock-and-bull story about being a journalist?"

"That's a good question, sir," Bosley replied, stalling for time while his mind performed cartwheels. "I suppose it was the long way around, but I thought if I contacted you personally, you wouldn't see me!" His voice rang with sincerity.

Armbuster smiled humorlessly. "You're quite right in your assumption, young man. Answer me this: just why are you so interested in drilling procedures?"

Bosley let his face go expressionless. "I want to specialize in oil recovery programs."

"You can't believe that we're *that* naive!" Armbuster retorted, and glanced at the two men, who sprang into action—one leaped behind Bosley, forcing his hands behind his back; the other slapped his face hard. The blows caught Bosley off guard, filling his head with stars.

Armbuster looked out of the window. "I want the truth!" he demanded loudly.

As Bosley absorbed more slaps, he tried to think. He felt no actual pain now, just a stinging sensation in his jaw—as if he had been bitten by a swarm of bees and was experiencing a delayed reaction, waiting for the poison to hit his bloodstream. "That's—the—truth," he stammered.

"I think you're probably working for the United States government," Armbuster said coolly.

"Not any more," Bosley found himself saying. "I've just finished a survey of some gypsum deposits." He did not dare say "in Indian Territory," that would pinpoint his location.

Armbuster whirled around, his eyes bright with interest. "Go on."

"That's it. . . ."

He was rewarded with another slap and felt the corner of his mouth catch on his assailant's ring. He tasted blood.

"You are either the stupidest man alive or the cleverest," Armbuster said, rubbing his thin jaw. "You think you've found oil in gypsum deposits?" He laughed hollowly, then demanded, "What is your *real* reason for coming here?"

"Like I said before, I simply want to find out more about drilling. . . ."

This time the man hit him in the stomach, but before his body curled forward, a second blow landed on his lower chest. He doubled up with pain; the man behind him forced his shoulders back.

"Now, I want the *truth*!" Armbuster spat out. "Who are you working for? Standard Oil?"

Bosley's breath was coming shallowly; each gasping lung contraction sent spasms of pain through his body. He was afraid that he would choke from lack of oxygen. He gasped for air and struggled feebly in the man's arms.

Larry Steele stepped forward. "Mr. Armbuster, I think if he was with Standard, he wouldn't have asked such simple questions. All he asked about was the basics of cable tool. Nothing technical at all!"

Armbuster grunted. "How would you know? You were drunk!"

"I tell you, Mr. Armbuster, he didn't get anything out of me. I didn't give him anything that he couldn't get from any roustabout." He paused. "Besides, I don't know any secrets."

Armbuster regarded Steele contemptuously. "He's not here for his health! There must be reasons for nosing around." He turned to Bosley, trying a new tactic. "You've just come up from Pennsylvania, right?"

"I—I've—never been to Pennsylvania," Bosley managed to get out. His body was beginning to throb, and his mouth was filled with blood, which dripped down his chin onto his frock coat.

"Clean him up," Armbuster said. "He's too dumb to work for Standard. Take him back to his room. But check his wallet first."

One of the men rifled through the billfold. "A hundred and twenty dollars in bills, a letter, and some business cards. That's it!" He handed the letter to Armbuster, who glanced at it briefly. "Well, at least he was telling the truth about working with gypsum. This is a government field report."

Three hours later, Bosley opened his eyes. There was

123

a terrible throbbing in his ears and an incessant joggling of his body. He was very, very cold, and ached from head to toe. He first thought that he was dreaming; surely he would awaken in his hotel room, cozy and warm. Gradually, his mind cleared. Then the events of the night before and the morning came back in sharp detail. He looked around at his strange surroundings. The sounds of wheels turning and the movement of something under him was very real. His head throbbing painfully, he rested on his elbow.

Very slowly, he reached down and removed his right shoe. He sighed with relief. He retrieved a piece of paper—the laboratory report that revealed a rich concentration of hydrocarbons of the naphthene series in the pitch samples of Letty's claim.

Bosley knew with certainty that if Armbuster had found that report, he would be lying in an unmarked grave instead of surveying the countryside through the half open door of a boxcar. . . .

Poppa Dice, dressed in a new pale gray serge suit and paisley Teck scarf, stood on one foot and then the other. "Miz Barrett," he said slowly, "I got somethin' personal to ask."

He was red in the face, and she wondered if he had been drinking. "Yes?"

He looked down at his feet. "I believe in progress," he said.

She looked up at him with wide eyes. "Well, so do I, Poppa Dice, so do I!" She separated a purple skein of embroidery thread, waiting for him to go on.

"I feel foolish comin' to you like this. . . ."

She had not realized that he was essentially a shy person. "What's on your mind?" she asked kindly. "Aren't the games going well from your point of view? I want you to know that I'm pleased." Perhaps she had not complimented him enough.

He grinned. "That's all fine and dandy. It's jest that I'm meetin' a class o' people far different than I ever been thrown with before. . . ." He worked his hands together behind his back, clasping and unclasping his fingers, then finally blurted, "Miz Barrett, I wanta learn to read and write!" He looked at her fearfully out of the corners of his eyes.

She almost burst out laughing, but contained herself by looking very steadily at the rosette pattern that she was embroidering on the hand towel. "Well, Poppa Dice," she said gently, "I think that can be worked out. Maybe we could devote an hour a day to the project. And if you study at home. . . ."

"Sam said he'd teach me. I don't want him to do it for free. I'm makin' good money and I'd be more 'n happy to pass a little of it to him." He paused, still working his fingers. "I meet so many of them educated fellas and they have somethin' in common that I don't. They're able to see things with their minds that I can't." He looked down at his feet. "And, Miz Barrett, I'm a mite jealous. I'm set in my ways at my age, but do you suppose Sam can teach an old dog new tricks?"

Leona's eyes shone, and the humor that she felt a few moments ago was gone. "Poppa Dice, you're a smart man. I don't see any reason at all why you can't learn . . . it hasn't anything to do with age." She paused and threaded a needle. "On my next trip to Angel, I'll bring back some books." She smiled. "Anything else?"

"No, Miz Barrett, that's all!" He was calmer now, and he felt a surge of affection for her. "Thank you kindly," he said, and headed towards Sam's room to tell him the good news.

Fontine set the mug of hot coffee on the kitchen table beside Poppa Dice, who was laboriously making large letters on a pad of foolscap. "I think you're out of your mind, trying to do somethin' that ain't natural for a man yore age. What kinda books you gonna read? Who you gonna write to? All your kinfolks is dead."

He looked up and rubbed his eyes. "I'm doin' this 'cause I want to understand what them men over at The Widders are thinkin' and talkin' about."

Fontine laughed hollowly. "All them men over there is for one thing only and it ain't got nothin' to do with books, Poppa Dice!"

"Now, hold on, girl!" he replied. "In the furst place, you don't know what in criminy sakes yore talkin' 'bout. The Widders' place is a kind of a club. . . ."

"Sure, Poppa Dice, with them women runnin' around without no clothes on and . . . and that Graphophone blarin' out ragtime. . . ."

"I told you to keep your mouth shut, Fourteen!" His voice was hard as a rock. "It ain't like that atall! It's like a proper social. There ain't no wild things goin' on so's you can see. It's all mannerly." His face was very red. "I'd appreciate it greatly if you'd not bring up the subject agin!"

"Very well, Poppa Dice," she replied and flounced out of the room only to run into John at the back door, who took a look at her flushed face. "Now, what's goin' on? I could hear you both goin' hammer 'n tong, clear out at the smokehouse. What's it this time?"

"I'm not allowed to talk!" Fontine replied through tight lips. "The old man in there is gettin' childish. . . ." She took a basket of wet laundry from the table and went out in the back yard, her jaw set stubbornly.

"Okay, Poppa Dice, out with it!" John said sternly. "What got you riled up so?"

"Fourteen has to learn not to bother me when I'm studyin'," Poppa Dice retorted hotly, "makin' fun o' me like I was some trashy—"

"I'll lay down the law," John said. "I jest think she's jealous, that's all. She was over at the parson's last week and wanted the recipe for a lemon cake from Mrs. Reverend. She got it too—on a piece o' paper! Fontine was too proud to admit that she couldn't read. Maybe you could help her."

"Whoa, Jaundice, whoa! I've only took three lessons." He paused. "The funny thing is, I already know the alphabet!"

John Dice frowned. "How's that?"

"So do you, only you don't know it!"

"Whadda ya mean?"

"Well," he explained impatiently, "it ain't much different 'n cipherin'. Ever' ranch, when we punched cattle, had a brand—the 4X and the 5W, the WW, the HP. We knew the Great Western Trail was the WT, the Chisholm was the CT—"

"—and the East Shawnee was the ES and the West

126

Shawnee was the WS." A light came into John Dice's eyes. "I see what you mean. Then half the battle is won!"

"Not yet, son, not yet! But the first step's easy. I can write the alphabet right now—and so can you. It's just makin' curlicues in the right order, starting with 'a' and ending with 'z'. See!" He held up a page of foolscap for examination.

"My God," John Dice cried, "I've never stopped to look at this afore! I can read 'em just as good as you can, Poppa Dice. Why didn't anyone ever tell us?"

Poppa Dice smiled widely. "If the beginnin' is so simple, the rest can't be too hard. It's just a matter of puttin' these letters together proper like. Hellfire, if a six-year-old kid can learn, why, it's gotta be a snap!"

John Dice scratched his head. "I never thought about it that way afore! Poppa Dice—ever'thing is sure clear this mornin'." He turned and called, "Fourteen, git yoreself in here. We're all a gonna learn to read 'n write!"

11

The Proposal

It was Saturday afternoon on Main Street in Angel.
The street resembled a miniature county fair. Farmers gathered in little knots in front of the livery stable and discussed the price of wheat and the problems of baling hay with the new three-gauge wire, while they lined up appointments to breed their heifers to the Stevens' new thoroughbred Angus bull.

The women formed circles in front of Baker's Mercantile Store, exchanged gossip about The Widows, chattered about a new calico that stayed crisp even in hot weather, and rhapsodized about a new Canadian baby powder that eliminated diaper rash. Rochelle Patterson then passed around a new recipe for a white sponge cake that required twenty-two egg whites and which, she said, was so divine it should be called Angel cake.

But the highlight of the afternoon was the drawing for a five-dollar bill. The merchants each contributed fifty cents, the names of customers were placed in a fish bowl and a child was chosen out of the group, blindfolded, and allowed to select a name.

October 8, 1901 was no different than any of the other hundreds of Saturdays that had come and gone in the Territory. But just before Little Luke reached into the fish bowl, Reverend Haskell surveyed the large crowd and addressed his wife. "Do you suppose if we gave away five dollars every Sunday, we could get a turnout like this?"

128

His wife patted his hand and shook her head. "More than you can hope for, I'm afraid, my dear."

He nodded. "I don't know what we would have done this last winter if the widows hadn't sent their tithes in regularly, but I still don't know if it's right to accept—"

Thelma held up her hand. "Let's not get into *that* again. They have the right to tithe, same as everybody else!" Then she smiled secretly. "At least, we're the only ones in the Territory who know exactly how successful their operation is, of course, assuming that they give ten per cent of their earnings!"

"Thelma!" he admonished sternly, "remember yourself!"

At that moment Baker announced the winner of the drawing. "*George Story*," he shouted above the cry of a baby. A murmur went up from the crowd. If everyone in the community knew everyone else, how did a strange name crop up in the fish bowl?

"*George Story*," Baker intoned again in a louder voice. There was a movement in back of the crowd and a tall, muscular man came forward. He wore his blue serge frock coat with an air of distinction and seemed completely at home with the gathering as he said modestly, "I only came into town for the day and purchased a new wallet at the store. I did not realize that the slip I filled out was to be placed in the drawing." He turned to Baker. "Would you please be kind enough to select another name?"

Letty and Priscilla, who stood a stone's throw from the man, exchanged glances. Priscilla whispered, "I haven't run into such chivalry since we left Minneapolis!"

Letty nodded, looked at the man again, and her throat grew tight. There was something very stirring about him. He was extremely handsome in a rugged, outdoor sort of way, and his face had a chiseled, sculptured look, with high cheekbones and a firm, protruding jaw. His naturally curly black hair was highlighted by the sun. But his most startling feature was his blue, aquamarine eyes, which flashed out of a dark, suntanned face. She was sure he was of some foreign extraction. Did Italian men have blue eyes?

129

"Thelma Haskell," Baker called, reading a scrap of paper.

The minister whispered, "The Lord is with us, my dear."

"Yes," she murmured before she went up to the fish bowl to claim her money, "we shall have smoked cod from Boston for dinner!"

George Story, in helping Thelma Haskell through the crowd, stepped on Letty's boot. He turned immediately. "I am very sorry," he said. She found herself staring directly into his clear, blue eyes.

She smiled in spite of herself. "It's nothing," she replied, but their gaze still held, then he broke away and joined Sam. Now that she saw them together, she discerned his ancestry. "He's *Indian*," she whispered to Priscilla.

"Well," Priscilla hissed back, "there's white blood in there somewhere!"

"Did you see his hands? Big as plowshares!"

"Yes, he could scalp a body without even using a knife!"

Letty stole a glance at George Story, who was looking intently in her direction. As the crowd dispersed, she turned in the opposite direction, not wishing to encounter him again. She grasped the handle of her pocketbook to stem the trembling in her hands. She had never met such an attractive man before, and she was ashamed of the feelings he had aroused in her. She turned away and walked to the livery stable, where Edward was hitching up the team.

"That woman with the blonde hair, who is she?" George Story asked Sam.

"The one with the blue bonnet? That's Letty Heron."

"Is the man with the horses her husband?"

"Oh, no, she's a widow. That's her brother-in-law."

"I must meet him."

"Very well." The two men came out of the crowd. "Mr. Heron," Sam said gravely, "I'd like you to know George Story. Mr. Story, Edward Heron."

The two men shook hands formally, and Edward introduced Priscilla and Letty.

"That was a very kind gesture to withdraw your name, sir," Edward said.

George Story laughed, showing an array of perfectly white teeth. "It was the right thing to do, because I know if *I* were a merchant and a stranger picked up *my* money, I would surely be hard put upon. I understand the minister's wife was the final recipient." He glanced up and down Main Street. "I gather the cash was appreciated."

Letty regarded the man in wonder. Not only did he have a magnetic personality, but he had humanitarian instincts as well.

"What brings you to Angel?" Edward asked.

"I am one of the attorneys for the Cherokee nation, and Born-Before-Sunrise—excuse me—Sam—was left a sum of money by a benefactor, a family with whom he used to live. I came down from Tahlequah to have him sign the papers. Even then, it'll be a year."

"Congratulations, Sam," Letty said warmly, "I'm delighted that you have an inheritance. I suppose, then, that you'll be leaving us?"

He smiled shyly. "It has always been my dream to be a medical doctor. I do not know that I can succeed. I am already a mature man, almost thirty, and college will be very difficult, but Mr. Story says that he will help me." He turned away, very moved. "So, I will try," he said to the horizon.

Letty smiled softly. "Sam, you will make a very fine doctor."

Priscilla gathered her skirts about her, and climbed into the carriage. Letty followed whispering, "Mind your manners!" It was then that they heard the sounds of the locomotive.

"That is my train, I believe," George Story exclaimed.

"I'll be pleased to drop you," Edward volunteered cordially.

"Thank you." George climbed into the back seat of the carriage and inadvertently hit Letty's open parasol with his hand. "Pardon me," he said coloring, "for some reason, I am very awkward today." He did not add that it was because, for the first time in many

131

years, he had met a woman that intrigued him emotionally and pulled at him physically. He took several deep breaths to calm the pounding of his heart.

Letty sat stiffly beside him, taking care that her skirts did not even touch his boots. She was afraid that if there was contact of any sort, the back seat of the carriage would ignite and throw a shower of sparks into the air.

As the carriage moved past the large watering trough and the hitching posts in front of the depot, the train came into the station at a steady pace, and without pausing, continued down the tracks toward Enid. Dumbfounded, Story looked at Edward. "It appears," he said grimly, "that I have missed my train."

"Didn't you tell the stationmaster that you would be taking the train this afternoon?" Edward asked.

"Why, no. I naturally assumed that it would stop!"

Edward smiled. "In a cow town like Angel, very few people go into Enid on the late train. If you didn't have a reservation . . ."

"When is the next one due?"

"Tomorrow morning at eleven-thirty!" Edward paused a moment. "We don't have a hotel in Angel, but if you like, you may stay tonight in the rooms over my cabinet shop, if you don't mind sharing the space with my apprentices."

George paused. "I am very grateful. I am sorry to put you out through my own stupidity. I have been in Washington for so long, I forget life on the frontier is very different."

Edward laughed, "Yes, especially when it comes to trains!"

Priscilla spoke up quickly. "Incidentally, we would be pleased if you'd come to supper this evening at six o'clock. Edward will fetch you."

George's blue eyes sparkled. "I am in your debt. Perhaps one day I can return the favor."

Letty rushed into the kitchen. "What are we going to fix, Prissy, in a bare three hours?"

"We were going to have corned beef and cabbage. . . ."

132

"Hardly suitable for company," Letty sighed.

"I wouldn't exactly call a red Indian 'company'!" Priscilla retorted.

"You shouldn't be biased. He appears to be a very nice man. After all, he's a college graduate and he's passed his bar examination. You and I were lucky to get through the eighth grade!"

"Letty, that's not true!"

"Yes, it is. If it hadn't been that old lady Myers liked you, you'd never have passed Civics." She paused. "I think I'll bake a cherry cobbler. And, don't we have some of that pork tenderloin canned from last year?"

"One jar left. I was saving that for Little Luke's birthday."

"That's very sweet of you, Prissy, but he won't know the difference. I say, serve it tonight with browned potatoes and carrots."

Priscilla looked at Letty out of the corners of her eyes. "You look very flushed. Are you sure you're all right?"

"Yes," Letty replied evenly, her heart pounding. "I'm fine. In fact, I have never felt better in my life."

"I thought so."

"What do you mean by that?"

"Exactly what you think I mean. You've set your sights on George Story!"

"That's not true!" Letty exclaimed. "I don't even know the man. . . ."

"An Indian in the family, really!" Priscilla scoffed. "I mean, that's worse than a Bohunk!"

Letty's face flamed as she worked the lard into the pie flour with her hands, added a bit of water and reached for the rolling pin. As she slid the wooden cylinder over the dough, she could feel George Story beside her in bed, their bodies so inflamed that the sheets were scorched. . . . In horror, she dropped the rolling pin. What was she thinking about? No decent woman ever entertained such thoughts! She had certainly never thought about such things during her marriage to Luke, who was the dearest man she had ever known. Yet, with all of Luke's passion, he had never stirred her in the way that George Story. . . . Angrily, Letty retrieved

133

the rolling pin. "I have butter fingers," she said aloud.

"Still mooning about that red Indian?" Priscilla asked sharply.

Letty whirled around. "Prissy," she exclaimed hotly, "If you know what's good for you, you will shut up this instant!"

The two women faced each other again, then Priscilla rushed into her arms. "Forgive me, Letty," she said contritely, "I don't know what gets into me sometimes." She paused. "I guess I'm just—jealous!"

Letty patted her shoulder, all anger gone. "But why?" she asked gently. "You've got Edward."

Priscilla's eyes filled with tears. "Oh, Letty, I feel *old*. Then, well, Edward is just Edward! My life isn't ever going to change. I'm going to be stuck here on this farm the rest of my life. You can do what you want, go where you want, do what you want. . . ." She paused. "Besides, I think I'm pregnant again!"

"Oh, *Priscilla*!" Letty's heart went out to her. "Come now, dry your tears. A new baby in the house will be wonderful."

"Yes," replied Priscilla sarcastically, "won't it be fun? Especially for Edward, who loves children so much! He's gone all day, sees the little ones on their best behavior in the evening. They play up to him, they're not fools! If only he had a diaper to change once in a while!" She put the potatoes on to boil. "Oh, Letty," she wailed, "why didn't I stay in Minneapolis and marry a rich man?"

Letty did not reply as she finished crimping the edges of the cobbler and put it into the oven. Then she went for a walk down by the creek. She had to get out of the house before she started to wail herself. Wasn't it always strange, she thought as she took a lungful of cool fresh air, how any conversation about herself always ended up about Priscilla?

Letty wore a pale blue watered silk dress for dinner with matching bows in her light blonde hair. She had burned a match and run the dark, sooty end over her upper eyelids and brows to give her face a bit of distinction. There was no need to rub a bit of rouge over her flushed cheekbones. Sitting across from George Story at the table, she knew that she looked pretty, and shivered inside at his obvious admiration for her. It had been years since she had basked in a man's courtly affection. His deep blue eyes gleamed and danced, and his physical presence engulfed her in waves of tenderness. She picked at her food, hoping that he did not notice her lack of appetite.

Conversation was lively and amusing, as Edward and Priscilla rose valiantly to the occasion. If Priscilla resented the man sitting next to her, she did not show it. It was one of her better performances. But under the gay facade of the supper-party atmosphere ran a marvelous current of feeling between George Story and Letty Heron. It was a memorable evening in more ways than one. . . .

In the parlor, the men ate the cobbler with relish. Over cigars and coffee, George Story, prompted by Edward, told of his reasons for his planned trip to Washington. "It is very simple," he explained, blowing a perfect ring of smoke over the footstool. "I go to stand up for the rights of my people. Several other attorneys who also represent the Five Civilized Tribes go with our tribal leaders to fight for the land given us by U. S. treaties." He paused, his voice low and commanding. "Now the Curtis Act of 1898, which goes back to the Dawes Commission of 1887, provides that this reservation land will be allotted to individual members of the tribe—and not the tribe as a whole."

"That *does* seem fair enough," Edward replied.

George held up his hands. "On the surface, and solely from the white man's point of view, it seemed fair to give each Indian eighty or one hundred sixty acres of land. But this idea was forwarded without consulting the Indian. We have continually been driven from our lands since the first Pilgrim landed on Plymouth Rock. The government did not take into consideration the fact that we have out own culture, our own government, loosely based on the Constitution of the United States. I do not know, offhand, what percentage of the white population has been educated to the eighth grade, but I venture to say that the Cherokee have a much higher

135

literacy rate, per capita. Of the Five Civilized Tribes—including the Choctaw, Chickasaw, Creek, and Seminole—we are the only tribe with a written language. We are a literate people."

"How come you have written language and the others do not?" Edward asked, lighting a cigar and blowing the smoke toward the ceiling.

"A brilliant man named Sequoyah, a mixed blood, eighty years ago devised an alphabet, which was so simple that it could be learned in less than a month. Thus we have had our own books and newspapers for many years. We have become so 'civilized' that our tribe has more mixed white blood than any other. We have our own schools and seminaries.

"The allotment act provided the machinery by which the government could take over our supposedly 'surplus' lands—territory given to us when our own lands were confiscated by the white man—and sell them publicly, with the money from the sales 'held in trust' for our tribes by the Department of the Interior. Congress, of course, can step in at any time and take money to minister to our people!"

"In other words, George, the government wants to confiscate tribal property, sell it, and then parcel the money back to the individual in the same way that the tribes would do in the first place! That's not fair."

"Of course not! That's what I've been telling you all along! That is why I—and others like me—must fight with every fiber of our being to right this control. Already some fifty-three thousand allotments of over five million acres have been handed out, reducing the total Indian lands from one hundred and fifty million acres to something like seventy-five million, and it still continues. The tribe must have proper legislation, or all is lost."

"I am still somewhat confused," Edward replied, taking a sip of coffee.

"So am I!" Priscilla whispered to Letty. Having finished the supper dishes, they sat in the dining room in the dark and listened to the men's conversation, knowing that if they entered the room, the topic would

136

change to the weather or some other harmless topic suitable for feminine ears.

George Story looked up quizzically, an evangelistic fervor creeping into his voice. "I should bring you up to date, sir. You see, before the Great War that turned our country into opposite camps, we Cherokee called ourselves 'real people' and llived in Georgia and a few other Southern states. Some even owned plantations and slaves. We sent our children to fundamentalist schools and lived much like our white neighbors. Missionaries had turned us into Christians. We believed in immortality . . . our ritual prayers referred to one God . . ." He smiled suddenly, leaning forward intently. ". . . even before we called Him Jesus!" He paused. "We learned English, not to be fluent in two languages but because we knew that if we dealt with the white man, it must be in his own tongue." He gestured with his hands. "We did not expect the white man to learn sign language or Sequoyah's syllabary in order to communicate with us!"

"But, George, if your people were so prosperous in Georgia, why did they emigrate here, of all places!" Edward asked.

"One very strange and perplexing word—*gold!*"

"But, there are no precious metals in the Territory!" Edward cried. "Only gypsum, red shale, sand, and cement."

"You misunderstand, my friend," George remonstrated, taking a puff from his cigar. "It was the white man's quest—gold was discovered in the Indian Nation. The governor of Georgia, sanctioned by the U.S. government, confiscated our land after the Treaty of New Echota, December 29, 1835. Washington then felt a twinge of guilt and gave us this Territory beyond the Mississippi, which was part of the original Louisiana Purchase, as a hunting ground. They also gave the Five Civilized Tribes land on which to live near Tahlequah. We were all forced to march here in the dead of winter. Have not you heard about Tsa–La–Gi—the Trail of Tears?"

"Ah, yes," Edward said. "It all comes back now. My mother told me about that journey when I was a little boy. Grandmother came from Atlanta and passed down the story. I always thought it was an old folk tale!"

George smiled bitterly. "It was no folk tale. My people—some barefoot, the elderly on litters, youngsters running along the path in the snow, pack horses loaded down with housewares and clothing—all creeping along in below zero conditions, urged on by troops." He paused and sighed heavily. "We lost one-fourth of our entire tribe . . . their bones are scattered all along Tsa–La–Gi. I did not mean to preach. I apologize. I will get down from my soap box." He smiled, only his intense blue eyes were not amused.

Priscilla arose and Letty followed her into the parlor. "More coffee, gentlemen?"

"Ah, the ladies grace us with their presence," George said. "No more coffee for me, thank you."

"Please do go on, Mr. Story," Letty said, "you are showing us a new world."

George held up his hands. "I am told by the settlers that the sheep this year are putting on a heavier coat, which suggests the winter will be unusually harsh."

Letty exchanged glances with Priscilla; the conversation had indeed turned to the weather.

The next morning Edward picked up George Story at the cabinet shop and brought him over to the farm for breakfast. After the women had finished washing the dishes, Priscilla began to plan dinner. "Chicken and noodles would be nice," she said. "Letty, if you'll knock down a few pecans, I'll make a pie."

"May I help?" George Story was standing behind them in the doorway.

"Why, yes, if you like. . . ." Letty said. Outwardly, she was composed, but inside she was suddenly apprehensive. Was it quite proper to be alone with him? Then she knew that her fears had nothing to do with propriety. As a woman, she was unsure of herself. His attraction was still almost overwhelming.

Once outside, they remarked about the warm, pleasant weather and the marvelous flavor of the home-cured ham that had been served for breakfast. Then there was a deep silence. Then Letty said, "I heard a bit of the conversation last night, Mr. Story. Would you clarify a point? Why do you think it wrong for every Indian to be on his own?"

"You see, Mrs. Heron," he replied gently, "we—the Cherokee nation—do not own property. We till as much land as we want, but the crops are shared. In fact, we divide *all* commodities." He drew in his breath slowly, and then expelled the air in a rush. "We prize our freedom above all else. If each family is given eighty or one hundred sixty acres to farm independently, the Cherokee nation will be broken up. We will be forced to assimilate into the mainstream of white life—which we cannot do. We have changed our culture to the ways of the white man, but we cannot change our souls."

"But you are part white."

"Yes," he answered proudly, "I am a mixed blood, which is no disgrace to the Cherokee, because we have much white blood. We have offered shelter to some three thousand freed Negro slaves, two thousand whites, and seventeen hundred Delaware Shawnee, and the other tribesmen. We are reduced to about twenty thousand all told." He paused. "That is why we must not be stamped out and brought into the mainstream. *We are individuals.* Without our ruling body. . . ."

"You are saying, Mr. Story, that your people are mainly spiritual?"

"Yes, to a very great degree. The wind and the stars and the crops; the feeling that exists between brothers; the fire under the roasting game; the first snow; the thaw; the prairie flowers; the birth of a child; the look of love between a man and a woman; the first steps a baby takes; the death of an elder; the respect for a great leader—all of these things are the essence of our people. How can all of this *feeling* be properly translated into words the leaders in Washington will understand? There is no simple way. The ways of the red man are opposite to the ways of the white man." He paused dramatically. "We used to use bow and arrows, but now we must battle with our wits. All we want is a life of our own." He paused. "By the way," he continued

139

slowly, "have you thought about having a life of *your* own?"

The question came so suddenly that she was caught off guard. "What do you mean, Mr. Story?"

"I mean it must be difficult to live with your dead husband's relatives, Mrs. Heron."

The tenor of the conversation had changed so abruptly that she was taken aback. "Why—not at all. . . ." She was not used to frank conversations with strangers. She smiled crookedly. "Well, I do occasionally feel like an old aunt." They had reached the pecan trees. "If you'll take a stick and knock the branches, I'll catch a few nuts in my apron."

He picked up a dried sapling and hit the loaded tree gently.

She laughed. "You'll have to use a bit more—power." She spread her apron.

"I am so awkward!" he replied, then went on tonelessly, "Have you ever thought of remarrying?"

Again, she was caught off guard. How could he speak about private things so casually? "Why—yes. If a man would come along who liked Little Luke, and . . ." A cluster of pecans fell to the ground.

He was hitting the branches with more force now. "Would you promise me something?"

"If I can." Her heart was beating very rapidly as she held out her apron under the branch.

"Promise that you will think of me as a man and not an Indian?" He hit the branch with fervor and was rewarded with a shower of pecans, which hit her apron with a soft swishing sound.

"I think that's enough," she said.

"Can you also think of me as a friend?"

She carefully tied the ends of her apron together, taking care that each end was folded over exactly and that the knots were perfectly even. She still could not look at him.

"May I see you again, when I am next in the Territory?"

She flushed and faced the tree. She was certain that he could see the movement of her pounding heart through her bodice.

140

"Do not turn away, lady," he murmured. "I have never before spoken to a woman this way . . . ." He paused. "May we at least correspond?"

"Letty!" Priscilla called from the top of the incline. "Little Luke has just thrown up over his new coveralls."

Letty smiled and sighed. "Back to a mother's duties. Yes, you may write to me, Mr. Story, if you like."

12

There Was A Man . . . .

Letty took a long walk around the farm.

She settled down on a tree stump in the deep, green meadow, and with her cape tucked in around her like a cozy blanket, read the letter with a growing excitement.

> Council House
> Tahlequah
> August 20, 1901

My dear Letty Heron:

Events are proceeding well here, but there have been many delays. Communications with Washington have reached another standstill, much to my regret.

I must take the train to Enid to research old survey records at the courthouse, then proceed to Gutherie to do the same. My time is very restricted on this trip, but I will be able to make a stop-over in Angel for four hours on the 5th of February. I will look forward to seeing you at that time.

I understand Baker's General Store now has a telephone installed. I wish that you also had one so I could talk to you personally now and again.

I send my regards to Edward and Priscilla and the children and, of course, a special greeting to Little Luke.

> I am in your debt,
> George Story

Postscript
I am hoping above all else, that you have decided to say yes to my proposal.

Letty called gently to Herbie, the new roan, as he smartly pulled the new shay into the hitching post area of the depot. The train from Enid was late. Finally, at one-fifteen, the locomotive chugged into the station. Letty was the only person in view; the railroad was old hat by now, and the townspeople no longer gathered to watch the crew untie the water funnel over the engine.

Suddenly George appeared on the steps of the passenger car and waved. He was dressed in an elegant new frock coat and wore a new style soft felt hat that she knew must have been purchased in Washington. She had forgotten how broad his shoulders were, and how narrow his waist.

"You are beautiful," he exclaimed, his blue eyes dancing. She was once more taken aback at his handsome face. Each time that she saw him, he seemed to have added stature. His closely shaved blue-black beard and medium long hair, combed back in waves from his forehead, were the personification of good grooming, and he wore clothes with elegant distinction.

"You look well," she answered. "The sun has turned you brown."

He laughed, showing his perfectly white teeth. "You forget that I am naturally dark."

She blushed, and as he took the reins from her, she opened a green parasol that matched her dress. Watching him out of the corner of her eyes, as he drove down Main Street, she suddenly knew that she loved him.

Letty nodded to several of Edward's customers on the street and saw their look of surprise at her companion in the carriage. They had never before seen her with a man. The townspeople stared at him, trying to ascertain his extraction. Was he Bohemian or Italian? Certainly, he bore no resemblance to the swarthy Indians who occasionally rode by on sleek mustangs, they were attired in an array of cast-off clothing, half deerskin, half cloth, and braids were not uncommon. But this gentleman with the masterful air . . .

George looked at Letty in her new Sears Roebuck finery. "May I say again that you are very beautiful?"

She smiled. "It's been so long since I've had a compliment, Mr. Story." As they passed God's Acre, she thought briefly of Luke. It was not that she loved him any less, she suddenly realized, but she also loved the man next to her. She had always assumed that when a woman loved a man, the other men in her life would cease to exist, but she found this old belief was untrue. She began to understand, then, that there were several levels of love . . .

George looked at her tenderly. Was there a new softness in his features? "Do you have an answer for me? Will you be my wife?" he asked directly.

"Let's drive by the Chenovicks," she evaded. "Their orchard is in full bloom. It's the prettiest sight I've ever seen on the prairie. Turn to the right on the Section Line Road."

They rode silently by the new barbed wire fence that enclosed the Stevens' pasture, which was spotted here and there by shadows cast from the sun through huge, fleecy white clouds. The countryside was peaceful, and the warm breeze moved her skirts slightly and fluttered the mane of the horse. She was content. "Look!" she cried, pointing to a vivid splash of deep pink that covered a slightly rolling hill.

"Whoa!" George Story exclaimed softly to the horse. "It is a picture postcard view!" He took her hand. "Mrs. Heron?"

She was suddenly touched by the sentiment of the moment.

"Do you have an answer?" he repeated.

She turned to him helplessly, and could not speak.

"Ah," he said, "there is a qualification!" His eyes were very dark. "You've been thinking about my mixed blood, have you not?"

She looked at him with wonder. "As a matter of fact, that isn't an important issue at all. I am a practical woman," she answered softly. "I know almost nothing about you," she continued quietly. "I mean about how you live. I have a farm, and, as you know, I own what may someday become a thriving town."

He smiled widely. "Do you think that I am proposing marriage because of your eventual wherewithal?"

She colored. "Of course not! But I don't know that I would want to move . . . ."

"Ah," he said, after a pause, "you do not want to live with my people. Is that it?"

"I love Angel," she replied simply.

He shook his head. "I do not live permanently in Tahlequah," he said slowly. "I thought you knew that. I love my people because they are a natural part of my life, but you must remember that I was reared by my white father in a white society. I move in both worlds because that is my privilege. I fight for the Cherokee cause as a lawyer because I can be of some service to the tribal leaders, but I would not ask you to move. I am also fond of Angel and I doubt that there would be much prejudice here." He paused, took her hand and looked out over the magnificent pink trees that were moving slightly in the wind. "I am not a wealthy man." He paused. "But neither am I poor. At thirty, I have practiced law for six years." He smiled. "I assure you that I can support a wife and a new son."

She drew her hand away. "I am embarrassed. I didn't mean to imply . . . ."

He nodded his head. "These are things that must be settled," he replied gravely, "and so we must talk. My work will take me away a great deal of the time—at least in the foreseeable future. But I promise to spend as much time as possible at the home that I will build for you and Little Luke." He paused and took her hand again. "May I make the announcement of our pending nuptials to Edward and Priscilla?"

"Oh, I've forgotten," she exclaimed. "Dinner is waiting, and it's already two-thirty!"

He urged the horse into a trot. "When your relatives hear the news," he smiled, "perhaps we will be forgiven."

"Edward is on our side, but I'm not sure about Prissy. But no matter what happens, George Story, you are the man of my choice."

George Story and Letty Heron were married by Reverend Haskell at the church in Angel on May 15, 1902, at two-thirty in the afternoon. George looked very tall in his blue serge, three-piece suit and gray cravat. Letty looked down at her pale blue dress and bouquet of vi-

145

olets and thought about her other wedding, when she had worn white satin and carried a spray of lily of the valley. That ceremony seemed now to have taken place a half century ago. I'm thirty years old, she thought, a bit stunned. I'm practically middle aged!

The minister's voice brought her back to the present and she found herself saying, "*I do*." Then before she knew it, George was holding her tightly and kissing her hard on the lips. She had expected a soft gossamer kiss, and was slightly taken aback. Had the wedding guests noticed his ardor? Then she smiled to herself. She was feeling giddy—as giddy as a young virgin.

Because of the heat of late summer, the reception was held on the lawn in front of the clapboard, under the towering maples that Edward had planted in 1893.

The women brought covered dishes, which were placed on one long table, while the other table was used to display the wedding gifts: a handmade crocheted bedspread, tatting-edged pillow cases, lace antimacassars, embroidered towels, and several hand-carved, pecan-wood bowls. The most striking gift, a sterling silver tea set, arrived with no card, but Letty knew it was from The Widows.

But the most precious gift of all, the one that meant more to her than any of the others was an antique silver water pitcher, a family heirloom that bore a laboriously handwritten card:

To a most admired couple
With love from
Fontine   John   Poppa Dice

At four-fifteen, the wedding reception guests and another small crowd of well-wishers gathered at the train depot to wave George and Letty on their honeymoon—two weeks at the Prince Hotel in Gutherie.

The happy couple stood for a moment at the rail of the observation car, and Letty looked at the town of Angel as if for the first time. The recently paved Main Street sent up heatwaves over the new buildings, and she could see the sign, EDWARD HERON, CABINET MAKER, standing out brightly over the second story of the shop building. Angel was growing by leaps and bounds, and best of all, she thought with pride, it was *her* town! Even the church and God's Acre, which had stood alone for years, were now surrounded on each side with small storefronts. If the town moved farther south, she would have a good view of Main Street from the upstairs window of the house that George was going to build for her!

As the train chugged out of the station, the happy couple waved once more to the crowd, and then settled down in the red plush seats for the long ride to Gutherie.

They had supper in the dining room of the Prince Hotel, which was filled with flashily dressed "drummers," salesmen who had invaded the Territory like squinty-eyed mice. The few well-dressed couples stood out among the land speculators, the businessmen who had come in for a quick supper before going to lodge, and the smattering of elderly spinsters taking respite before going to Wednesday night prayer meeting.

Upstairs in the bridal suite, which was decorated in pale blue and yellow, George took Letty into his arms. "I love you, lady," he said. She clung to him, feeling his broad chest, and kissed his chin; his beard smelled faintly of witch hazel. She looked up at him. "I can't believe that we're alone. Do you realize that we have had very little time together, Mr. Story?"

He nodded. "Now we have the rest of our lives."

Suddenly she was filled with horror. Those were the exact words that Luke had uttered on their wedding night! Oh, God, she thought, I can't lose you, George. I must never lose you!

She went to the long pier mirror at the dresser, filled with panic. She had not been with a man in ten years. In the mirror, she saw that he was casually undressing. She turned her head away, then gathered up her new nightgown of ecru lace and went into the small dressing room, where she carefully removed each article of clothing. She delayed her re-entry into the bedchamber as long as she could.

Her new husband was standing by the bed—unclothed. Letty's face went scarlet and she averted her

147

eyes. In their three years of marriage, she had never seen Luke completely undressed. How bold her George was turning out to be! Had she made a mistake? He was always so proper with other people present, and his manners were impeccable.

He drew her into his arms, dextrously unfastening the bow at her throat. The nightgown fell to the floor, and she trembled. He laid her back gently on the bed, but made no move to blow out the lamp. She and Luke had always made love in the dark. She closed her eyes tightly, lying loosely in his embrace, her heart beating wildly. She did not want to behave as one of those women who catered to . . . . Suddenly she thought of Leona Barrett. She was almost certain, now that she thought about it, that the widows did not extinguish the lamps when gentlemen came to call.

Then George was kissing her, and suddenly she was filled with new warmth and she found herself responding to his caresses. For the first time in her life, she felt *free*, reveling in the sensation of being completely unclothed, which allowed her to feel the fire of his body. How powerful he was as he lay over her, resting lightly on his elbows. How cool her breasts felt pushed against his smooth, broad chest. Then her heart began to beat wildly again and, filled with new panic, she began to tremble.

"What is the matter, my dear?" he asked softly.

"I'm frightened and I don't know why!" She began to cry, and as the tears rolled down her cheeks and onto her neck, he held her close, comforting her with his strong sinewy arms.

"I am apprehensive, too," he answered quietly, "but that is very natural. I only want what is good for you. We need not hurry. I am not a schoolboy and you are not a schoolgirl—that is what is so wonderful about being our age. We never need to be impatient with each other."

Her tears dried on her cheeks. "It's as if—well, as if I was never with a man before . . . . It's almost as if holding me is enough . . . ."

He smiled slowly. "It is. Let us not concern our-

148

selves." He got up slowly and blew out the lamp, then slid back into bed beside her.

Now that the room was dark, the electric street lights threw a glow through the window blinds, turning the place into dusk. George kissed her. She had always known that Luke was a very special man, but he had never stirred her as George was doing now. Her body was encased in warmth; she could not remember such accommodation with Luke. Obviously George was an accomplished lover, while Luke and she had discovered love together—hesitantly. Now, as George moved over her, all apprehension vanished. So little was required of her. . . . She had forgotten in those nine years between men, that she was a woman—*inside*. And as she opened herself to him, she realized that her body had lain dormant. It was as if Letty Heron had gone into hibernation and Mrs. George Story was being awakened. She blushed in the dark, the heat rising up from her neck to her forehead like the fire from a blast furnace. Suddenly she wanted him to possess her entirely—but it was not yet possible. She tried to relax completely under him so that her tension would abate. Very patiently, kissing her all the while, touching her back with his fingertips, caressing her buttocks with the palms of his hands, he very slowly and gently completed the journey.

She sighed sweetly, feeling herself against him at last. Here was joy! Here was the indescribable feeling of all womankind! Here was the completeness that she had missed without Luke! Was this union God's sweet reward for all the trials and tribulations of life?

She lay back now, fully relaxed as he moved over her. Then, as their bodies generated new life-giving warmth, his body shuddered with a deep spasm, and she shivered. She had not reached the peak of excitement yet, but was enthralled with the feeling that she was giving him pleasure. He paused a very long moment, breathing heavily, then began his slow, rhythmic movements again. She was now participating in a way in which she never had with Luke. This was a new experience altogether! She sighed softly, and waves of euphoria emanated from her body. It was as if she was somewhere in

149

the room, looking down on her own body suspended on tiny, silken threads. *"Oh, George!"* she cried at last.

They lay together for a long while. She luxuriated in the feeling of him—the very presence of him. Then, as she became drowsy and started to drift off on new waves of euphoria, she felt her empty body expand. At that moment, she felt life form, divide, form, and then divide again, and she knew that she was with child.

Bosley returned to Angel on the 1st of June with his entire savings of two thousand dollars tucked into his shoe. After waiting at the depot for fifteen minutes, he finally decided to walk the two and a half miles to the Heron farm.

It was a sunny day, but the air was sharp with a cool breeze. He was pleased to see that the town had grown in the year he had been away. There was now an undertaker, he noticed, and new houses now stood on several lots that had been inhabited only by tumbleweeds and briar patches. Four new buildings had been built nearer Letty's farm, including a small clapboard frame with a new sign in Edwardian script: *The Angel Wing*. He smiled; the town now had a newspaper. Angel was beginning to acquire *character*.

He was still smiling as he walked down the new wooden sidewalks. He had his proposal to Letty already framed in his mind. He started to whistle and checked himself. A gentleman did not whistle on the street, even in Angel! He turned into the entrance to Edward's shop and went into the showroom, where several pieces of completed furniture were being labeled by an apprentice. He nodded politely and opened the door to the room at the rear of the building. The place was a beehive of activity. Four men in coveralls were working at various jobs. Edward, who was planing a four-by-six, looked up; his face broke into a wide grin. "Bos!" he exclaimed. "My God, how good to see you!" He came forward, wiping his hands on his apron.

They shook hands. "We've been expecting word from you."

"I wrote that I was coming, but I guess you can't trust the mails."

"If you'll make yourself comfortable for about fifteen minutes, we can go home for supper. Prissy and the children will be as glad as I am to see you." He paused. "Letty is still on her honeymoon, but—"

"*Honeymoon*?"

Edward saw the look of dismay on Bosley's face and drew back. "You mean, you hadn't heard?"

Bosley shook his head numbly. "No. . . . Who did she marry?"

"A man by the name of George Story."

"A mixed blood Cherokee?" Bosley asked incredulously.

"You know him?"

"No, Edward, only his name. He's rather well thought of around Washington." He paused. "I wish that I had know about the wedding."

"Letty wrote to you," Edward replied gently, "but apparently you were in transit."

Bosley went to the door and looked out through the showroom to the street outside, his mind whirling in confusion, his dream of wealth receding into the background. The oil on Letty's property would now go to a red Indian! He smiled wryly to himself. Armbuster and his henchmen, and all of the months of oil-drilling research wasted, as well as a good deal of his own money. What a fool he had been! Why hadn't he proposed to Letty the moment he had received the chemist's report?

"I hope they will be very happy," he said flatly. There was one alternative left—he could simply not say anything about the oil reservoir under Letty's creek. No one would ever know! But, no, he was an honorable man. He had made one mistake; he would not make another.

Edward placed his hand on Bosley's shoulder. "I know you cared for Letty," he said sympathetically, "and if you had been around more, I think you could have won her. Although, frankly, I think your resemblance to Luke hurt your chances. . . ."

No doubt, Bosley thought. It had been his luck to resemble the dead husband of the woman who could have lifted him from the ranks of poverty to untold riches!

151

* * *

The next afternoon, Bosley hitched up the horses to the carriage and drove to the railroad station. He had regained his composure and felt almost lighthearted. He had formed a plan, a very good plan, he thought. . . .

George got off the train first and held out his hand as Letty alighted. Bosley waved as the couple came toward him, faces wreathed in smiles. Letty had never been more beautiful, and there was a new femininity about her. The couple exuded an aura of love. Always a dignified man, George carried himself even straighter and seemed to walk with new purpose.

Letty made the introductions. Bosley had expected to dislike George Story; instead, to his surprise, he found him to be warm and sincere. "I didn't get your letter about the wedding. I was moving about a good bit."

"It all happened rather suddenly. What job has taken you to so many places?" Letty asked breathlessly. "Each letter had a new postmark."

"I've been doing some research on my own," Bosley replied. "We can get caught up after supper." He turned to George. "Angel has grown a good bit since I was here last."

He laughed. "Yes, it's prospering, all right." As they passed the newspaper office, he pointed to the sign. "How do you like the name, *The Angel Wing*?"

Bosley smiled. "Who thought that one up?"

"A contest was held," Letty replied. "Bella Chenovick won the prize—a lifetime subscription!"

That night, after the children had been put to bed and the second serving of coffee had been poured, Bosley held up his hands. "We must have a very serious discussion," he announced. He turned to Edward. "Remember when we went riding down by Letty's creek and saw all those dying cottonwoods? I took a sample of the pitch that was seeping out of the ground and had it analyzed in Washington. I wasn't sure then, but the sample was positive."

"Positive of *what*?" Edward asked.

Bosley looked from one to the other, then turned to

Letty. "As far as can be determined, it appears that there is an anticline under your property."

"An anticline—what's that?" she asked, frowning.

"I should explain. Millions of years ago, during the Ice Age, plant and animal life turned into hydrocarbons through pressure from the slow-moving glaciers, and as the layers of strata were pushed up and down and wrinkled into mountains and valleys, this material was trapped and became petroleum."

"Then," George said, "petroleum is trapped under Letty's creek! Is that it, Mr. Trenton! *Is that what you have been saying*?"

Bosley nodded. "There is an anticline—an inverted dish effect—which I noticed when I crawled down the water well. But you see, there is no way of telling how big the dome or reservoir is without drilling."

There was a deep silence in the room. Letty, George, Edward, and Priscilla looked at each other in wonder, trying to digest the import of Bosley's announcement.

"I don't understand," Priscilla said finally.

"It means, Prissy," Bosley explained patiently, "that there is oil down there, and the decision must be made whether to drill for it or not."

Edward laughed. "We may be sitting on a fortune."

Bosley nodded. "Or it may not be worth going after. . . ."

"What is the next step?" Letty asked, her face glowing with anticipation.

"That depends." Bosley paused. "In Pennsylvania or Texas, for instance, large oil companies lease oil rights from people like you. They move in drillers and spudd wells, sharing the profits with the landowners. The companies bear the burden of the expense of drilling—which can be considerable."

Letty frowned. "Why can't we drill our own well? Then we wouldn't have to share the profits. After all, we *know* oil is here!"

"That's the other possibility, but it would take a great deal of money. You've got to employ four men at least. Tools must be bought and a derrick has to be erected. Drilling is a long, wearying experience. It may take months."

153

George clicked his tongue. "How much money do you think it would take?" He suddenly looked very dark, very Indian.

Bosley shook his head. "I don't know, perhaps several thousand dollars."

"That much, eh?" Edward asked.

"I've done a bit of research," Bosley put casually. "Wildcatting is a very chancy business."

"Well, then," Letty said, "why can't we form a company? I have a bit of money—not much—but I do have income from the stores. If we fail, at least we have made an effort."

Edward smiled sadly. "I'm in debt over my ears. Is there any oil under my property, Bos?"

He shrugged. "I didn't see evidence of an anticline in either your well or the widows', but that doesn't mean—"

"I have some savings," George interrupted, "but I think we must be careful in promoting this scheme. How much cash is needed?"

"Again, it's hard to say. There's a great deal more involved than may be apparent. The usual procedure, before the first well is even contemplated, is to lease the oil rights on all the surrounding property. If petroleum is found, everyone and his brother is going to descend upon Angel. Leases will fly right and left. But you have to pay something for the surrounding leases, even if no oil is discovered. It's a huge undertaking. . . ." He paused. "I do have a few connections among the oil companies. But they may be hesitant about drilling in Indian Territory without states' rights. . . ."

George nodded. "It gets very complicated. I think we are only examining the tip of the iceberg, Mr. Trenton. There must be many more factors involved than we know about."

"It's going to take a great deal of thought and money, Mr. Story."

Letty clapped her hands. "Why don't we all contribute what we have and go into partnership?"

"That is a very good suggestion, my dear." George nodded.

154

Edward shook his head. "I have no cash whatsoever."

George glanced at Bosley. "We need brains as well as money."

"But, the oil is on your land. . . ."

"Yes," Letty agreed, "it is! But we don't know anything about drilling. If you'd put in a like amount of money, Bos, I'll contribute the land—you have the knowledge—this certainly evens things up."

George sighed. "I think that is quite fair."

"I've got two thousand dollars," Bosley said, thinking how long it had taken him to save that much money.

"I've got three and Letty has a couple. Is seven thousand enough?" George asked.

"To start."

George stood up. "I'll draw up the papers tomorrow."

Letty laughed. "Isn't it marvelous to have a lawyer in the family?" She stood up. "I'll fetch some wine. This is an occasion! We should all drink a toast to the *Heron Oil Company*!"

13

The Proposition

George stood back and admired the new clapboard house as he drew Letty close.

"I think, my dear, that it will pass muster. However, I do not see how one more bit of gingerbread can be added!" It was true—the front porch, the cupola that extended the upper sitting room, and even the eaves around the second story, were fitted ingeniously with small, hand-turned wooden curlicues—courtesy of Edward's new lathe. "It's a handsome place," he added.

Letty looked at her husband with shining eyes. "It's a *mansion!*" She squeezed his hand again. "I'm glad we have four bedrooms," she said casually. "One for you and me, one for Little Luke and one for the baby that will arrive next January."

He looked at her with wonder, and kissed her cheek, doing some swift calculations. "You've known for three months?"

"Yes," she laughed, "but I wanted the house to be finished before I told you."

He grew serious. "What if he is red?"

"All babies are red!"

"You know what I mean."

"He may be pink or yellow or candy-striped for all I care. I'll love him just the same."

"I notice you keep saying 'he.'"

"I do?"

"Yes."

"Perhaps it's an omen, but it would be nice if Little Luke had a sister."

He drew her close again. As a slight wind blew over the prairie and dark clouds began to gather over the horizon, he took her by the hand and led her down the path by the wild rose bush toward their new home.

"George?"

"Yes?"

"Little Luke has a proud heritage. He's English and Dutch." She paused. "The new baby will have an equally proud heritage. Not only will he have Dutch, Irish, and Cherokee blood, but he will also have the added strength of his father."

Forty-two members of the community of Angel attended the church service commemorating the ninth anniversary of the founding of Angel. Everyone brought boxed food for the traditional picnic, which was held—even in chilly weather—on the lawnside next to God's Acre.

Reverend Haskell, dressed in a new blue serge suit (tithing was an established practice now that the area was growing more prosperous) stood up and waved for silence. Dessert had long been consumed, and the ladies of the church paused in their cleanup duties. "It is only proper and fitting," he said gravely, his thin, reedy voice causing some of the bluebirds headed south to tarry in their flight, "to ask Letty Heron Story, who contributed the land for this church and parsonage, to say a few words."

He helped Letty, who was seven months pregnant, to her feet. She felt calm, free of the stage fright that had accompanied her first attempts to speak to the congregation at previous anniversaries. She wore a billowy blue faille dress with a ruffled white blouse that had been especially made for the occasion to hide her ballooning figure. Her wide-brimmed hat with a blue rose shaded her face from the sun. Letty had been prepared to stay home because of her condition, but the community women had insisted she come to the affair. "It wouldn't be the same without you, dear," Bella Chenovick had said. "We're all practically family, anyway."

Letty acknowledged the applause with a demure smile. "Thank you," she said looking out over the

157

group made up of the Dices, the Stevenses, the Chenovicks, the Trunes, the Bakers. . . . "It is once again my pleasure to welcome everyone in the community. During the last eight years, with God's help, we have made successful lives for ourselves. Surely, all of you must be filled with pride at your own handiwork. Through all of your great efforts, you have built a section of Garfield County that is second to none."

Now was the difficult part. She paused and softened her voice. "Now, we may or may not be on a brink of even greater prosperity." Everyone leaned forward expectantly. "Our geologist friend, Bosley Trenton, whom most of you know, believes that there may be the possibility of a petroleum deposit in this area."

She looked over the group, waiting for the murmuring to cease. "While this is anything but certain, my husband and I are willing to take a chance and drill the first well on our property." The crowd stirred, there was heavy applause and an exchange of glances among the men. Letty went on, her voice rising above the tumult. "My husband and I are willing to speculate. If no oil is discovered, then we have made a very costly mistake, but we will have at least tried."

She did not know if the ensuing silence was good or bad. She must proceed very carefully now. "This is a small community and most of us know all about each other's finances. I'm not a woman of means, nor is my family, or my husband, yet we're prepared to take a chance with the little cash that we do have and share some of it with all of you."

There were looks of disbelief, and Letty hurried on. "A large oil company would acquire leases on your property, and we would like to arrange a similar deal. We are prepared to pay fifty dollars to every head of household in the community for a five-year lease." She raised her hand as the cacophony of voices rose in the Sunday air. "This isn't a great deal of money, I realize, but a fortune to us, if oil isn't struck. However, if our well does come in, then we'll certainly drill on your property also."

She silenced the wild applause by a wave of her hands. "I admit the possibility is dangerously speculative, so none should get up hopes that an oil industry here is a foregone conclusion. We are, in a way, all in this together." She paused dramatically, looking at the expectant faces. "There is one more item that may be the most difficult of all. I beseech all of you to keep this matter to yourselves." She looked directly at the young editor of the *Angel Wing*, William Truscott. "Please don't publish anything about our endeavors. We have been, in the past, a close-mouthed community." She thought about the outlaw whom Luke had shot in self-defense. "Now, we're all in this venture together. If word should leak out about the possibility of discovering oil, the big companies are apt to move in and speculators by the hundreds will overrun our land. . . ." She paused and blushed. "But, if we *don't* find oil, Garfield County could become the laughing-stock of the entire Indian Territory!"

John Dice stood up in the back of the group. "Folks," he said, shuffling his feet. "What Miz Story has said makes sense." He paused, aware that this was the first time he had ever spoken in public. "My claim is next to the Herons', and if George and Letty are lucky enough to hit pay dirt, and then drill a well on my place, I don't want anyone nosin' around!" He scratched his head; the sentences were coming easily, to his surprise. "And it's not as if there's a lot of us land-owners. I think we can sure'n hell—excuse me, Rever-end Haskell—keep our traps shut!" He sat down to a round of quick applause.

Torgo Chenovick was next. He stood up proudly in his new broadcloth coat. "Bella and I came here like everyone else—without anything—and we've worked hard in good times and in bad. There'd be no town of Angel if it were not for this brave woman and her kin-folk. I say support her. I'll be the first to sign my name on a lease!"

There were nods and "amens" from the group. Letty stood up again. "I want to thank you folks for the vote of confidence. Please drop by my house on your way home today. I have the papers ready to sign."

There was a wave of handclapping and cheers. Letty sank down on the chair next to George. "Thank God

159

that's over!" she whispered, "Did I do all right? Did I remember all the words?"

He took her hand. "Perfectly."

"I wish that you'd given the speech."

"They would never have taken it from me. After all, I'm the newest member of the community. It's you, my dear, who have the power."

"Power?"

"I firmly believe, my dear, that if you had asked everyone to send their children into bondage, there would not be anyone under fifteen in the community!" He grinned, and suddenly it occurred to her how much she cared for him.

The group began to break up into little knots. Priscilla was helped to her feet and brushed off the back of her dress. "With a pitch like that, Letty, it's a wonder that you weren't elected mayor!" She turned and joined Edward, who shrugged his shoulders behind her back.

"What's wrong with Prissy?" George asked.

"Oh, nothing really," Letty said lightly. "She's just being—Prissy!"

That night after supper, George counted the signed leases. "Everyone came through," he said triumphantly.

"Yes," Letty nodded sadly, "and we are two thousand dollars poorer." She signed. "Oh, George, I hope we're not making a mistake!"

He took her in his arms. "We've got to go on faith— faith and Bosley Trenton!"

"Speaking of faith," he said gently, "I am loath to leave you in the family way, but my presence is desperately needed in Washington."

"But George, you've said yourself that the other tribal lawyers can handle the situation. The winter is going to be very cold and I'll need you here."

He took her hand. "You knew when I married you, my dear, that I had obligations elsewhere. I will, I hope, return by Christmas." He looked out the hoar-frosted windows at the white landscape. "If only I were like any other man!"

"If you were," Letty smiled softly, "I wouldn't have been attracted to you." She sighed. "I've been selfish.

160

Of course, you must go and help your people." She stood up straight. "I'll manage."

On December 8th, 1901, George Story stood in the back of the gallery and listened to Theodore Roosevelt's message to Congress, a rather boring report delivered with much spirit and raising of eyebrows and flashing of strong teeth. Not really concentrating on the words, George suddenly heard the word *Indian* mentioned and leaned forward intently.

"In my judgment," the president was saying, "the time has arrived when we should definitely make up our minds to recognize the Indian as an individual and not as a member of a tribe. . . ."

George clamped his jaws together. This stubborn man was ignoring, as so many presidents before him, the fact that the Constitution of the United States was written for setting controls upon the white man, and not the Indian, who then belonged to quasi-foreign nations. . . .

". . . The General Allotment Act is a mighty pulverizing engine to break up the tribal mass. It acts directly upon the family and the individual. Under its provisions some sixty thousand Indians have already become citizens of the United States. We should now break up the tribal funds, doing for them what allotment does for the tribal lands; that is, they should be divided into individual holdings. . . ."

George shook his head sadly. At least now, it was official. The president had spoken in the most public way possible—before the Congress and the world. George reached out on either side and grasped the hands of lawyers from the Creek and Choctaw Nations, then the trio left the gallery.

In the corridor outside, George lighted a cigar and threw the match contemptuously on the marble floor. "The government is going ahead, by God or by damned," he said furiously, "and gentlemen, we might as well get used to it! We have fought the wild bears for years, and no matter how many lawsuits we file, or no matter how many treaties are broken by the government, our cause is lost. I have a new home, a new business, and a baby on the way, and up until now I have given freely of my time. But from this day forward, I will take no more salary from the Cherokee Nation." He threw his cigar on the floor and crushed the shaft under his boot.

"Does this mean you are giving up?" St. Clair, his Cherokee lawyer friend, asked incredulously.

"No, I am not giving up! I will fight to the end, but on my own time. Why spend months on end here in Washington, waiting for such accounts as today to filter down from on high? I will take our crusade to the people!"

On January 15, 1903, during a fierce electrical storm, Sam brought little Clement into the world. "It is a good sign, lady," he said. "Babies born when the sky lights up always have musical talent."

Letty smiled softly, looking down at the wrinkled face at her bosom. "Well," she said with a laugh, "I'll love him just the same!"

Bosley Trenton alighted from the stage of Bartlesville, a sprawling town of wooden buildings, not unlike Angel. But there was a frenetic air about the town, as if it were on the brink of something very special. Already one well was being spudded outside of town, and preparations were underway for other explorations. Equipment was being brought in by wagon, and an excitement was engendered on the streets by the land speculators, oil men, and roustabouts lounging about in their Sunday suits.

Bosley glanced up and down the street and was momentarily overcome with trepidation. Somehow, somewhere, he had to locate a drilling crew that he could cajole or bribe into returning with him to Angel. I'm crazy, he thought, absolutely crazy. I've come on a wild goose chase! He turned into the saloon on the corner and ordered a whiskey, then lounged with his elbow on the bar and surveyed the crowd. After a bit, he was able to piece together some information: A banker by the name of Frank Phillips was one of the persons responsible for putting up the drilling money. No oil had been struck yet, but hopes were high. Bosley downed his second drink and went out into the street.

He had heard talk of huge bonuses if oil was found. He might as well go back to Angel empty-handed. What could he offer? The Heron group barely had enough money to last a few months, and he had heard one of the men at the bar say that drilling on the local number one well had been going on for almost a year. Disillusioned and weary, he made his way across the dusty street to the hotel; his valise seemed to weigh a ton. He saw the big, brawny sheriff escorting a tall, sandy-haired man from the local jail to the stagecoach.

"See that you and your kind shake the dust from your heels. Don't ever come back to Bartlesville again!" the sheriff exclaimed angrily, opening the stage door. He stood by while four men, escorted by a deputy, entered the coach.

"What have they done, sheriff?" Bosley asked.

"Blew the town wide open, that's all!" the man replied gruffly. "Got drunk last night and shot up the Midtown Saloon. Someone might have got killed." He lowered his voice. "They're all broke—got cleaned out by some fast women." He peered at Bosley suspiciously. "You in the oil business?"

Bosley shook his head. "No."

"I never seen you around here before." The man was becoming belligerent. "What's your game?"

Bosley smiled. "Just passing through. In fact, I'm taking this stage."

"Well, don't have no truck with those men," he replied sternly, "they'll skin you alive!"

Bosley nodded and climbed into the coach. Even with the windows open, the interior smelled like a privy. "Well, I declare," a vaguely familiar voice said, "we meet again."

Bosley swung his head in the direction of the greeting and gazed into the face of Larry Steele, whose wide smile showed off his rotted front teeth.

"How's our friend Armbuster?" Bosley asked nervously, experiencing the pain in his jaws again.

"That sonofabitchin' teetotaler?" Steele laughed hol-

163

lowly. "Fired me off the rig, me and my crew! We went up to Caldwell, Kansas, where we heard there was a strike. Turned out a rumor, so we ended up here in Bartlesville. We were gonna work for Phillips, in fact got an advance in pay, but we ran into some rotgut last night." He shook his head, he was not smiling now. "Turned us inside out, it did. I swear, I'm off booze forever!"

Bosley made a quick decision. "If you behave yourself, Steele, you can go to work for me. . . ."

While the drillers waited for the heavy equipment to arrive, a large platform supporting a huge wooden derrick was built over Letty's creek, at the exact spot where the black pitch seeped through the red shale. The jarhead, Larry Steele, whom Bosley still did not like personally but admired because of his knowledge and experience, supervised the raising of the structure.

On a slight incline near the maple tree, a pine bunkhouse had been built that contained five beds, a potbellied stove, a few chairs, and one long closet. A few feet away was a sturdy outhouse. The tool dresser, Clarence Harcourt, and two roughnecks, Jed Sims and Patrick Fegan, made up the crew. Pat ran the mail pouch and did the cooking. After the third scorched supper of beans, bacon, and lumpy grits, a conference was held with George.

"My wife cannot be expected to cook for five extra people," he said, "so why not make arrangements with The Widows?"

Larry Steele showed his rotted teeth in a wide grin. "Ain't that a whorehouse?"

George coughed discreetly. "Why, yes, but it started out as a restaurant, and food is still served to hungry customers." He looked up at the derrick. "I imagine that you men will be going over there occasionally, anyway. See Leona Barrett."

"I guess anything would be better than the victuals we been getting." He glanced at Pat. "No offense, cookie."

Patrick held up his fists in mock attack and threw back his head and laughed. "I ain't no housewife, and

164

that's for sure! No one likes home cookin' more'n me! At this point, I'd eat in a rat cellar if the food was good!"

Poppa Dice poured a cup of coffee from the pot on the back of the stove in Leona's kitchen and stretched his back. The poker game had lasted for eleven hours and he was tired. Larry Steele was dressed, as were his companions, in freshly laundered coveralls, and his left hand, holding the cards before him, looked like a giant paw. The pot contained three hundred dollars.

Poppa Dice went into the living room, where the three men from Enid dressed in frock coats were smoking cigars. "If the U.S.A. recognizes the Republic of Panama," Everts, the banker, was saying, "what will happen to the Canal?"

The other two men sipped their bourbon, and Poppa Dice clicked his tongue. "I'll tell you what, gents. I think that Colombia should be consulted. I know that President Roosevelt is against an alliance, but, after all, Colombia borders . . ."

Everts looked up with a slow grin. "Mr. Dice, would you kindly refresh our drinks?"

"Of course." The old man went back to the kitchen. He knew it wasn't fitting to engage in conversation with the guests, yet he wanted to talk. Now that he could he read the *Angel Wing* from front page to back by the light of the coal-oil lantern every night after his stint at The Widows.

Poppa Dice had always been interested in politics. Now that he was able to get his information firsthand and was not dependent upon the opinions of others, he was able to take a long-range view. For the first time in his life, he could see *ahead*.

If he had known that so much knowledge was out there in the world, just to be had by reading, he would have abandoned his days on the Chisholm Trail and gone to school in Santone along with the first graders. With John and Fontine also perusing the paper every day, talk around the house was no longer limited to crops and weather and what to have for supper.

* * *

165

Reginald Savor held Mary Darth in his arms. "This is a very special occasion," he said quietly. "It's our last time together. I'll be going back to Louisville for good. My old aunt in Garber can no longer live by herself. She's coming home to live with me. There will be no need to return to the Territory."

"I'm sad," Mary said. "I'll miss you very much." She kissed him on the lips, surprised at his warmth.

He kissed her again, running his hands over her breasts, which were suddenly responding to his touch. She drew against him and in a moment, they were together.

As Reginald Savor started to make love to her, Mary Darth felt a pleasant twinge in her solar plexus, and she became more alert. She had always been detached in her frequent encounters with customers, as if she were somewhere in the room looking down at herself on the bed. But now she was totally involved in what was happening to her. She had never felt so *alive*.

The pleasant feeling built up until she was enveloped in a strange, new yearning. As he moved, she also moved, and a delicious sense of belonging came over her, before she shuddered once, and then again.

He looked down at her in amazement, then kissed her deeply. He held her close, feeling her body vibrate against his. *"Ah-h-h,"* she breathed, *"ah-h-h-h . . ."*

He lay there for a long moment, taking delight in the close embrace, then broke away very gently. His eyes were very bright. "I can't think of ever giving you up entirely," he said at last. "I love you too much, Mary Darth!"

She lay completely relaxed beside him, at peace, content to be held loosely in his arms. For the first time in her life, she felt like a woman. All the things other females had told her about their husbands over the years made sense to her now. She understood the joy, the feeling of freedom, of giving, of taking, of being whole. Not just a person on the outside looking in, but a person who had experienced love.

"I wish that you'd come back to Louisville with me," he murmured. "Didn't you feel a very special—glow—tonight?"

She nodded. "Yes, oh yes, I did!"

"Please marry me," he said in the voice of a small boy.

She caressed his face with her hands, running her fingers along his sideburns. Suddenly she knew that she loved him.

"Reggie," she whispered, "I'll be your wife."

He hugged her to him suddenly. "I can't believe my ears!" he exclaimed, tears coming into his eyes.

Then they were speaking about the move, the house in Louisville, transportation on the train, giving up her interest in The Widows. At last, she got up and stretched her arms to the ceiling. She knew that she was very beautiful, and very soft, and very feminine, and she sighed with contentment.

"Just think," she said, standing up very straight and summoning a stern look on her face. Mentally, she was standing in the doorway of a great southern mansion. "May I announce," she continued, in the tones of a very proper butler, "Mr. and Mrs. Reginald Savor."

He looked up at her and smiled. "A small correction my dear. We would be presented as *Senator* and Mrs. Reginald T. Savor!"

14

The Plague

The well situated over Letty's creek was now down a hundred and thirty feet.

Larry Steele shook his head at George and Letty. "We'd have struck it by now, I think," he said sadly, "if we'd had another crew to work nights. But we can only put in ten hours a day. Cable tool drilling is much slower than rotary."

George nodded. "I can't criticize," he replied. "I've never seen men work so hard." Then he and Letty went back to the house. They were determined to economize even more; money was getting scarce.

The winter was severe, and there were many days when the men lounged in the bunkhouse, huddled next to the pot-bellied stove. With temperatures running four below zero, work on the rig was impossible; even the trip to The Widows at mealtimes was a trial. With a good portion of the drillers' weekly pay siphoned into Leona Barrett's pockets, she did not miss the usual clientele, who could not venture out because of the icy roads.

At Christmastime, the men traveled east to spend the holidays with their families, and the snow-bound community of Angel counted the days until the first thaw.

By April, when Bella Chenovick's peach trees were in full bloom, Larry Steele announced that the well was down to two hundred and forty feet. Work was progressing at a snail's pace. Her face pinched and worried, Letty avoided the townspeople as best she could, weary of inquiries about when the well would come in.

168

She was inclined to lay her financial woes at the feet of the crew, to beg them to stay on without pay, but George shook his head. "I won't allow you to ask favors, Letty. Any move like that on our part means they take over. Steele is a hard man. I do not ever want him to get the upper hand."

In June, Bosley cashed in his life insurance policy and put the two hundred dollars in the Heron Oil Company account in the Enid bank, then took a three months' job at Bartlesville helping Frank Phillips complete a geological survey. He kept his ties in Angel secret, fearful that his employer would discover he had petroleum interests.

In late July, thirty dollars remained in the Heron account.

Letty tied up her horse at the hitching post outside the washhouse and knocked at Leona's back door. Audrey, holding floured hands up in the air, peered through the screen door. "Why, if it isn't Mrs. Story," she said with surprise, her face flushed. "Do come in, I'll get Mrs. Barrett." The big woman ushered Letty into the kitchen, her face still red as a beet. "I'm making apple turnovers," she explained as she poured water from the bucket over her hands and wiped them quickly with a huck towel. "Just go on into the parlor, she'll be down in a minute."

Letty had not seen the inside of the house for years and was surprised at the quiet good taste. Not that she had expected gold-framed mirrors and scarlet wallpaper, as Fontine had speculated, but neither did she expect to find the decor so genteel.

Leona Barrett came down the stairs, placing a comb in the back of her auburn pompadour. "I hope nothing is wrong, Mrs. Story," she said, coming forward quickly, knowing that an emergency must have occurred to have brought her neighbor to her door.

Letty smiled. "No, Mrs. Barrett, there has been no catastrophe!"

"May I get you a cup of tea?"

"No, thank you." Letty looked about the room. "You have such lovely things."

169

"Thank you." Leona sat down on the Morris chair opposite. There was an uncomfortable silence, then she went on. "Such lovely weather . . ."

"Mrs. Barrett," Letty broke in, "I've come to see you today because I think we can do business."

Leona's eyes opened wide. "Business?"

"I think you appreciate a good deal when you see one."

More perplexed than ever, Leona held out her hands in a helpless gesture.

Letty leaned forward. "I'll be frank. As you know, we've been drilling the well for fourteen months."

Leona nodded. "The drillers keep me up to date. They think oil sand is very near. There's been a sulphur smell."

"It could be any time now." Letty paused, then said plaintively, "You see, we have no cash flow. We're broke."

Leona's eyebrows shot up—so *that* was it!

"All of my husband's cash is gone, as is Bosley Trenton's. And," she looked strained, "I have mortgaged every piece of property I own. . . ."

"Including the lots in town," Leona added. "I've heard."

Letty started. "No one is supposed to know!"

Leona nodded. "The banker is a client. But I don't believe anyone else in the Territory is aware of your plight." She paused, and then added gently, "You want me to loan you some money, is that it, Mrs. Story?"

"No. It must be a business arrangement, an investment in the Heron Oil Company."

Leona smiled wryly, but her voice was not unkind. "And, what would happen if it became known that I was one of your backers?"

Letty blushed to the roots of her hair. "I did not mean . . ." she stammered.

Leona held up a jeweled hand. "You said that we were to be frank!" she replied. "I have no illusions, Mrs. Story."

Letty looked down at her hands, red and rough from washing clothes. "What I'm offering you, Mrs. Barrett,

170

is stock in the Heron Oil Company." Her voice was flat. "One fourth ownership for five thousand dollars."

"But surely you could go to a bank."

Letty fought back tears. "I have—eight to be exact—two in Enid, one in Wichita, one in Perry and four in Oklahoma City." She shrugged. "They simply will not speculate."

"How about other oil companies?"

Letty nodded. "We could go to Beaumont, Texas. A big well called Spindletop has started an enormous oil boom there. A big company would bail us out, but gobble up most all the profits! There's also the added problem that since we're not a state yet, working the Territory legally is most difficult."

"Edward?"

Letty pursed her lips. "It's all he can do to support his employees, and then Priscilla . . ."

"Jealousy is a strange bedfellow, eh?" Leona's eyes were bright.

"She won't let Edward invest. It's as simple as that." Letty sighed, "And so you . . ."

Leona laughed. "I'm the last resort, eh? The town madam!"

"I don't blame you for being bitter."

"I'm not bitter, only realistic, Mrs. Story." Leona paused and smoothed the back of her head. "I've always liked you. We've always gotten on," she waved her hand, "and had things turned out differently, we might have become good friends." She paused. "All right, I'm game. I have a lawyer client—" She saw Letty's look of shock and hastily went on. "No, my dear, *not* your husband—who will get together with Mr. Story and draw up the papers . . . this afternoon, if you like."

Letty shook her head. "Not so soon." She leaned forward. "You see, I must prepare the men. . . ."

Leona looked at her, amused. "You mean they don't know that you've offered me a deal?"

"No, that's why I have to have time to break the news."

"Well, Mrs. Story," Leona smiled broadly, "you are certainly a very courageous woman!"

"Not really, Mrs. Barrett," Letty repllied softly. "After all, it's *my* property!"

Summer turned lazily into fall. Lavenia Heron came down from Minneapolis and surveyed the town with wonder. "It must be a pleasure, Letty," she said grandly, "to sit back and bask in all this pride of ownership."

"Not really, considering it's all mortgaged to the hilt, Mother Heron," she replied wearily. Letty still called Lavenia "mother"—out of habit, not affection. Their relationship had not improved on this latest trip.

Later Lavenia told Priscilla, "Letty's scared to death that the well won't come in."

"I know. Thank God, Edward and I stayed out of it." Priscilla was measuring Betsy for an underskirt. She looked up at her mother-in-law and grinned. "I think that Letty's luck has run out! It's rather ironic, isn't it, that she owns practically the whole town and yet she may lose everything if the bankers foreclose."

"Is there really any danger?"

Priscilla nodded. "I'm not told *anything*, of course, but Edward says that she's three months behind in her payments. . . ." She looked down at Betsy's stomach. "Mother, look at this rash. What do you make of it?"

Lavenia brushed her hands over the baby's chest. "Welts." She paused, and leaned forward, keeping her panic from showing. "I'd best fetch the doctor. I'll take the trap into town."

QUARANTINED—SMALLPOX

read the sign tacked on Edward Heron's clapboard; soon signs appeared on other houses.

Angel's new, young Doctor Schaeffer paid a visit to Leona Barrett. "I have a great favor to ask," he said earnestly, and she smiled inside. Could it be that the young man was about to become a customer? But no, his expression was too grave for dalliance.

"I wonder if I might borrow Sam. He's had the measles, I'm told; therefore, he's immune to the pox. I need help, and from what I've heard, he would make an ideal assistant."

"He may go with you, if he likes. But borrowing is quite another matter," Leona retorted. "He's a person, not a thing. Just because he's an Indian does not mean he doesn't have feelings."

"I thought you were accustomed to dealing in flesh," the doctor replied tartly.

"Putting it crudely, Doctor—yes, I do deal in flesh." She flushed. "But if you had any understanding. . . ." She cut herself off; it was ridiculous to quarrel with a man she barely knew.

"I have understanding," he replied sharply, "otherwise, I would have chosen another profession. At the moment, however, I am striving to help the community at large. I will pay you Sam's salary. . . ."

She shook her head defiantly. "Make your own terms with him. Next September he's going to college, then on to medical school." She smiled coldly. "I shouldn't be surprised if he then settles here in Angel to practice medicine."

The doctor's lip curled. "Be that as it may, I am still not equipped to deal with a person of his class."

She looked at the callow young man with wonder, knowing that he had hung up his shingle in Angel just after receiving his degree. "Unequipped you may be, Doctor, but if you want his services, there is no other way."

"You are an impossible woman!" he exclaimed hotly.

She regarded him dispassionately. "I think that you could probably pick up a pointer or two from the boy—especially about birthing babies! From what I've heard, Cissie Baker could have been relieved of pain during her twelve-hour heavy labor. None of Sam's women endured that kind of torture."

He marched stiffly to the door. "Where is the boy?" asked furiously, the huge vein in his forehead standing out.

"I think," she said with a slight smile, "you'll find him in the washhouse."

* * *

173

Doctor Schaeffer closed his black bag wearily and regarded little Betsy with tired, red-rimmed eyes. The child had calmed down now, but her face was very pale under the splotches of red. "I can't do any more for her," he said dully. "Sam, keep changing the wet cloths on her forehead and continue to take her temperature every fifteen minutes. Don't forget to write down the results on the pad. I have to go over to the Bakers, but I'll drop by again on my way back to town." He turned to Priscilla. "Pray that she passes the crisis."

"Will she be scarred?"

He shrugged his shoulders. "It's inevitable."

"But to go through life . . ."

"Mrs. Heron," the doctor replied sharply, "it is not a queston of whether she will be scarred or not, it's a question of whether she will *live!*" He slammed the door.

The moment he had gone, Priscilla whirled on Sam. "If you can't do anything for her—with all of your *mystical* knowledge—you might as well go back to The Widows!"

"I'll stay, Mrs. Heron. If she gets worse . . ."

"I suppose then you'll recite some mumbo jumbo."

"Leave the boy alone, Prissy," Edward ordered. "Your place is upstairs with the children. If they come down with the disease . . ."

"My place is with my baby. I can't keep running back and forth."

"All right," he replied stoically, "I'll check on the children." He went into the kitchen, where he filled the fly spray can with fumigant and dusted his clothing, then walked slowly up the stairs, the weight of the world on his shoulders.

Reverend Haskell stood in front of the small gravesite. Fearful of spreading the disease, no one in the community of Angel except Priscilla, Edward, Letty and George had ventured forth for the services. This was the fourth funeral that he had conducted this week, and the second for a child. "Although," he said sadly, "little Betsy Heron was only six years old when the Lord took her, she was known for her sunny disposition. . . .

174

Letty marveled at Priscilla's composure, but it was Edward's stricken face that she would always remember: gray with jaw jutting outward, teeth clenched tightly together, his stark, lean profile silhouetted dramatically against the buttermilk sky. How terrible, she thought, to lose a child. Her heart went out to them.

After the service, Priscilla hugged her close, their differences momentarily forgotten. "Oh, Letty, what's to become of us?" she wailed.

Over Priscilla's shoulder, Letty saw Edward walking into the woods, east of God's Acre. She knew he must be alone with his grief.

After the funeral, Larry Steele came by the house. "Mr. Story," he said, "me and my men will be leaving on the afternoon train."

"What do you mean?"

Steele stood on one foot and then on the other. "We'll be going down Beaumont, Texas way." He paused. "Your farm is surrounded by families with the pox. We don't want to die, and we don't want to end up with scars all over our bodies. We may not be the handsomest fellas alive, but we don't want to look like freaks. We're sorry we couldn't stay to see the well come in, but I'm sure you understand our position."

George nodded numbly. "Come by on the way to the train and I will pay you off." He closed the door and turned to Letty. "We are broke. We might as well kiss everything goodbye. With the men gone . . ."

Letty turned to him angrily. "We can't give up now, George, we just can't! That well is going to be brought in—if we have to do it ourselves!"

George assumed duties of jarhead. Bosley, the tool dresser, also ran the wheel used to operate the block and tackle on the rig, while Letty, a bandanna wrapped around her hair and her skirts tied in large knots, became the operator of the mail pouch. Luke Jr., nine, looked after the one-year-old Clement in his crib.

"After you get the hang of it, it's not difficult work," Bosley said, after the first week of operating the rig. "It's the long hours that are the hardest."

175

"Amen," Letty replied. She did not remind George that her work began two hours before the men, when she arose to clean house and prepare food, and ended two hours afterward, when she wearily completed the other chores and put the children to bed.

Learning to work on the rig, the threesome drilled twelve inches per day for the first week, then fifteen per day afterward. They prayed for bad weather so that rest periods could be taken without feeling guilty, but the winter of 1904 was exceedingly mild and few days were spent indoors.

As Easter, 1905 approached, a depth of four hundred and two feet had been reached. Bone weary, Letty searched the upstairs closet for a dress. "We haven't been to church for six months," she said as she added new veiling to a tiny straw hat and fastened some cornflowers to the brim. "We've simply got to go—and besides, we need a change of pace."

Easter Sunday was bright and unusually balmy. "You and George go to the services," Bosley said. "I'll stay with the rig."

George and Letty bade him a reluctant goodbye. The spring wheat, pale green and hardy, peeked up from the plowed fields, and the early primroses, dotting the fences that separated the claims, opened their faces to the sun. Letty looked down at her rough, callused hands and touched her weather-worn face, then brought the dotted veiling down under her chin. She looked, she knew, like a sharecropping farm woman with twelve kids, played out from overwork. As exhausted as she was, when they approached the church she grew warm inside. In the ten years since The Run, Angel had become a thriving community, and prosperity showed in the new coats of paint on every clapboard farmhouse. She sighed and looked in the direction of Luke's grave, then reached over and pressed George's hand.

"What was that for?" he asked.

She smiled softly. "Just for being such a good man."

Letty could not remember much of Reverend Haskell's sermon, which had to do with the Resurrection; her thoughts kept slipping back over the years. Priscilla

176

men, I give you the constitution for the new State of *Sequoyah*."

As he expected, George did not receive applause, but he felt exuberant. He was followed by St. Clair, who was to present the articles of the new constitution.

After closing a deal in Chicago with the Ellenfarm Refinery whereby the Heron Oil Company would provide eight thousand barrels of oil each month for six months, with an option to increase the barrelage according to demand, George Story returned to Angel. When he came into the kitchen, the supper dishes had been washed and Letty was punching down the dough for breakfast rolls. He tiptoed behind her and placed his arms around her waist. She stiffened as if she had been struck with a hot poker and whirled around. "You scared me," she said, still holding her floured and doughy hands up in the air, "but—I'm glad you're home!" He kissed her on the back of her neck, and she shivered.

"The children are in bed?"

She nodded. "Luke has the pinkeye. I purchased some smoked eye glasses for him to wear and he looks like a twelve-year-old version of Benjamin Franklin. Clement stubbed his toe. . . ." She smoothed a mixture of butter and nutmeg over the rolls and wiped her hands on her apron. "But enough of this. How did it go?"

"I'll recount it all later. I made the proposal for Sequoyah." He kissed her on the cheek. "Let us go upstairs."

She pressed his arms. "You've been away so long this time—six weeks. The crew found heavy oil sands yesterday on the new well."

"Oh? Well, right now," he whispered, "I am only interested in making love to you."

She drew back playfully. "Don't be so forward."

"As a man who has been deprived of a woman's company for so long, I demand my rights!" He ran his hand along her thigh.

She grinned. "You mean you intend to dally with a matron of thirty-four?"

"You will never be a matron, even if you reach ninety!"

She laughed, took his hand and led him up the stairs to the bedroom, where she lighted the kerosene lamp. "I used to hate the fumes," she said, sniffing the air, "but now that we've struck oil, the smell spells m-o-n-e-y. Just think, all over the country, citizens like us are lighting lamps . . ."

"Or turning on electricity," he added wryly as he undressed, "cutting down kerosene sales."

She removed her vest. "Edward is going to electrify his shop," she replied.

George nodded. "He should. With mechanized machinery, he'll be able to double or even triple his daily production." He made a motion to blow out the lamp.

"No," she said, "leave it on . . ."

He smiled. "Remember how shocked you were on our honeymoon when I left the lamp lighted?"

She laughed. "I was a very properly brought up young girl," she admitted, "and I thought you were the height of, well, decadence!"

"I still am," he replied softly, removing his Balbriggans, and standing before her quite unclothed. He looked down. "For a middle-aged man, I think my body is in good proportion. . . ."

"You're becoming egotistical; imagine standing there admiring your own body!"

"Take off your corset," he said. "I've forgotten what you look like without clothing."

"You want me to undress for you—like those women in the machines in the Peep Shows Parlors?"

"And what do you know about Peep Shows?"

She giggled. "Fontine Dice went into the one in Enid last week, and she said the pictures were scandalous! She put a nickel in the slot and peeped into this big cabinet, and two men in *tights* were *boxing*! She said it was very obvious that they were men!"

"Oh, Letty," he laughed, "boxers wear metal cups under their tights, that's why they look so large!"

"I don't think I'll tell Fontine. She confided to me that Jaundice is not nearly so . . ."

182

"Letty! Is *that* what you women talk about when we men are not around?"

She removed her corset cover, then her corset. "I never say a word about you. I get so tired of Priscilla complaining about Edward's strawberry birthmark. . . ."

He looked at her cream-colored body. "After I am away a while, I forget what a fortunate man I am, Letty. You are *so* beautiful!"

She kissed him. "We must be very careful, George," she said as they lay down on the bed. "This is only the third of the month, and we must be very careful until after the sixth—"

He kissed her full on the mouth, inserting his tongue between her lips. Then he began to lick her breasts and she felt herself responding as if she were a newly-married virgin. He started the ritual that had long been established between them, and once more carried her aloft on wings of feeling.

He disengaged himself from her embrace for a moment, which she found strange; always before he pressed into her at this point in the foreplay. Opening her eyes, she looked down and then drew back. "What are you *wearing*?" she asked with wonder.

"I purchased some of these tube sheaths made of lambskins when I was in Chicago."

"It's unnatural!"

"Well, my dear, as unsightly as it may be, it will enable us to make love as often as we like, *when* we like, and with no more worry about conception."

"Will it hurt?"

He smiled. "No, of course not." He began to kiss her bosom wetly until she was again euphoric, then he moved over her and she felt him reach out. Truthfully, the extension of his body felt the same; she could discern no difference. Her mind free of care and worry, she relaxed and drew him to her entirely.

She began to sigh and make the intimate sounds that she knew increased his own pleasure. At last, when the moment arrived for them both, she responded as she had during the early months of her pregnancies, without worrying about the possibility of a child starting with her. The warmth of his body gave comfort and then she knew no more until morning.

Contemptuously, Priscilla looked out over the prairie at the unsightly wooden derricks that towered grotesquely over the naked cottonwoods. At least when the trees leafed out, she would not be able to see the clumsy wooden structures! She closed the kitchen window with a clatter; some days, when the wind was right, she could hear the pump wheezing as plainly as if the wells had been spudded in her living room! There was, it seemed, always *something* that drew her attention to the Story farm. She poured a cup of coffee, which she brought to Edward, who had his accounts receivable spread over the dining room table. "Aren't you finished yet?" she asked crossly. "It's almost time for supper."

"One more column to add, then I'm through." He bit the pencil eraser. "You know, Prissy, with that order from the Orion Furniture Company in Gutherie last week for those fifteen Birdseye Maple bedroom suites, we're going to finish our second quarter in high style." He made a fast calculation. "I figure about forty percent profit for 1905—about five thousand dollars! And that," he added, "as Poppa Dice would say, 'ain't hay'!"

"It's about time we made money, Edward—working our fingers to the bone. Mother Heron inquired in her letter yesterday if we had opened the retail store in Enid yet."

"She never gives up, does she?" Edward sighed, "She thinks outlets should be opened up all over Indian Territory."

"Which we will—eventually." Priscilla replied smugly. "It's only a matter of time."

"I wonder," he paused. "Instead of trying to find a good manager for a new store, I still think it would make more sense to throw in with George and Letty. . . ."

Priscilla whirled around, her skirts flashing about her legs, and shook her finger angrily. "So, we're back to *that*! Not on your bottom dollar! What we have is *ours*."

"But the hardest part is over—they've struck oil!"

184

"And it's so expensive to transport the crude out of the Territory, they'll go flat broke. Mark my words, before it's all over and done with, Letty will lose every piece of property in town. People will always need furniture, but oil?"

"You don't understand, Prissy," he replied heatedly. "With all the new machinery being manufactured, powered by gasoline engines, petroleum is bound to become a prime commodity. The Model T . . ."

Her lips curled. "And, how much fuel will be required to run a horseless carriage that no one can afford anyway? There's no smooth road to travel on and . . ." Her voice grew loud. ". . . And Letty told me herself that the market price for oil is only three dollars a barrel, and the railroad takes a dollar and a half just to transport it to other states."

He closed the account book with a snap. "You don't understand, Prissy, I'm not thinking about now but the future." He leaned forward patiently, his voice persuasive. "Smart money should be invested NOW, before the Heron crew starts drilling on our land. We won't be able to get into an oil company in five years!"

"And," she replied hotly, "we may be dead in five years, just like little Betsy!" She looked at him out of the corners of her eyes, and knew she had hit home when his face crumpled.

"All right," he said brokenly, "we'll open the store in Enid." He got up and went out into the yard. She knew that he was headed for God's Acre.

Priscilla addressed the members of the Angel Study Club, which was meeting for tea at Rochelle Patterson's tiny apartment in back of the school house. The ladies, having attended a matinee production of *Uncle Tom's Cabin* in Enid the week before, had arrived quite breathlessly in rented hacks at the depot just in time to catch the five o'clock for Angel. With many households of the community going without a proper dinner that night, husbands had passed the word around in no uncertain terms that further trips to Enid for entertainment were to be cancelled; men, changing diapers and

185

eating sandwiches made six hours ahead, made it clear that the woman's place was in the home.

No one was more vociferous than Edward. "Priscilla, I won't have it! We should have finished the Chenovick's cedar chest this afternoon. With Mitchell teething and having to be held all afternoon, my work is already a day behind. Why can't you stay home like Fontine Dice? You don't see Letty making a fool of herself!"

"At least," she replied angrily, "I keep my child home, while Letty spends half her time wheeling Clement up to the rigs. I declare, she's so afraid a well will come in when her back is turned, and as far as Fontine is concerned, she doesn't have the brains of a bunny rabbit!"

"Just the same, I expect you to stay home, instead of traipsing all over the Territory attending vaudeville."

"*Uncle Tom's Cabin* is not vaudeville, it's legitimate theatre!" Priscilla retorted.

"I still think it is unwomanly to go to these—plays— without an escort. What would you do if a man . . ."

"What" Priscilla countered, "could happen to nine women bunched together? A man wouldn't dare . . ."

"What defense would you have against a drunk, for instance?"

"Oh, Edward!" she replied heatedly. "In broad daylight! After all, we were not on the streets, we took a hack directly to and from the depot to Zoo Hall." She paused, and then stood, hands on hips, for her next announcement. "And, furthermore, how can you say life in Enid is fast, when we live practically next door to a whorehouse!"

"Prissy!"

"Well, it's true. I didn't mean to say that word." Her voice had calmed down somewhat and she was afraid she had gone too far. "But that's what it is and everyone knows it! What may I ask is Angel famous for? It's certainly not our Angel Food Cake—it's The Widows!" It was then that she decided to bring up the subject at the next Study Club Meeting.

Priscilla looked over the heads of the twelve ladies gathered at Rochelle Patterson's. "There is just one more piece of business before this meeting is dismissed. I think it is time that we ladies of the community did something about The Widows. The place is a disgrace to the whole area. Here we are, hard-working citizens while they are carrying on. . . ."

Bella Chenovick raised her hand and stood up; her normally rosy apple cheeks were scarlet. "Torgo says that we should be fortunate that our men folk do not patronize the place."

"How do we know?" Priscilla demanded. "Most of the men are gone from morning until night. They could just as well sneak over . . ."

Bella sat down in a flurry of petticoats and Rochelle Patterson took her place on the floor. "Ladies, I think that it would be the better part of valor to continue to ignore The Widows."

"But if we go to the town fathers—"

"What could they do?" Miss Patterson continued softly. "How could they place pressure on The Widows? If there were gunfights, if someone had been killed, if there had been any trouble whatsoever, we might have a case. But apparently Poppa Dice keeps order. I'm told the place is run like a sort of men's club."

"Men's club!" Priscilla spat out, her face splotched with anger and embarrassment. "Those women should be tarred and feathered and run out of town on a rail!"

Rochelle Patterson smiled coldly. "We must be realistic, ladies. If I may say so, the places on Two Street in Enid, or so I've heard, are conducted in quite another manner, and with those saloons facing the square, the temperance ladies have not been able to do anything."

She looked at each lady in turn. "And, Angel, a growing town as it is, has only some thirty families. Most of our strength lies in the members of the farm community. Remember, we are not yet a state. With no laws on the books . . ." She gestured helplessly. "I really don't see how much headway can be made." She paused. "Now, I do believe that a study club, based as ours is, on cultural events, should not concern itself with—conditions beyond our control. And furthermore," she continued quietly, "even our social events outside of Angel, I understand, must be curtailed."

Bella Chenovick drew her shawl around her shoulders. "If you will close the meeting," she said to Priscilla, "I think we have 'studied' enough for today! Torgo will be in from the field shortly, and he has every right to expect a good, hot supper."

Priscilla knew when she was beaten. "Very well, ladies," she said with resignation, "that will be all for today." She looked over her foolscap pad. "Don't forget to read *The Lay of the Last Minstrel* by Sir Walter Scott for discussion next week."

Only as the buggy headed home did she realize that perhaps the choice of reading material was unfortunate in the light of the main discussion of the day.

Edward's new store in Enid, on the north side of the square across from the courthouse, sported a hand-painted sign—THE HERON FURNITURE COMPANY; the tiny showroom inside featured one bedroom suite, two library tables, a sideboard, and a footstool. "It doesn't look like much," he told Priscilla, "but it's a start."

She smiled and took his hand, her eyes filled. "This is a very special occasion," she said, "the first step in an empire!"

He laughed. "You've been reading novels again," he chastised gently. "No one builds an empire today, times are too uncertain." He glanced at his watch. "Now, if you will sit here in the office, I'll pick up Mr. Pederson at the depot."

Priscilla had barely settled herself at the desk when a tall, elegantly dressed gentleman entered the store—her first customer. She examined the expertly tailored frock coat and the highly polished boots. She wondered whether he would order a dining room set or a parlor suite. He was definitely the parlor suite type, she decided.

"Good afternoon, sir," she said politely, assuming the arch tone of a lingerie saleslady for Sears & Roebuck.

He nodded. "Good afternoon. Is Mr. Heron hereabouts?" He looked her with such dramatic intensity that

188

she almost swooned. She felt undressed! His dark, brilliant green eyes in a handsomely sculptured face held a strangely unsettling magnetism, like the eyes of a cat. "No, he's out of town at the moment," she found herself saying, "but perhaps I can service you. I—I mean, I am Mrs. Heron, his wife . . ."

He seemed unconcerned at her discomfiture. "Manford Pederson is my name."

"Oh!" She flushed. "Edward left just a moment ago to meet you!"

He smiled and his teeth were very white. "The train was a bit early." He glanced at the sketches on the walls. "Are these designs currently in production?" he asked, looking at Priscilla as if she were the first woman he had ever met.

"Yes." She was confounded by his appraisal of her.

"Sturdy pieces." he replied. "As I was being driven from the depot, I was impressed with the number of tree-lined streets with beautifully designed houses." He looked at her directly and she felt a surge of electricity emanate from her solar plexus. Then Edward came in and hurried over to Pederson. "Our hacks apparently passed each other," he explained. "The trains are most usually late." The men shook hands. "Priscilla, I hope that you've been entertaining Mr. Pederson?"

"She's been charming," Pederson said, glancing at her, and she knew at that moment that he was as attracted to her as she to him. Then he, too, had felt that first flush!

"When I answered your advertisement in the Grand Rapids paper, I had already made up my mind to travel westward, perhaps even to California," Pederson said, "but Indian Territory seems just as adventuresome." He smiled indulgently. "Grand Rapids is a good little town, and the Hollanders are fine people, but the furniture manufacturing companies are steeped in the Old World tradition of craftsmanship." He paused. "I think that new methods should be employed—my boss thought otherwise. How do you feel about the situation, Mr. Heron?"

"We're a very small outfit," Edward replied, warm-

189

ing up to the man, "not very adventuresome, but I do want to modernize some."

Pederson nodded. "It must be taken in steps. Now, I don't want to give the impression that I'm a hothead, but I'm just weary of working for people with no imagination." He inclined his head slightly in what Priscilla figured was an habitual gesture. "I firmly believe that the future of the furniture business lies very much in marketing techniques."

"Which is our weakest factor," Edward replied and glanced at his watch. "The train for Angel is almost due. We'd better pick up our wraps. By the way, you did not mention in your letter if you had a family."

"I am divorced," he said matter-of-factly, and looked out of the window.

Edward exchanged glances with Priscilla. Manford Pederson was the first man they had ever met who had gone through the scandal of divorce.

"When dessert is finished, let's go over to the shop." Edward suggested to Priscilla the next afternoon. "I want to show Mr. Pederson some new designs. We're doing ornamental woodcarving that's going to be very popular next season."

"Letty and I will stay," Priscilla sniffed. "I have some new Graphophones discs. I can't wait to play 'She May Have Seen Better Days,' which must be delicious."

"Thank you," Letty replied, "but if you don't mind, I'd like to look at Edward's new electrified lathes. I also want a new sofa. Perhaps we can hear the discs later."

"Very well," Priscilla sighed. "Far be it from me to interfere with a business deal." She paused. "But we can't be making very much money when we give forty per cent off to the family!" She went into the kitchen, her swishing taffeta skirts underscoring her displeasure. Letty followed her into the kitchen to smooth over her hurt feelings.

"Oh, don't mind Prissy, Mr. Pederson," Edward said with a smile. "She's been feeling testy all week." He lowered his voice. "She has an appointment with Doctor Burgen tomorrow. We think a little one's on the way." Edward frowned. "She says that thirty-seven is too old to be having a baby." He sighed. "But, God willing, the little duffer will be bright and healthy." He brightened, "One good thing though, Prissy's moodiness always vanishes in the second month of pregnancy. I can count on about seven months of pure serenity."

George's eyes gleamed. "Would it were that you could always keep her in the family way."

But it was not to be; Priscilla lost the baby four weeks later, and Doctor Burgen shook his gray head. "You'll have no more." He sighed, "and it's just as well at your age!"

The addition to the back of the store had enabled Edward to add the new electrified equipment. He put on a smock, a pair of goggles, and turned on the current. The machine held six long pieces of wood upright between vice-like cams. He guided a template pattern down the side of the first piece of wood.

"Look, George!" Letty exclaimed. They watched each of the other five pieces of wood exactly duplicate the engraving Edward was making on the first; three minutes later the six pieces of wood had become six identical chair arms.

Edward then picked up an electrical tool that looked like a hair curling iron to Letty. "Look closely," he said as he applied the bit to the upper part of the chair arm. As he moved his hand, a flower design was cut deeply into the wood.

Manford Pederson scratched his head and examined the wood carefully. "What you did just now would take three men a half a day to carve by hand!" he exclaimed. "And, you can't tell the difference!" George shook his head. "That's a wonderful tool, to be sure."

"It's called a 'router'."

"Let me look at it," George countered, "Would you turn on the electricity again, Edward?" The blade began to turn rapidly. "Look, Letty, how it cuts down into the wood!"

She laughed. "That's very handy. I wish we'd had such a thing when we were trying to bring in Number One!"

George stared at her with a growing excitement, took

up a pencil, and drew a design on the table with quick, bold strokes. "I'm going to have a drilling bit made that works on the same principle, with a turning edge that will bore down and bring the core up at the same time."

Letty looked at the drawing. "I can see it! It should go very fast. Instead of the old cable tool method, it will work like a rotary."

He laughed. "Exactly, my dear, exactly—it will be used for rotary drilling."

Letty broke in. "I remember one day we only got down six inches. This bit should go much faster." She paused, absorbing the impact of Edward's idea.

George held up his hand. "I'm going to send a telegram to Bosley in Washington to work out the logistics. With his background in geology, he will know whether this bit will cut down through rock or not." He sighed and held out his hand to Edward. "If this works, my friend, we have you to thank!"

Edward shook his head. "I didn't do anything, George. I just showed you my new routing tool."

"I am most grateful. If we place this on the market, you deserve a percentage."

"No, George. I'm happy to have been of some service to you both. What are you going to call this new bit? It's got to have a name!"

Letty looked at the pencil sketch on the table. "It looks like some animal, with those two big round bits. They look like cheeks! And those two little screws, or whatever they are, that hold them together look like eyes." She paused and laughed. "You know, gentlemen, it looks like a cat—a wildcat!"

"Then," replied Edward smoothly, "why not call it the Wildcat Bit?"

16

Allegro

The new Wildcat Bit, forged by the blacksmith in Angel, was used for the first time to spud a well on the Dice farm.

Bosley Trenton, who had just returned from Bartlesville, had brought back rotary drilling equipment and a seasoned crew who, at first, looked skeptically at the strange double-fisted bit. The jarhead had seen sophisticated bits, magnificently designed but made out of inferior metal that broke off forty feet in the hole. A tool dresser had unsuccessfully fished for three weeks trying to locate the bit before the superintendent announced that the well had to be abandoned. But the Wildcat drilled down smoothly and swiftly on the rotary rig. After two days of trouble-free operation, the jarhead had to admit that the Wildcat was a superb drilling tool.

Three weeks later, at two hundred and eight feet, a thick, pungent, sulphurous mud bubbled to the surface, followed by a four-foot spout of oil. This time the men were prepared to cap the well immediately, knowing that there was no dangerous gas present. Soon a pipeline was screwed in place that quickly transferred the oil to a nearby wooden holding tank.

"I would never have believed it, if I didn't see it with my own eyes," Bosley said to George. "Imagine, bringing in a well in twenty-one days! Our new bit is a Wildcat in more ways than one."

George smiled gravely. "We'd better apply for a patent. I must go to Washington anyway on tribal business.

193

We can make the trip together. Somehow we must raise new money for expansion without giving the whole company away."

"It's not going to be easy, my friend."

"I know, Bos, I know." George ran his hands through his blue-black hair. He was as worried as he had ever been in his life.

It was raining in Washington on the 31st of May, 1906, and it continued to rain for eight days. The steps of the Capitol Building were a dangerously slick thoroughfare. While Bosley was busy at the patent office, George talked daily with the bureaucrats, who met in committee and then brushed off his inquiries. He felt helpless and insecure, knowing that he and other tribal lawyers could do nothing in the face of opposition . . . . Theodore Roosevelt signed the Enabling Act on June 16, 1906, which made possible the uniting of Indian Territory and Oklahoma Territory into the State of Oklahoma.

George Story purchased a bottle of Kentucky bourbon and got quietly drunk in his room at the National Hotel.

After a month of standing dissolutely in the corridors of the Capitol Building, trying unsuccessfully to see Curtis, George was preparing to return to Angel, when Bosley arrived from Pittsburgh. "I didn't get anywhere," he complained. "Everyone I talked to told me to go to Standard Oil or hell, and not necessarily in that order!"

"I have not had much luck, either—for the Cherokee Nation *or* the Heron Oil Company!" George shook his head sadly. "I do not really believe in omens, but luck has never come my way during bad weather. Let us pack and go home." He looked up with a smile, "For one thing, I am hungry for home-cooked food . . ."

There was a knock on the door, and a telegram was pushed under the door.

194

GEORGE STORY
NATIONAL HOTEL
WASHINGTON, D.C.

APPOINTMENT MY OFFICE GARVEY AND TWENTY-THIRD TODAY ONE FORTY-FIVE.

J. C. ARMBUSTER

George threw the yellow square of paper on the chiffonier. "What do you suppose *that* means? Do you know the name?"

Bosley shifted his position, avoiding George's eyes. "He's in oil. Used to be in Beaumont, Texas."

"Well, I am not going over there on a wild goose chase. I'll telephone his office." Before Bosley could stop him, he had picked up the telephone. "Please connect me with the office of Mr. J. C. Armbuster." He paused a moment, then said, "This is George Story." There was a long pause. "Yes, it is true, we *have* applied for a patent," he replied with some surprise. "Yes. Yes. Very well." He replaced the receiver and turned. "Armbuster said not to wait until one forty-five, but to come over now."

Bosley shuffled his feet. "I met Armbuster once. He's a strange and difficult individual."

"Are you sure it is the same man?" George inquired.

"How many J. C. Armbusters can there be? I doubt very much," Bosley added, "that the initials stand for Jesus Christ! If you don't mind," Bosley rubbed his jaw with remembrance, "I'll stay here."

"Bos," George replied, taking his arm. "We have not found back-up money to manufacture the Wildcat Bit." He paused, and then added humbly. "I do not want to go back to Letty empty-handed. Let us at least *see* the man."

"I'll make a couple of telephone calls to find out about his finances. If he's broke . . ."

"If he has no money, that will be the end of it."

But, Bosley's government source reported that the Armbuster Tool Company, Incorporated, was worth in the neighborhood of two million dollars, but that the

195

old man's personal fortune was reputed to be twice that amount. Bosley whistled through his teeth and opened the door. "What are we waiting for, George?"

Armbuster's office was located on the fifth floor of a new building complex in downtown Washington, within walking distance of the National Hotel. His secretary, a Miss Cuthbertson, who looked as cool and aloof as one of the statues in LaFayette Park opposite the White House, led the two men down a long corridor, through two reception rooms, and another long corridor to the main office.

Armbuster was looking out of the window, from which could be seen the dome of the Capitol. Bosley wondered if the man had directed the building to be erected in that precise location so that when seated at his desk, he would be framed by the most famous edifice in America. Armbuster turned around slowly, a bit of dramatics that was not lost on either man, and held out his hand. "I'm J. C. Armbuster, and I presume you're George Story?"

"Yes," George shook his hand, "and I believe you know Bosley Trenton."

Armbuster's thin, aesthetic face took on a vague look. "I'm afraid . . ."

Bosley forced a smile that he did not feel. "Beaumont, Texas, 1901."

"Were we talking leases?"

"No, I was posing as a reporter for the *New York Times.*"

Slow recognition passed over Armbuster's sensitive face. He smiled faintly. "I hope that you hold no grudge. Those were perilous times. If I remember rightly, I thought you were one of Standard's men. Didn't you have something to do with gypsum?"

"I'm a geologist, and was studying oil drilling techniques at the time, shall we say, *sotto voce?*"

"Ah, I see," Armbuster sniffed the air. "I was *not* wrong, then. My instincts *were* right. If I remember, I told my men to strip you and send you out of town in a box car." He paused. "I hope you didn't catch cold."

"As a matter of fact," Bosley replied, warming up to

196

the man against better judgment, "your—friends—left my clothing intact."

Armbuster pursed a thin mouth. "Beaumont was wild and wooly, if you remember." He chuckled. "It still is . . . . I hope that I will have an opportunity to reinstate myself in your opinion. Are you a business associate of Mr. Story?"

"He is one of my partners in the Heron Oil Company," George volunteered.

"Ah, I'm beginning to see the light!" Armbuster exclaimed. "Please make yourselves comfortable, gentlemen." He sat down at his desk, the Capitol dome framing his head like an aura.

Armbuster leaned forward confidentially. "I am essentially a cable tool driller, but I lost my shirt in Beaumont. After six months with no success, I discovered that the peculiar rock formations in the sulphur dome would only give up their bounty of oil to a rotary rig." He smiled. "However, if my drilling operation was a disaster, my brokerage firm was not. I made over a million dollars in trading and selling leases, and the atmosphere was such—well, you saw it, Mr. Trenton—that I bought and sold lots as large as an acre and as small as one/thirty-second of a acre that I never saw, or never hoped to!" He shook his head. "I use cable tool now only where geologists tell me there's soft shale. I'm into rotary now, and frankly, I need a new bit. You call yours Wildcat, right? How appropriate!"

George laughed. "Not at all. It has nothing to do with the term 'wildcatting'. It got its name because it looks like the head of a wildcat." He paused. "How did you learn about it? We only applied for the patent three weeks ago."

Armbuster opened his eyes wide. "I've been in the oil fields for twenty years, and before that I lived here in Washington for another ten. To use a cliche, my spies are everywhere. Now what I want to know is this: do you plan to manufacture the bit yourself?"

"No," George said, impressed with the man's straightforward approach, "our money is tied up in spudding wells at the moment. You see, we only have four partners and one of those is silent."

"Good," Armbuster nodded his head approvingly. "Keep it that way. I also own my company. The more stockholders you have, the more trouble there is, take it from one who knows."

"What we would like to do," George replied enthusiastically, "is to farm out the actual production, then place the Wildcat on the market."

"So that every Tom, Dick, and Harry could buy it?" Armbuster's voice was hard.

"Why not?" Bosley put in quickly. "We can't personally drill every well in the United States!"

Armbuster laughed. "Forgive me, but I was only testing you. As you know, the business is overrun with upstarts who not only are amateurs themselves but who *think* like amateurs—which is worse." He paused. "Of course, I would have to see the bit in operation. If it's any good, and time will certainly tell, perhaps we could make a percentage deal wherein my company would take over the manufacturing and distribution." He leaned forward. "You don't happen to have a prototype with you, perchance?"

"Yes," Bosley said, "we do, but we've decided not to show it before the patent is issued."

Armbuster threw back his head and laughed, and his face did not look so thin and aesthetic. "I would probably do the same in your seats. But you realize, of course, that I must watch it operate."

"Then," George replied cordially, "you come to Angel. There are several first-class hotels in Enid, and we're only eighteen miles east—not far by motor car, and there is also a morning and afternoon train."

Armbuster consulted his calendar. "I'm due for talks with the Union Oil Company in Santa Paula, California, in August. I'll arrange to visit the Wildcat rig on the way west." He got up quickly and held out his hand. "My card, gentlemen. Do you have telephone service?"

George laughed. "Only the general store." He did not state that The Widows were also connected, which made listening in on the party line a rare treat. "I suggest the mails. Let us know when you will arrive."

The men shook hands, and Miss Cuthbertson appeared as if by magic and escorted them through the labyrinth of corridors to the elevators. She was as beautiful and as silent as a statue.

In the lobby, Bosley said. "He's on to something, George, otherwise he wouldn't be stopping over in Angel."

George nodded. "I think you are right, Bos. Word must be out that we have the drilling industry by the tail—the tail of a wildcat!"

The day before leaving Washington, George Story sent Senator Curtis a telegram:

THE ACT OF 1906, PERMITTING PRESIDENT ROOSEVELT TO REMOVE PRINCIPAL CHIEF CHOCTAW, CHEROKEE, CREEK, SEMINOLE AND GOVERNOR OF CHICKASAW BRINGS FURTHER GRIEF TO TRIBES AND OPENS WAY FOR COSTLY LITIGATION STOP YEARS OF TURMOIL WILL RESULT STOP YOU PERSONALLY WILL BE INVOLVED IN NEST OF HORNETS.

GEORGE STORY

Armbuster spent four hours a day for five days observing the Wildcat at work. Then he told George, "It's the smoothest operation I've ever seen. I'll have my lawyer contact you to negotiate a deal."

"I'm a lawyer. Why don't we talk?" George asked.

"Oh, no!" Armbuster replied, his thin face breaking into a grin. "That wouldn't be proper! I never deal personally with lawyers, especially about money matters. You see, Mr. Story, I like you, and if onerous details must be ironed out, I want to be far, far away. We'll get together over a glass of French Champagne after all the blood has been cleaned away!" He dropped his archness. "Now, I've been observing your operation here. The railroads have the upper hand. If you don't mind telling me, how much does your transportation cost?"

"Too much—a cent and a half a barrel."

"And the market is set at three cents a barrel, right?" Armbuster frowned. "I have a suggestion. Let it be known to the railroad that you're going to lay a pipeline to the refinery in Tulsa."

George smiled. "If we had enough ready cash, we

199

would set up a refinery in Angel. I do not get your reasoning."

"I think, from the railroad's point of view, they would rather transport your oil for a little less profit—say a half a cent a barrel—than have no profit at all!"

George tipped his hat. "You're a smart man, Mr. Armbuster. How far do you think we'll have to lay that line before we get an offer from the gandy dancers?"

"Gandy dancers, that's a good one!" Armbuster laughed. "Not long, but you've actually got to start laying the line or they'll be suspicious. Lay the line from your wells south to a farm—say the Stevenses, which is about four miles. By that time the gandy dancers will come through, and you'l already have lines put in that you've got to have anyway! That way you won't need to go to the expense of putting up wooden tanks. You can have several tanks placed together, perhaps near your Number One. Now, I'll be leaving tomorrow for Santa Paula. I'll stop by on my way back to Washington in eight weeks. By then, our contracts for the Wildcat Bit will be ready for signatures."

Sam was almost unrecognizable in a new bowler hat. George and Letty had difficulty picking him out of the crowd at the Angel Depot, but finally discovered him arguing with a porter over a Gladstone bag claimed by a nattily dressed urbanite.

Sam greeted them formally with an outstretched hand and a wide smile.

"I miss your turban," Letty cried.

"So do I," he replied in that peculiarly high pitched voice that they remembered so well, "but in the halls of Harvard Medical School, it is best to be as inconspicuous as possible, I have learned—especially if one hails from Indian Territory!" Sam glanced over his shoulder at the crowd of men still pouring from the train. "Who *are* they?"

George scowled. "It is like this every day, Sam. Out-of-staters come nosing into town, trying to buy up land. The farmers around here will not sell; still these carpetbaggers have purchased mineral rights to much of the property outlying the Heron leases. They hope that

200

Angel will produce another Spindletop! Fortunately, the independent drillers have not been successful." He smiled tightly. "All the wells have been dusters."

Sam glanced slyly at Letty. "How many dusters have you had, lady?"

"None, so far," she laughed. "Knock wood. Bosley Trenton is most careful in laying out the drilling sites. Most of these men," she gestured at the group behind her, "have no truck with geologists—they're wildcatters, pure and simple."

"Then Angel will not be a boom town after all?" Sam asked.

"We do have three new hotels filled to overflowing, and the cafes do excellent business," George replied with satisfaction, "so the merchants are doing a landslide business. There is good in all things."

"May I take the reins?" Sam asked. "I miss being around horses."

"Of course," George replied, handing them to Sam as Letty got into the back seat of the carriage. Sam spoke gently to the horses, and they started down Main Street. Men were already lined up in front of the Red Bird Cafe, across from the Post Office.

Letty indicated the queue. "Most of these men will end up at Tulsa. The Glenn Pool, a very rich dome, was discovered last year, and when word finally gets out that Angel has made no overnight millionaires, the town will be ours once more. You see, Sam, we're content with small pickings. Our royalty checks may not be large, but hopefully the wells can be pumped for years, bringing a gradual prosperity." She sighed and suddenly felt a surge of affection for him. "How long can you stay with us?"

"Thirty days, then I must return to school. In two years I will graduate." He sighed. "I can scarcely believe I'm going to be a bonafide doctor, lady! There is a God in heaven!"

"Are you going to give young Doctor Schaeffer competition?" George asked.

There was a pause before Sam spoke. "I think not. Now that our tribal lands have been divided, our people will be poor. I will be needed. I have just returned from

201

Tahlequah, which is almost a ghost town. A Senate investigating committee is there now." He paused, his dark eyes glowing out from under the bowler hat. "Under the old regime, when our people enjoyed estate in common, there was, as you know, great prosperity. Now the farmers who had three hundred acres apiece and have been cut to sixty acres under the Enactment Act simply cannot survive." His voice faltered. "Farmers with corn ready to harvest had to give up all except the sixty acres provided by law. Out-of-state people who had filed for the land took over and harvested the corn, pocketing the money."

George nodded gravely. "I know, and it is heartrending." He sighed. "I have fought for years. I am tired of fighting."

"But you are a brilliant lawyer!" Sam cried. "It is not your fault if the government . . ."

George shook his head. "I am not very good if I have not been able to accomplish anything. The lawyers involved with me have returned to private practice, and I have neglected my oil business much too long." He looked at Sam out of the corner of his eyes. "We can only do so much, my friend."

For a reply, Sam pressed his arm, and they shared a moment of sorrow and communion of spirit.

Sam transferred his luggage to the guest bedroom and came downstairs wrapping his familiar white turban loosely around his head. "Now lady," he said with a smile, "I feel like I am home again." He paused. "What is that I hear?"

Letty laughed. "Clement practicing his scales. Bella Chenovick is his piano teacher. Not bad for a four-year-old.

"So, I was right when I said that a baby born in an electrical storm was imbued with musical talent, remember?"

"You're right!" Letty exclaimed. "I had forgotten." She paused. "Sam, I wish we could go back to those days, sometimes."

"I am content with the present. Mrs. Barrett wrote me about coming back to work during my vacation, but I declined." He looked up. "I am not ashamed of my former occupation, but I have been out in the world for

202

six years now and I could never go back to servitude."

Letty nodded. "I understand, Sam. The world is moving much too quickly for all of us, I think. Yet, I suppose progress is the important commodity."

"Yes," he replied quietly, "progress and maturity." For some reason, she did not ask him what he meant.

17

A Blade of Grass

Bosley arrived from California in time for dessert.

He had been away for five months, studying new geological theories being used by Union Oil in Los Angeles. The house was empty except for Fontine Dice, who was placing candles on a large, three-tiered cake. "I can't believe Luke is thirteen," she said. "Soon he'll be flying out of the nest and getting himself a wife."

Bosley nodded and fumbled in his watch pocket for his timepiece, which he wound habitually before placing back in its hiding place. "Where is everybody?"

"Down at the orchard, except the men—they're spudding another well. George, as usual, is in Washington. We set up the tables under the trees. It's a pretty sight with all those peach blooms. Give me a hand with the cake?"

He took the huge plate. "I'll take it down."

Luke's classmates were dressed in Sunday best. The girls in long pastel dresses with ribbons in their hair made a charming tableau, but the boys in dark suits and uncomfortably high collars looked stiff and uneasy, obviously wishing they were back home, playing stickball.

Letty waved. "Just in time, Bos."

She was more beautiful than ever, he observed. She looked more like a naive young girl in her flowing white dress than a woman with a half grown son. After being away, it was always a special treat to see her shining face and graceful demeanor. He realized suddenly that he was still in love with her and was ashamed of how he had once tried to court her only because of money. Ah, youth! What a fool he had been. Now he would be single for the rest of his life.

In the middle of the night on long journeys, lying in bed in some cramped hotel room, he sometimes thought of what life would be without Letty. She belonged to George Story, his greatest friend, yet she had become his beacon of light, his source of power and strength. . . . He shook Luke's hand. "Congratulations," he said.

"Thank you, Uncle Bos." The boy replied gravely, suddenly aware of his own importance.

He was a handsome lad, Bos suddenly realized, and quite mature for his age. His dark upper lip had been closely shaved; eventually he would have a blue-black beard. Luke obviously had his major growth—he was almost six feet tall and broad-shouldered. His voice had already changed; it had a soft, mellow timber.

Luke awkwardly blew out the candles and carefully cut the first piece of cake. Letty laughed. "Thank you, I'll take over now." After the cake had been served and the lemonade poured, Letty took Bosley's arm and they walked up the small incline to the house. "This is his last ice cream social," she said quietly, "his farewell to childhood. I suppose next year it will be a dance."

Bosley nodded. "Where does the time go, Letty?"

She smiled softly, the afternoon sun turning her hair into golden shadows. "I've been feeling nostalgic all day. I haven't thought about Luke, Senior for a long time, yet I can still see the look on his face when we finally reached the homestead that day of The Run. We found him lying down there by the creek, paralyzed by bullets." Her voice faded to a whisper. "I held his head in my lap. I'll never forget the look in his eyes, a kind of wonder and surprise. He knew he was dying. In fact, I think he had held on, waiting for us to return, afraid somehow that the claim would be forfeited. . . . I remember his eyes stayed wide open, and the light just went out. . . ."

Bosley changed the subject as they reached the smokehouse. "When do you expect George?

"In a week, if all goes well."

"Each time he returns from Washington, it's the same thing, Letty."

"I know. There's no real point in going again and again. Now, the Indian Bureau has taken charge of the Cherokee school system, and the federal government is making contracts with sectarian schools for the children's education, using Indian funds. George and the other lawyers are preparing a suit—which they will carry to the Supreme Court if necessary—to restrain the government from using Indian monies." She paused and threw up her hands. "It's all so complicated. And, he's giving his own time while he should be concentrating on our own oil business. He's getting nowhere with the Indian cause."

"It's become a gesture, Letty."

She nodded. "Yes, and that's what makes it so hard for George, he hates gestures."

"What about Sam?"

Letty smiled and tears came into her eyes. "He's gone back to Harvard Medical School. Oh, Bos, isn't it truly wonderful that he's been given his chance? So often, we see boys who have talent that's just wasted. They don't have an opportunity to become anything. But Sam, with his wonderful hands and his Indian knowledge, why, there'll be no stopping that boy!"

"We're going to be proud of him one day."

"Bos, I'm proud of him *now*." She turned away. "Sometime ask George to tell you about what happened to Sam when he was a boy. . . ."

"I know. Sam told me himself a long time ago." He sighed. "Thank God he has his medicine. He'll likely become famous. He's got to work out his life in the right way—what else has he?"

Letty nodded. "Years from now, I hope, when he looks back on all of this—his working at The Widows and all, and helping us women here in Angel with the birthings, that he'll be *proud* of himself. . . ."

"By the way, when the party breaks up, I'd like to take Luke out for a ride. I want to talk to him."

Luke sat easily in the saddle; Bosley envied his nonchalance. He could ride for the next fifty years and

206

never achieve that casual grace that only comes from being around horses since birth. Being a city dweller, Bosley had not learned to ride until he was eighteen when he had come West.

They drew up their mounts at the summit of a rising glen, two miles from the Heron homestead, and surveyed the rolling hills that meandered into flat prairies fifteen miles beyond. It was late afternoon, and the sun, shining through high, fleecy cloud patches, cast huge lazy shadows over the terrain.

"Where are we going, Uncle Bos?" Luke asked, his eyes squinting under the wide brim of his felt hat.

"Don't ask so many questions, just follow me."

As they rode down from the rough pasture land by the giant oak, the horses' hooves kicked up a fine cloud of dust over the new asphalt road. Bosley swore and Luke laughed. "Might as well get used to it, Uncle Bos. More automobile roads are going in all the time. There won't be any free country left soon.

Bosley nodded his head. "The farmers load stock on oil-burning railroad cars, powered by fuel from our wells. That's progress!" They turned to the right and headed into the pecan groves by the creek.

"Should have brought my fishing gear," Luke said, looking enviously at a small inlet, fed by the stream, where the water was dark with catfish. "Say," he exclaimed, suddenly realizing where he was, "Isn't this Widows Pond?"

"Well," Bosley replied with mock surprise, "I *do* believe it is!"

"They won't be too pleased that we're trespassing on their land." Luke replied. "I've heard Leona Barrett, especially, can get a bit testy." They were now within a hundred feet of the farmhouse, its gabled roof rising above the tree tops. "They keep it up nice," he continued, looking at the spacious porch that encircled the lower story. "Fresh paint every two years. . . ." He paused. "Uncle Bos, we'd better turn back before Audrey chases us up to the road."

"I'm thirsty, Luke, aren't you?"

The boy smiled nervously. "To tell the truth, I am."

"Let's go in for a cold drink."

Luke reined in his horse; his face suddenly red. "I'm not so thirsty that I can't wait until I get home. . . ."

Bosley dismounted and tied up the reins at the back yard hitching post. "Oh, come on," he remarked casually, "maybe Leona has opened a new keg of cider." He ambled up the steps and knocked on the back door. Audrey appeared instantly, a wide smile on her face. "You're expected, Mr. Trenton," she said, her dark eyes bright and snapping. She nodded to Luke. "Good afternoon, Mr. Heron," she said politely.

It was the first time that any one had ever called him *Mister*. He drew up to his full height and replied. "Afternoon, Audrey."

Leona was seated in the parlor, feathering the bright plumage of a peacock on the antimacassar encased in a huge embroidery hoop. She wore a pale beige-colored dress of chambray, and the back of her molasses-colored pompadour was covered by a lace square that reminded Luke of the doilies placed over the communion plate at church. She asked them to sit on the tapestried sofa. "We've got some hard cider from Seattle or, of course, Kentucky bourbon."

Bosley chose the whiskey, Luke, the cider. The squat glasses were served on a silver platter. The taste was sharp to Luke's tongue, but smooth on his palate: his stomach warmed. Suddenly the room took on a new aspect. He began to appreciate the fine furnishings and enjoy the small talk about the weather, the new crop of wheat, the price of pork bellies, and the possibility of striking another productive well on the Dice Farm.

As the second round of drinks was served, a young lady in a lacy, pale pink dress came into the room. "The vegetable wagon is here, and the cook wants to know if she should order a sack of limas or pintos."

Leona arose. "Excuse me, household duties call. Bosley, what do you think of using new copper kettles? I've heard they cause heart disease." She paused. "Pardon me. Luke Heron, this is Stella Manners, a visitor from Wichita." Leona led Bosley out of the room.

Luke looked at the girl out of the corner of his eyes. She was about eighteen, he judged, blonde and blue-eyed; her white complexion had obviously never been

208

touched by the sun. He was immensely attracted to her. "Wichita must be a big city," he said at last. "I hear they have miles and miles of stockyards."

She smiled. "Yes, with all of the accompanying smells, and the town is dusty and the streets are foul in wet weather." She paused. "I like it very much down here. The sky is so blue—heaven-blue." She suddenly sat up very straight. "I have some post cards of Wichita in my room. One shows the new bridge over the Arkansas River." She stood up. "Come on, I'll show you."

Luke looked into her wide blue eyes. He knew the reputation of The Widows. Who in five counties did not? But, he could not believe that Stella was anything but a beautiful young girl, just a few years older than he, who was wanted to show off her collection of post cards. His early nervousness disappeared, and warmed by the second glass of hard cider, his step felt as light as air on the stair.

Stella's room, located at the rear of the house, was decorated in white and blue, the very shade of blue that matched her eyes. His boots pushed down into the burgundy and rose Aubusson carpet; the many-paned windows were covered with sheer white Priscilla curtains. It was a very feminine room, and yet for some strange reason, he did not feel ill at ease. It was the bedroom that a rich oil family might provide for their daughter.

Stella knelt gracefully by the chiffonier, revealing a bit of ankle, and removed a stereoptican and a box of cards. "See," she said, looking up with wide eyes, "here is a scene of Central Avenue at Christmastime."

He inserted the double photo card into the stereoptican and held it up to his eyes; suddenly the street, with its decorated Christmas trees, sprang into three dimensions. In the foreground, a team of horses drawing a carrige of merrymakers looked so real that he could almost smell the gritty dust that billowed around their hooves. He drew in his breath. In the background, a woman was holding a little boy by the hand, and his balloon almost hit Luke in the eye. He had never seen anything so real! The next photo card depicted the exterior of the Union Depot, a massive building with a porte cochere under which a hundred people seemed to be milling about. How breathtaking!

"Here's the stockyards," she said. The cow pens stretched as far as the eye could see, and he could make out thousands of Holsteins, Jerseys, Longhorns. . . .

He automatically took the next card from Stella without looking up. What would it be this time? A view of downtown Wichita? But no! It was a double photograph of—could it be? Yes, it was Stella, but what was she doing? There was someone else in the picture also. A slow blush started up the back of Luke's neck and slowly spread over his scalp and face . . . and when the flame reached his thighs, he felt another sort of warmth. Meanwhile, she had thrust another revealing card in the stereoptican.

Stella moved closer to him, and when she placed her hand on the back of his neck, he wondered why her flesh did not fry and wither, he was consumed with such heat. Indicating the new picture, she whispered softly into his ear: *"That is what I would like you to do to me . . ."* and deftly exchanged the photo card for another scene, which was, if possible, even more graphic than the first.

Having lived on a farm all of his life, Luke, of course, understood the basic facts of life, but it was the human positions that had always caused him the most mental anguish. He wondered how one went about it with any grace? But with the poses so ingeniously captured in the photo studies, he knew three different positions already!

He saw that she was standing in front of the bed in her petticoat, and while he watched, she smoothly raised the snowy material over her head without disturbing her pompadour. She was now down to her knee-length cotton vest, made of some soft fleecy material that hugged her body. She looked very fetching indeed.

"Shall I help you with your coat?" she inquired.

Since the age of five when he had begun to bathe himself, no one had seen him nude. "No, thank you." He really did not want to undress in front of Stella, but if they were going to do—what they were going to do—

how could it be accomplished without disrobing? The men in the photographs were as naked as jay birds. Very slowly, he took off his coat, collar, vest, and shirt. At this juncture, Stella picked up a copy of *The Ladies' Home Companion* and began to study it quite intently.

He sighed with relief, removing shoes, stockings, and trousers, then stood for a moment in his Balbriggan summer underwear that now featured a protrusion for which the thoughtful manufacturer had provided. Stella looked up, smiled sweetly, and unfastened her vest while he carefully removed his Balbriggans and climbed on the bed beside her. She looked him in the eye. "You're very attractive, Luke," she whispered and kissed him on the lips. "Especially down here."

He had never thought he was very special in that department, but after all, she was a connoisseur of men—if she thought that he was extraordinary, then it must be so! He swelled with pride.

He cleared his throat, his heart pounding wildly. She was so soft and warm. He kissed her hesitantly and felt the tip of her tongue dart between his lips. Was this the famous French kiss that he had heard his classmates talk about? But whatever the national origin of the kiss, it was very wonderful, indeed. Lying side by side, holding each other tightly, they experimented with different lip pressures.

Which of three positions illustrated in the photo cards should he try first? Suddenly he felt very awkward. They could not continue holding and kissing each other all afternoon. Supper was served promptly at six o'clock, and he knew that there was a fresh apple pie in the oven. How would he explain his lateness? And Bosley was sure to be questioned, too.

Somehow he had to start or it would soon be midnight! He made a little motion with his hips, and very adroitly, Stella moved on her back and suddenly he found himself straddling her. So it was not going to be so difficult after all! Now, they were positioned like the couple in the first photo card.

He froze as her hand encircled him. He had not been touched there since he had grown man-sized. She gave a little sigh, moved quickly, and he felt a moist warmth engulf him. He moved instinctively. He could not believe it had happened so effortlessly. He had always imagined that love making was a very complicated business, but it was not at all complicated! He was enjoying himself immensely, encased in her warmth. Tentacles of feeling spread out over his body. He heard himself breathing quickly and unevenly. Then a new and unexpected burning sensation enveloped him. His body convulsed once, twice, thrice and he collapsed upon her. She whispered in his ear. "Oh, Luke, that was *marvelous*."

Downstairs in the parlor, Leona snapped the embroidery hoop. "If nothing else, Bos, my needlework has improved out here on the farm." She checked her watch. "They should be down soon. Would you like another whiskey?"

"I think not." He reached for his wallet. "I appreciate the fact that you arranged for us to be alone here this afternoon."

She smiled. "Oh, there really isn't much business daytime Wednesday anyway, so I simply asked my regulars to come a little later than usual." She paused. "The first time is terribly important—it mustn't look contrived. I don't know nor want to know how you first lost your virginity, Bos, but I imagine it was probably less than satisfactory."

He nodded. "Yes, that's why I wanted Luke to come here."

"You might say that this sort of thing is Stella's speciality. She was orphaned at fifteen. Three years ago, I discovered the poor thing working the Union Station in Wichita. There she was, so forlorn, standing up against a pillar. It was raining outside and she looked like a bedraggled pullet. I brought her back with me and I must say she has turned out very well. . . ."

There was a slight noise on the stair, then Luke and Stella came into the room, holding hands. They might have just come in from a local dance, flushed and happy, and filled with the joy of youth.

As goodbyes were said, Bos pressed a ten-dollar bill into Leona's hand, which she palmed back to him. "The first is always on the house," she whispered.

Back on their horses, halfway up the path, Luke turned to Bosley. "Stella's a wonderful girl," he said, eyes bright. "But, we better get home quick. It's getting very late."

"We've plenty of time, Luke."

"We don't dare be late for supper. We were in there an awfully long time."

Bos smiled and pulled his timepiece out of his vest. "Sixteen minutes, all told," he said.

"What? I can hardly believe that." The boy looked incredulous. "Surely your watch is wrong!"

"No." Bosley replied gently. "But one thing worth remembering, Luke, is that love can't ever be measured by the position of the sun in the sky!"

18

High Finance

Five weeks later, when the crews had put down pipe-lines to the Stevens claim, the railroad recapitulated.

A contract was signed to transport Heron crude for one-half cent a barrel. Three weeks later, J.C. Armbuster returned from California with an order for five hundred Wildcat bits.

"This is a fortune!" Letty exclaimed to Priscilla. "We'll realize a profit of about eight dollars apiece, and this is only the first order of many."

Priscilla sniffed, patting her pompadour. Her dark eyes flashed. "It may be a fortune for you, my dear, but a dip in the bucket to Mr. Armbuster. What's a million-aire like him doing peddling equipment in the field?"

Letty sighed. "It's not the money, per se, I'm sure." She looked out of the window at the rolling prairie and the naked derrick of Number One. "I think it's the feel-ing of discovery, of being a part of a great industry."

"Remember, you can go bankrupt any time, Letty, if production of oil ever exceeds the demand—something I'm pleased to say that we'll never have to worry about in the furniture business."

"Oh, Prissy," Letty had had enough. "You're just jealous!"

"I am? You're wearing dresses we made three years ago! I don't see you wearing any jewelry, either." She waved her hand in front of Letty's face. "See what Ed-ward bought me from the profits from the store in Enid!"

Letty observed the one-carat diamond ring with care.

"It's very beautiful," she said at last, thinking that the profits from the new store should have been ploughed back into the business. "Now, if you'll excuse me, I promised Sam I'd help gather mushrooms for canning."

Outside in the meadow, she had sudden misgivings about the oil business. What if Prsicilla was right? What if supply did ever exceed demand? Then she brightened when she saw Sam on his knees gathering the fragrant caps in an apron, just like the old days.

"Good afternoon, lady," he said, looking up, his white turban slightly askew.

"Sam, aren't those mushrooms by the oak tree spectacular looking?" She gazed in wonder at the golden brown specked with scarlet that had sprung up overnight.

"Yes," he nodded solemnly. "I did not know they grew hereabouts. Avoid them, lady, destroy them whenever they sprout up."

"But they are so beautiful!"

"They have a purpose, lady, which we should not discuss."

"What are you saying?"

"They contain a powerful medicine that must only occasionally be used." He answered softly.

"I don't understand you."

"It can be said that they give a pleasant death."

Letty stepped on the luxuriant fungi, grinding the caps down into the red soil. Then Sam said, "While we are on the subject of medicines, could I gather a quart of petroleum to distill for cough syrup? Thelma Haskell has a very bad cold."

"Of course, but how do you know how to make this elixir?"

"My people have always known about its wonders, although we didn't know it was valuable. We use the oil mixtures in a variety of ways. It provides a very good water-tight bottom for wicker baskets, for instance. We have always called it 'running rock'."

"You mean, Sam, that your people have always known where oil seepages occurred?"

He nodded. "Because it smelled so badly when burned, we used it for fumigation purposes, too. It is

unfortunate that we did not know anything about *oil!*"
He laughed, showing all of his white teeth, "otherwise,
we would have been a very rich nation indeed."

Bosley Trenton slammed the door of the new field
office, a hastily constructed one-room building near the
church, and hurried to his geophysical survey map on
the wall. He felt very discouraged, and yet he did not
want to show his concern to either George or Letty.
From what he knew of the anticline, he had laid out
what he thought was an excellent base plan. Heron No.
1, 2, and 3 wells had been spudded in a direct line from
the creek, five hundred feet apart and drilled down to
depths of over four hundred feet. The Chenovick No. 1
and 2, in a direct line over the pasture to the right, and
the Stevens No. 1 and 2, in a direct line to the left, were
producing about two hundred barrels each per day, but
there had been no gushers since Heron No. 1. It was a
modest oil dome apparently. From what he knew, the
anticline should extend to the upper forty acres of the
Dice farm, where a new well was scheduled to be spudded the next Monday. After that well came in, he knew
that he would have to give in to the pressure of drilling
on Edward's property. Nothing was ever certain where
oil was concerned, yet he had found no upward dish in
Priscilla's water well. The company, still in grave financial straits, would simply have to amortize the drilling
expense of Edward's well if it turned out to be dry.

That night, he sat next to Armbuster at George and
Letty's table and made what he thought was amusing
small talk, then after generous helpings of delicious
homemade strawberry ice cream, Letty asked Luke to
take Clement upstairs to bed. The boy asked, "After I
tuck him in, can I come back down?"

George exchanged glances with his wife. "I think not,
Little Luke. We're just going to talk business."

"I know quite a lot already," the boy countered,
brushing his sandy hair back from his face. "Please?"

Letty frowned. "Listen to your father," she said
firmly.

Little Luke stood up straight. "In the first place,
while I love you very much, you are not my father. In

216

the second place, if I understand it correctly, I will one day be a major stockholder in the company, after all, I am a *Heron*." His suddenly husky voice rang out clearly in the room. "And furthermore," he continued earnestly, "I'd prefer not to be called Little Luke; after all, I am almost fourteen years old!"

There was a deep silence in the room, then Armbuster laughed softly. "It is none of my business, but perhaps Luke should be permitted to listen to our discussion tonight."

Bosley nodded. "I'm only a misplaced uncle, but sooner or later, he must be apprised of the facts."

Avoiding Luke's eyes, Letty said quietly. "We shall speak about this at another time. . . ."

"No," George replied softly, but there was an urgent tone underneath. "After all, we are among friends, there are no strangers here." He paused. "Let us discuss your viewpoint, Luke. It is true that I am not your father and Letty should not have presumed to refer to me by that name." He leaned forward. "I only wish that you had spoken about this before. I have never had a wish to replace your own father. I am only a stepfather who has evidently not done his job well. . . ."

Luke stood on the bottom of the steps, holding Clement, who was pulling him toward the kitchen. "I meant no disrespect just now, sir." he replied, looking at him intently. "It's just that it seemed to me that everything was piling up tonight. After all, I'm an individual also, and I have rights. You are always speaking about Indian rights, sir. I feel I have my rights too."

Bosley thought of the incident at The Widows and felt a guilty pang of regret. Perhaps, after all, the boy was too immature for such an experience.

"I want a drink of water," Clement screamed to get attention.

Letty rose and took the boy by the hand. "I'll take care of him," she said softly to Luke. "You join the other men at the table."

When she returned from Clement's bedroom, Armbuster had placed a stack of papers on the table. "Now," he addressed each one of them with his eyes. "I have a rather shocking proposal." His sensitive face was

217

slightly more pale than usual. "But first, we must look at the facts before us. The Heron Oil Company, as of this date, is composed of four equally divided blocks of stock, owned by Letty Heron Story, George Story, Bosley Trenton, and," he glanced at Luke, "by an unidentified party with whom we are acquainted. . . ."

Letty sighed with relief, thankful that Armbuster had the delicacy not to mention Leona Barrett by name.

"Each block of stock is worth, if Bosley's calculations are correct, in the neighborhood of twenty-five thousand dollars, with the income from the wells now in operation. However, from the debit ledger, including notes owed various banks and current operation expenses, each block of stock, if sold now, would be worth eight thousand dollars, for a grand total of thirty-two thousand dollars."

Letty smiled crookedly. "That's not really much to show for four years' work, is it?"

"If I may say so, Mrs. Story, it is, to put it mildly, quite disgraceful."

George leaned forward, lighted a cigar and blew a perfect ring of smoke over the potted irises. "What is this plan that you referred to as shocking?"

"Before I get into that," Armbuster replied gently, "we must discuss our various roles. At the moment, I am an onlooker who would, frankly, like to become involved in the destiny of the Heron concern. You, George, have spent most of the last few years in Washington, fighting for the Indian cause, which we all agree is admirable. Under the circumstances, you could hardly have done otherwise. But, I dare say, you were needed rather desperately here."

He paused and took a long sip of cold coffee. "I'm afraid I'm being brutally frank, but you have asked me for certain opinions, which I must give honestly. Bosley, you have not done badly as a field superintendent, but you should have been freer to scount leases. Your special knowledge of geology is intensely invaluable, especially in these times when many small oil companies use wildcat methods and know or care nothing about underground strata."

218

Bosley nodded. "What are your suggestions?"

Armbuster's voice dropped an octave until he could hardly be heard. "On the table is a list of nine men whom I would like to appoint to the board of directors of the Heron Oil Company. Each man has very special talents: Sebastian is a financial wizard with important contacts in government; Clarry is a social butterfly from one of the finest families in America, but underneath his dilettante air he can smell out money; Morgan's family is deeply into railroads; Everts, the banker, whom all of you know, has the pulse of every bank account in Indian Territory. After we become a state, he will figure even more importantly . . . and so on down the line—every man has been hand-picked."

"We have been remiss," Letty said, her voice steady. "What must we do to obtain the services of these men?"

Armbuster turned his diamond ring around and around on his finger. "I propose to offer a new stock deal, on the basis of one hundred and eighty thousand new shares. You four principals would receive twenty thousand shares each, and the ten new men, including myself, would receive ten thousand shares each."

Letty colored and her mouth worked. "But, Mr. Armbuster, that means we are *sharing* the company with these men!"

He held up his hand. "In return for these shares of stock," he said quietly, "each man will, in turn, invest twenty-five thousand dollars, for a total of two hundred and fifty thousand dollars of new money."

There was a stunned silence. Finally George spoke. "I do not quite understand the logic. For that kind of investment, each man could speculate on his own." His voice was hard, his blue eyes cold. "Apparently these men think that our potential is far greater than we do!"

Armbuster nodded. "They have had great experience in these matters. Remember also, twenty-five thousand is nothing to these men—they gamble twice that much on riskier prospects than we have to offer." He pursed his lips. "But to be fair, the Heron name is one of the most respected in the Territory, and you also have a geologist who has proven his worth. You also have obtained leases on thousands of acres of potentially oil-rich land. So both sides have quite a bit to offer."

"You make sense, Mr. Armbuster," Bosley said. "What do you think, George?"

"I am all for it, but the final decision must rest with Letty."

"If my former husband was with us now—" She turned to George. "I'm sorry to mention him in your presence, my dear, but it is important—he would agree totally with Mr. Armbuster. Luke was a man of courage, imagination, and vision, and he died delivering this land to me." She turned to the boy seated at the end of the table, who was mesmerized by the proceedings. "What do you think, Luke?"

He looked up with clear, bright eyes, and at that moment resembled his father so much that Letty had to look away. "I think," he said slowly, "that we should take in these men. It is time that the Heron Oil Company is run by professionals."

They all looked at the boy in surprise. His flat appraisal hit the core of the matter. George's dark blue eyes became even darker. He was delighted to find that Luke had a good mind.

"Then it is settled," Letty said.

Armbuster shifted the papers on the table. "One other piece of business remains to be decided. Before drawing up the necessary papers, Mr. Story, we need a logotype—a symbol—to represent the company. I was thinking about some sort of block design, perhaps a seraph treatment of the letter 'H'."

"If we're going to use a symbol that everyone will remember," Luke blurted, "why not use the drawing of a bird? Miss Patterson says the flying heron is a very commanding sight."

"Why, that's a brilliant idea!" Armbuster exclaimed. "A very distinctive emblem, indeed."

In future years, the long, graceful outline of a Heron in flight, wings and long legs outstretched, would become one of the most famous trademarks in the world of petroleum.

Six weeks later, the Wildcat bit had bored down four

hundred feet, when Bosley called a halt to the drilling.

"I'm so humiliated!" Priscilla screamed, "Imagine—us having the first duster in the Heron field." She furiously turned to Edward. "Well, just don't *stand* there—do something?"

"What would you suggest? I have blood in my veins, not petroleum!"

A week and a half later, the drillers had reached three hundred and six feet on Dice No. 1 and were preparing to shut down for the night when a low rumbling sound was heard. The crew had barely retreated twenty feet when a column of oil and gas shot up in the air a hundred feet, spraying the surrounding pasture land with a heavy black mist. The men stood back in wonder; the jarhead held his hand out and rubbed the thick green crude between his fingers. "It's good," he said, "mighty good."

As the golden twilight settled over the landscape, the drillers were joined by John Dice and Fontine, who had run out of the kitchen, her hands still sticky with biscuit dough. "My Gawd, Jaundice, ain't that the purtiest sight you ever seen?"

He put his arm around her waist. "Indeedy, it is," he said softly, his eyes very bright. "Aren't you glad, honey, that we left our little house in Santone?"

She nodded, then suddenly looked up at the heavy geyser of oil. "Jaundice, what are we all standing here for—look at all that oil going to waste!" She stomped over to the jarhead. "Do something, man, that's our money shooting up there!"

He smiled. "Well, Miz Dice, we cain't do nothin' now. It'll be dark in five minutes. Best wait 'til mornin'."

"Nit on your bottom dollar!" she spat out furiously, her blonde curls quivering in indignation. "Get a light out here and *do* something!"

The jarhead smiled softly. "Why, Miz Dice, we cain't have no fire out here—even in a lantern. The whole rig'd go up in flames."

Fontine whirled around and faced her husband.

221

"What'll happen if it stops shooting? We've got to save what's there!"

He took her hand. "Now calm down, Fourteen. These men know their business; it won't hurt if it spouts all night. There's plenty more down there where that come from!"

She smiled sheepishly. "I guess you're right." She paused and looked up at him with wide eyes. "You've got my permission," she said slowly, "to slap me silly if I get to acting up again!"

The next morning, as word spread through Angel that John Dice had hit it big, a line of carriages, shays, and buggies lined up on the section road. Men, women, and children made their way up the pasture, now slick with petroleum, to look at the gusher as men worked frantically to control the flow of oil. During the night, petroleum had blackened the pasture grass and flowed into the creek. Four days later, the well was under control. "We've got the biggest producer yet," Bosley cried triumphantly to George and Letty. "We figure Dice No. 1 will be bringing in a thousand barrels a day."

It was the morning of November 16, 1907. A mounted deputy ordered the few gas buggies in the streets of Gutherie to be parked two blocks away from the center of town. "Otherwise," he shouted, "you'll frighten the horses!" George turned the team into the livery stable and helped Letty down from the carriage. Luke looked longingly at a Model T coming down the street. "When are we going to get a motor car, Dad?"

"When they make one that won't break down every ten minutes, and when a decent asphalt road is put in between Enid and Angel."

"I think it would be good for business to drive around in an automobile. How can we expect other people to buy our products when we don't use them ourselves?"

George nodded. "You do have a point, Luke. Perhaps we'll look into it when we get home."

The statehood celebration was scheduled for seven days, but George and Letty had decided to leave for

Angel immediately after the opening ceremonies so they could visit the new Heron Tool Company plant in Perry on their way home.

"Just think, Dad, we're on the brink of a whole new world. With railroads giving up coal and converting to oil, and heating furnaces going the same route, the gasoline engine can only rise, too."

"That's why the oil business is so exciting; we're in on the ground floor, so to speak."

"*Under* the ground, you mean!" Letty said. They all laughed, and joining arms, weeded their way through the crowds with Clement eagerly following. Shopkeepers had set up display tables, presenting a variety of wares; several merchants were doing a big business selling arrowheads. George stopped by one stand to examine some Indian artifacts, which sparkled in the sun. He picked up a beaded headdress. "Made recently, I expect, for just this sale," he whispered to Letty, then noticed a tray of arrowheads labeled 'Cherokee'. "These are Osage," he told the clerk, who laughed and replied, "Who'll know the difference?"

George sighed, took Letty's elbow, and guided her past a group of square dancers cavorting in a roped-off section of the street. The Chenovicks were buying cotton candy and the Haskells were lined up at a soft ice cream stand.

The crowds grew larger as they reached the courthouse, where a number of tipis were pitched on the lawn. Indians in war bonnets smoked long pipes, seated cross-legged on benches. George turned away furiously. "This is like a circus." Tourists who obviously had never seen a red man stood with open mouths watching a group of youngsters in buckskins chanting and dancing in a circle. "That is supposed to be a sacred rain dance," George exclaimed. "It's a mockery; those children don't even know the right steps!"

As they walked along the brick sidewalk, a man in front of a large tent was shouting from his cupped hands: "Ten cents to hear about the Trail of Tears . . ."

"Can we go in and listen?" Clement asked, looking up expectantly.

223

"No," George said sternly, pulling him back from the entrance.

"But, it's only a dime, Dad."

"You know far more about Tsa-La-Gi than that man does!" George reprimanded, and when Clement stamped his foot, George bent down and whispered: "One more outburst like that, young man, and you will be sent to the carriage." Clement straightened his face at once, and a moment later was distracted by an organ grinder and a monkey.

The opening ceremonies began promptly at 10:12, but the crowd was so large that Letty and George could hear very little of what was being said. After a series of long speeches, an Indian maiden dressed in buckskin was escorted from one side of the platform crowded with dignitaries, and a white man was escorted from the opposite side. Standing, with their backs to the crowd, the couple were united in a mock marriage ceremony. George turned to Letty, "Let's go home," he said sadly. "There is nothing more for us here. He looked over the hushed crowd. "This is the end for the Indian Nations," he said brokenly. "Our cause is lost. We will now be expected to disappear in the mainstream. . . ." He sighed. "I will go to Washington no more. What has been precious and holy to us, is now only history. Once our generation is gone, so will our heritage be forgotten."

Riding out of Gutherie on the dirt road that led to Perry, he was still much disturbed, and Letty knew better than to engage in small talk.

"I wonder, too, if we are doing the right thing," he said pensively, "this drilling for oil, disturbing what God placed under ground."

"But, Mr. Armbuster says that oil will 'grease the wheels of progress,' " Luke replied.

"Perhaps," he said, then shook his head. "Let us speak of other things, other times. . . ." And, as he talked, he suddenly came to the realization that, for the first time since he was a small boy, he was thinking in Cherokee even as he spoke in English. . . .

224

One afternoon in early summer, Leona Barrett took a walk over the meadow to see the wild flower display under the cottonwoods. The sharp, crisp air made the skin tighten on her face. She had a long Saturday night in front of her, and she needed the peace of nature to restore her equilibrium. She paused by a giant oak and was startled to hear a clear, plaintive voice singing an old cowboy song. She looked over the fence and saw five-year-old Clement lying on a log, looking up into the dark blue sky that was host to a hundred fleecy white clouds. He sang:

> *"Come along, boys, and listen to my tale,*
> *I'll tell you of my troubles on the old*
> *Chisholm Trail.*
> *Coma ti yi youpy, youpa ya youpa ya,*
> *Coma ti yi youpy, youpy ya . . ."*

She smiled at the incongruous words slipping so easily and so melodiously from the little boy's lips. When he had finished the song, she tiptoed around the tree and took the cowpath home, careful that the sound of a broken branch or a kicked pebble would not disturb the boy's solitude. . . .

19

Affluence

Poppa Dice lighted a cigar and blew the smoke out in a perfect ring.

He picked up the mail from the post office and rode back to the farm. John had just come in from the field, perspiration pouring from his face. He opened the letter clumsily with callused fingers and drew out a long piece of blue paper. A bead of sweat dropped on the Heron logo of the flying bird. "My God," he exclaimed, with shaking fingers, showing the check to Poppa Dice, then called loudly: "Fourteen. Fourteen. Come here!"

She appeared around the corner of the henhouse, her apron full of eggs. "Well, what do you want me for?" she asked crossly. "I just got pecked by the old setting hen. She's a caution!"

"You'll be a caution too," he replied, "when you see this!" He held out the check to her.

Fontine's mouth flew open and she staggered back, the eggs plummeting one by one to the ground, until she was surrounded by broken shells, white pools of albumen, and splattered yellow yolks. Poppa Dice caught her as she reeled. "I never thought I'd see the day," she exclaimed weakly, "when I be smitten . . ." She corrected herself, ". . . when I would be in such a faint-hearted state. Why, Jaundice, it's the same as the morning sickness." She took another look at the check. "Whatever are we going to do with five thousand dollars?"

"Let's declare a holiday, Fourteen, tell Emma to get

ready. Poppa Dice, hitch up the wagon—we're off to Enid!"

They stopped by the Heron farm. "Letty, would you have the hired man milk Gracie and Buttercup?" Fontine waved the check in the air. "We're going to Enid, and we won't be back until late tomorrow!"

Letty had just placed the lemon pie in the oven to brown the meringue when she heard the loud volley of shots. She ran out on the porch and met George coming up from Number One. "What was that?" She asked. "Did you hear it?"

"Yes, it was coming from the Dice place. Come on, Letty, let's ride over." They saddled up the horses and quickly rode down to the lower forty behind the barn. "Go easy," Letty said softly. "There's liable to be shooting if outlaws are about."

"My dear, there hasn't been outlaws in Garfield County since Dick Yaeger was captured!"

"Just the same, we must be careful, with the Dices away. . . ."

They dismounted, tied their horses to a fence post, then made their way up over the stile to the barnyard where they stood back in wonder as a new volley of sounds rent the air in quick succession.

John Dice, dressed in a duster that had once been white, was maneuvering a new Model T Ford, which was backfiring, into the barn. He was obviously having trouble with the reverse mechanism. "Hallo," he called, waving. "I'll get it right, sooner or later!" He tried once more and succeeded in running the front of the automobile into a bale of hay. "That's it!" he said, turned off the motor, and jumped down from the seat. "I don't think I did so badly, with only a half hour's instruction this morning in Enid."

"How long did it take you to drive out?" George asked.

"Two and a half hours. . . ."

"But that was because we got stuck in the mud twice," Fontine said, coming out from the stable. She was dressed in a bright red watered silk taffeta dress with a matching hat with yards of veiling. She pirouetted,

227

then drew on a long ankle length duster of cream colored faille. "This is what one is supposed to wear when one goes driving," she said archly, then dropped her pose and ran into Letty's arms. "Oh, I've got trunks full of new things," she exclaimed, excited as a schoolgirl. "And Jaundice bought six pairs of expensive boots, and I got Poppa Dice two stetsons—one gray and one brown—and lingerie for Emma, who's getting big, and we hired a man to bring out a wagon full of new furniture tomorrow, and I got a sewing machine and a Graphophone with four dozen cylinders, and I ordered a whole passel—excuse me, a great deal of merchandise from Sears & Roebuck in Chicago, and Jaundice is going to run a line from Angel so we can talk on the telephone, not that I'll be calling many people, because I don't know anybody who has a line in yet, except Baker's store, but we want everything new. . . ." She ran out of breath.

Letty patted her arm and laughed. "You are a joy, Fontine," she said, "and we love you very much."

"Well," she stammered, "what brought that on?"

"There's no one like you in Oklahoma!"

Fontine beamed, eyes shining. "I have some dessert inside, if you don't mind day-old cherry pie."

"Pie!" exclaimed Letty. "I forgot my meringue!"

When Letty reached home, the kitchen was permeated with a burning smell. She rushed to the stove, flung open the door, and removed the black, charred mass from the oven.

George stood quietly in the doorway. "Well, my dear, no longer can you say that you have never had a failure!"

"Don't you dare make fun of me, George Story! It wasn't my fault at all. It's all because of the Dices becoming rich overnight!"

"With John and Fontine Dice having two motor cars and George and Letty having one," Priscilla said to Edward over breakfast one morning, "I don't see why we can't have one too. The stores in Enid and Gutherie are very successful, according to the books."

"What are you doing going over my accounts?" Edward asked.

"Well, it's my money, too!" she replied peevishly, setting a fresh plate of pancakes on the table in front of him, and admonishing Mitchell: "Lazy boy! Come properly dressed to table. Great balls of fire! You haven't been reared in a barn. Comb your hair!"

"Next thing you'll want is a hired girl!" Edward said, pouring blueberry syrup over the cakes.

"I'll wait for a hired girl if you'll get a motor car. Is that a bargain?"

He threw his napkin on the table. "No, and that's final! People are very slow in paying bills, especially in Gutherie. With statehood, everyone's saving what they have until the wheels of government start turning properly. We merchants have to wait—it's understandable."

"People not paying honest debts is never understandable," she exclaimed hotly, then went on in a soft, insinuating voice. "Until you purchase a motor car. . . ."

He looked at her contemptuously. "Prissy, after all these years, you are still pulling that old saw?"

She raised her eyebrows. "I'm only preserving my rights."

"Your rights!" he shouted. "Don't you think that *I* have rights—as a husband?"

"Don't carry on this way in front of Mitchell!" she cried.

"You started this argument in the first place!" he replied, and stalked out of the house.

He walked carefully over the red, damp, pounded earth of the section road toward Angel. It was a crisp autumn morning and the mist was rolling in over the prairie. When he came to God's Acre, he opened the wrought iron gate and went to Luke's grave. "Brother," he asked softly, "what would have happened had you lived?" He glanced up at Heron Number One; he could hear the gentle *swish-pip, swish-pop, swish-pip* of the pumps amid the cries of the early-morning birds. Then he sighed softly and visited Betsy's little mound. He could hear her merry laughter. He loved Mitchell, yet most of all, he missed the sweet face of the child as a baby, whom he could see in his mind's eye in the high chair at supper, reaching out for him to hold her.

At nine o'clock, Edward telephoned a motor car distributor in Enid and ordered a brand new Model T Ford.

That afternoon, Manford paced the floor in the factory, observing the new electrified machinery with new eyes, then came jubilantly into Edward's office. "Eddie," he said, his gray eyes dancing impishly because he knew his boss disliked being addressed by the diminutive. "Eddie, you know all those newly rich people in Tulsa who've never had anything in their lives, would just as soon purchase veneer pieces. Our profit would triple. I'd like to put in a line of Birdseye maple veneer bedroom and dining room suites."

Edward got up from his desk. "No, Manny," he said, knowing that Manford hated his nickname. "I'm a *cabinet maker*. As I've told you before, I won't prostitute my name. If a man doesn't have integrity, what does he have?" As soon as Manford went into the showroom, he placed a call to Enid and cancelled the order for the Model T.

Edward could not sleep. He lay motionless in bed, watching the dawn turn the window blinds a deep pink. Priscilla lay beside him, breathing evenly. It had been eight weeks since they had been together. His body cried out for release, yet he would not touch her. At first, the issue of the motor car had seemed crucial; she needed to be taught a lesson. But as the weeks overlapped and money from the various stores swelled the bank account, he thought how foolish it was to let money stand between them. But on the other hand, a stand had to be taken or he would be forever downed in any argument.

He longed to reach out and touch her breasts, to feel the softness beneath his finger tips and move his body over hers in a close embrace. That was what the "old Edward" would have done—anything to have peace restored to the household. But, he realized he must be strong, stronger than he had ever been in his life. He arose quickly and pulled up the blind. It was light out now, around six o'clock, he judged. In the old days, Priscilla would already have been up for two hours and his breakfast would be on the table.

Now they did not eat until seven o'clock. Going down the stairs, he felt a pang of conscience—certainly he would not lose face by hiring a serving girl. Then he heard Mitchell rousing and went back upstairs to play with him for a few moments before waking Priscilla.

Clement, like other boys in his class, played baseball after school on Fridays, the only afternoon that he was not required to study music. After the game, he walked home, appearing just in time for supper. He kicked a few pebbles along the section road, listened to a whip-poor-will, and daydreamed about being allowed to go into Enid alone one day to see the circus. It was unlikely, he thought, considering the way that his mother kept an eagle eye on him, and his father did not believe that children should be left to themselves.

He decided to take the short cut home and climbed over the fence that separated The Widows from the Heron Farm. As he made his way around the giant oak, he saw a familiar figure take the stile over the fence by the Widows' pond. He was about to call out to his uncle Edward but decided he was too far away to be heard.

Clement picked up a horned toad, which angrily spouted a minute stream of blood, saved for such confrontations, from a growth on the head. He petted his back and made a cooing noise, and soon the animal, lulled by the unusual feeling of being stroked, closed its eyes. Clement carefully laid the sleeping toad on a rock and proceeded up the incline. When he turned to survey the prairie below, he saw his uncle knock at the back door of The Widows. What was he doing over there? The door opened and big Audrey came out of the house and began to take down sheets from the clothes-line. Then a movement in the upper story of the house caught his eye—a window shade in an upper bedroom was being lowered. How very strange that his uncle would be . . . He knew vaguely what transpired at The Widows, but how they went about it was another matter. Could he do it? He opened his trousers and looked at

231

himself, then shook his head. He guessed he wasn't old enough.

"You're late!" his mother admonished from the kitchen. "Wash up, supper's almost ready. Where have you been anyway?"

It was on the tip of his tongue to say that he had just seen Uncle Edward visit The Widows, then he thought better of it. . . . When he had asked one day why Leona Barrett and the other ladies were never invited for supper, his mother had said that the widows were all recluses. The smell of fried chicken worked on his salivary glands, and he forgot all about recluses who stayed up every night past every one else's bedtime, and who didn't get up until it was time for dinner. . . .

Liza cradled Edward's head on her bosom. "It's almost five-thirty," she said softly. "I don't want you to be late."

He touched her cheek. "The hired girl will be preparing supper, and Priscilla and the other members of the study club have gone to Enid to attend a performance of some Shakespeare play or other at Phillips University. They'll be back on the seven o'clock train." He roused in her arms, and she encircled him, then turned on her side, her long dark hair falling down over her shoulders. She shook her hand lightly.

"I'm an old man, Liza—thirty-five years old. I don't know that I can be ready again so soon," he laughed.

"The prime of life," she replied.

"Shall we just be warm together?"

"All right." She began to slowly run her fingers over his back. "I find your strawberry birthmark very exciting. Only one other man. . . ."

"Yes?"

"A very long time ago . . ." Her voice grew flat. "I had a lover. His name was Louis Fennell, and he was a schoolteacher from Covington."

"Yes?"

"He had a strawberry mark on his thigh. . . ."

"How come you never married him?"

"He . . . died." Then thinking of all the men with whom she had been intimate over the years, she laughed hollowly. "That experience actually started The Widows in the business, strange as it may seem."

"I often wondered how it all started. Still you're almost the same as that girl I met in 1893."

"Not quite. Relationships between males and females don't change basically. It's want and desire, cause and effect."

"Yes," he agreed, running his hand over her buttocks. "Me being here, for instance." He looked up expectantly. "No offense."

"None taken," she replied. "Except that your wife doesn't realize that when she doesn't behave like a wife to you, what she's really doing to herself."

"What do you mean?"

"She's not being fulfilled as a woman." Liza paused thoughtfully. "Sometimes I'd give everything to be married." She sighed. "I'm the same age as you, Edward, and I don't know how long I can continue. . . ."

"You have a beautiful body, Liza."

"If you don't look too closely. I'll keep on until I'm fortyish, then retire from the business."

"What will you do?"

She smiled wryly. "I'll probably crochet baby booties, or some other such inane thing. It's too bad there isn't a special home for retired, worn out ladies of my profession. I dream of sitting on a large porch overlooking a peaceful river, drinking tea and eating tarts." She laughed suddenly, a high-pitched, hysterical sound. "I didn't mean that as a pun, honestly I didn't. I don't know what's wrong with me today—I'm in a peculiar mood. If I hadn't known you for so many years, I could never be the way I am now—myself. Regular customers would never understand. To them, I've got to be quiet and mysterious. But I enjoy men. Most women in my, uh, profession don't really like male company."

"You can be yourself with me, Liza, you know that."

"And vice versa. When a person sees you on the street, they'd never guess that you were such a lonely man."

"I've always been lonely. Never had much spark, either. Luke was the bold one, full of life and humor and get-up-and-go. He had the talent. . . ."

233

"I never met him, of course," Liza said, "but I think you're underestimating yourself—you always do!"

"What do you mean by that?"

"You're not appreciated."

"That comment could fit any of the men who frequent The Widows," he replied reproachfully.

"Yes and no." She kissed his neck and rubbed her cheek against his closely shaved beard, then she ran her hands over his hairy chest. She liked men with a thick mat. "What started the trouble between Priscilla and you?"

"A motor car."

"What?"

"She told me that she wouldn't perform her wifely duties unless I got her a motor car. She's always been like that, but this time I decided not to give in—and I haven't."

"But you have a new Packard."

"Yes, *now*, but I waited for six months before I ordered it from Enid, but by that time, we were sleeping in separate beds."

"I think that's absolutely criminal," she replied heatedly, then sighed. "But you'd be surprised how many women in Oklahoma lose interest in making love. Our business wouldn't be half as good if wives paid proper attention to their husbands." She encircled him again and moved her hand back and forth slightly, then swung over him until she was looking down into the rather boyish sunburned face. "Lay still," she cooed, "we still have a bit of time." She started to shake her body expertly in a never-fail method of exciting response, and he was engulfed with pleasurable sensations.

But after a few moments, he deftly switched positions until he was staring down into her eyes, and she understood that to preserve his masculinity, he had to be the aggressor.

In the heat of passion, as he moved swiftly within her, she felt herself responding to his thrusts. She guiltily allowed herself to climax sweetly. Then his dry breath was reduced to a series of little gasps, and he cried out, "Oh, Prissy!"

234

* * *

That night, before supper, Leona Barrett paced nervously through the house. Liza and Stella were booked solidly from seven to twelve. She knew that Everts, the banker, and three of his cronies would be driving in from Enid for a game of Faro. Five men who were spudding a new well on the Dice Farm were in the washhouse and would soon be gathered around the kitchen table, digging into large helpings of liver and onions. For the first time since she had built the house fifteen years ago, she felt cloistered, trapped; the place had become a prison.

During the evening, she played hostess in her usual brusque manner, scarcely able to contain herself until she had sent the last man off into the night. Then Audrey made a fresh pot of coffee, and Poppa Dice, Liza and Stella, as was their custom, gathered around the dining room table to discuss the evening's activities. Leona stood in the doorway, mug in hand, and listened to the gossip until she could stand the chatter no more, then sighed. "Come on, girls, it's very late. It's time to turn off the lights."

When they were alone, Leona poured Poppa Dice another cup of coffee and sat down wearily beside him at the table. She took his hand, and he looked up in surprise—this was the first time that she had shown any outwardly affection toward him. He cleared his throat. "You've been acting peculiar all evening," he said quietly. "What's on your mind?"

"Politics."

He grinned and shook his head. "You're probably the best informed woman in Oklahoma," he replied with a twinkle.

"Yes, and I'm feeling great pressure. The governor frowns on establishments like this."

He scratched his white head thoughtfully. "It won't ever be the same again, will it, Leona?"

She looked down at her coffee mug. It was the first time he had ever called her by her first name. "Do you know," she said finally, "you've worked here for nine years and yet I've never known your Christian name."

He threw back his head and laughed. "Outside of

235

Jaundice and Fourteen, no one else does, either!" He colored, then went on in a small voice that did not go with his big frame. "My name is. . . ."

"Yes?"

". . . Lancelot!"

She held back the laughter that threatened to bubble up in her throat. "I think that's a very nice name." She carefully examined her coffee mug. "Didn't your family call you Lance?"

He shook his head. "No, I could have borne up with that. My mother was an ignorant dirt farmer's wife who couldn't read or write. She'd heard the name from a schoolteacher and thought it was, as she used to say, 'charmin.' For years, I didn't know why every one laughed at me, until I was told about Lancelot and his quest for the Holy Grail. The name certainly didn't go with the big, rawboned cowboy that I was as a young man, so for years I called myself 'Dice', then when I raised a family, the 'Poppa' was added." He looked at her out of the corners of his eyes. "You won't ever give my secret away, will you, Leona?"

"No, Poppa Dice, I promise, but I still think Lancelot is a beautiful name."

He finished the coffee and got up slowly. "My bones ache tonight, and I'm feeling kind of funny-like," he said, "but what can an old man expect? I guess it's time I stayed home more."

"Let's have another cup of coffee. I want to talk about what's been on my mind all night."

"If you don't object, I'd like a little more whiskey."

"Sit still, I'll fetch it." She returned a moment later with the whiskey; he took a long sip from the glass and swallowed slowly. "Thanks," he said. "Maybe it'll make me feel better."

She leaned forward, her eyes dark and luminous. She was still a handsome woman. "Conditions here in Angel are going to change very drastically. The ladies of the community are putting pressure on the new mayor. Time is catching up with all of us." She paused and looked down at her manicure. "I'll be forty-four years old this year. I want to see something of the world before I get too old and cranky to enjoy it!" She paused, expecting the moment to be dramatic, the atmosphere filled with electricity, but it was not—there was only a chilled feeling in the room. "Poppa Dice," she said flatly, "I'm going to close The Widows."

20

Pianissimo

Poppa Dice staggered up the stairs, his boots hitting each step with a resounding thump, thump, thump.

Fontine was out of bed in an instant and ran out into the hall, her hair wrappers bouncing around her head like spools of wire. "Poppa Dice, what's the matter with you?" Then she saw his puffy, red face and drew in her breath sharply. "You're drunk!"

"Yep!" he announced, "that I am! It's a sad day, I can tell you."

She did not call his attention to the fact that it was four-thirty in the morning. "Just don't wake up the children," she said irritably. "The very idea, you coming home in this condition!"

"What *is* all of this?" John Dice stood in the doorway, pushing the sleep out of his eyes with his fists.

"Your father is reeling all over the place, that's what!" Fontine replied, interrupted by the crying of a child. "Now Mitch is up!" She placed her hands on her hips. "Might as well bid sleep good-bye when that one rouses." She flounced into his room, and a moment later all was quiet.

John Dice placed his hands around his father's broad shoulders. "Now," he said gently, "what upset you so?" With difficulty, he guided the heavy, lumbering old man into his bedroom.

"It's the Widders," Poppa Dice said, reverting to his old way. ". . . closin' down!" His face crumpled as he fell, outstretched, on the bedspread. "Miz Barrett tole me tonight. She's a takin' off for Europe. Gonna spend all her money seein' canals and big churches . . . Nothin' ain't ever gonna be the same again." John took off his boots and loosened his Teck scarf. "I'm broke, son." His face took on a hang-dog look.

"I wouldn't worry about that, Poppa Dice. It's time you retired. How old are you?"

"Seventy."

"You're lying. You'll be seventy-six years old your next birthday!"

"But there won't be any more paychecks, son!"

John Dice chuckled. "Our days of being dirt poor are over. You've got money in the bank, and our two wells are producing, and the third is about to come in. Our oil checks will keep us in high style. You don't have to work."

"I've got to earn my keep. I won't . . . sponge off nobody."

"But, we're *rich*, Poppa Dice, *rich*."

"Yep, I know, rich in love and feelin'. But Jaundice, we gotta git enough cash together to get us to the Territory. . . ."

It was then that John Dice realized with a shock that his father had gone back in time to the days when they had lived in the tiny white house in Santone, long before they had made The Run. . . .

Poppa Dice was seated in the shade of the white mulberry tree, where he could see the road and the barnyard, where the chickens, ducks, and guinea hens pecked their way across the gravel driveway to the large, flat basins of water by the silo.

Fontine summoned the hired girl to the back door. "Look out after Poppa Dice, will you, Helen? I've got to go into town. Come out and crank up Bertha Mae.

Helen, a large Bohemian woman, dutifully went into the barn and performed the hateful task while Fontine sat in the front seat. The motor coughed twice and sputtered to life.

In Baker's Mercantile Store, Fontine purchased embroidery thread, several yards of ecru lace, and a needlepoint pattern. "I never did learn much fancy work," she confided to Mrs. Baker, "but now that I've got time on my hands, I'm trying to learn. It takes so much patience! My cross stitch still looks like hen scratching."

Mrs. Baker smiled. "You'll improve," she said kindly as Rochelle Patterson and Portia Stevens came into the store. The schoolteacher was saying, ". . . . and, my dear, they caught them *en flagrante!*"

"Isn't that near Enid?" Fontine asked, and she did not understand why Rochelle Patterson and Portia Stevens leaned back against the coffee grinder and doubled up with laughter.

Poppa Dice was napping, Fontine saw coming up the walk, but he roused. "What's fer dinner?" he asked.

"Oh, beefsteak, I guess, and maybe a fudge cake with redhots."

"I didn't realize it was Sunday," he said, shaking his snow white head. "It's like when I was on the Old Chissolm, easy to lose track of days on end."

"It's *Wednesday.*"

"We got company comin'?"

"Why, no, just us."

"How can you afford beefsteak, then?"

"Poppa Dice, we can have anything we want!"

He shook his head. "Puttin' on the dog, that's what yore doin', puttin' on the dog."

Fontine stomped her foot. "We're not in Santone, Texas, we're in Angel, Oklahoma, and we've got plenty to eat, Poppa Dice, plenty. We've got *money*, and so have you!" She went into the house and returned with his bank book. "Look," she showed him the figures. "See! You've got four thousand dollars in the bank in Enid."

He looked at the figures blankly, then threw back his head and laughed uproariously. "You're a caution, Fourteen. Where in sam hill would I git that kind o' money? Don't play your tricks on Poppa Dice." He reached into his pocket and produced a fifty-cent piece, which he held up in the sunlight. "That's all I got, all I got between me and starvation. . . ."

Fontine's eyes filled with tears and she went back into the house with a heavy heart. Poor old man, she thought, here he should be enjoying his last days, and all he could think about was poverty. What made people's minds go soft? Young Doctor Schaeffer had said that the blood couldn't reach the brain properly and had wiped out part of his memory. She couldn't understand how the brain could have so many different rooms, but he had said that the room that contained all the information for Poppa Dice for the last fifteen years was vacant.

Jaundice drove in at four-thirty. Fontine knew when he greeted her with a kiss on the cheek that he had forgotten to bring some new Graphaphone discs. "Honey, I forgot your records, but I had a most successful meeting with Mr. Armbuster and George Story. I've really got a surprise for you! What do you think I've been up to?"

She sniffed the air suspiciously. "You didn't go into a saloon?"

He grinned and suddenly looked very boyish. "Matter of fact, we *did*, long enough to toast our new enterprise. We're all going to put some money together in a kind of partnership. Angel is going to have a bank, the *Dice* Bank!"

She giggled and took his hand. "Oh, Jaundice, that's wonderful. We're coming up in the world. If our friends in Santone could see us now." Her eyes grew misty. "Whatever I thought when I married a dirt farmer, I never ever dreamed that one day I'd be the wife of a *banker*." She paused and grew serious. "Speaking of money, Poppa Dice is off again."

Jaundice shook his head. "I wish we could get him to Oklahoma City to a brain specialist, but he won't travel." He sighed. "But I suppose we should be glad, as Doctor Schaeffer said, that he isn't paralyzed. It's so sad to see him so childish."

That night, after they had tucked in the children and put Poppa Dice to bed, John took Fontine in his arms. She snuggled down into the warmth of the bed. "You're gone for two days, and it seems like a month," she said.

He kissed her soft, moist lips. "I could barely sleep last night, thinking about you, Fourteen. I miss you so much, because if we can't make love every night . . ." He massaged her hips lightly and felt a spark spread over her flesh. ". . . no matter what happens during the day, good or bad, I know that we'll be together after dark. I love you, so much, Fourteen. I suppose the time will come when we won't want to do it so much—with age and all . . ."

She giggled. "Maybe so, but I've not noticed any appreciable difference, especially since we don't have to worry about unwanted babies. George Story surely did us a favor when he showed you those lambskins. We have lots more fun."

He turned her body and brought his legs up over her thighs. "You're very precious, do you know that?"

She luxuriated in his presence. "Not any more precious than you are to me," she whispered. "Jaundice, do you suppose Letty and George carry on like this?"

He stopped moving. "I never thought about it," he replied. "I imagine so."

"Do you suppose they enjoy it as much as we do?"

"How should I know!"

"Well, Priscilla says that she and Edward have given it up."

"Then he should beat her twice on Sundays." He started to move again, and then they were lost in each other; thoughts of Letty and George and Priscilla and Edward vanished as the heat of the moment spread out and love renewed itself again and again. Afterwards, as they lay totally relaxed and spent, he brought his big hands protectively over her breasts. "I could never do without you, honey," he said. "I love you more than ever."

"You say such sweet things to me, Jaundice. You make me feel like I'm the only woman in the world."

"You are, Fourteen," he answered before falling asleep. "You are—to me . . ."

Poppa Dice climbed the incline by the oak tree very slowly. He was held back by the heavy grasses wet with early morning dew. His old stained overalls hung down over his muddy boots. He scratched his white head, sat down on a blackjack log, and looked out over the pasture. It was a peaceful time of day, yet he felt no peace.

He had awakened early and when he opened the

242

closet to take out his work clothes, he had stood back dumbfounded—his closet was filled with fine clothes; herringbones and twills and gabardines. He drew back in fright. He had suspected for some time that Jaundice and Fourteen were planning to ship him off to the old folks' home in Santone, and now they had moved in a stranger's wardrobe.

He placed his head in his hands, and tears stung his eyelids. It was terrible to be so poor, so down and out. Jaundice tried to hide the fact that he was broke, boasting about how good the times were, but he couldn't fool an old man with experience in money affairs. And Fourteen set a fine table. He never ate much, because he knew the food was stolen. Why, just yesterday he had seen her bring a coconut cream pie over from the Heron Farm!

He wiped his cheeks with a bandana and looked down at his worn boots, moving his toes around the holes. Even in the old days on the Chisholm, he had never been so broke that he couldn't get together enough cash to buy a new pair of boots! What was he going to do? He looked furtively behind him to see if he was being followed. Then, from the barnyard, he heard the sound of that infernal motor machine that reeked of evil-smelling oil and gasoline. He knew Fontine had pinched the car in Enid, just as she had stolen everything else in the house. Oh, to be old and feeble, living among thieves. "There's got to be a way out," he said out loud, "there's just gotta be . . ."

The members of the board of directors of the Heron Oil Company sat around the conference table at the Donley Hotel in Enid, annual reports spread out before them.

J. C. Armbuster, who had been speaking all morning, was hoarse. "Gentlemen, while the Angel field is producing a modest amount of petroleum, the cost of transportation is taking all the profits. I think we should put in a refinery at Angel. If our leases at Pawnee and Osage pay off, we can easily put in pipelines to the new plant. We'll make far more profit by distilling our own crude." He coughed. "Also, I think we should send you, Bosley, into new areas to search for leases. I'm now speaking of out-of-state. We've got to increase our holdings."

"I agree," George said. "I'm available for consultations. I can draw up papers whenever I'm needed." He looked over the men seated around the table, all brilliant in their own fields; he appreciated their acumen in running the company. "I know that there has been pressure placed upon us to go public, and Standard Oil is willing to step in any time, but we must resist. The Heron Oil Company must remain privately owned."

Armbuster raised his hand. "Amen," he croaked. "We are all fairly young men. I don't think there's anyone here over fifty—except me, and I don't count. It's too early in the game to be bought out, and then sit back and receive a pittance. Let's be content to grow slowly." He paused, "Now, if all business on the agenda has been negotiated, may I hear a motion that this meeting be adjourned?"

Everts, the banker, stood up. "There is one other order of business that I would like to discuss, but it has nothing to do with Heron. Would the following men please stay for a moment: Sebastian, Clarry, Morgan, and you, too, George. Thank you."

Armbuster grinned. "Am I to be excluded?"

Everts nodded his head until his jowls shook. "No offense, J. C., this is just a—private matter."

When the other men had gone, Everts took a sip of tepid water. "I have something both rather controversial and humane to speak about. First the controversial: As most of you men know, Leona Barrett has closed The Widows . . ."

Sebastian, a red faced man with a strong Baptist background, frowned. "Pray tell us what this world shaking event has to do with *us*?"

"Did you ever visit the place?"

"No, of course not!"

"Have you ever ridden by it?"

"No!"

"Then I must explain that the house is quite commodious and beautifully appointed. Most of the hundred and sixty acres are under cultivation . . ."

Clarry snorted, and rose to leave, his pink cheeks pinker than usual. "I'm going to be late for supper, and furthermore, I find this conversation most distasteful."

"Just a moment," Everts replied, "I was just getting down to the humanitarian part."

Morgan, a rotund man with a glass eye, sighed and retorted: "Pray tell me, what is humanitarian about a former whorehouse."

"Patience, gentlemen, patience." Everts said slowly, "As I said before, Leona has closed down and moved away, but of course, she still owns the property. Mrs. Barrett was a very proficient . . ."

"No doubt she was in her profession," Sebastian said, going to the door.

"Just a moment, please let me finish. She was a very proficient musician. In fact, she played the harpsichord."

"You are the most exasperating man alive!" Morgan said.

"Leona Barrett is a very wealthy woman," Everts went on triumphantly, "and she has authorized me to turn The Widows into a privately endowed conservatory of music!"

Sebastian closed the door and faced the group. "*What?*"

The banker smiled widely. "You heard me." He leaned forward intently, "And, we are going to need a board of directors."

"You can count me out!" Sebastian said, making a quick exit.

"Me, too," Clarry said, standing up in righteous indignation.

"I'm not going to get mixed up in this mess," Morgan shouted, waving his report in the air, "and I'll thank you, sir, to not bring up the subject again!"

When they were alone, Everts faced George Story. "Well, are you going to bow out too?"

George stood up, went to the window and looked out over the sprawling city of Enid, a prairie town that was becoming more like a big city every week, then turned and faced the banker. "You were a regular client at The Widows, right?"

Evert nodded solemnly. "And I'm not ashamed of the fact that I was—and am—a close friend of Leona's."

"Then I know that you can keep a secret."

"I've never broken my word yet, George."

"I'll be pleased to be on the board of directors of the conservatory of music, because you see, Mr. Everts, when the Heron Oil Company was in dire financial straights—before our Number One came in and we were on the verge of bankruptcy—Leona Barrett bailed us out with five thousand dollars."

"No!"

"To this day she is still a large stockholder in the company."

"Ah, *ha*!" Everts exclaimed, pounding his knee. "So all of her money didn't come from gambling, liquor, and fucking?" He threw back his head and laughed until the tears ran down his cheeks. "So she was even far more of a humanitarian than I thought!" He paused. "Well, then, now, more than ever, we've got to make this conservatory a success. It won't be easy, with the stigma attached to the place."

"We will surely be required to put on our thinking caps, Mr. Everts."

He nodded. "The free scholarships should help. You know that she's willing to pick up all expenses. She wants to build dormitories, hire the finest teachers. There is no half measure with Leona Barrett."

"No," George replied softly, "and there never has been . . ."

The ensuing silence was broken by the sharp ring of the telephone. Everts answered and then placed his hand over the mouthpiece. "It's for you, George," he said in a worried tone. "It's your wife."

"Yes?" George said, knowing the call was important if Letty contacted him during a business meeting. He listened, and then an incredible look of sadness came over his features. "All right, my dear," he said gently, "I'll be right home." He hung up the receiver slowly and turned to Everts. "They just found Poppa Dice. He hung himself in the barn."

* * *

246

Bella Chenovick answered the telephone. "Oh, Jaundice," she said in a hushed tone. "Our hearts go out to you and Fontine."

"Thank you," he said brokenly, "I have a great favor to ask. Poppa Dice loved you and Torgo so much, and I was wondering if you would play at the funeral? Now, I know," he went on quickly, "you don't come to Reverend Haskell's any more now that we've got a Catholic church in Angel, but I know Poppa Dice would be so pleased."

"We'd be honored, Jaundice," she said with pride.

Bella Chenovick, seated at the new organ, looked out pensively over the congregation, the largest ever assembled in the church. There was standing room only at the back. Finally, Reverend Haskell opened the door so that two dozen late comers on the steps outside could hear the services. While the community of Angel was represented well, there were at least fifty men, patrons of The Widows, some from as far away as Pond Creek, Perry, and Hennessey, who had driven or ridden over rough country roads, to pay their last respects to a man they had all admired.

But the touchstone of the afternoon occurred just before Reverend Haskell gave the nod for Bella to start pumping up the organ for the first hymn. A slight wind seemed to move through the crowd as a tall, elegant woman in black with a veil down to her shoulders appeared in the doorway. The standees made way for her and she walked down the aisle with a firm step, her back as straight as a ramrod. The flutter continued throughout the congregation as Thelma Haskell set up a folding chair for her next to the first pew, on the opposite side of where John and Fontine Dice were seated.

Leona Barrett had come home.

Reverend Haskell, who was known to preach for forty-five minutes at a funeral, spoke very briefly, his voice quavering with grief. Poppa Dice was the first man that he had met in The Territory, sixteen years before—a lifetime, really, considering what had happened to the community since. And he loved the old man, despite his lack of religious fervor. He finished the services by leading the congregation in the Lord's Prayer, then nodded to Bella Chenovick.

Knowing that his presence would condone what was to take place, Reverend Haskell very slowly walked down the aisle and out of the front door of the church, while the stunned congregation heard Bella stomp out the opening chords of the song they all knew well. Then Torgo stood up, placed his violin on a red bandana on his shoulder, and played very softly, "And Her Golden Hair was Hanging Down Her Back."

21

The Sounds of Music

When the dormitories at the music conservatory were completed, wagonloads of Heron furniture—solid maple beds, chiffoniers, and foot lockers built by extra cabinet men from Enid—arrived.

Brochures printed in the spring of 1909 were mailed to prospective students all over the United States by Dean Harks, the hatchet-faced new president who, Rochelle Patterson learned enviously, had been hired away from the Julliard School of Music in New York City for the sum of eight thousand dollars a year. The other fifteen members of the faculty, drawn from all over the country by enormous salaries, had settled down in the little cottages under the cottonwoods. The women were inclined to wear tweeds and pince-nezes; the men were tall and willowy and smelled of scent.

John Dice carefully set the cornerstone for the first bank of Angel in the wet cement and straightened up carefully, hand on his back. "I'm not as young as I used to be," he joked to Torgo Chenovick, who was at least fifteen years older. John posed for the photographer from the *Angel Wing* with trowel in hand, then addressed the large crowd gathered on the corner where the three-story brick building would eventually stand.

"Folks, we have known each other much too long not to be candid. I want all of you to know that I'm opening this bank for one reason, and one reason only—I want to invest not only money but *time* in this community. If you have a financial problem, I want to hear about it, but," he grinned, "if you have a medical problem, of course, that's in Doc Schaeffer's domain; any mental quirks will have to be taken to that psychiatrist fellow in Enid who has just returned from Vienna!"

There was a ripple of laughter from the crowd and Letty sought out George's hand. "He's like an actor," she whispered. "He has every one in his palm." For a moment she thought about the other Jaundice, that fumbling, inarticulate Texan whom she had first known, and marveled at the poised man standing before them.

"My door will always be open to any of you. Remember that!" He bowed slightly, and waved his ten-gallon hat.

Heavy and prolonged applause filled the fresh prairie air. In back of the crowd, standing against the doorway of Baker's Mercantile Store, Fontine, still dressed in mourning black for Poppa Dice, cried softly into her handkerchief. A few moments later, she was joined by her husband, who looked at her red eyes and exclaimed, "What are you sniffling about?"

She looked up with wonder. "I'm so proud of you, Jaundice," and she reached up and brushed his cheek with her lips.

"Aw, honey," he said softly, "behave yourself. You just kissed the new banker in public!"

Every morning, promptly at nine o'clock, eight-year-old Clement walked the short distance from the Heron farm to the conservatory, where he studied piano. At ten-thirty, he walked to the schoolhouse and spent the rest of the day on reading, writing, arithmetic, civics, and science—but his heart remained in Leona's former parlor.

After the flurry of excitement of having some forty out-of-town students that first year and seventy the next, the citizens of Angel got quite used to the flurry of youthful activity; in the third year, the community boasted openly about the excellence of the Conservatory. By 1912, the settlers had conveniently forgotten that their now-famous music school was formerly a bordello. And when Clement gave a recital in Angel's new opéra house in 1913, there was not an empty seat or a dry eye in the place.

"What's it like having a musical genius in the family, Mrs. Story?" asked Mrs. Baker at the general store one day.

"Rather tiresome," Letty retorted, "and with Luke away at Harvard and Mr. Story gone for weeks at a time, I'm to the point of wearing ear mufflers! Clement is studying the Grieg piano concerto for his recital in Oklahoma City. I've always thought the Norwegians were a simple, peace-loving people, but if this music is an indication of their temperament, the whole kit and kaboodle must be war-crazy!" Letty smiled crookedly.

Bosley came back from Toronto for Clement's graduation from grade school. "I can only stay for two days," he told George. "What we should do, I think, is form a Heron Tool Company of Canada. I fear we are going to run into problems importing Wildcat bits. There's no point selling to the drillers up there unless we can make a good profit."

"I'll talk to Armbuster," George said frowning, "but I don't know where the money will be coming from to open a new shop."

"I'm thinking about the future, George," Bosley replied quickly, trying to counter George's conservatism.

"So am I. We haven't any men to spare to send up to manage the place, and quality control is essential with the Wildcat. On the other hand, with the legalities that may be involved, it may be cheaper in the long run to start a small place. I'll look into it . . ."

"You'll look into what, Dad?" Luke came into the living room. At nineteen, he was, it seemed to Bosley, looking more like Luke, Senior, then ever. He was slightly over six feet tall, with tousled sun-streaked sandy hair and deep brown eyes. He looked like one of those advertisements for shirts and neckties that were featured regularly in the *Angel Wing*.

"Your dad and I were just talking about the possibility of opening a manufacturing plant in Toronto."

"Capital!" Luke exclaimed with a bit of swagger.

"How about letting me manage it? I hear the Canadian girls are very beautiful!"

Bosley laughed. "They *are*, but you shouldn't be thinking about getting married so soon!"

Luke threw him a knowing look. "I wasn't, Uncle Bos."

George held up a hand. "Let's think about getting an education before joining the company, Luke. There will be plenty of attractive girls in Boston." He paused, "That is, there were when I went to Harvard."

"Oh?" Luke was a bit taken aback. George had never before alluded to a premarital romantic life, and he wondered if this was an attempt to establish their relationship on more of a man-to-man basis? His father could be awfully inscrutable at times. He looked up and grinned. "You must give me some pointers, Dad," hoping his daring comment would not be taken the wrong way.

George laughed, showing all of his teeth and his blue eyes deepened. "Oh, you young sprouts have no problems today—at least not the problems that I had when I went to college."

"Or me," Bosley added with a smile. "Prior to the turn of the century, college boys were thought to be 'fast'. No self-respecting girl would have anything to do with a campus rat."

George nodded. "Especially an *Indian* campus rat!"

"Can you talk about something more uplifting?" Letty said, coming in from the yard, her apron filled with apricots.

Luke laughed. "You must have gotten in on the end of the conversation, Mother."

Letty turned pink. "Which reminds me, George, you must set some traps in the barn. The place is overrun with mice!"

"All right, I will," he replied. "If Poppa Dice were still alive, he'd mix me some poisoned grain to spread around. But the formula died with him."

They all paused, thinking about the old man whom they had loved so much.

"When he went, it was like my own father," Letty

said sadly. "I didn't realize that he had become so much a part of our lives."

Luke sighed. "He taught me to fish," he said, "when I was a little boy. Remember, Mother, he also showed me how to tie my shoelaces?"

She smiled crookedly. "I'd forgotten that, son." She turned to the porch. "We'd better get washed up for supper. It's getting late." If they said any more about Poppa Dice, she would start to cry, and she had not cried for a very long time.

Priscilla padded down the stairs and answered the telephone. Two long rings and one short ring was Heron's signal number. She was out of sorts at having her breakfast in bed interrupted. Who could be calling at nine o'clock in the morning?

"Prissy," It was Edward's voice. "I've wonderful news!" She had not heard him so enthusiastic in years. "Manford and I have just found the perfect location for the new plant, two buildings with about forty-two hundred feet each; we'll use one solely for refinishing . . ."

"Yes, yes," she interrupted impatiently, "but *where*?"

"Oh," he chuckled, "I forgot to tell you—in Dallas."

"Dallas?" She brightened. "Oh, Edward, how marvelous." Her voice caught in her throat. "Imagine a cosmopolitan city! At last, to get away from Angel. When are we going to move?"

"I'm certain that Letty will let us out of the lease on the store, so as soon as we can get the equipment loaded—not that we'll be using much of it, because we've ordered so much new . . ."

"No, Edward, I mean when will *we* move?"

There was a long pause and when he answered his voice was very strange. "Why, we're going to stay on the farm, Prissy. That will be our home base. I wouldn't want to give up my claim."

"If you think that I'm going to be stuck out here on this damned old place, you're very much mistaken, Edward Heron, while you go galavanting all over the country . . ."

"We're on the telephone, Prissy!" He knew the regulars would be listening.

"I don't care! As it is, you're home so little, you're like a stranger to poor Mitchell. No siree, we'll be moving to Dallas, too!"

"But, Prissy," he replied, shocked, "our *roots* are in Angel. All of our friends, and Letty and George, and the Dices . . ."

"You know very well I've never been close to anyone here in Angel. I can't wait, positively can't wait, to get out of here."

"But Letty . . ."

"Letty can do what she wants to do, and frankly I'm getting tired of her mealymouthed ways." She paused for breath and went on hurriedly. "Now that we can afford a better house, I want something that's fit to live in, a place where we'll be proud to entertain. After all, your customers . . ."

"Prissy, we will talk about this later. I'm on long distance, remember?"

"We can afford the calls! After all, you talk to salesmen all over the country every day." The connection was getting progessively weaker, and she knew that more of their neighbors were picking up their telephones all along the line.

"I'm going to hang up," said Edward.

"When will you be coming home?"

"It depends on this deal. I can't let Manford take care of *all* the details. Maybe by the fifteenth." His voice was very distant.

"But that's ten days! You've already been gone since the seventeenth of last month."

"I can't help it, with business affairs going so well."

"We are moving to Dallas. Then you won't have any excuse for not coming home!" Before she hung up, she heard a series of clicks, and she knew that by dinner time every one in Angel would know that she and Edward had had a fight on the telephone, "all the way from Dallas, Texas."

* * *

254

Audrey hung the wash on the clothesline in back of the tiny one-story farmhouse near Perry, then called: "Liza, look at the lupin—it's out early this year!"

Liza, who had just washed her waist-length hair in vinegar water and was drying the long strands in the sun, turned to the gently rolling hill blazing with blue. "It's very pretty." But her manner suggested otherwise—she was obviously bored.

"Here, let me comb your hair," The large woman took the comb. "I hardly have enough work to keep me busy, Liza. It's certainly not like the old days at The Widows, is it? Why, I used to have six or eight lines of clothes drying every day, besides cooking all the meals for all those hungry men."

"Do you miss all the excitement, Audrey?"

She paused, and placed her hands on her large hips. "To tell the truth, no. Oh, it was awful tenseful the time that Dick Yeager came to call, and when Everts, the banker, lost the two thousand dollars and had to pledge his diamond stick pin, and when Reginald Savor took Mary away to become his wife . . . . but all in all, it's a nice, quiet peaceful life we've got here and it's a good change of pace—at least for me. I'm no spring chicken, you know."

"Nor am I, Audrey," Liza sighed, "except I get so lonely out here on the farm.

"Well, Mr. Edward does get away when he can . . ."

Liza got up from the stool and shook out her hair all around her shoulders, and held up her hand for James, the blue jay, to swoop down and light on her forefinger. They appraised each other for a moment and then he took off for his favorite perch in the chinaberry tree.

Audrey looked at Liza's face for a long moment. "You should have had babies, Liza, many babies."

She whirled around. "I should say not! I've never had one ounce of maternal instinct. Oh, if Frank had lived, I suppose he would have wanted children." She paused, growing nostalgic. "I wonder what my life would have been like if he hadn't been trampled in The Run?"

"You'd probably be the mayor's wife in Angel instead of Fontine Dice!"

Liza laughed out loud.

"Or who knows, maybe you'd have married Louis Fennel."

Liza walked towards the Chinaberry tree and her heart ached once more for the young schoolteacher. She could see him standing tall and straight, the sun making a halo around his brown-auburn hair. "It's the funniest thing in the world, Audrey, but you know I still love him. We were only together three times, yet if he walked up the lane this minute, I'd go with him without even getting my wrap . . ."

The sound of a distant gasoline engine startled the guinea hens in the barnyard into a rampage of screeching. "That's Mr. Edward's Packard," Audrey said, "you'd better get dressed properly."

Liza threw back her head and laughed. "Only to get undressed again?"

Audrey shook her head. "Mind your manners!"

Edward drove by the mail box, waved, and parked the car in the barn, causing the goose and her goslings to run, helter-skelter, out into the sunshine.

He took Liza in his arms. "I must say you look fetching," he said, lifting her up and whirling her around so that her hair blew out in all directions.

"Why didn't you telephone?" she asked. "I would have been properly dressed!"

"I like you exactly the way you are now." He turned to Audrey. "What's in the larder for a starving man?"

Audrey laughed. "Cold duck, some candied yams, and if I remember rightly, a bit of prune cobbler."

"And lots of hot coffee?"

Audrey went into the house, and Edward clasped Liza around the waist. "I can't stay long. I'm expected home for supper."

"But it's been two weeks since I've seen you!" She pursed her lips and pouted.

"I know, and I'm sorry for that, and it may be six weeks before I'm back again. We're opening a new store in Houston and a large plant in Dallas. We're growing by leaps and bounds." He grew pensive. "I wish that you could live nearer me so I could see you more often. Perhaps we can move you to Dallas."

256

She looked up, her dark eyes wide. "You know that's impossible, Edward."

"But you're alone so much . . ."

"That really doesn't bother me. Besides, I wouldn't know how to act in regular society. All those years at The Widows, with just men for companionship. I wouldn't know what to do in the company of other women. I'm used to being looked after." She smiled wryly. "If I were Catholic, I would have made a good nun, shut away from the world." She turned to him suddenly. "You know, Edward, there are some women who are like hothouse flowers—they can't take too much of the sun."

He smiled and took her hand. "I don't think you're like a hothouse flower at all."

She laughed. "You're thinking of one of those delicate varieties, I suppose, all soft and pink and transparent. I'm a hardy breed; it's the sun I can't take. I'm a night-blooming jasmine."

"This conversation is getting rather esoteric," he said, "That's a new word I picked up—it means secret or private."

She laughed suddenly, a trill that startled the blue jay in the chinaberry tree. "That fits our relationship perfectly, doesn't it? Secret and private."

He threw a quick look at her, and brushed his grey-blond hair back from his forehead. "Did I detect a tone of regret, Liza?"

"No." she took his arm. "It's just that I have so much time to think out here. I sometimes wish I'd been better educated so that I would get more enjoyment out of reading, and I'm bored with handiwork. How many bedspreads can one crochet? Audrey takes me into Perry to church, but the minister is a bore and so is his wife, and so is the congregation for that matter. No one can understand why I live out here by my lonesome, and then too, Edward, it's getting so that I'm afraid at night. The nearest neighbor is a mile away . . ." She stopped and looked down the road. "Oh, I don't know what's the matter with me. I should be the happiest woman alive."

"What's really bothering you?"

257

"I thought that when we closed The Widows, I'd be on the top of the world. I'd settle down out here—and you'd be my man, and I wouldn't have to keep climbing those stairs all hours of the day and night or keep changing clothes or taking Japanned plunges or seeing young Doctor Schaeffer every week." Her face crumpled. He took her in his arms, and patted her head. "Don't do that—treating me as if I was a pet—a dumb animal." She ran into the house and slammed the screen door.

Edward looked about in dismay and sought out Audrey, who was rinsing lingerie on the back porch. "What's wrong with her?" he asked, eyes troubled.

Audrey worked the ecru lace gently between thumbs and fingers. "Oh, Mr. Edward, I wish I knew. She's fine for days, then she'll pace back and forth in her room all night, and I'll catch her looking at her face in the mirror as if she's trying to find somebody else's face." She sighed and brushed her dyed red hair back from her forehead. "I have an opinion . . ." She dried her hands on her apron. "I think she's starting the change of life. She's forty."

She paused a moment and then looked in his eyes. "We've known each other long enough that we can talk frankly. Sometimes women in the profession go into menopause early." She looked away, "Then, too, Liza's physical make-up is different. She always *liked men.* Mary Darth didn't, you know, until old Doc Burgen fixed something in her female organs, and she married that Kentuckian. She told me she was finally able to feel what it was like—being a woman—after all those years . . ."

Edward turned to her and took her by the arm. "Audrey, what are you trying to say?"

"Oh, Mr. Edward, I may be wrong, awfully wrong . . ."

"Look," he replied gently, "you've always worked around—the profession, haven't you?"

She nodded. "Since I was fifteen. I started as a scullery maid in a big house in New Orleans."

"Then you've had a lot of experience with women of

all temperaments. I mean, you've seen a lot in your day."

Audrey nodded. "That I have."

"I value your opinion."

"I don't mean to insult you, sir, you know that. It hasn't anything to do with you. You're a good man, a fine man, a respected man. But, seeing Miss Liza over the years—oh, I don't know how to say it so you'll understand and not downgrade her."

"I would never do that," Edward replied earnestly. "You must know that I love her dearly."

She inhaled deeply and blurted: "Personally, I think she misses the company of other men."

Edward turned away. "I don't think you mean that she's lonely," he said at last, "I think you mean she misses them—physically."

Audrey nodded numbly.

He patted her arm. "Thank you, Audrey."

Upstairs, Liza was waiting for him in bed, the sheet pulled up over her breasts, and she was trembling. He saw that she had blended rouge high on her cheekbones and had added a bit of kohl to her eyelids. With the pink window shade pulled down and the sun casting a soft, rosy glow over the sheet, she looked very desirable.

He removed his clothing quickly, not bothering to hang up his trousers or his coat. Finally he stood naked before her, and as her eyes looked appreciatively over his midsection, a shiver of want ran up his backbone. He quickly pulled down the sheet, exposing her body, which was delicately mottled with pink as if blood had just rushed to the surface of her skin.

He drew himself over her and started to kiss her eager lips. She was passionate at once, but he was not yet aroused. Kissing him all the while, she lightly ran her fingertips over his back and down over his buttocks to his thighs. Her caresses encouraged him to relax and then grow tense. His body responded. The weeks without physical release were spanned in an instant.

She was panting under him now, and she received him eagerly, moving forward frantically and backward under him. He cried out once, then again, and slumped against her. "Oh, Liza, I'm so sorry," he cried. She did not reply, but continued writhing under him. Still firm, he responded as best he could, although he was experiencing an uncomfortable tenderness. Finally she reached a climax, then fell back on the bed, exhausted, perspiration running down her cheeks and onto the embroidered pillow case.

"I'm behaving like a sixteen year old boy," he apologized.

She smiled serenely. "It's been too long. Was I the last?"

"You know you were," he admonished. "I have no truck with other women."

"Don't you get—upset—when you want to make love and there's no one there?" she asked, a strange look in her eye.

They were lying side by side now. "Sometimes, but I'm very busy, you know, Liza, traveling from store to store, overseeing the new designs. I have to make sure that the operation is running smoothly."

"But you have Manford Pederson."

"Yes, but he makes contacts and takes orders mostly, and then when I'm home, there's Mitchell to take my mind away off sex. Priscilla is away a good deal of the time now, too. She's so involved with her women's clubs and social obligations and charity work." He paused. "No, I don't get—upset that way very often." He smiled foolishly. "I suppose my days as a hot blood are over. After all, I'm forty-two . . ."

"I'm almost as old, Edward, and I . . ." She got up and pulled on the pegnoir he had purchased for her on his last trip to Oklahoma City. She raised the window shade and looked out over the brown, parched prairie. A misty whirlwind of dust was moving erratically down the dirt road, creating its own dark spiral. "Edward," she said slowly, "I've been thinking." She turned and faced him. "I would like to visit my family in Virginia. I've never seen any of my nieces and nephews, and I think the change would improve my outlook. The Blue Ridge Mountains will be beautiful this time of year. I'm sick of the drought here. Lately I've been going back over my childhood, and for the first time in years, I'm *homesick*."

He considered the proposition for a moment. "I think that would be an excellent idea. Why don't you take Audrey with you as a traveling companion? Take six weeks or two months or so, if you like, make a regular trip of it. When would you like to leave?"

"In a week or so, if that's all right."

He nodded. "I'll add some extra money for the trip to your monthly check." He looked up quickly. "I want you to go first class."

She sat down beside him on the bed and her fingers moved in little circles over his hairy chest. "The monthly check I'll take, but not anything for the trip. I'll pay for that." She lay down beside him again, and her fingers continued their intimate exploration. "I have saved money over the years, Edward. I'm not penniless. You should nōt be expected to pay for me to see the Galbraiths."

"Leave your money in the savings account," he advised. "John Dice is a good banker. He'll get you top dollar for all your investments."

She smiled. "I know that, but I insist. The trip is on *me!*"

"Very well." He drew her close. "Now will you allow me to make up for being such a jackrabbit a few moments ago?"

"I'd be very disappointed if you didn't," she whispered in his ear, and they began the motions of love once more.

After they had bathed and dressed, Edward took her hand. "I think I'll call home and say that I've been detained on a business deal . . ."

She pressed his hand. "Then you'll be able to stay all night?" She was ecstatic. "Wonderful, wonderful! I'll tell Audrey." She bounced down the stairs, happy as a young girl.

They had dinner by candlelight in the dining room. The flickering tapers cast strange shadows on the polished mahogany table top that Edward himself had hand-rubbed to perfection. He looked around the room, appreciating every piece of furniture, all of which he had selected himself. It was among his best work.

Liza was very beautiful in the soft light; her eyes were large and mysterious, and suddenly he knew that this was a special occasion. A new feeling streamed between them. He had never considered himself a very perceptive individual, but tonight was different. He knew somehow, that he would always remember the very special ambience of the room.

Audrey sat in the darkened kitchen and sighed. She, too, felt that the atmosphere was charged with wonder. She had never regretted not marrying, never felt that peculiar need that caused people to want to build a home, to raise a family. She had always been content to live on the periphery in the various houses where she had worked and lived. She knew that Leona Barrett had regarded her as a deep, personal friend. But tonight, sitting in the kitchen in the remote little farmhouse, seeing two sweethearts sharing a rare communication, she was sorry that she had not ever found a man who thought that she was attractive enough to marry . . .

During the next month, Edward received two post cards at the office from an "L. G." postmarked Bowling Green, Virginia. Two lines about the weather told him that all was safe and sound with Liza and Audrey. Three weeks later, he drove by the farm, expecting to see signs of life. But the Hudson was in the barn, and the house was closed tight, storm windows still firm against the glass. He was about to get back into the car when he decided to check the house. He located the special hiding place for the key under a rock by the well, and opened the front door. An unfamiliar musty odor hit his nostrils, and he was about to close the door, when he saw a large white envelope propped up on the mantle with his name in large, childish letters. He took out a large square of paper, upon which a message had been laboriously scrawled:

Dear Edward:

I have decided to move away. I had already made up my mind the last time you were here, but I couldn't tell you then. You are a fine man and I wish you success in all things. You were good to me and I will always value your friendship. Audrey will look after me when we choose our new location. Before going home, the wanderlust has come over me very strong. The car is in the barn, and you will find the deed you gave me to the farm in this envelope. You don't owe me anything, Edward. I only hope you will understand.

Sincerely,
Liza Galbraith

He crumpled up the sheet of paper and closed his eyes tightly to imprison the tears. He bowed his head in agony, clenching his fists together so that he would not cry out. Now he had no one. There would never be another time like that last night they had spent together. He had thought she loved him, but she had not even signed the letter in an affectionate way. That one word—sincerely—was the most cruel of all. He would never be able to forget it . . .

22

Sixes and Sevens

Bosley returned from the British Isles in the fall of 1913 and immediately telephoned Armbuster in Washington, D.C. "J. C., my vacation paid off. I learned in London that the British Navy is finally deciding to convert to fuel oil. They had another practice skirmish with battleships, using coal-burners against fuel-oilers, and guess who won?"

Armbuster laughed. "The fuel-oilers ran circles around the coal-burners, right?"

"Right. Now contracts are going to be issued to an oil company. I've learned that a British syndicate is already after Union Oil in California, trying to either buy into the company or establish a separate English franchise. Now's the time to move, because Union is going to have a change of top personnel. The word's out that old Lyman Stewart is going to resign as president."

"How would you like to proceed?"

"You must go to London. Mr. Huxley-Drummond, our British contact who has his finger in many international financial deals, has offered the use of his house. He and his family have gone to Switzerland with a tubercular child."

"Unfortunately, I can't, Bos. My wife has just had a serious operation and she will be an invalid for some months. I dare not leave her. I'll call George. You'll need a lawyer, anyway."

"But he's not as keen in negotiating as you are, J. C.!"

Armbuster snorted. "You mean he can't look an opponent in the eye and stretch the truth a bit?" He chuckled. "He will be an excellent bargainer. He's a gentleman, for one thing—which I'm not always—and this is one time when his mixed blood is going to work for him, not against him. The Britishers will be impressed that a half-breed Indian is the president of an oil company. He's the personification of the American way of life!"

"Maybe you're right," Bosley replied. "Do you want to call him, or should I?"

"I'll handle it." Armbuster pressed down the receiver hook and then placed a long distance call to Angel. "George," he said smoothly, "how would you and Letty like a vacation in London?"

Letty and George Story docked in Southampton on February 14, 1914, and took a carriage to the railway station. The day was gray, foggy, and quite cold. Letty's eyes were bright as she tried to peer through the mist. "I was hoping to see so much," she exclaimed. "But we might as well be home, being driven down Main Street in the midst of a prairie fog!" She shivered. "Oh, I'm so cold, George."

He smiled indulgently. "And you've been cold during the entire journey."

The horses' hooves resounded hollowly on the cobblestone street, and suddenly she was afraid. On the ship, she had also been afraid—overwhelmed by the strict protocol required even for a simple meal, intimidated by the patronizing attitude of the staff. How unsophisticated they must have appeared.

An hour later, ensconced in their train compartment, Letty was aghast with wonder. "Imagine," she said breathlessly, "why don't American trains have aisles along one side of the car with doors opening into separate compartments, instead of an aisle down the middle?"

George laughed, "These are called wagon-lits, my dear. We will also be sleeping here."

She sighed at the wonder of it all and looked out the window. "Look, George, it's clearing up!"

It was true—frosty sunshine now illuminated the

pale, damp green and brown mottled hills. The rails were laid along what appeared to be a country lane, and here and there were stone houses with thatched roofs. "Why didn't the settlers think about growing grass on the roofs of our sod houses in the old days? Did you ever live in a soddy?"

He shook his head. "No, I was born in a wooden house. My father was a Condederate soldier. I was conceived, or so my mother said, when he came home on furlough at the beginning of the war."

"What was your mother like?" Letty asked, leaning forward. "Was she beautiful?"

George thought for a moment. "I always thought so. She had a strong face, browner then mine because, of course, she was a full-blood. She died young, at thirty-five, I think. She was born just after the Trail of Tears and educated at the seminary in Tahlequah." He paused, reflecting over the years, his blue eyes dark and troubled. "Father became a clothing merchant after the war, and frankly, I don't think ever got over the fact that she was better educated than he. At seventeen, I was sent to Harvard. My father died of smallpox . . ." He paused. "Look at the mist in the trees." He pointed at the passing landscape.

Letty wanted to ask more questions about his younger days, of which he seldom spoke, but she saw that he had set his jaw and knew he felt that he had spoken too much already.

The next morning, after a restful night, the train rumbled into Victoria Station. Letty was awe-struck at the huge, ornate structure, teeming with what seemed to be thousands of people. "Oh, look, George, there's an Indian in a turban!"

He glanced at the brown-skinned man dressed in a white wrap-around. "Oh, he's from *India*!"

"But your people must be related." Her mind went back to the old daguerreotypes of the Cherokees that rested among the relics in George's study at home.

"There is a vague similarity," he said, "but our people's head gear was wrapped quite differently. Sam's turban is very carefully constructed." He paused.

"Well, I suppose we must have our luggage man get us a cab."

Strange how he did not want to talk about his people or the past, she thought. Was it because they were in a foreign country and he, too, felt subdued?

George gave the address of the house to the carriage driver, who tipped his hat, smiling widely, and helped the luggage man strap the heavy steamer trunk to the back of the vehicle. Unaccustomed to the currency exchange, George held out a handful of change. The luggage man took three coins, nodded and chirped, "Thanks, Guv'nor."

The carriage stopped in front of an imposing three-story house; a wrought iron railing enclosed a strip of grass on either side of the massive double front door. The house was built on a square with a large park in the middle.

"We're 'ere!" the cabbie announced solemnly. "This is Number 14 Bentley Square."

"Are you *sure*?" George asked.

"You wanted the residence of the 'uxley-Drummonds didn't ye? Well, this 'ere's it. I've come 'ere often in the past."

The door was opened by a tall, ascetic-looking man with a hawk nose, who vaguely reminded Letty of J. C. Armbuster. He looked confused for a moment. "Oh," he said apologetically, "Gerald must have missed you at the station!"

"We did not know that we were to be met."

The butler smiled coldly. "It's his fault, sir, not yours. He had a photograph of you both. Please come in. I'll have the footman collect your luggage."

"The tip . . . for the cabbie . . ."

"Oh, I'll take care of that."

George took Letty by the elbow and ushered her into the enormous foyer; to the left, a huge winding staircase led upward, culminating in a turret on the fourth floor. To the right, the open double doors of a book-lined room revealed a roaring fire in a cavernous fireplace, so huge that it seemed to take up half the wall. "I thought this was to be a kind of cottage!" Letty whispered to

George. "Whatever will we *do*?" She shivered, suddenly feeling insignificant and small.

He shrugged his shoulders and whispered back: "Just be—gracious!"

She threw him a perplexed look. As the footman in a smart blue and maroon uniform brought in the steamer trunk, with the help of the cabbie, the butler was gesturing to a man who had driven up behind the rented carriage—obviously the driver who had missed them at the station.

A moment later, the butler returned. "I'm terribly sorry, but it has been a confusing morning. My name is Higgens." He turned to the staff who had lined up in front of the staircase. This is the housekeeper, Mrs. Helm . . ."

Letty nodded at the tall, bone-thin woman with piercing dark eyes.

"Mrs. Soams, the cook . . ."

Letty smiled at the plump, matronly figure with a large mouth and watery green eyes.

"Bertie, the head parlor maid . . . and Jessie, the upstairs maid."

Letty nodded. Bertie was very young and nervous, obviously having been in service a short time; Jessie was quiet and reserved.

"Not all of the staff are present," Higgens apologized. "Dorlene is in the scullery, the laundress is ill, and Timothy, the footman, will be down shortly. Your suite of rooms is on the second floor, the apartments once occupied by the master's mother."

Mrs. Helm stepped forward. "I'll show you the two wings of the house that have been opened up for your arrival. Madame carefully instructed us by post to render the same service as the family receives." She paused. "And, of course, we're pleased to comply." But something about her manner suggested that she was not pleased to comply at all, and perhaps resented being ordered to serve foreigners.

Still wearing their coats and hats, George and Letty were given a tour of their rooms, which made the interior of the clapboard in Angel look like servants' quarters. When they were finally alone, Letty sat down on the chaise longue. "I know I'll get those people's names and duties confused. We would have been much more comfortable at a hotel!"

Laughing, George looked about the exquisitely appointed room with its high ceilings, paisley moire drapery, and Louis V furniture. "I agree," he said reproachfully, "but I could hardly refuse. I was given to understand that some sort of lodging would be provided, but this . . ."

"I had visions of a vine-covered picket fence and a white clapboard house with leaded windows." Letty replied regretfully. "Whatever are we to do?"

"I assume that the staff has been organized to perfection and that you'll not have to bother with details."

Letty smiled ruefully. "I do hope so, my dear. I haven't the foggiest notion what to do with a household this large."

Downstairs, Higgens looked at the battered steamer trunks and snapped his fingers for the footman. "Get the driver to help you transport these pieces upstairs," he said, then turned to Mrs. Soams. "I have no idea what Americans prefer to eat."

"Nor do I," Mrs. Soams said and shook her red head, which, streaked with wings of gray, made her look somewhat like an Irish setter. "I've prepared a joint of mutton for tonight. They do have mutton in—Oklahoma—don't they?"

Higgens shrugged his thin shoulders. "I've no idea. I'd never heard of the place until a fortnight ago."

The cook waved her hands. "I don't know what Indians eat, either. Maize, I suppose." Her face was furrowed with doubt. "The Storys do look like a nice couple, but I do wish . . ."

Higgens nodded. "They must be very important in the petrol industry—you can count on that, or the master and mistress would never have turned Bainbridge over to them for three months."

Mrs. Helm looked distraught. "Mrs. Story did not even bring a personal maid!"

"Tim," Higgens said, "I suppose you'd better act as a temporary valet for Mr. Story." He paused, "And don't pull a long face, either!" He turned to Jessie, "And you,

269

my girl, look after Mrs. Story. We must make the best of this situation. No matter what we all think about this intrusion, I want no complaints to reach Switzerland!"

"Do you suppose, Mr. Higgens," the housekeeper ventured, "that the Storys will be entertaining much?"

"It's highly possible," he replied. "They're over here on important government business." He paused. "We will bear up," he added, "after all, to them, we are the English way of life, and they are guests not only in this household, but in this country. I want no insubordination!" He clapped his hands. "Now, we must get back to our duties. It's almost four o'clock."

There was a discreet tap on the door. "Yes?" Letty asked.

"Begging your pardon," Higgens said, standing on the threshold, "but would you be wanting tea, madame?"

Lefty brightened. "That would be nice, Higgens."

"Since it's still rather cold out, madame, I thought perhaps you would like it served in the library downstairs. We haven't cleaned the flue in the fireplace in the drawing room. I'm afraid some birds have taken up residence since the master and mistress went to Zurich."

"We'll be down in a moment." She turned to George. "A cup of tea does sound good."

"Well, I think it's rather more than that, my dear."

"What do you mean?"

He smiled and took her hand. "You'll see!"

They seated themselves before the fire, feeling rather lost in the large room. Dancing shadows from the fire played on the bookshelves lined with ornate volumes.

Higgens appeared a moment later, carrying an enormous silver tray. "How delightful!" Letty exclaimed, looking at the array of small sandwiches, tiny cakes, and pastry tarts.

The butler smiled. "I thought you might enjoy a high tea, since railway food is usually insufficient."

Letty poured the pale liquid into the thin bone china cups, then looked at George and laughed. "I feel very grand," she said.

She took a sip of tea and nodded her head with approval. "It's good, but I would enjoy a cup of coffee more." She set down the cup and looked at him with trepidation. "Do we have to stay here? Can't we make some excuse to leave? This is supposed to be a vacation for us—me especially, you said so yourself. It's the first time we've ever been able to get away since our honeymoon."

He took her hand. "We must not insult Mr. Huxley-Drummond, Letty," he replied gently. "He's treating us like family, and we don't even know him! Would you turn your house over to strangers?"

She looked up guiltily. "I'm afraid I wouldn't be so generous." She paused. "We'll make do somehow. But you've got to help me, George."

For an answer, he kissed her cheek.

Higgens glanced through the leaded glass doors that led from the solarium into the library at the tender scene and shook his head. "Ah," he whispered to himself, "these Americans!"

It was an exclamation that he would often be making during the next twelve weeks.

After tea, George brought his gladstone bag of company papers into the library, then began flipping through the textbook on English corporate law. Letty went into the sitting room upstairs to write to Clement, who was in boarding school in Oklahoma City, and to Luke at Harvard. At seven, Jessie knocked on the door. "Madame," she said quietly, "what would you like to wear for dinner?"

Letty sighed. She had forgotten about changing; on board ship, of course, she had worn evening gowns. She had brought two with her, one she had made herself out of a rose watered silk, and the other a green taffeta she had purchased in Enid. "I suppose the taffeta," she replied. "I'll be finished here in a moment." She glanced at the clock on the mantle. It was seven-thirty. She sighed. She was tired and not at all hungry. After a long, long day, she wanted to go to bed.

George and Letty sat at either end of the twelve-foot-long polished table as course after course was set before them by Higgens and taken away by Bertie. The heavy atmosphere could be cut with a knife. They ate in strained silence. The main course of mutton, strong and heavily spiced, remained almost untouched. The dessert, a mixture of cake, jam, wine, and a sweet sauce, would have been delicious if only she had an appetite. Neither she or George touched the wine in the tall glasses.

George had lighted a cigar and they were prepared to leave the table when a small plate containing bits of toast was set before them. He took a morsel in his mouth. "Fish?" He looked at Letty who shrugged her shoulders and took a small bite; she had difficulty not making a face. Higgens, his thin face a mask, and Bertie, her eyes wide and staring, stood in the background as if waiting to pounce on the dishes.

George got up. "Shall we go upstairs, my dear?"

Higgens pushed her chair back and Letty got up, feeling awkward, but strangely contained at the same time. George took her elbow and they went up the stairs to their bedroom, where Letty collapsed on the chaise longue. "Oh, George, to think we've got to push ourselves through the paces *every day*. Seven courses, not counting that nasty fish dish! Higgens must have forgotten to serve it earlier!" She paused. "It's like we're prisoners here, pampered prisoners."

He nodded. "We'll get used to it, my dear."

After a breakfast of four different kinds of meats and coddled eggs served from the sideboard, there was a timid knock on the sitting room door. "Yes?" Letty answered nervously.

Mrs. Soams appeared, foolscap in hand. "I thought we might select the week's menus, madame."

Everytime she was called "madame," Letty flinched inside, conjuring up a picture of Leona Barrett . . . "All right," she replied evenly, waving at a chair opposite the sofa on which she was sitting. When Mrs. Soams ignored the gesture, Letty knew that she had made another mistake in etiquette.

"I bought some Channel sole from the fishmonger this morning for luncheon, and I thought I might prepare a joint of spring lamb with a nice bread stuffing. About the vegetables . . ."

"Mr. Story and myself like *everything*. Select what you think would go well . . ."

"For luncheon tomorrow . . ."

She sighed as the cook droned on and on, discussing each meal for the week in exquisite detail, until Letty thought she would scream. By the time Sunday dinner had been dispensed with, Letty's brow was dotted with perspiration. "Thank you, Mrs. Soams."

"Oh, one other thing, madame. Did you like the savory last night?"

"Yes, it was very nice. Mr. Story and I are very fond of dessert . . ."

Mrs. Soams colored and looked into the fireplace. "I was referring," she said, "to the sardines on toast."

Letty blushed to the roots of her hair. "In America, we don't serve . . . anything after dessert . . ." She looked up. ". . . but, of course, being here in England, we want to observe . . ."

Mrs. Soams nodded. "I've some minced kidney for tonight." She puffed up like the pouter pigeon that she resembled.

Letty swallowed quickly. Neither she nor George could bear kidney, minced or otherwise. "Is that all, Mrs. Soams?"

"Yes, madame." She inclined her head and closed the door.

Letty walked to the window and looked out across the park. Already nursemaids were wheeling baby carriages around the long walks that crisscrossed the square. Her eyes filled. Oh, to be home! Suddenly she missed the sounds of the pumping oil wells in the distance. Oh, how good it would be to hear the sound of a rooster crowing! She had been reading about Mary, Queen of Scots, shut away in her prison cell. She knew exactly how she had felt. . . .

George returned at five o'clock, reserved and quiet, and Letty knew that his day had been very demanding. "I was delayed a half hour in traffic," he said apologet-

273

ically. "There was a collision of motor cars in the Strand." He paused wearily. "How was your day?"

"Higgens is like a little martinet, and I found that miserable Jessie rearranging my wardrobe twice. She's so critical. I caught her smiling at the sewing machine stitches on my new evening cape this morning." Letty began to cry. "I feel so out of place . . ."

A large vein in George's temple began to pulsate. "I have enough legal problems to work out without having to listen to your women's problems," he said sharply. "I, too, sometimes feel that protocol here is over my head." He paused and his voice became kinder. "We are essentially simple people, Letty."

"But, you've gone to college, been involved in Indian affairs in Washington for years. You're the president of an oil company. You've moved freely in high political places."

"That's all quite different. Washington is a place unto itself." He smiled wearily. "If the Dices could learn to read and write, we can certainly learn how to conduct ourselves in English society."

Suddenly she was furious with him. "You are acting as if we aren't *good* enough for these people!"

"I didn't mean that, and you know it!" he shouted. "But, my God, Letty, Oklahoma isn't the hub of the universe."

She looked at him with wonder. "Do you realize that we have been married for thirteen years, and this is our first quarrel? And what are we fighting about—stupid details—things that shouldn't concern us really . . ."

He glared at her, his blue eyes frosty, and she realized that she had never seen him really angry before. "We are fighting about something far more important than you realize! You are having great difficulty in coping with a very insignificant cultural problem—the proper behavior between mistress and servants." He paused and swallowed to calm himself. "Now, I think, you may understand what it is like with someone of my mixed-blood background to come up against persons with different cultural values every day of my life! I was supposed to represent my people, who share a different background than I do, in Washington. But how do I *really* know what the average Cherokee on the reservation thinks? With the oil company it's been much the same thing. I have a powerful position, but every time my associates look at me, what do they see? A red man in white clothing, that's what they see! And every time I speak, they think: what does he know—he's only an *Indian*!"

She looked at him, stunned by his outburst. "I can't believe this is you speaking, George!"

He sighed. "Perhaps, then, my dear," he replied sadly, "you are seeing me for the first time!"

"But you've always been so confident and strong. You stand for everything I've believed in all my life."

"You really think that?"

"Of course!"

He smiled wryly. "Then perhaps we are both naive— me with my idealism that everything will eventually turn out right, like this British oil contract, you with your home-sewn dresses . . ." He went to the window. "Maybe we're both naive. Maybe we should look long and hard at our own lives . . ."

She was horror-struck. "George, you are a complete revelation to me tonight. Suddenly we are two different people, people neither of us know . . ."

His shoulders sloped forward. "I think we have been trying to tackle events that are beyond our scope. I think we have too much power and don't know how to use it . . ."

She set her jaw and her voice was very faint. "Then if you think like that, we'd better go back to Angel on the next boat and never stir out of that town again." Tears filled her eyes, and when she turned to the door, he had left. The house was as quiet and melancholy as a tomb. She would give anything to hear Clement practicing his saxophone in his room.

George spent the next morning around the conference table at the admiralty, then sent a cablegram at noon.

275

FEBRUARY 26, 1914

BOSLEY TRENTON
NATIONAL HOTEL
WASHINGTON, D.C.

BRITISH NAVY WILLING TO CONVERT TO OIL STOP GOV-
ERNMENT POLITICAL SCENE EXTRAORDINARY COMPLEX
STOP SUGGEST FORMING NEW CORPORATION CALLED
HERON—BRITISH PETROLEUM COMPANY WITHOUT LEGAL
TIES TO HERON OIL COMPANY OF OKLAHOMA STOP BRIT-
ISH INTERESTS FORTY-EIGHT PERCENT STOP HERON
INTERESTS FIFTY-TWO PERCENT GIVING US CONTROL
STOP REPLY URGENT.

GEO.

The next day, a cablegram was delivered by Higgens:

FEBRUARY 27, 1914

GEORGE STORY
BAINBRIDGE HOUSE
14 BENTLEY SQUARE
LONDON, ENGLAND

BOARD OF DIRECTORS HERON OIL COMPANY OF OKLA-
HOMA CONCUR ON PROPOSAL TO FORM BRITISH HERON
PRTROLEUM COMPANY STOP NEW BOARD OF DIRECTORS
STOP HALF AMERICAN STOP HALF BRITISH STOP WITH
YOU AS PRESIDENT ESSENTIAL STOP DRAW UP PAPERS
QUICKLY ARMBUSTER ADVISES STOP PERCY ROCKEFEL-
LER IN WINGS.

BOS.

George read the message again and then gave the cablegram to Letty. "We have bitter competition," he said
slowly, "if old John D. is sending Percy into the fray,
Standard Oil, you can be sure, will be prepared to offer
better terms than we can. I'll make up the contracts tomorrow and get those signatures!"

The next afternoon, George arrived for tea with a
crestfallen expression on his face. "We've lost the contract, my dear, pure and simple."

Letty set her jaw in a hard line. "Rockefeller won
out after all, then?"

He smiled wryly. "No, at least Standard got bamboo-

276

zled too! Union Oil Company of California won—but it is a tenuous victory."

"What do you mean?"

George waved his hands in an old Indian gesture that Letty had not seen him use in years. "Simply this, my dear, the rumor is that the new concern is to be called the British Union Oil Company, which will purchase one hundred fifty thousand shares of Union Oil treasury stock at par value. Union needs the cash desperately, or so my informed source tells me. But the deal may eventually backfire. Perhaps we are best out of it!"

"I don't understand."

"Well," he explained patiently, "this will give British interests a stake in Union Oil of California. Now, I'm told that the first payment of two million, five hundred thousand dollars will be due soon, and the rest will mature in several future payments. Now what happens if there is a war and the British Navy does not have time to convert all of their men-of-war battleships from coal to oil?"

Letty shrugged. "But—war, George, war. . . ."

"It may come, my dear. The Austrian situation is very bad and Germany may face a showdown, and Britain has treaties . . . it's very complex." He paused. "But, the outcome, whatever, war or not, means that Union Oil *could* eventually be under British control." He walked to the window and looked out over the mists that obscured the mansion across the street. "You see, my dear," he turned toward her, "that is why Armbuster advised a separate corporation that could never gain control of Heron of Oklahoma!"

She sighed. "Then it's just as well that we're out of it! We're a small company, George, and we must not become too ambitious. Why try to fight the giants?"

He smiled softly and gazed at the tapestry on the wall that depicted a fox and lamb in furious combat. "You know, Letty," he said solemnly, suddenly turning around. "I think we've been making a mistake."

"What do you mean?"

"I've gone over in my mind at odd times today the conversation that we had the other night." His eyes were very blue and his expression was very earnest, "and I believe we've forgotten some of the things that made us successful."

She frowned. "I don't follow you at all."

"Let's see, Number One came in on Easter Sunday, 1903, right? So, we have been in funds for about ten years. We have not grown very much in this decade that has placed American industy on its feet."

"But you're wrong, George, dead wrong. The wells are still producing, the refineries, the hundreds of miles of pipelines, and certainly the Wildcat bit . . ."

"Yes, yes," he said excitedly, "but most of that success has been due to Armbuster and the board of directors. I mean, we—you and I—we're still the same . . ."

Letty tossed her blonde head; the deep waves over her forehead looked as if they would come tumbling down any moment. "*Thank God, yes*—money hasn't changed us at all!"

"Oh, but is has, my dear, in a very insidious way, I think." He was speaking with such fervor that she could see him standing before a jury, giving a long summation. "We've been wrong. We haven't taken advantage of what we have." He paused. "I admit that I've gone to meetings—important meetings like the one yesterday—with hat in hand, figuratively. I haven't been honest with either myself or the company. It's so clear now, so very clear! I should have been more positive. I should have said that the Heron Oil Company could *guarantee* certain shipments of oil; that's what Armbuster would have said, and then work like hell—excuse me, dear—to do it! When they wanted to buy stock in the company, I should not have acted horrified, but said, positively *no*; why not keep most of the money here in Great Britain; form a separate English-American company." He was pacing up and down. "Our talk the other night may have been the most important one we've ever had in our lives! You are as guilty as I am. We've been thinking *small*. You've even allowed the servants here to intimidate you, and those old biddies at the tea last week . . . Have any of them ever sat beside their husbands in a ramshackle buckboard and made a historic run for a free claim? Have they had a baby in a sod house? Have they helped bring in an oil well? Have they cut out a dress from a pattern? Have they sat in on a board of directors meeting? Have they cooked for threshers?"

Letty was entranced. "I'm beginning to see what you mean," she replied, her past life a kaleidoscope of moving pictures . . .

"I think we've been tackling the problems in the wrong way! It's like we've been looking through the wrong end of a telescope! We've got to change, Letty, change! We don't meet them on *their* terms, they meet us on *ours*!" He picked her up and whirled her around the room. "I feel like I am eighteen instead of forty-two. Why, Letty, we've just begun to *live*!"

23

Changes

The next morning, Letty arose early, before the servants had gathered for their "cuppa" in their sitting room in the basement of the house.

She went for a long walk in the park across from Bainbridge House. Warm and snug in her heavy cloak, she planned the day as carefully as George prepared a court brief. She must gauge the "feeling" of the morning. For the first time she understood what Clement, as young as he was, meant when he said that an audience must be understood in emotional terms; that performing was only part of what took place in an auditorium. She would be performing alone on a stage that was not of her own choosing.

"I would like to make certain changes in house schedules regarding meals," Letty told Higgens when she returned. "Mr. Story and I have had difficulty adjusting to the set routine. We will function better if we go back to the hours food is served at home." There, she had spoken without fainting!

"Tea?"

"I think the custom is charming." Letty paused, choosing her words carefully, "but in Angel we do not eat substantial food before dinner." Ah, she thought, I'm learning. I did not say *supper*! "A cup of tea by itself is very nice in the afternoon, but let's eliminate the other dishes . . ."

Higgens swallowed with difficulty. "But with such a long time between luncheon and dinner . . ."

"Would it be possible to serve dinner about six-thirty? We retire early and eight o'clock seems so late."

Higgens opened his eyes wide. "Of course. I will tell Mrs. Soams, madame." He paused. "And if there is any other household routine that you would like to change, speak with Mrs. Helm."

Letty stood up and went to the window. "I'm afraid it's most difficult to conform to our ways, Higgens, and I know that it must be a great inconvenience . . ."

"It is understood perfectly," he said graciously. "The master was most insistent that your wishes be carried out fully. It is no hardship on the staff, I assure you, madame."

That afternoon, Mrs. Soams sought out Mrs. Helm. "You won't believe the changes she wants to make!" Tears gathered in her eyes, which she quickly brushed away with her apron. "Turning the house topsy turvy, she is! Now it's plates of food from the kitchen she wants served for breakfast and luncheon, no tea, and dinner at six-thirty . . . The next thing, she'll be invading my kitchen, showing me how to make cornbread, I suppose." She sat down on a kitchen chair. "What's the world coming to when people don't know how to . . ." This time she could not hold back the tears.

"There, there, Mrs. Soams," Mrs. Helm said, patting her shoulder. "This turmoil will last only for a bit. When the Huxley-Drummonds return, everything will be back to normal . . ." Although she tried to comfort Mrs. Soams, she felt old and rejected inside. It was obvious that the Storys were *common*. They might be rich and he might be a highly respected barrister, but they were still common. For the next few weeks, Bainbridge would be run like a hotel. Well, she thought, as she squared her shoulders and prepared to go upstairs to see Mrs. Story, it will be run like an elegant hotel!

Letty had barely settled herself down by the fireplace in the sitting room and was collecting her thoughts, when there were two taps on the door. "Yes, Higgens," she called; she knew his knock by this time.

He appeared with the usual apologetic look on his

281

face. "While you were out, madame, this message arrived."

She opened the long, cream-colored envelope, glanced at the contents, and looked up with a smile. "Lord and Lady Morris are going to be able to come to dinner on Saturday after all. He's over his indisposition."

"Then all guests have accepted. Very good, madame." He paused.

"Yes?"

"I think perhaps we should review the protocol," he replied quietly.

"The *protocol*, Higgens?"

"Yes. I believe Lord and Lady Morris will be the only titled personages present . . ."

"Why, yes."

"Then certain rules must be observed. Lord Morris should be seated at the left of Mr. Story and Lady Morris must be seated at your right—"

"But I've only met them *once*, Higgens. I'd thought that the Motleys . . ."

"Begging your pardon, madame, but . . ."

Letty arose, brushing her soft pompadour with her fingers. "Higgens," she said as gently as she could, "I appreciate your concern, but I want this dinner party handled differently. In the store room upstairs, I noticed several small tables . . ."

"Yes," he replied. "They are used for garden parties in the summer."

"I want you to move the long dining table, and we'll scatter those little tables around the dining room." She paused. "We're going to serve buffet style from the sideboard."

Higgens cleared his throat, trying to keep his face composed. "*Buffet* for a formal dinner party, madame?"

"Instead of giving an English dinner party, I want a totally *American* flavor." She grew enthusiastic as the plan began to form fully in her mind. "For instance, I'm going to answer the door myself, just as if I were in my own home in Angel. We'll gather in the drawing room, and I'd like you to hire someone to play the piano very softly in the background—perhaps some gifted student.

"We'll serve sherry—that's a concession, because I don't serve alcoholic beverages in my own home. We'll go into dinner in two's and three's." Ignoring his stricken face, she continued authoritatively. "And the food will be a complete American menu, which I will give to Mrs. Soams, along with recipes."

She paused. "The main course will be fried chicken, with waldorf salad, mashed potatoes and cream gravy, and perhaps green peas with little onions, or string beans cooked with bacon. Fried green tomatoes would be nice, and relishes, like celery and carrot sticks, Sally Lunn soft bread—no, cornbread would be better. For dessert, an apple pie—a real pie with a top and bottom crust, not like yours with only a top crust—and I'll personally bake an Angel Cake." She paused. "Also, while every one is having sherry, we'll pass around some salted nuts and popcorn . . ."

"Popcorn?" Higgens was leaning against the door jamb, his face drained of color.

"Yes, Higgens, believe it or not, that is a typical American dinner, usually served on Sunday, around two-thirty or three o'clock in the afternoon."

"The *afternoon*, Madame?"

She smiled widely. "Yes, Higgens, in the afternoon. Of course, over here we'll make a concession and serve dinner at eight."

His eyebrows appeared permanently attached to his hairline. "I see . . ." He cleared his throat. "I think this will be a very interesting—experiment. . . ."

"Well, for one thing, it will solve the problem of who sits next to whom. The married couples will be seated together. Oh, yes, I forgot—coffee and dessert, I will personally serve in the drawing room. While everyone is having dinner, the dessert table can be set up in there, along with plates and cutlery and additional napkins."

"Very well, madame. I shall inform Mrs. Soams. Is that all?"

"Yes," Letty replied with a smile, "that is all—for now!"

* * *

283

Letty supervised the setting up of the tables for dinner immediately after four o'clock tea. She had become accustomed to the "pause in the afternoon," as she had written Priscilla, but she would accept no side dishes.

After cut flowers had been distributed in strategic areas around the drawing room, she borrowed an apron from Jessie and went below stairs to the kitchen. "Ah, Mrs. Soams!" she said warmly, "you've iced the Angel cake superbly."

The old lady smiled reluctantly. "Thank you, madame. I couldn't find any cocoa to be had anywhere, so I used German chocolate. Here, have a taste." She handed Letty a spoon filled with the dark, lustrous mixture.

"Oh, that *is* good, very rich!"

Mrs. Soams smiled, her eyes filled with admiration. "A cake that takes twenty-four eggs deserves something special. You must give me the recipe, madame." She paused. "It was nice of you to bake one for us below stairs, too. We all had a sample for tea. It's rather like a sponge."

Letty nodded. "Yes, but it shouldn't be baked on a damp day or the moisture in the air will make it soggy. The texture must be light as air."

"It is that," Mrs. Soams said. "Now, I've got the chicken marinating in the buttermilk as you said, and I'll mash the potatoes at the last moment." She paused and looked about the kitchen. "And I think that everything else is under control."

"With you in charge, I knew it would be, Mrs. Soams. Now, I think I'll go upstairs and rest a bit before the guests arrive."

Promptly at seven o'clock, the knocker on the door trembled once, and Letty, dressed in her pale blue watered silk dress with a wide skirt, opened the door. Bertram and Gertrude Motley stood on the threshold. "Welcome. Do come in," she said warmly, ignoring their looks of utter surprise. As they gave their wraps to Higgens, she continued small talk about the weather. After she had asked them to be seated in the drawing

284

room, there was another knock and she opened the door to the Hoovers. Herbert quickly looked over the foyer, and seeing Higgens standing beside the door, understood the situation at once. "How nice of you to make us welcome," he said warmly, and then crossed to shake George's hand. As Lou was being led into the drawing room, she whispered. "How nice *not* to be announced!"

One after the other, the guests arrived, and as the clock in the hall chimed seven-thirty, Lord and Lady Morris made their appearance. "I'm so pleased that you have recovered from your indisposition, Lord Henry," Letty said. "We're having an 'American night'," she explained, pressing Lady Sybil's arm.

After glasses of sherry had been passed around, Higgens opened the double doors into the dining room. "Shall we go in," Letty asked pleasantly. "We're having a buffet tonight, an American custom when very special people gather."

Higgens helped with the serving, managing somehow to adopt an informal air. Letty had the feeling that he was enjoying the evening in spite of himself. From the adjoining music room, the first phrases of "In the Gloaming" wafted pleasantly through the french doors as the guests, their plates filled, found their place cards.

The music continued throughout dinner, and Letty could have kissed Herbert Hoover when he rose nonchalantly and took a second helping of fried chicken that she was sure he really did not want to show that it was entirely proper to take more food. He was followed by Lord Morris, who, she was happy to note, took a generous portion of mashed potatoes and two ladles of cream gravy. The moment that he put down his fork and dabbed his lips with a napkin, Letty rose. "Let's have dessert and coffee in the other room," she announced quietly.

Later, Gertrude Motley, who was seated next to Letty, took a bite of the cake and her eyes widened. "What an extraordinary—confection. It's absolutely delicious."

"Thank you," Letty smiled crookedly. "It's called Angel cake."

"Aptly named, I should say. It's divine. I assume this is totally American, too?"

"Yes," Letty replied, "in fact, I made it myself "

Gertrude's eyes grew wide. "You *did*?"

"Yes. The cook, Mrs. Soams, contributed the icing."

"Wherever do you find the time?"

"Well," Letty smiled, "on our farm, I used to cook for threshers—the men who travel from county to county, harvesting the crops each year. Traditionally they are given a daily wage, plus three meals, and I must say they're hearty eaters! So whipping up a cake is child's play when you've cooked for an army!" She sighed. "I do quite a bit of my own baking at home. It eases the daily burdens somehow. Cooking is therapeutic."

Gertrude laughed discreetly. "You're making me want to learn how to sauté and bake." She became serious. "One thing I do *so* approve of, Letty," using her Christian name for the first time, "you've a sense of value, you plunge into things, I can see that." She became wistful. "I sometimes think we women who actually have so little to do are much too pampered. Our husbands treat us like china dolls—which is rather nice once in a while, but on a day-to-day basis, quite stifling. Don't you dare change!"

The music became more lively as the young pianist played modern pieces and the conservation soared.

At ten o'clock Lord and Lady Morris stood up. "My dear," Sybil said, "what a *delightful* evening," then she lowered her voice. "Where did you get your gown? It's breathtaking."

"I made this one myself for my son, Clement's, graduation from the fifth grade last year. You see," she continued quickly, "our small town is very remote. Oklahoma has only been a state for six years, and we've been experiencing difficult growing pains. We simply do not have salons. I envy you London and Paris." She almost told about ordering clothing from Sears & Roebuck!

Lady Sybil smiled, and took her hand. "I so admire you, my dear. I wish I had some of your American spirit."

286

Lord Henry shook George's hand. "A very interesting evening," he said gruffly, a twinkle in his eye. "First time I've not been truly bored in a long, long time. I actually *enjoyed* myself tonight." His voice dropped an octave. "I'd like to see you on Friday, if you can manage it. I need some advice—on petrol matters . . ."

When the last guest had left, Letty kissed George. "Well, was it a success or not?"

He grinned. "You have to ask?" He placed his arms around her waist and looked down into her eyes. "As Bertram Motley said, 'It was a *smashing* evening'!"

George wrote a letter to the Huxley-Drummonds, which both he and Letty signed. After a polite introduction, he carefully composed the following paragraph:

The fact that you have turned Bainbridge over to us, strangers in a strange land, was a kind gesture that we will never forget. We are sure that by now you have the contracts with Union Oil in hand, and since the Heron Oil Company will not be involved in further negotiations, we shall be leaving tomorrow for the United States. Again, we must tender our heartfelt thanks, and if ever we can return a favor, remember that we are greatly in your debt.

24

Progress

George walked quickly into the board room, keeping his face as blank as possible. J. C. Armbuster, Chairman of the Board, called the meeting to order and stood up. "First of all, gentlemen, I'm going to ask for our president's report."

George rose slowly and put on his glasses. "As all of you know, Union Oil won the contract to supply His Majesty's . . ." He smiled wryly and looked over the top of his spectacles at the men seated around the table. ". . . Excuse me, living in a foreign country does that to one . . . to supply the British Navy with fuel oil."

Tension was very evident among the group of men, and he could feel their displeasure. "However, I was approached with an offer that I hope you'll consider most carefully." He paused. "I wish to place, for your consideration, a proposal to form a new company called Heron–British Oil Company, Ltd., with British and Dutch interests to be headed by Bertram Motley. We will supply petroleum to a great many Commonwealth industries. Mr. Motley feels that we will be able to dispense some two million barrels of Heron oil a year, and if war comes, perhaps a great deal more . . ."

The tension that had been so evident before broke as the men broke into a quick round of applause.

Sebastian nodded. "I assume this means building seaworthy tankers?"

George nodded. "Motley advises that the head office should be set up in a country other than England—in fact, he thinks The Hague, Holland, will be ideal." He paused. "Do any of you gentlemen happen to speak Dutch?"

The prairie around Angel was brown from a long drought. The fields of golden wheat, moving like a yellow ocean in the breeze, yielded the poorest crop in half a decade—barely sixteen bushels to the acre. The Story clapboard looked small in comparison to Bainbridge House, and Main Street, with its motor cars and buggies, also looked forlorn against the hustle and bustle of London. It was like times out of the past, reflected Letty.

Clement came home from school and filled the house with the music of Grieg once more, only this time he also played modern melodies, to the delight of Fontine. For the first time in her life, Letty was nervous and skittish. She went riding over the pasture land, attended quilting bees, prepared box suppers for the church, helped make costumes for the annual school pageant, and commiserated with George when Britain entered the war in August of 1914.

On September 16th, dressed in a poke bonnet and a calico dress, she took part in the twenty-first Cherokee Strip celebration in Enid. Riding around the square in the old buckboard, George at her side, she was suddenly very tired. She had seen the territory grow from scattered tents to clapboards, attended the statehood celebration in Gutherie, helped bring in the discovery well, Heron Number One, and she was weary of it all. . . .

Late that night, she could not sleep and went downstairs to make coffee. She heard George's step on the stair. "I guess you can't settle down either," she said glumly.

He shook his head. "I'm like a fish out of water, my dear." He stood with the mug in his hand. ". . . And so are you."

"What's come over us since we got back from Europe?" she asked.

He smiled. "Frankly, I think we've outgrown Angel," he replied quietly. "With the new field office in Tulsa, and all of this government talk about breaking up various trusts, I really think we belong in Washington. Our life has become very political, whether we like it or not." He took her hand. "Let's hire a caretaker for this place, Letty." He smiled suddenly. "I'll build you a new house on a fine street in Washington." He paused. "And if we're not happy, we can always move back to Angel!"

"Oh, George," Letty cried with the exuberance of a young girl, "Let's do it. I think it's time we left the womb!"

The architectural blueprints for the new twenty-room house on Connecticut Avenue in the nation's capital were approved on April 12, 1915, and the ground breaking took place on July 21st, but only George was present for the ceremonies. "Build the house," Letty had said. "I don't want to see it until it is completely finished, landscaping and all." Then she had smiled. "Somehow I don't feel like a pioneer any more!"

George and Letty attended Luke's graduation at Harvard, then spent a few days together in New York before taking the train to Chicago and thence to Angel via Wichita and Enid. They had avoided talking about what was uppermost in mind: the international situation. Finally, after supper on the first night home, Luke brought up the subject. "I'll enlist if war comes," he said stoically. "And I don't think there is any doubt that it will, especially with the sinking of the *Lusitania...*"

George nodded numbly. "I'm afraid you're right, Luke," he sighed. "We lost our two tankers when Germany began treating the water surrounding Britain and Ireland as a war zone. We can't get the oil through now, and I've those contracts to worry about. I was hoping you could come into the company now, Luke."

"I'd like nothing better, Dad, but . . . tell me, was England able to get all of their man-of-war battleships converted to fuel-oilers?"

George shook his head. "No, only about half. But Union Oil has those contracts. Ours deal with oil for industrial purposes—factories and so on."

"You see," Letty said, "that's why it's so important to have you in the company. We can get you a defer-

290

ment. It is vital that we continue to furnish petroleum to our own government. A great deal more gasoline and fuel oil will be needed."

Mitchell Heron came back from Stanford in July and went riding with Luke. The boys had never been close, but by the time they had watered their horses down by the creek, a sort of camaraderie had been established. They sat on a log in the shade of the cottonwoods. Mitchell gave a long sigh, lighted a cigarette, and ran a hand through his rust-colored hair. "Damn it," he said, automatically flicking the ash into the cuff of his trousers, "I don't want to go into the furniture business. And, my Dad thinks I'm crazy." He glanced at Luke. "What are you going to do?"

"Join the company if I don't enlist. I like the oil business. Hell, Mitch, I remember when I was a kid and old Number One came in and we were all soaked to the skin. I liked the smell of that green crude then—and I still do!"

"You're fortunate that you like the business." Mitchell turned his palms upward. "These mitts were not made for rubbing wood."

"But you used to help Uncle Edward in the shop!"

"Sure, sweeping up, carrying lumber—you know—odd jobs. I got an allowance for working, but I don't want to go into the business."

"Well, what do you want to do?"

Mitchell shook his head. "I suppose you'll think I'm crazy, Luke, but I don't know what in the hell I want to do. Sometimes I think I'd like to teach, but I know I'd be bored stiff after a while." He sighed. "I wish I had the talent to paint or write. It would be fun to work with clay, or play the piano like Clement." He shrugged, blinking his eyes, and grinned. "But I think what it all boils down to is that I don't have much ambition. I guess I'm just lazy."

Luke shook his head. "I learned one thing in college, Mitch, and that is the sun does not rise and set in Angel, Oklahoma! I could never be cooped up here. I want to travel, I want to learn, I want to take my place with—well, with people of substance." He walked a few

291

paces and looked out over the prairie, then suddenly whirled around. "Do you know, Mitch, that we're the only boys from this area who've gone to college? The kids we went to high school with are all married and have children. The fellows are farmers or pipe fitters or work in the oil fields. A couple have businesses in town." He laughed ruefully. "They're content with so *little*."

Mitchell ground out his cigarette under his boot. "I understand that. They've found their niche. I wish the hell I could." He looked up and grinned. "Dad has a genius for working with his hands; I guess my talent is in my body. I'm a lover, not a carpenter."

"I'm a lover, too!" Luke laughed. "It's too bad The Widows is closed. We could go over and get a piece of ass. Say, that gives me an idea! What are you doing this afternoon?"

"Nothing."

"I'll borrow Dad's car and we'll go over to Two Street in Enid! My asparagus hasn't had a workout since Boston!"

"Sounds like fun . . . but I don't know that I'm really in the mood . . ."

Luke spat in the grass and mounted his horse. "C'mon, let's go home," he said with disgust. "I bet you've never been to a whorehouse!"

"A couple of times in college we went to a place in Palo Alto, but I was drunk and . . ."

"Mitch, you're twenty-two years old. I'll bet you've still got your cherry!"

"I lost it years ago."

Luke snorted. "Then it must have been one of the girls in Angel. Which one? Martha Stevens, I bet, she'd go with any fellow."

"No."

"Abigail Baker?"

"Stop asking." He paused. "I guess I'm not very, well, very—sex-minded."

Luke laughed as they rode over the incline past The Widows Pond. "I got mine when I was thirteen, right up there in that bedroom." He pointed to the Conservatory. "It was Stella, a hot little piece from Wichita." He paused. "Dollars to doughnuts, you're still a virgin."

"Well, you could ask Belle Trune."

Luke whirled around. "Belle Trune? She wouldn't drop her bloomers for anybody."

"Well, she dropped them for me—in a haystack with a couple of other fellows."

"Well, I'll be damned! I suppose you got it often after that?"

Mitchell shook his head. "No, only once. She got scared, I guess, because she avoided me like the devil." He sighed. "I've changed my mind, I'll go into Enid with you."

Supported by President Wilson, Congress declared war on Germany on April 6, 1917, and Luke at age twenty-three enlisted the next day. Three months later, he was on his way to France.

Clement spent the long hot summer at the farm in Angel. He practiced the piano four hours a day, and John Dice, driving home from his office for dinner, became familiar with the classical melodies that swept out over the prairie from the Story clapboard. Even with Germany in such discredit throughout the world, he decided that he liked Wagner best. Something about the soaring music stirred his imagination, and he fought many battles with the Huns on his drives to and from his noonday meal. "If I wasn't an old man, I'd shoulder a gun myself," he often told Fontine, who was not impressed with his derring-do.

Clement was restless. When not studying, he would ride over the farm, sometimes stopping at the conservatory to talk to the young students, who to his amusement regarded him with awe. He lectured them: "Just because I was a so-called 'child prodigy' doesn't mean that I'm more talented than you are!" He brushed his black hair back from his forehead and his dark eyes swept over the callow young group. "You must *study*. Persistence is the most important quality for a musician. Practice and study."

"What's it like to give a concert?" asked a redheaded girl, whose eyes were full of stars. "What's it like to stand up there on the stage before all those people and perform?"

Clement laughed. "It's a little like what the Catholics call 'purgatory'. You're in a 'between world' until it's over, and even then, you don't know if you'll go to heaven or to hell." He laughed. "I'm taking license . . . but what I mean is—you know if you've played well or not, if you've struck any wrong notes, but you don't know if you've really interpreted the music well until you get a review. Audiences applaud sometimes because you've created a certain mood. Many don't know the difference between a bad performance or a good performance." He paused and smiled. "It often depends on whether you're a good showman or not!"

"What do you think about popular music?" a boy with horn-rimmed glasses asked in a nasal voice.

"As an alumnus of this conservatory, I probably shouldn't say it, but I *like* popular music."

"Would you illustrate what you mean?" The lad's brows were furrowed.

"I go to local dances," Clement replied. "I can waltz and schottische and polka. I hum along with the Graphophone discs. I like to go to a place where someone plays in the background. In fact, in Oklahoma City, I used to go to tea dances with my instructor and his wife. Once I took the place of the pianist who was ill." He laughed. "It was fun, but I'm afraid I startled the orchestra leader. I added a few embellishments . . ."

The bell rang for class, and Clement clapped his hand. "Back to your instruments!" he cried and shooed them out of the room.

The boy with the horn-rimmed glasses came up afterwards. "Will you come back and talk some more during noon hour?"

"I just might," Clement said, laughing, "if someone would share their food with me!"

The students looked blankly at one another. They had forgotten to invite their "professor without portfolio" for lunch!

Priscilla followed the housekeeper through the eighteen rooms of her Dallas house. "You're getting worse all the time, Mrs. Bellows," she snapped, running her finger along the paneled walls in the library. "This is filthy, absolutely filthy! Dallas has more dust than Angel!"

Mrs. Bellows, a fat, squat little Irish woman, drew in her breath and retorted. "There's a war on, ma'am, and I can't get any help except young girls that have to be broken in, then up and leave when they get a little experience. They don't knuckle down to nobody. Good servants are scarce as hen's teeth!"

Priscilla had to smile. She hadn't heard that old expression in years—not, in fact, since they had moved to Texas. "Well, Mrs. Bellows," she said more kindly, "do what you can. I know conditions aren't easy." She looked down at her manicured nails and flexed her fingers. Her diamonds, which she had just cleaned that morning with a toothbrush and baking soda, sparkled in the refracted sunlight. "Raise the windows a bit, Mrs. Bellows, it's stifling in here." She paused. "Today is Thursday, so don't worry about having the cook perpare luncheon ahead. I'll serve myself some cold meat." Anything to get the woman out of the house!

Mrs. Bellows smiled. "Thank you. The girls and myself thought we would go to the picture show this afternoon. There's a new Mary Pickford playing at the Bijou and then we'll eat downtown."

"If you stay out late, be quiet when you come in, I'll probably be asleep."

"When is Mr. Heron expected?"

"Lord only knows. For sure not until next week. He's in Oregon now, trying to purchase some lumber acreage for the factories. Everything is so complicated."

"I'm sure it is," the housekeeper agreed, reflecting privately that it seemed that everything about the Herons was complicated. She shook her head and went downstairs. If the family was not one of the richest in Dallas, and if she wasn't able to pinch a few dollars every week from her household budget, she would go elsewhere . . .

* * *

Manford Pederson waited around the corner in his Cadillac until Mrs. Bellows and the two maids got on the street car before he drove into the driveway.

Upstairs, Priscilla stepped out of her shift and slipped between the sheets. Manford liked her to be waiting for him. She arranged the pillows behind her head and smoothed her hair, feeling for a moment like a young girl. She lifted up the sheet and looked at her body. Her breasts were still firm, considering the fact that she had had three miscarriages. Her stomach was rounded—not flabby yet.

However, she knew that Manford, for all of his attractiveness, never really looked at her body the way that she did. He had once told her that he loved her because she was someone else's wife and supposedly unobtainable. He had been drunk, but she knew it was the truth. Knowing how he felt about her, she dared not tell him that Edward and she had not been intimate for ten years. If Manford suspected that he was not sharing her charms, she would lose her attractiveness for him. Priscilla was not a fool. She had been in love with him from that first day he had strode into the store in Enid. But she had carefully let herself be pursued, always keeping herself beyond reach—desirable, teasing, withdrawing, only finally giving a hint that she might consider him as an object of her affection. Even then, she kept him successfully on the hook. Then one night that first year in Dallas, when Edward was out of town, she had some champagne and allowed herself, reluctantly, to acquiesce. And, frankly, she did not enjoy the experience very much.

In the old days with Edward, she enjoyed their bedtimes, especially when she was pregnant. She loved to lie back on the bed and drowse. However, even that luxury now did not seem so crucial. It was the *attention* that she craved now most of all, to know that she held a man in her power for even the short time they were together. She had become expert in prolonging the sexual excitement—so expert that finally when Manford at last was permitted to go to sleep, he was always exhausted and she, triumphant.

He came quietly into the room and kissed her cheek,

then undressed quickly, throwing his clothing on the floor. He tossed his B.V.D.s on the chair and crawled into bed beside her. "Did Edward get home last night?"

She raised her eyebrows slightly. "Yes," she lied, "he just left for Portland this morning. Didn't he call you?"

"No, but then I just got in from Houston myself." He paused. "Did he make love to you?"

"Oh, yes!" she replied, stepping into the necessary formula. "Once last night, and then again this morning."

"Was it good?"

She allowed a long sigh to escape her lips. "Wonderful . . ."

"Did you make it last a long time?"

"Oh, yes." She paused. "Both times. We must have carried on for at least an *hour*."

She knew that he was very aroused, and she changed her position to accommodate him.

"Was he very passionate?"

"He always is," she replied smugly, "he could hardly wait . . ."

"And did you hold him close—like this?"

"Of course, and I ran my fingers along his back, like this—very slowly. He was shivering just as you are now."

Manford's voice was very husky. "Could you feel him, I mean, *inside*?"

"Not as much as I feel you, my darling . . ."

He let out a long, low moan, and increased his tempo.

"I love your body," she whispered, "you're so *big* . . ."

Again he moaned as she caressed his back with long finger strokes. Then she knew that she had lain still long enough, and began to move her body in slow, agonizing circles. Then there was no more need for words. She lay back, imagining herself as a temptress. Looking over his perspiring shoulder, she conjured up a line of men waiting in the hall for her pleasures. It was then that she cried out and Manford answered with a cry of his own.

* * *

Clement graduated from Angel High School two months after his fifteenth birthday. After the ceremonies, he took one of the family cars out of the garage and motored to Enid on the new asphalt road. He returned in time for the dance that night in the ballroom of the new four-story Hotel Stevens. But before he left to pick up Charlotte Dice, his date, he carefully hid the paper that showed that he had enlisted in the United States Marines.

He watched the mails most carefully and when his summons arrived, he waited impatiently the five days until he was to report to the Armory in Enid, then, leaving a note for his mother and father, took the morning train. He stood on the train's little observation platform and watched the town recede in the distance; he did not feel the expected wave of nostalgia. He went back to the chair car and idly watched the passing prairie from the window. The last thing he saw before the train reached the depot in Enid was the oil tank farm and the new refinery that his dad had erected six months before. The Heron logo of the flying bird, emblazoned in bright blue paint, seemed to mock him . . .

That night when Clement did not appear for dinner, Letty found the note in his room. She was beside herself with grief as she handed his short letter to George. "I can't believe he would go and do such a thing," she cried. "He's not even dry behind the ears. What can we do? We've got to bring him back."

"I will have him tracked down," George replied, his jaw set, "but it will take time! I'll call Washington tomorrow, but with so many young boys enlisting, I'm afraid he will already be in training in some of the camps that are being set up all over the country." He paced back and forth and finally telephoned the induction center in Enid. He hung up wearily. "The line is busy." He paused. "If he was to show up at the center this morning at ten a.m., he's probably on a train." He placed his fingers up to his eyes and turned. "I'll try to bring him back . . ."

A week later, a postcard arrived from Louisiana:

Dear Mother and Dad:

I had to do it. For me there was no other way. Don't worry about me, I'll write when I can.

Clement.

Two months later, another postcard arrived:

Dear Mother and Dad:

Training is very difficult and I'm so tired that I fall into my bunk at night completely exhausted. But, I'm learning so much and I feel very confident. I'm glad I made the decision. I'll live by it.

Clement.

George clapped his hands. "It's mailed from Camp Meade! At least we know he's in Maryland. I can have him traced now. We'll find him yet."

But their letter was returned with a stamped entry: *Shipped out of state.*

The meeting in the Roosevelt Hotel in New Orleans had run late and Edward was very tired. His fight with Manford Pederson over the opening of the twelfth furniture store had taken a great deal out of him. He did not feel like taking the midnight train to Memphis, though he was due at a convention the next afternoon to give a speech. Thankfully it was the same speech that he had given many times before. The Furniture Association meetings were all very much the same, but he was expected, as a leading manufacturer, to put in an appearance, say a few words, and shake a few hands. It was part of the public relations aspect of the business that he did not enjoy.

He decided to walk the block and a half to his hotel. It was misting outside, and water dripped from the awnings. Distracted as usual, he had forgotten to bring an umbrella. One aspect of New Orleans that he had always hated was the terrible humidity and dampness.

The street walkers, who normally worked the French Quarter, had sauntered far from their usual haunts, he saw; apparently there were several large conventions in town. One woman came out of the doorway in front of him and began walking alongside him. "Five dollars," she said huskily. "I don't live too far."

He smiled to himself. Even if she was young and beautiful—which she wasn't—tonight he was too tired to care about anything but drawing up the covers and going to sleep.

"I can tell you're lonely," she continued in a strange voice that caused a memory to stir, "and I'm lonely, too." She paused and then whispered, "I promise that I can get it up for you. I guarantee."

Panic seized him and he began to tremble. They had reached the street corner by now. Afraid that his legs would give out from under him, he leaned against the side of the building.

"Had a little too much to drink?" the insinuating voice continued. "That's okay with me. As I said before, I can get it up for you. I'm very clever."

He could not stop trembling. He pushed his homburg lower over his gray hair. He could not look at the woman, and he was too weak to run.

Suddenly, she took him by the shoulders. "Honey, I told you I was *good*. You can put your wallet away. If you'll come with me, I won't even charge you, how's that?"

He thought he was going to faint. "That's all right, I'll help you," she said solicitously, misinterpreting his reaction. "Come along now, come along." She turned his face to hers and stared into his eyes, then drew back in astonishment, the bright street light turning her face under a mop of bright orange into a grotesque overpainted doll. Edward Heron stared into the face of Liza Galbraith.

She staggered backward, then ran down the side street, slowed by her lemon-colored, tight-fitting dress and high-heeled shoes, which clicked over the cobblestone alley. He called after her, "Liza! Liza!" But she had turned a corner. All he could hear was the hollow, fading clicks of her heels. He leaned against the cold glass window. Had he imagined the old woman was Liza? Was his mind playing tricks on him? That creature with the dyed hair and the awful painted face couldn't be his Liza. *His* Liza was tall and beautiful and exquisitely dressed, and never wore makeup. Then he counted the years. She had left him in 1912; this was 1918. If she was forty-one then, she'd only be forty-seven, now, but that hag was sixty-five if she was a day! Then he thought about those years and the thousands of men that had separated them. His face crumpled. He gathered up his strength and crossed the street. The mist had turned into light rain. The doorman greeted him at his hotel. "Nasty night out, Mr. Heron," the rosy-cheeked young man said.

"Yes, Jim," Edward replied slowly, "a nasty night indeed."

25

The Battlefields

All night long, the boxcars filled with marines of the 5th Brigade rattled through the Chateau–Thierry area of France, each car cryptically marked:

HOMMES 40, CHEVAUX 8

Clement, crowded into one of the cars, laughed. "This crate may hold eight horses—but forty men?" He was greeted with jeers and shouts: "That's right, Breedy." There was so little room, the men could not smoke. At the rear of the train, two giant guns, capable of firing 1200-pound shells, were tied down on two flatbed cars. The next train was carrying members of the U.S. Coast Artillery Corps, who would man the guns that the Germans at St. Mihial desperately wanted.

There was an explosion, and Clement was aware of being lifted on a stretcher. He heard the medic shout: "I've got the sonofabitch here. I need two strong men to carry the bastard." Next he was conscious of a pain in the back of his head, of great heat and cold, and then being jostled unmercifully.

Gradually the white room took shape. He was in a large dormitory, filled with cots dressed with army blankets. A fat nurse in a nun's garb rearranged his pillow. She saw his confused expression. "You're in the hospital, son."

He looked down at his body under the blanket, fully expecting to see a space where an arm and a leg should have been, but he seemed to be complete. Through very thick lips, he asked, "Where did I get it, ma'am?"

She patted his shoulder. "You were lucky. A small shoulder wound and a concussion."

"What's a concussion?" he asked.

"Let's say," she replied, "you've been shaken up a bit."

"Shell shock?" He was frightened.

"No," she laughed, her eyes and cheeks bright. "You'll recover very soon, if you're able to ask so many questions!"

"What day is it?"

"Tuesday."

"Is it still 1918?"

She nodded her head, her jowls shaking. "You've only been here three days." She took his temperature and pulse.

"Am I going to die?"

"I'm afraid not, my boy. You're almost as good as new. The concussion was apparently very slight. Can you move your shoulder?"

A pain shot up as he moved his elbow. "Yes, but it hurts."

"You've just lost a bit of flesh." She lowered her voice. "The doctor said you'd have what will look like a strawberry birthmark on your left shoulder blade."

He smiled. "Just like Uncle Edward . . ." Then he drifted off to sleep.

Two days later he was sitting in the sun on the patio of the great house that had been turned into a convalescent center for the troops. He looked out over the lawn at what looked like hundreds of marines, a few in complete uniforms, some dressed as he was in green trousers and shirt. His head ached dully, yet he was extremely fortunate; some of the men had limbs missing and others were wrapped in tremendous bandages, but all were in the last stages of recovery. He was bored and listless. He knew no one, and his inquiries about his buddies went unanswered. He finally located two marines from the 5th Brigade, but they were wary and uncommunicative.

A day later, he was walking on the terrace when he

heard a commotion behind him. A diminutive woman in a cape paused in the ornate doorway to what had been an enormous drawing room. "I can do one of my monologues, I suppose," she said, "but I'd rather sing."

The colonel, a blustery middle-aged man, shook his head. "We've never lost a musician before—heh, heh," he quipped.

She faced him. "It may be very amusing to you, sir, but I assure you it is *not* amusing to me! How could this have happened?"

"There are four hospitals in this area," he replied, and Clement saw that underneath the jaunty manner, the man was totally exhausted, and from the strange look in his eyes and his shaking hands, near hysterics as well. "Obviously he was taken to another location, heh, heh!" He paused. He'll turn up sooner or later, Miss Janis."

Clement stared at the woman. Was this the famous Elsie Janis? It was then that he saw the lead sheets in her hand. He turned and saluted the colonel. "Private Clement Story reporting for duty, sir!"

The colonel saluted. "Duty?" His bloodshot eyes danced.

"Yes, sir. I am a graduate of the Conservatory of Music in Angel, Oklahoma," he said proudly. "Could I fill in until Miss Janis's pianist arrives?"

She turned to him, smiling, her hand outstretched. "I would be most grateful. Have you seen a piano hereabouts?"

"Yes, ma'am, there's an old upright covered up with a sheet in the corner."

"Would you play something for me?" she asked. "Of course, with the colonel's permission."

"Permission granted," he answered, and Clement saw that his hands were still shaking.

Clement removed the dust cover from the piano and sat down, then dusted the keys with a handkerchief and ran his fingers lightly over the keyboard. The resulting chords pierced the low rumble of soldier-talk and reverberated from the giant ceiling. The room was acoustically perfect. He started another trill, limbering up his fingers. The piano must have been recently tuned, he marveled.

The woman watched his fingers fly over the keys and smiled. "He'll do, Colonel." And when he started the first few bars of *The Wedding at Troldhaugen*, she exclaimed, "Indeed, he will! If he plays Grieg that well, he certainly can thump through my little sunshine number!"

After she finished the song, Elsie Janis wrapped her cape around her shoulders like a cocoon and began one of her famous monologues. She received an ovation from the entertainment-starved men and sang an encore. Then she introduced Clement, who took a bow. "I have an idea," she announced, eyes bright. "The boys near the front lines need cheering up. Surely in the four hospitals here there are other boys who can play musical instruments." She leaned forward conspiratorily. "If I speak to the colonel, do you think you could organize a doughboy band?"

Clement looked at her with surprise. "If I can find the men—I'd like that very much."

She glanced at the colonel, who was conversing with one of the nurses; even with his hands clasped firmly behind his back, he could not entirely stop the tremors. She lowered her voice. "I think at this point the old boy would agree to anything." She approached the officer, who looked at her with suspicion, but as she spoke, he nodded once and then again.

Within a week, Clement had found a clarinetist, a saxophone player, a violinist, and a trumpet player. As they rehearsed before making the rounds of the hospital wards, Clement looked heavenward and prayed that whatever deity was looking down over the battlefields of France would please come to his rescue. The men played badly, often out of tune, and always with the expressions of frightened high school band students. However, the soldiers, half-dead from horrific wounds, could not have been more appreciative. Within a fortnight, the little band was bravely performing from the back of a truck near the front lines.

The fighting had become very intense. Now the Germans were only forty-four miles from Paris. During the

305

last part of June, the combat areas of Belleau Wood and Chateau–Thierry once more became a bloody battleground. But when the American Marines pushed the enemy back, saving Paris from plunder, the grateful French government officially changed the name of Belleau Wood to *Bois de la Brigade de Marine*. One old-time sergeant exclaimed: "Hell, it wasn't the Marines that drove the Kaiser's troops back—it was the racket made by that damned Breedy and his godawful band!"

In September, the band played on the average of forty-five minutes every three hours. Traveling in the back of an old ambulance that had seen better days, they would pile out of the truck, stretch their legs. Clement would stand at the small portable piano that rested in the back, and the music would pour out over the large gatherings. They often played while half asleep, but the troops, who had not heard any music for months, always applauded loudly.

Late one night, the ambulance broke down in a battered little village and the musicians were billeted in a barn. It had begun to rain, and the exhausted men climbed into the hayloft and fell to sleep. The next morning, they gathered in the village square and played several numbers. Trucks full of soldiers paused to listen for a moment before being driven on to the front.

Clement had just closed the back door of the ambulance when he heard his name called and whirled around to see his brother standing behind him. Joyfully they shook hands. "My God, it's good to see you, Luke," Clement cried.

Luke laughed. "I was wondering when we were going to meet. I've known you were in this area for a long time. You're very famous, you know." He shook his head. "They say the band is winning the war . . ."

"We can't be *that* bad!" Clement replied with a smile. "Have you heard from Mother and Dad?"

"About three weeks ago, I guess. Mother's up to her elbows in war work and Dad is his old self, trying to supply more oil for war industries." He paused. "I guess they've finally forgiven you for enlisting without their consent."

Clement nodded. "I was *sick* of Angel. I don't think I can ever go back."

"Me, either," Luke replied, soberly. He looked rakish in his captain's uniform, as he glanced at Clement's sleeve. "Damn, I should think they'd have given you a promotion by this time. After all, you're risking your ass every day of the week." He paused. "It's not fair. I'll see what I can do." He glanced behind him, saw that no one was listening, and whispered. "There's an *estaminet* on the back street, behind the hotel."

"An *estaminet*?"

Luke laughed. "You know—a place like The Widows. Why don't you boys take an hour or so for a bit of fun?" His eyes were full of mischief.

Clement equivocated, and Luke laughed again and punched him on the back. "Don't mean to tell me that you've still got your cherry?"

Clement flushed crimson. "It's just that I'm afraid of picking up some social disease . . ."

"Suit yourself," Luke grinned, "but there's a girl called Lisette who is *magic*. Not as good as Stella used to be, but *nice*."

Clement looked at his brother, eyes wide. "You mean you used to go to The Widows?"

"Sure. Uncle Bos took me over there on my thirteenth birthday. For the next couple of years, before I went on to college, Stella got all my allowance." He laughed. "Dad never could figure why I was broke all the time!"

A sharp whistle was heard in the background, and Luke held out his hand. "I've got to go back to the chart room. A batch of new aerial photographs are due in, and we've got to check the enemy lines."

They shook hands, and when Clement climbed into the ambulance, his eyes were misty. How strange it was to encounter Luke here in the wastes of 'no man's land'. They had never been close because of the difference in ages, but now that they were young men, the disparity did not seem so great.

When Luke returned to the chart room, his commanding officer looked up from the stack of photographs, and grinned. "Thinking about deserting us to play with that terrible band?"

"The leader, sir, is my brother."

"I thought he was a half-breed Indian." The old man puffed on a cigar. "He is," Luke said, not smiling, "but he's still my brother, sir."

With great alacrity, the major went back to shuffling photographs.

Luke sighed and stepped out in the courtyard. The sound of whining engines caused his gaze to wander skyward, where two planes, a DeHavilland and a Fokker, were engaged in a dog fight.

The pilot of the De Havilland, obviously an old pro, was probably an old barnstormer from the Midwest from the way that he maneuvered the craft. The other pilot, less adroit even with a superior engine, was headed off again and again. The dog fight turned into a game of cat and mouse, with the DeHavilland as the aggressor. Finally, the other pilot grew tired of the foreplay and turned his craft into the path of the DeHavilland, which opened fire. The game was over. The enemy plane circled quickly and headed swiftly for a cloud bank, puffs of smoke spurting out of the engine.

Luke's shouts of joy brought the major out of headquarters. "What's up?" he cried.

"Look, Major, look. Watch that Fokker go!"

Twenty kilometers away, Mitchell Heron climbed out of the foxhole and wiped the mud from his boots. Night was falling and the artillery fire had slacked off as the mist settled over the countryside. The sky was illuminated now and then by mortar explosions.

"Wher'ya off to?" Vern, his buddy, asked.

"Be back in a minute," Mitchell replied. "Going to take a leak." He crouched down and ran into a clutch of trees. The woods seemed to absorb the battle sounds, but his ears still ached from the continuous noise. After he answered the call of nature, he lay down on a log for a moment, protected by the tall pines. He was truly exhausted, and a moment later was snoring.

When he awakened it was dark and his body was chilled and stiff. Somewhere nearby an owl hooted eerily. Making a protective shield of his palms, he lit a match and looked at his watch. It was three o'clock in the morning! Coming out into the clearing, he saw the moon was full. Obviously, the company had moved out, lock, stock, and barrel. If he had slept through all of that commotion, he could sleep through anything.

He walked down the foul-smelling trench that he knew would lead eventually to the road that the troops would have taken. He stopped, then retraced his steps. To hell with the company! He had had enough war to last a lifetime. Paris was about thirty-five kilometers away. He had been taught how to avoid the Huns; certainly the same tactics would work hiding from the Americans. If he was careful—sleeping by day and traveling by night—he might reach Paris. If he was picked up, he could always say that he had become separated from his company and lost his bearings. It was worth a try—anything to get out of those trenches.

For the first time in months, Mitchell felt almost happy. He silently thanked Sam, who had taught him how to survive in the wilderness, as he examined the underbrush. Yes, there were the markings of a rabbit, a bit of blood near the place where his tail had rested. If he followed the trail though the underbrush . . .

Fontine Dice telephoned Letty. "You've got to see George."

"I see him every day."

"That's not what I mean," Fontine snapped. "I've just come back from Enid and I had to wait three hours at the refinery to get gasoline. People were lined up around the block. It's getting worse all the time. George has just got to open a filling station away from the refinery fumes."

"I'll see what I can do, Fontine," Letty replied, "as soon as George returns from California. Maybe when the Armistice is signed, we can expand a bit more. Most of our crude oil products have been exported."

"I know that, Letty, but it's time George paid some attention to his gasoline buyers here at home!"

Peace came to the world in November of 1918; the

first Heron two-pump filling up station opened on Broadway in Enid in February, 1919, and one month later, a smaller one-pump station opened in Angel on the same property that had once housed Edward Heron's cabinet shop. "Nothing like keeping it in the family," Rochelle Patterson remarked to Bella Chenovick, looking up at the famous blue heron logo.

"Well, why not?" the old woman replied tartly. "If it hadn't been for Letty Heron, there wouldn't be a town of Angel. Do you know, young lady, I was *here* when she named it!"

The Heron Oil Company bought the Armbuster Building in Washington as soon as Luke had taken off his captain's uniform for the last time. "I've redone the office next door for you, son," George said. "I want you to eventually be on the board of directors, but first I'll break you in as my assistant."

Luke, who stood an inch above George, chuckled. "Fine with me, but as I told you before, I want to spend a year or two out in the field, at the wells that are being spudded, at the refineries, and I'd also like to go on a couple of geological trips with Uncle Bos."

"Smelling prairie dog holes for tell-tale signs of gas?" George laughed.

"Why not? I've got to learn as much as I can, and with old Armbuster near retirement . . ."

"Mind your manners, Luke. Armbuster will always be a king as far as I'm concerned. You don't know what that man had to put up with all those years when we were building the company." He sighed. "Luke, we didn't know beans about what we were doing. If it hadn't been for Armbuster, we'd still be a small company selling a few barrels of oil out of Angel, and making a few extra dollars out of the Wildcat." He paused. "Always treat J. C. Armbuster with deference."

Three months later, Luke came back from a trip through the Midwest and marched into George's office. "I've got an idea, Dad," he said, excitement in his voice. "'A lot of the oil companies are redrilling their

310

old wells to get down to deeper sands. I'd like to bring in rotary drilling equipment into the Angel field. Some of the first wells are producing so little petroleum, we're going to be forced to close them down. Heron Number One has dried up."

George nodded. "It'll cost a great deal of money. What does Bosley say?"

"He agrees. Several years ago Harry Sinclair leased mineral rights on quite a few farms near Garber/Covington, and Frank Phillips is going to town in Bartlesville . . . J. Paul Getty has done the same thing. They're all bringing in wells right and left. Champlain has a new refinery in Enid. Everyone's making money."

But in eight weeks, Heron Number One was abandoned at 1,958 feet. Bosley scratched his head. "Luke, I think we should go on over to Dice Number Two, the old anticline may run deeper over there." When a rotary rig was set up, another strata of oil sand was discovered at 2,068 feet. The well was brought in at 4,000 barrels a day. "Not bad, Luke," Bosley crowed, "for a redrill!"

Soon Stevens Numbers One and Three and Chenovick Numbers Four and Five were brought in at various depths over 2000 feet. Luke shook his head. "I had a feeling, Uncle Bos . . ."

"Which paid off, I might add," he replied. "Our business is based on chance. A gut feeling is all some of the old timers had—it's invaluable. I'm pleased to see that you apparently have the same gift. You'll make a wildcatter yet!"

Luke flushed with pleasure. "It's peculiar, but look at the Three Sands field near Tonkawa, so named because oil has been found at three different depths." He paused. "I'm sorry now that I didn't take up geology in college, Uncle Bos."

Bosley laughed. "You've got a business brain, which I never had. You'll be running the company one day, Luke."

"Yes," he replied darkly, "and everyone will say that I've got the world by the tail, but underneath it all, I'll be scared to death . . ."

Bosley laughed. "I never knew a successful business-man yet who didn't pull off the really big deals by the seat of his pants."

Clement celebrated his return to civilian life by having dinner at Luchow's, which one of his Army buddies had said was a famous Chinese restaurant on Fourteenth Street in New York. Much to his surprise, the place turned out to feature German food! He paused in the doorway nearest Union Square and Broadway for a long moment before entering, the fetid smell of the trenches coming back to his nostrils; once more he was biting down on hard rations and hearing the terrible sounds of rifles and cannon and the cavalry charging, the Sergeant drawling: "Get that piano out of here, Breedy," the Huns bayonetted during the rise on the Marne, crying out. Gradually the sounds of the war quieted; he squared his shoulders and opened the door to the restaurant. The war was over. Why should he resent Germans owning the place, Germans who had established American citizenship a long time ago? He had fought a war so that there would be no more prejudice.

He was standing in the Gentlemen's Grill, obviously a male refuge, located next to the dining room. Seated in the dim place near the figure of Lohengrin, he suddenly felt comfortable ordering *Sauerbraten mit kartoffel Klosse*, which turned out to be a spiced pot roast with potato dumplings. He also asked for a bottle of Pommard Burgundy and a piece of coconut cream pie—which was almost as good as Aunt Priscilla's.

Looking down at his beautifully tailored gray serge suit, which he had bought in a small men's shop around the corner from the Sherry Netherland Hotel where he was staying, he did not care if he never saw another mufti uniform. In the elegant surroundings, among the very rich, he felt on top of the world.

After dinner, he took a cab back to the hotel and went up to his suite on the twelfth floor, where he opened his new suitcase, took out a bottle of the very best Kentucky bourbon, and got quietly drunk.

The next afternoon, his head still spinning from the

drinks of the night before, he walked unsteadily into the elevator; during the quick descent he almost became ill into the pink straw hat of the little lady standing in front of him. When the door of the elevator opened, he came face to face with a woman in a red veil, who looked at him in surprise. "Why hello, Breedy."

He stood back and blinked, his throat suddenly very tight. "How do you do?" he replied, wondering who she was. Then the night in the crowded hospital at Chateau Thierry came back, and for a moment he was seated at the portable piano and she was singing softly to a blind boy.

"Fancy you being in New York, Breedy. Have you been mustered out?"

"Yes, Miss Janis."

"My running into you like this, I suppose, in a way, is providence. My pianist is ill with the influenza, and I'm supposed to sing at Madame Elder's intimate salon tomorrow afternoon." She fluttered her rather large eyes. "Would you, perchance, be free to accompany me?"

"Why, yes . . ." he managed to stammer.

"When can we rehearse, then?" She handed him a card. "Here is my address. We only need to run through the songs once. I'm doing two of the numbers I did for the doughboys, but no encores."

The Holden Elder mansion, as it happened, was located only two blocks up Fifth Avenue from the Sherry Netherlands. The salon played host to a hundred and fifty of Manhattan's upper crust. The large living room would have accommodated another twenty-five guests without a potted palm being removed. Wherever Clement looked he saw a famous face, but strangely enough he was not at all nervous as his name was announced by the butler. He stood aside politely as Elsie Janis stood grandly on the threshold. After her name was announced, she took his arm and ushered him into the room as if he were a lap dog.

A tall, elegantly tailored man with a lean, ascetic face came forward and kissed her cheek. "May I pre-

313

sent our host—Holden Elder—Clement Story," she said. The men shook hands. "It's the strangest thing," she continued, "but this boy served as a pianist for me a year or so ago in France when I was entertaining in the Allied hospitals, and I just ran into him again yesterday. He's marvelous, Holden."

At the mention of his name, a woman in a large silver pompadour, who had been talking to a small group of people nearby, turned and appraised the boy, a smile firmly planted on her face. Leona Barrett Elder stepped forward and held out her hand. "Welcome to my home," she said. "Perhaps after you play for Miss Janis, you will honor us with a solo."

Leona sat in the back of the room and listened to Elsie Janis, but her eyes kept returning to the boy at the piano, whose hands flew over the keyboard with controlled fervor. She had not seen him since he was five years old, riding with his mother into Angel. He was not very good-looking—he had not inherited his father's fine bone structure nor his mother's fair complexion. He must be a throwback to his dark and swarthy forebears. Yet there was a certain elegance and grace about him that was very impressive, and his personality was very outgoing. However, the real surprise came when he played "Sheep May Safely Graze" in classical style, then, very slowly, began to ornament the passages with outrageous grace notes until he was rendering a full-fledged jazz version of the piece. The delighted gathering laughed and applauded loudly and Elsie Janis, wise enough to know the afternoon belonged to Clement and not her, held up her hands for silence. "I want all of you to know that this young man is my discovery. I found him, in the war zone in France, and he accompanied me on a tour of the hospitals." She turned to Clement. "Please honor us with an encore!" There was a fresh burst of applause, and he began a deceptively gentle version of "When You and I were Young, Maggie," which turned into a robust cacophony of jazz. After he acknowledged the applause, the group would not let him go and Clement then launched into "Tiger Rag," the rage at the moment.

The skin on the back of Leona's shoulders tingled, and she felt a wave of nostalgia engulf her: it was as if, having lain dormant for years, she was suddenly infused with new life. This boy with a talent that shone out of every pore had rekindled her ability to feel. It was like the old days when she stood at the bottom of the stairs at The Widows and surveyed her territory—Reginald Savor holding the winning hand in the dining room; Steele, the driller, losing money hand over fist in the kitchen; and Liza taking a bath in the Japanned plunge in preparation for the next customer. For a long moment, she longed for those days when she had to be ready at a moment's notice to step in to prevent a catastrophe. Then she looked around at the elegant room and the guests and her husband, and she was glad to be in New York.

She noticed Lester Mainwaring, the hotel magnate, sitting uncomfortably on the Louis XIV sofa with his fat wife, Elaine. For once the old man was not observing his manicure, examining his boots, or picking lint from his superbly cut trousers, but was staring intently at the absorbed pianist.

At last Clement stood up, but the applause continued. Finally, his face suddenly very grave, he announced. "One more number, then I must leave. I will play and sing for you a song dedicated to my home state of Oklahoma." He hit one note, then began to sing very softly a cappella:

> *"Come along, boys, and listen to my*
> *tale.*
> *I'll tell you of my troubles on the*
> *old Chisholm Trail.*
> *Coma ti yi youpy, youpa ya,*
> *Youpa ya,*
> *Coma ti yi youpy, youpy, ya . . ."*

Leona turned her face to the wall, moved by the words to the plaintive old cowboy tune:

> *"I woke up one morning on the old*
> *   Chisholm Trail,*
> *Rope in my hand and a cow by the*
> *   tail.*
> *I'm up in the mornin' afore daylight*
> *And afore I sleep, the moon shines*
> *   bright.*
> *It's cloudy in the West, a-looking*
> *   like rain,*
> *And my damned old slicker's in the*
> *   wagon again.*
> *Crippled my hoss, I don't know*
> *   how,*
> *Ropin' at horns of the 2-U cow . . ."*

Leona got up very quietly before the tears started
and slipped into the powder room in the hall, where
she splashed cold water on her face and repaired the
makeup. She calmly rejoined the gathering who were not
aware that she had left the room. Dry-eyed, she listened
to the rest of the song:

> *"I won't punch cattle for no damned*
> *   man.*
> *Goin' back to town to draw my*
> *   money,*
> *Goin' back home to see my*
> *   honey,*
> *With my knees in the saddle and*
> *   my seat in the sky,*
> *I'll quit punching cows in the*
> *   sweet by and by.*
> > *Coma ti yi youpy, youpy ya,*
> > *   youpy ya,*
> > *Coma ti yi youpy, youpy ya . . ."*

Fresh applause rippled over the salon; Clement
bowed once and left the piano. Many from the audience
gathered around Clement, who was filled with a kind of
touching dignity. Leona was pleased to note that although the boy was enthusiastic and gracious, he was
not at all condescending. She waited until most of the

crowd had left before going up to congratulate the boy, who held Lester Mainwaring's card in his hand. "You were a very big success," Leona said. "I believe theater people would call it a 'smash'."

"Thank you, Mrs. Elder," he replied, his face flushed. "I'll be going back home with very good news. Because of this afternoon, Mr. Mainwaring has asked me to form an orchestra made up of men of Cherokee descent. If we're good enough, he's promised us a long booking at the Wyandotte Hotel in Kansas City." He shook his head. "I can't believe it, I just can't believe it! I didn't think that things like this could happen."

Leona laughed, but she was very moved. "As you grow older, young man, you'll discover that the most surprising events occur at the strangest times." She patted her silver pompadour, thinking about that extraordinary morning when Mary Darth had shown her a fistfull of bills and she had known that life would never quite be the same again at The Widows. "A bridge has been crossed today, Clement," she said, inadvertently using his first name. "Thank you so much, Mrs. Elder," he said fervently. "While Miss Janis may say that she 'discovered' me, it was *you* who gave me the opportunity. I'll never forget that."

No, Leona thought, nor will any of your family! She was tempted to tell him about their relationship, then thought better of it. No, there would be no point in recounting a tale that would no doubt sound like the fabrications of a half-senile Fifth Avenue dowager. Some stories, she decided, should remain untold.

That night after dinner, she went upstairs to her bedroom and placed a person-to-person call to Letty. It was the first time she had spoken to her in fifteen years. "This is Leona Barrett Elder," she said clearly into the mouthpiece.

Letty replaced the receiver in the cradle, and turned to George, who was removing his tie in the dressing room. "You'll never in the world guess who that was on the telephone just now," she called. "Leona Barrett!"

"Does she want to sell her stock? We have the first option, you know."

"Nothing like that. She's just met Clement!"

"*Clement?* Where on earth . . ."

"He came to her house to entertain and apparently got a job out of it . . ." Letty shook her head. "Do you suppose she's taken up drinking?"

"Possibly. I do know that she married a very wealthy industrialist."

"Anyway, she doesn't want Clement to know who she is."

"That's not surprising, my dear. And all of that happened so long ago."

Letty sighed. "You're right, of course. But, just to be on the safe side, I think we should keep this completely under our hats. If Prissy knew . . ."

George laughed and brushed the gray hair back from his temples. "She'd be the first to spread the tale that Leona was entertaining Clement, and you know what people would think!"

"One hundred and twenty-five million gallons of gasoline will arrive in Los Angeles within the next ten days," the newspaper proclaimed. George Story chuckled and turned to Letty. "About two hundred thousand gallons of that is Heron gas, all the way from one of our refineries in Texas! That should make a story in the *Petroleum Record*. With so many automobiles in Southern California, this gas shortage has been very acute."

Letty nodded. "Better get dressed for dinner. Luke is bringing a date." She paused. "I wonder what she'll be like?"

He took Letty in his arms. "Like you, I imagine, soft and pretty and . . ."

"Oh, George!" she cried, holding him close. "You say the nicest things!" He kissed her on the lips and she drew back. "Now, dear, we haven't time—the children will be here momentarily . . ."

"They can wait. Luke will probably want a glass of sherry, and she may even want a cocktail!"

Letty sighed. "I still can't get used to serving spirits in my home."

He laughed. "When the Volstead Act goes into effect, there will not be a 'spirit' anywhere—except the Holy One." He kissed her again, then went into the bathroom; when he returned, he was naked. She looked at him and smiled. "How bold you are, sir!"

"Let me undress you, lady. You're very beautiful."

She was thankful that she had kept her body young. There was not an ounce of extra flesh, and her breasts were still firm. She was not like Fontine Dice, she reflected, who had gained at least ten pounds, but John still only had eyes for his wife and called her honey, even in public!

Letty lay down on the cool sheets. It was summer, and a cool, fragrant breeze blew in over the lawn through the upstairs windows. George lay beside her, his warm body touching her side. She moved toward him and they started the familiar ritual. They both relaxed, and the extensive foreplay turned into passionate response. Outside, they heard Luke's Packard in the driveway, but the tender tentacles of feeling were upon them now, and the climax came in a rush.

Downstairs, Luke poured a glass of rum. "Here, Jeanette," he called, "come and get it."

She turned and took the glass. She was very beautiful, he thought, with her black hair drawn up over the top of her head in a gentle swell that complemented her long, graceful neck. She looked rather like a drawing of a European woman, and he thought briefly of Lisette, whom she resembled so much. He wondered whatever became of her. Was she still at the *estaminet* at Chateau Thierry? He shook the thought away and looked into Jeanette's deep green eyes.

They had met at a party in the National Hotel, introduced by J. C. Armbuster, of all people. The old man had tottered up with her on his arm and said, "Luke, please dance with her. I don't understand these new steps." Luke and the girl had looked at each other and they both knew that she would accompany him back to his apartment after the dance.

She had obviously had affairs before, because there was a touch of the liberated woman about her. Girls looked differently at sexual affairs since the war, and he was flattered that she found him attractive. She had even complimented him on his asparagus!

At that moment his mother and father came down the stairs, arm in arm. His mother's eyes were suspiciously bright and his father's handshake not as firm as usual. There was the certain aura about them that could only mean one thing—they had just been to bed. He smiled to himself. So they were still doing it after all these years!

He smiled and said, "I'd like you to meet my fiancee, Jeanette Landau."

Luke and Jeanette had not planned to marry until June of 1922, but after a session with the doctor, Luke visited his mother and asked that it be a Christmas wedding. Letty glanced at him out of the corner of her eyes, but his look was pure innocence. That was one thing that she did not like about her son. He was not always completely honest—not that she expected him to confide in her, because he had always been standoffish in that regard—but she felt it odd that he did not even mention Jeanette, and she was very nettled when she telephoned Priscilla in Dallas and told her the news. "Well," replied her former sister-in-law, "if they want to hurry it up, it only means one thing."

"What do you mean, Prissy?"

"Well you know the old saying, my dear, 'The first baby can be born any time after the ceremony, but the second child always takes nine months'!"

Clement and his Cherokee Braves Dance Band traveled down from Philadelphia to play for the wedding, which was held in the ballroom of the Connecticut Avenue house, decorated incongruously with red poinsettias. "Well," lamented Letty to George, "It *is* holiday time, and furthermore, trying to get gladiolus or chrysanthemums this time of year is impossible. I didn't *ask* them to tie the knot with Santa Claus looking over his shoulder!"

Edward and Priscilla arrived in a rented limousine. Priscilla shook out her sables and flashed a huge new

320

diamond bracelet. "Every time Edward opens a new store, he buys me a bauble."

Letty laughed. "George, did you hear that? If I had a jewel for every filling station we've opened lately, I couldn't raise my hands!"

George excused himself for a moment, then returned with a square velvet box. "I think the timing is right," he said.

Letty's eyes shone as she opened the box. The Heron logo had been fashioned into a broach with an outline of tiny aquamarine chips, the bird itself set in fiery diamonds. She gasped, "Why, George, I've never seen anything so—so grand." And she kissed his cheek.

Priscilla glanced at the brooch. "It is rather nice, my dear," she said with raised eyebrows, "but, really, wearing the company insignia is like an advertisement for Heron Oil!"

"So what's wrong with that, Prissy?" Letty replied with a crooked smile. "I happen to be very proud of our organization, just as you must be very proud of Edward. The name of Heron means something!"

Priscilla shrugged her shoulders. "I'm rather tired of it myself," she retorted. "Every time you go out anywhere, all you see is that damned flying bird!"

26

High Times

Secretary of Commerce Herbert Clark Hoover looked very uncomfortable standing beside the fireplace, a glass of lemonade in hand.

Letty wasn't quite sure whether he looked so depressed because of the drink or his companion, who was Henry Ford. Having only taken his oath of office as Secretary of Commerce a few months before, he obviously was impressed with the man at his side. He nodded intently again and again.

Lou Hoover took Letty's arm. "I am so pleased that you and George could come tonight," she said warmly, "especially since it was a last-minute invitation."

Letty smiled. "We are very honored. You have a lovely home, Lou."

She laughed. "You don't know how nice it is to be settled. You know, we've lived all over the world. In our twenty-two years of marriage, I've set up housekeeping in England, where we lived the longest, China, Central America, Italy and Australia. For a girl from California, that's quite something! We still keep our old home at Palo Alto." She saw her husband move away from Henry Ford. "Would you bring George into the library?" she murmured. "Mr. Hoover cautioned me not to let him leave before they had a private word. The time is right, just before we go into dinner."

Letty singled out George in the crowd. "*He* wants to see you in the library," she whispered excitedly.

"I wish you could come with me." George frowned.

322

"I know him only slightly. I've got to feel him out on this exporting of oil without him knowing about it!"

"Good luck. Remember, he's a self-made man. You'll get along."

Five minute later, the men stood before the roaring fire in the library, and Herbert Hoover, who almost never smiled, was smiling now. "I'm glad that we could be together," he said with an Iowa twang. "I want you to know that I've always admired your background."

"That's very kind of you, sir," George replied modestly, "but I hope I'm more successful with the Heron Oil Company interests than I was with Indian affairs. I'm afraid I failed miserably in furthering the cause of my people. I don't have much influence any more."

"Neither do I. After all, Lou and I lived eighteen years abroad and when President Harding began asking my views prior to my appointment to his cabinet, there were those here in Washington who confused me with the other Herbert Hoover—the one who makes vacuum cleaners!" He chuckled; although he was becoming less austere and was obvious trying to be friendly, George had difficulty trying to warm up to his rather odd personality. "Bureaucracy—that's what we've both had to fight," Hoover said. "When I get to know you better, I'll tell you about some of *my* battles!" He paused, then went on slowly. "My work is cut out for me now. I want to expand foreign trade. What are your thoughts?"

"Well, sir," George replied, a bit taken aback, having expected to gently lead up to the subject. "Of course, we want to expand Heron's operations, but we have much more work to be done."

Hoover nodded. "That's what I'm told by other oil companies. But in the next ten or twenty years, I see the United States firmly entrenched in foreign oil production. Henry Ford sees his automobiles all over the world. There's a great deal of petroleum in South America and the Middle East. Those countries will need men with great foresight and engineering genius. New techniques must be developed—along the lines of your Wildcat bit. Any other ideas up your sleeve?"

George flushed. "Not really."

"Another thing I want to stress—there is entirely too

much waste in the manufacturing and distribution of products, and I'm afraid the petroleum industry is no exception."

"I agree wholeheartedly, sir." George replied with conviction. "And we're all guilty. When I think of the folly of placing hundreds of wells twelve feet apart to drain one small underground pool of oil that could be recoved by a half dozen, I get a very clammy feeling. Yet we all did that sort of thing in the beginning."

Hoover nodded. "Another thing, I don't think the cracking of crude oil in the refineries has produced nearly as many by-products as possible. We need more chemists. I believe that hundreds of products can be refined from crude besides gasoline, naphthas, asphalt, illuminating fuels, and jellies."

"Exactly," George said excitedly, "and the research arm of Heron is looking into all these possibilities."

"Will you keep me personally informed? Feel free to telephone me. I want to keep in touch with all men of industry." He squinted up at him. "You see, Mr. Story, I don't want legislation enacted to compel manufacturers to adhere to certain standards—that would be cumbersome and probably wouldn't work, in my estimation. I believe that standardization must be achieved through willing cooperation, not government force!"

"Again, I agree. You have my word that the Heron interests will stand behind you one hundred per cent."

Hoover laughed for the first time. "I knew we would get along, even though you *are* a Democrat! Lawyers and engineers who have come up the hard way often see problems in the same light."

The door opened and Lou Hoover came into the room. "Excuse me, gentlemen, but cook tells me that if we delay dinner much longer, the spinach soufflé will be as flat as a pancake."

"Good!" Herbert Hoover said with a grimace. "I'm not terribly fond of spinach anyway!"

"Neither am I," George Story said *sotto voce*, and received a knowing look in return.

Over the dessert, a *blancmange,* Letty looked down the long table of twenty-six guests, twelve on each side, with the host and hostess at the ends. As her gaze swept over the group, her eye came to rest on a svelte blonde bobbed head that was vaguely familiar. The woman turned away from her companion for a moment and their eyes met, then the woman looked quickly away.

Letty took a sip of coffee. That delicately sculptured face! She seemed to see those large eyes and that wistful expression under a hat. How very strange, she thought. Then time flew backward almost thirty years and the past came back with a rush. She could see the woman clearly now, prim black hat set securely on a blonde pompadour. The woman was standing beside a mound of deep red earth and Reverend Haskell was leading the group in the Lord's Prayer. She was certain that this very chic, middle-aged lady was Mary Darth!

After dinner, when the men had gone into the library for cigars and the ladies had retired to the drawing room, Letty took her hostess aside. "Lou, who is that attractive lady by the sideboard?"

"That's Judge Savor's wife. He's just been appointed to the Supreme Court."

"Could her first name be . . . Mary?"

"Why, yes. Why?"

Letty smiled softly. "I think I used to know her!"

"Really? Well, she's a dear. I've known them since he was a senator. She's very active in aiding crippled children, besides heading many committees here in Washington. I always say, if you want something done, appoint Mary Savor. Would you like to say hello to her?"

Letty turned away. "On second thought, Lou, I may have confused her with someone else."

"Well, at any rate, you two will be traveling in many of the same circles." Before Letty could protest, she was being guided to the sideboard. "Mrs. Reginald Savor," Lou Hoover said, "I'd like you to meet Mrs. George Story."

"I am so pleased about your husband's appointment," Letty said graciously.

"Thank you. I've been admiring your necklace. It glittered all during dinner. Isn't Lou a marvelous hostess, Mrs. Story?"

"Yes," Letty replied, peering at her again. The

woman was unmistakably Mary Darth! It was not possible that Mary did not remember her, although they had never been close and seen each other only during the very early years in the Territory. It might be, she reflected, that Mary was unfamiliar with the name Story. She debated whether to reveal her identity. She looked around the room at the cabinet members and their wives and the senators and thought, why bring back memories that were perhaps best forgotten? "Yes," Letty found herself saying, "It is a lovely party."

That evening on the way home to Georgetown, Mary held her husband's hand in the back of the limousine. "I had a bad scare tonight, Reggie."

"What bit of gossip is being passed back and forth?" he replied humorously.

"No, nothing like that, but I did meet George Story's wife and I swear she used to be Letty Heron, but I didn't get a chance to ask Lou Hoover."

"I hardly think . . ." He snapped his fingers. "Say, George Story is a mixed blood Cherokee Indian from Oklahoma." He turned to her. "You may very well be right, my dear, he could have married her!"

Mary looked stricken. "My God, Reggie, what if it ever got out that I . . ." She paused and began to cry. "I told you years ago that some day my past would catch up with me."

"No, don't worry," he replied gently. "We've been married for twenty-three years. Even Letty Heron could not prove that you were the Mary Darth of The Widows. You were a mere child then. All of that has been behind us all this time."

"Yes," Mary said quietly, "up until now. Oh, my God, what are we going to do if rumors start all over Washington?"

"I doubt that it will happen," he said casually, but his heart was beating furiously. To have come this far, to be appointed to the highest court in the land . . . Would it be for nothing?

On the morning of April 9, 1922, George was summoned to the telephone by Hans, the new butler. "It's Senator John B. Kenrick of Wyoming."

"Yes, Senator, what can I do for you?" George asked. He had only met the man once or twice in the corridors of the Capitol Building and barely knew him by sight.

"I'm calling a few key people, Mr. Story," came the cordial, off-the-cuff reply. George had been around long enough to recognize the tone. The senator wanted something, and he wanted it very badly. "You know that the navy has been in control of the Teapot Dome oil lands in my state for some time?"

"Yes," George replied, "that's common knowledge."

"Has anyone ever approached Heron Oil Company to lease this land?"

George was taken aback. "No, sir, not to my knowledge."

"Good." There was a pause. "Do you know Harry F. Sinclair?"

"Yes. He used to be a druggist from Kansas. He took over leases next to some of ours near Garber, Oklahoma."

"Do you know Edward L. Doheny?"

"Casually. I met him once, I think, in Los Angeles."

"Have you ever had any dealings with Doheny?"

"No."

"Good." He hung up, leaving George looking at the receiver in his hand. He quickly dialed a number. "Is Luke in?" he asked his secretary, and a moment later he was on the line. "What's up, Dad?"

"Has anyone contacted us about taking over any of the Teapot Dome land in Wyoming?" he demanded.

"Hold on, Dad, what is this? You sound . . ."

"Never mind how I sound. *Have they?*"

"No."

"Thank God." He sighed with relief. "Keep this under your hat, my boy, but there's going to be a scandal the size of which will shake every oil company in this country." He went on, excitement raising his voice an octave. "Sinclair has just leased some of the Teapot Dome acreage."

"But, that's navy land, Dad!"

"It was, but the Secretary of the Navy has turned it over to the Department of Interior, headed by Albert B.

327

Fall. Also some of the old navy land in California has been leased to Edward Doheny."

"How do you know all of this, Dad?"

George chuckled. "I just received a call from Senator Kenrick."

"He told you?"

"Yes and no. He gave me all the clues. He was checking to see if Heron had any interests in Wyoming." George paused. "I have a feeling Kenrick is going to blow the whistle on Albert Fall. Thank God we're not mixed up in this thing." His voice grew urgent. "Always tell me about everything, or write a report. Never agree to anything verbally before consulting the board of directors. Understand?"

"Yes, sir."

"When the whole Teapot Dome story is revealed, mark my words, son, heads will fall!"

And heads did fall. E. Denby, Secretary of the Navy, was forced to resign. When the Attorney General, Harry M. Daugherty, also implicated in the scandal, declined to turn over his files, President Coolidge asked for his resignation. Though Fall, Doheny and Daughtery escaped prosecution due to legal loopholes, the scandal reverberated through the business community, and large corporations began to look more carefully into government ties.

Edward Heron finished his speech at the annual employees' picnic held at the huge Dallas Park, then handed the megaphone to Manford Pederson, who cracked a very bad joke, to end the formalized program. A large group of revelers, nine hundred strong, including husbands and wives and children, lined up at twelve-foot-long tables where chefs in tall white hats served thick slices of barbecued beef and pork. The crowd helped themselves to hot baked beans, and eighteen different kinds of salads.

Edward and Priscilla left the band stand where the ceremonies had taken place and lined up at the buffet. He took a plate, then served himself a large helping of mustard potato salad while Priscilla clicked her tongue. "You're supposed to be slimming down," she reminded

328

him with a sigh, "and besides, those potatoes look green."

He laughed. "It's the mustard."

She picked at the Waldorf salad, and finally placed her plate in a disposal can. "I can't eat a thing." Her eyes swept over the huge gathering scattered over the lawn and under the trees. The hubbub of voices rose in the air like so many chickens in a barnyard. Several infants were crying, and children were running about playing tag, while a group of men shared a flask behind a catering truck. It was like all of the other Heron 'family' picnics held over the years—too bucolic, too reminiscent of certain times gone by that she would just as soon forget. She glanced at her watch and turned to Edward, "If you're going to get to the depot on time, we'd better hurry. That interview with the newspaper in Tulsa is important." She caught Manford Pederson's eye and nodded faintly. Edward finished the potato salad, took her arm, and they made their way to the Packard limousine.

Edward arrived at the railway station forty-five minutes early, bought a copy of *The Saturday Evening Post,* and had just sat down in the waiting room when he suddenly became violently ill. He ran to the men's room and vomited twice, then, felling better, resumed his seat. He was about to board the train when he became ill again and returned to the men's room. He looked in the mirror. The face that stared back at him was barely recognizable. He knew that he had aged over the last several years; his head was tinged with gray, but his complexion was yellow-white. To hell with the press interview. Very slowly, as if in a daze, he went out to the street and gave his address to the taxicab driver, then leaned back against the seat, trying to stop his hands from shaking.

Priscilla lay back on the bedspread, looking as seductive as she knew how. She had drawn the blinds so that the late afternoon sun would send a soft glow over the room and soften her features. She turned on her side so that her breasts would look more voluptuous, and tried to assume a provocative pose. A little shiver of desire ran over her body as she heard Manford's automobile pull into the driveway.

By the time that he reached her bedroom, he had removed his coat, shirt and tie, which he flung on a chair. He quickly took off the rest of his clothing and climbed beside her on the bed. "I've waited so long," he murmured, taking her quickly into his arms. "Did Edward make love to you this morning?" he asked, his eyes glazed with want.

She smiled slowly. "Yes, he was very passionate, as always."

"Tell me all the details." He was breathing heavily.

"Well," she said, "just before we went to the picnic, he was dressing and I just came in from having a tub . . ."

"Yes?"

"He took me in his arms, and pressed my body up against the dressing table, and I could feel him . . ."

Edward came up the curved staircase, colors dancing before his eyes. He would ask Priscilla to call Doctor Abramson. At the top of the stairs, he paused for breath and held the balustrade for support. He was afraid that he was going to retch again. He gathered his strength and with a palsied hand, opened the door to Priscilla's room. The scene before him swirled in a pink mist. He tried to call out her name, but his throat was parched and his mouth dry. Gradually, the room became clearer. It was then that he saw the moving figures on the bedspread. The last thing he saw before falling forward into oblivion was the stricken look on Manford's face as he glanced over his shoulder.

EDWARD HERON,
DALLAS FURNITURE MANUFACTURER
POISONED

Edward Heron, 54, president of the Heron Furniture Company, died this morning of food poisoning from potato salad consumed yesterday at an employee picnic. Heron was among two hundred taken ill at the annual affair, all but twelve of whom were released after treatment at a local hospital.

Pathologists worked most of the night trying to discover the source of the Salmonella bacteria, usually found in spoiled food. The culprit was discovered to be a mustard potato salad, which apparently had been left out of the refrigerator at the Bostic Catering Company.

Services are pending for the socially prominent manufacturer, who moved his family to Texas from Oklahoma twelve years ago.

The funeral was held at the First Baptist Church in Dallas on November 16, 1925. George, Letty, Luke, Jeanette, and two-year-old Luke III sat in the back of the first pew, directly behind Priscilla and the children. The service was unmercifully long and drawn out. The minister, a tall, reedy man with an unctuous voice, spoke more about the "brave widow" than he did about the deceased.

Priscilla had flatly refused to have the funeral at Angel. "I never did like Reverend Haskell," she had proclaimed, strangely dry-eyed. "The children can accompany the body back to Angel if they want to. I have no intention of ever going back."

Manford had stood beside her. "You belong here, Prissy," he had agreed, avoiding George's eyes.

Letty had remained silent. She had long ago given up trying to reason with Priscilla. They had known each other for fifty years, yet they were almost like strangers now. "Thank God, George, for Manford." Letty said after the funeral. "Prissy so needs someone to look after her, and with Edward gone . . ."

George opened his mouth to reply, then took her hand instead.

Four days later, Edward Heron was buried beside little Betsy in the family plot in Angel, with Reverend Haskell reading a brief eulogy. A large group of townspeople made the short journey to God's Acre to pay their last respects. But the only real mourner was Bosley Trenton, who stood back from the gravesite sheltered by a giant maple tree and very softly cried into his handkerchief.

* * *

331

Manford Pederson sat on the brocade sofa in Priscilla's huge living room, lighted a cigar, and looked at her obliquely. "You've taken Edward's death so calmly," he said. "It's not natural."

"Fiddlesticks!" Priscilla replied. "I've never believed in putting on public displays. It's not in good taste for one thing." Then afraid that she was giving herself away, she went on in a softer tone, "I miss him so much—especially at night . . ." She perceived a glint in Manford's eye and smiled to herself. "But now that I'm free . . ."

Ignoring this remark, he looked at her directly. "I have several points of business that I'd like to discuss today. We are losing a great many potential clients."

"I don't understand."

"It takes a long time to manufacture furniture, even with the modern equipment I've managed to install. Every piece has six hand-rubbed coats of stain and varnish—"

"Yes, yes," she said irritably, "but how does this affect management?"

"Well," he continued intently, "it takes such a long time to bring a piece out of the factory, and we have to charge so much . . ."

She sighed impatiently. "I don't know what you're trying to say, Manford."

"I would like to retain our high-quality line, to skim the cream off the crop, but I think it would be prudent to feature a new line of more reasonably priced furniture that the middle classes could afford. The profit would be enormous."

Priscilla patted her short hair, dyed a dark brown, and glanced out the window over the lawn. "How much do you think profits would increase?"

"The sky's the limit. Offhand, I should say anywhere from forty to sixty per cent."

Her eyes flew open. "That much?"

He smiled. "Perhaps a great deal more if we go public. After all, money attracts money. We'd need a lot of new financing to open up several manufacturing plants, necessary if we sell to large chains."

Her eyes narrowed. "You mean, list on the stock exchange?" She paused. "Edward was always so careful, I don't know . . ."

He got up quietly and threw his half-smoked cigar into the fireplace. "It all depends," he replied casually, "on where the company is going. Lots of manufacturers are becoming millionaires . . ."

Priscilla's eyes glittered, and she laughed, showing all of her teeth. "It would be nice to be very rich." She paused. "Are Letty and George millionaires?"

He looked at her with quiet amusement. "I shouldn't think so, at least not personally. Their holdings must be enormous; I suppose if they liquidated everything . . ."

"If we sold all the stores and the plant, how much would I have?"

He shrugged his shoulders. "Possibly seven hundred and fifty thousand."

"That's not a million, is it?"

"No." He paused. "We don't have much inventory, Prissy, we're still small."

"But, if we did go into cheap furniture . . ."

"Not *cheap*—reasonable. But stores all over the country would buy our line. See, the selling point is the Heron name. It's become rather famous, you know."

She laughed hollowly. "Yes, that damned bird! You know it's always stuck in my craw that Letty kept Luke's name, particularly after marrying that Indian!"

"It was perfectly legitimate. After all, Bosley discovered the oil years before she met George."

"I'm sure Luke has been spinning in his grave." She paused, and went to the window. The lawn, she noticed, needed reseeding. It was brown as the prairie that surrounded Angel. She grimaced. When she turned, there was new purpose in her voice. "Manford, let's go public. As you said, 'money attracts money'." She paused. "And besides, I think it's time to cash in on the Heron family name."

He laughed out loud. "That's what I was hoping you would say. We can really fly now!"

"Speaking of flying . . ." She came up very close to him and put her arms around his neck, but he drew back slightly.

He looked down at her, and she was amused to see

333

that the look in his eyes was not of passion, but of greed. But she would change his expression as soon as they were in the bedroom, because she knew exactly how to excite him . . .

He kissed her lightly on the forehead. "Today is a big day," he said, "and I must be getting to the office. There is much to do."

She placed her arms tightly around his waist. "Indeed?" She put her head against his broad shoulders. "But surely we have time . . ."

"I've got to make some telephone calls to New York," he interrupted, "and with the time difference . . ."

"If we go public," she asked sweetly, "the new corporation will need a president, right?"

"Of course."

"And, you are the logical candidate, right?"

"Well . . . yes."

"And you *want* to be president, right?"

"Well . . . yes."

"Then," she said, her voice a soft purr, "I think we should go up to bed."

Very meekly, he followed her up the staircase, suddenly feeling all of his fifty-seven years.

27

The Hottentot

*Clement looked over the bandstand at the huge
crowd of tea dancers at the Balmoral Hotel in St. Louis.*
He was weary. Over the top of the piano, he raised
his right hand and made a gesture; the band neatly
segued from the jazz tune into his signature, "Lady
Luck." They had played for a wedding reception earlier
and the men were tired. One more set and they could
rest. He sauntered to the tiny dressing room, which also
served as an office, and poured himself a cup of cold
coffee. A moment later, he answered the small tap on
the door. A young woman with red bobbed hair and
great green eyes stood on the threshold.

"May I help you?" he asked, suspecting that she
wanted an autograph.

"I think it's dreadful what you are doing!" she exclaimed, her head quivering with indignation.

He smiled slowly. "Most people like my music."

Her eyes blinked. "I'm not referring to your *music*,"
she cried, "I mean the way that you're exploiting your
heritage! I think it's distusting."

"I'm sorry, ma'am," he replied indulgently, "but I
don't know what you're talking about."

"Your *Cherokee* heritage, what else?

"Oh, you mean the band!" He held up his hand.
"Now, every member has Cherokee blood. There's not
even a trace of Black Foot or Navajo!" He looked at
her with amusement. "Do you want an affidavit as to
our authenticity?"

"Don't make fun of me," she replied angrily. "Capitalizing on the fact that all of you have Cherokee blood is what's so awful. Where is the dignity . . ."

He glared at her. "Are you, perchance, part Cherokee?"

"One quarter."

"Ah hah," he replied hotly, "I'm beginning to see the light!" He paused. "Now, just what is your problem?"

"I have no problem!" she shouted.

"Then why are you carrying on?"

"I am *not* carrying on! But you are advertising the fact that you're Indian."

"I'm very proud of my background."

"Then why do you persist in demeaning it!" She went on contemptuously. "Clement and his Cherokee Braves Jazz Band! Cheap and unworthy . . ."

"I really don't know what you mean," he replied testily, "I'm letting the American people know that we Indians are just as creative as . . ."

"Who said we *weren't* in the first place? You've raised a question and answered it at the same time! It's a wonder you don't have the band members dressed in feathered headdresses . . ."

"Well," he replied, "we did think about it, but frankly we don't have the money to hire a wardrobe mistress to polish the beads and oil the feathers!"

"Oh, you're impossible!"

He shook his head. "I really can't be angry, because you're too beautiful for one thing. What's your name?"

She had quieted down somewhat, obviously not expecting him to be interested in her as a person. "Sarah Morton."

"You mean you don't even have an Indian name?"

She blushed. "That has nothing to do with it! Sarah is a perfectly good . . ."

". . . old biblical name," he finished for her.

"My father was a missionary," she said, somewhat deflated, "but my mother taught me the Cherokee syllabary."

"So you could read the Bible in our language? I also learned the syllabary."

She looked at him in amazement. "You can read Cherokee, too?"

"Of course," he replied calmly, "and the portions of the Bible that I've read haven't been translated all that well. I prefer the King James version."

She glanced at him out of the corner of her eye, obviously in a quandary whether to believe him or not. "Are you pulling my leg?"

He smiled. "Indeed not! Now, I'm sorry if you think that I am holding our people up to ridicule, but nothing could be further from the truth. As a matter of fact, the Cherokees that I've spoken with think that the idea of a native jazz band is calling attention to our cause."

She shook her head. "I don't know. If John Ross, Redbird Smith, or George Story were still around . . ."

"George Story is still very much around," he replied quietly. "He's my father."

She looked at him in amazement. "George Story is your *father* and he approves of what you're doing?"

"Of course."

"I'd like very much to hear it from his own lips."

"You can't—at the moment, he's in Washington."

She sat down on a small stool shaking her head from side to side. "I can't believe that the Cherokee people like their tribal name plastered over bandstands." She got up stiffly. "I can see that I won't get anywhere *here*." She avoided his eyes. "I shouldn't even have bothered to come. Now, if you were giving classical concerts in a big hall . . ."

"I went through all of that when I was a boy in Oklahoma. I only decided to go to popular during the war when I formed a doughboy band. Now I sometimes play the classics at home, but I like modern music much better . . ."

"I give up!" she exclaimed and turned toward the door.

"Miss Morton?"

"Yes?" She still would not look at him.

"If you're free tonight, I would very much like you to have supper with me."

She turned her head and threw him an amused glance. "You mean dinner?"

He laughed out loud. "No, in this case, I mean sup-

337

per. I have to play for dancing after dinner. Are you staying in the hotel?"

"Yes."

"Then may I call for you at ten-thirty?"

She frowned. "Frankly, I don't know whether I should or not."

"Let me prove myself. If you're willing, perhaps we might go on to a speakeasy later—unless you don't approve of 'fire water'!"

"I told you I was the daughter of a missionary."

"Well, fire water or no fire water, will you let me take you out?"

"I'll have supper with you," she replied reluctantly, "but I won't stay out until all hours." .

He grinned. "That's really swell of you. I promise I'll have you home by midnight."

Suddenly she smiled endearingly, and Clement was reminded of his mother.

"I'll eat with you tonight," she said soberly, "but that doesn't mean that I approve of either you or what you're doing to our cause."

It was on the tip on his tongue to say: Then why are you going out with me? But he knew that she was propelled by a greater force than she knew, and he was filled with excitement.

Sarah Morton was the first girl with whom he had felt even a twinge of what Uncle Bos referred to as "passion."

London had changed very little since 1914, Letty thought as she gazed out the window of the wagon-lit. Of course there were automobiles everywhere, and fashions were a bit more daring than in Washington, but otherwise, the atmosphere was the same. She sighed and looked at George, who was taking a cat nap, his head resting against the plush upholstery of the opposite seat. In repose, he looked very Indian, but as she examined his face, she thought suddenly: why, he looks—old! There were deep lines under his eyes and the corners of his mouth were turned down, but the gray wings that swept up over the sides of his head gave him a distinguished look . . . still, for all his dark skin, he was very pale.

He had been driving himself too hard, she decided, and he tired so easily nowadays. She could not remember when he had last seen a doctor. Perhaps he would see a physician in Harley Street. After all, England was only the first stop in their trip around the world.

Bainbridge House had taken on an uncomfortable, weatherbeaten look, and when Higgens opened the door, he, too, thought Letty, looked aged and weathered. He took her fur and his eyes sparkled. "Good to see you again, madame."

"Thank you, Higgens, it's good to be back," she said, smiling to herself at the "madame."

Higgens bowed. "And you, sir, welcome home."

George laughed. "Thank you. The journey from the hotel has been memory lane tonight."

Letty glanced over the foyer and the curved staircase and shivered involuntarily. The place was exactly the same, and when they were announced in the drawing room and joined the other guests, she saw that not one ashtray had been moved. It was as if time stood still, and for a moment she felt apprehensive and unsure.

Mr. and Mrs. Huxley-Drummond came forward. They were the same body size, possessed the same dark coloring, and were both dressed in shades of brown. Letty thought that surely they must be joined together exactly like Siamese twins. They greeted George and Letty graciously.

Gertrude Motley came forward and kissed Letty's cheek and shook George's hand. Gertrude, except for a shorter hairstyle, and a higher hemline, could have stepped forward out of the past. Letty began to feel stifled. It was as if she were back in charge of the house.

"Ah, hah, my American partners!" They turned as Gerald Motley wheeled himself in their direction. They had heard that he was confined to a chair but were unprepared for the man's bird-like appearance. He had lost so much weight that he looked like a caricature of himself. Even his voice seemed to have shifted upward an octave.

It took all of Letty's considerable will power to get

through the interminable evening; the twelve-course meal seemed to last three days. She watched the clock while making small talk after dinner, and the moment the women joined the men in the drawing room, she took Mrs. Huxley-Drummond's hand. "It was a magnificent dinner, my dear, but we have a very heavy schedule tomorrow."

"It is so good to see you. Do come again." Letty detected a note of relief in her hostess's manner as if she, too, were weary and depressed and wanted her guests to depart.

"Oh, George," Letty exclaimed in the car on the way back to the hotel. "What's wrong with me? I felt absolutely claustrophobic tonight!"

He took her hand. "I felt the very same way."

"That old house, spic and span, and yet somehow moldy and . . . well, decadent. In a way there is a touch of Mrs. Faversham in *Great Expectations* about Bainbridge." She shook her head. "Oh, I'm imagining things. Here we are, among the privileged few, and yet . . ." She turned to him. "I can't wait to leave England. Maybe Germany will be better."

But they did not go to Germany, because in the middle of the night, George Story suffered a hemorrhage of the throat, and Letty awakened to find the sheets stained with blood.

Letty and George wintered in Switzerland. "Have you lost your minds?" Priscilla wrote. "With all the Americans in the south of France, what are you both doing in the coldest part of the world?"

Letty could not reply that they had no choice about the matter. Old gray-bearded Dr. Helmer thought that he could cure George's 'complaint,' never once referring to the fact that George had cancer. "I think the injections are working," he said each time. "Your condition seems improved." He looked over his glasses and winked. "Nurse tells me that you've gained a pound and a half, that is goot." Everything with Dr. Helmer was *goot*!

Finally, after six months of looking over the snow-capped peaks in the distance and bundling up against

340

the rigors of winter, George came back from a short walk around the rented chateau and announced, "Letty, pack up. We're going home."

"But we can't go now, Dr. Helmer . . ."

"Dr. Helmer is an ass," George replied. "I am not better, and I won't stay in this unfriendly country one day longer." He turned to the window. "As it is, I've lost valuable time. Luke is a very progressive businessman and extremely capable, but there are certain things he must learn that only I can teach him. In the time that I have left, I want to prepare him—"

Letty faced him furiously. "I won't have you talking like this! You *are* getting better, anyone can see that!"

He turned to her. "Look at me, my dear, not as a loving wife, but as a woman. I'm fading, fading. You've got to admit it . . . they told me in London that it was hopeless . . ."

"This is not like you, George. You can't admit defeat!"

"My God, Letty, I am not admitting defeat! I am going to die. You are going to die. We are all going to die. Only I am going to die sooner . . . I'm lucky if I have three years left! They can't operate, they don't know where to start! I've got to go back to Washington where I belong and work as long as I can. In the last analysis, I've got to prove very many things that I've put off proving . . ."

"Oh, George!" Letty cried. "I can't bear to even think . . ."

He took her hand and his voice was gentle. "I love you, lady, but you've got to help me in this. I can't pretend that everything is progressing well any longer. And you shouldn't either. You've got to stand behind me as you've always done and bear with me. We've got to work this out—together."

She choked back the tears. "We've always faced everything." She squeezed his hand. "And we'll face this too—and conquer—"

He shook his head. "No, this we will not conquer, but we will make the best of it . . ."

* * *

Bosley Trenton picked up his new Packard touring car in Detroit and made the long journey to Angel, taking a month to stop off at various refineries, either owned by Heron or doing business with the company.

He drove up to the small place off Main Street that John and Fontine Dice had rented while their new house on the farm was being built. Fontine answered the door herself. "I can't believe it's you, Bos!" she exclaimed. "Do come in." He kissed her cheek and she drew back, blushing. "Oh, it's always good to see you. You never change."

He laughed, patting his sandy-gray hair. "Nor have you!"

She shook her head. "I've put on too much weight. You're kind, indeed, sir to be so gallant. Where's your traps?"

"At the Stevens Hotel."

"You go fetch them right now. You're staying *here*."

"No, thank you, Fontine, there's so much business to transact and telephone calls to make to be your guest this time around."

"Well, you've got to at least stay for supper. It's a simple menu—ham and fried potatoes, with an Angel cake for dessert." He shook his head. "Good times come, and good times go, wars are fought, wells come in, but you're always Fontine Dice!"

She looked at him obliquely. "I *hope* I've changed."

"I mean, you're still the same person inside. Money hasn't done anything to you."

"Yes?" She laughed and her blonde curls danced. It suddenly occurred to him that she had touched up her hair—it was as golden as the first day he had met her all those years ago. She had to be in her mid-fifties, yet with the added weight, she didn't have a wrinkle in her face.

"Jaundice will be home from the bank any time," she said, then leaning forward, went on confidentially, "He sometimes comes home at two o'clock."

"He's earned his freedom, Fontine."

"He has that." She went to the mantel and examined the antique Napoleon clock. "Bos, will you tell me something? You still have *your* freedom."

342

"I'm just an old bachelor." He shuffled his feet. "With me on the road all the time, it wouldn't be fair to a wife."

"Yet of all the men I've ever known, I think that you'd probably make the best husband."

"No, thank you. Some men are not meant to be tied down."

"Yet there have been women, I'm quite sure."

"You know, Fontine, I'd appreciate a cup of coffee."

"My stars, where are my manners? I've got some java on the stove, as usual. Come in the kitchen." She filled a mug and handed it to him with a small curtsey.

He bowed and laughed. "Thank you, Ma'am."

"You know, Bos, Jaundice and me always thought you'd eventually settle down here in Angel. There are one or two music teachers at the conservatory—quite educated . . ."

"Will you stop trying to marry me off?"

"But you should have *someone* to care for you."

He placed the mug down firmly on the kitchen table. "Fontine," he said firmly, "I am fifty-three years old and too set in my ways to take on a wife."

"Well," she sighed gently, "then there must have been someone a long time ago that upset you good and proper!"

He smiled. "There was. But, I was a young whippersnapper then, and I let dollar signs interfere with logic. By the time I got around to asking her, she was already taken." He paused. "Now, are you satisfied?" He was about to go on, when heavy boots were heard on the porch.

"Son of a gun!" John Dice exclaimed, holding out his hand. "My old friend!" They shook hands and suddenly the past returned and they were standing together at a church social talking about alkali when Bosley was still surveying the Gyp Mounains.

Over supper, the men spoke about business matters, then Bosley lighted a cigar and Fontine got up to go into the kitchen. "Come back," Bosley said.

"No. I'm sure you both want to talk 'men talk'."

"What I'm going to say concerns you, too."

She sat down and nervously picked at her dress. "I

343

don't know very much about business. Jaundice never tells me a thing!"

John Dice laughed. "It's true, but you don't have a mind for money affairs. You can barely get by on your allowance."

She nodded. "It's true. But it's awfully nice to have money. I mean, if I want something, I can wangle a way to get it!"

"Well, I think there's a bit more that we can 'wangle,' Fontine, if you'll support John in running for state senator."

Her eyes grew as big as saucers. "Would that mean that we would have to move to Oklahoma City?"

Bosley laughed. "No, but you'd get to visit Letty and George in Washington."

John Dice cleared his throat. "If you're going to talk about politics, I wish you'd have dropped by my office instead of setting off a bombshell like this at home!"

"Excuse me, John, but it's essential that we discuss this with Fontine. You've both got to change a bit if we put your hat in the ring."

"It's too sudden for me to think," John Dice replied. "You come in here and just make an announcement, just like that! I'm a small-town banker. I don't know anything about politics and I don't know that I want to find out any more, from what I've seen and read."

Bosley leaned forward. "That's just the point. I think the people of this state would vote for a self-made man."

"I'm not educated . . ."

"What *is* education, Jaundice? A degree from Stanford? That doesn't mean much. After all, you were a marshal in Texas as a young man. You were one of the most respected pioneers in the Territory, and since statehood, you've become a rich man in oil, mayor of Angel, and now a well-known banker. Whether you know it or not, you've got a wonderful reputation. Mention your name in most of the towns around here and people smile and say: 'Sure I know old John Dice, he's a fair and square shooter'."

He smiled awkwardly. "I don't know about *that* . . ."

344

"Well, I do." Bosley paused. "Besides, I spoke with George Story yesterday."

"How is he?" John Dice asked, his brow furrowed.

Bosley sighed deeply. "It's only a matter of time now, I think. He never talks about his condition, and neither does Letty." He paused. "But on the phone, he said he would back you 100 percent. With Coolidge not running for a second term, we think that Hoover will get the Republican nomination. He's done a good job as Secretary of Commerce, and he's a personal friend of the Storys—not that it means much now." He leaned forward. "It's our belief that you could get the rural vote. There has to be some relief for the farmers . . ."

"I'll agree with that," John Dice shook his head. "The boys around here who haven't had the luck to bring in a well on their property are hard up . . . I know, because I've advanced them seed wheat money for years."

He turned his hands over. "I'm soft now. Used to have calluses a mile thick." He smiled softly. "Do you know, Bos, times were so bad after The Run that first year, that Poppa Dice and I had to use some of the seed wheat we'd brought from Texas to make bread. We almost starved that first year." He looked up. "You didn't know that, did you, Fontine? That was before you came up from Santone."

She nodded numbly. "I knew. I didn't say anything, but I knew. That seed wheat had to go somewhere, and I figured it went into your bellies."

Bosley crushed out the tip of his cigar in the ashtray. "With all your background, I think you'll get the grass-roots vote."

"But what would I talk about, how would I build a platform? I don't know anything about politics."

"That's just the point, John. You run on the *farm platform*. You know more about the problems of agriculture than any man I know. And with the Heron Oil interests behind you, I think you'll carry the state without a problem." He paused, "In fact, if I were running against you, I'd probably take my name out of the race."

Fontine opened her eyes wide and looked up at the

ceiling. "Wouldn't it be something to walk down Pennsylvania Avenue as a big politician's wife?"

It was then that Bosley knew for certain that John Dice would run for the Senate.

Sarah Morton, deep in Clement's arms in the back seat of the Stutz Bearcat, which was parked on the lonely road, suddenly shifted her position and shook her short bobbed head. "Oh, no, you don't, my fine feathered friend!" She raised up and adjusted her blouse. "We've gone far enough!"

He blushed. "What do you mean?"

"You know very well what I mean, Clement Story."

He grinned laconically. "Don't tell me that an emancipated girl like you has never . . ."

"In the first place, I am not emancipated—yet—and in the second place, I don't believe in going all the way."

"Who said anything about going all the way?"

"Well . . ." She was flustered. "You intimated . . . I mean . . . We were . . . you were . . ."

"I wasn't trying anything."

"Oh, no?" She set her lips firmly together for a moment and then went on in a rush. "This is *so* like you! Turning everything around and making it sound different . . . You make love just like you play the piano—with a lot of chords to hide the melody."

He laughed out loud. "For a college girl, you surely don't express yourself very well."

"Express myself?" she replied hotly, fastening her skirt. "I think I've made my intentions known. I won't be taken advantage of."

"Ending a sentence with a preposition—see what I mean?"

"You're mad, absolutely mad, and I think I'll walk home."

"Suit yourself," he replied slowly, "but it's a long way back to town. And in all my experiences with women, it's never been necessary for my dates to get out and walk."

"Oh? Well, perhaps they gave in."

346

"You just ended another sentence with a preposition!"

She glared at him, got out of the back seat, and started down the road.

"You're very beautiful when you're mad," he called after her, but when she did not reply, he shouted: "Okay, come on back."

Without turning around, she said, "Are you in the front seat?"

"Yes."

"Will you stay there?"

"Yes."

"Will you leave me alone?"

"Yes."

"Promise?"

"Yes."

"All right, then." She retraced her steps and climbed into the front seat beside him. "Now, can we have some ice cream? I think the parlor across from the college is still open."

He grinned. "Need ice cream to cool you down?"

"No, it's not that at all. But we've got to do *something*."

"Ice cream is a poor substitute."

She faced him angrily. "Then take me home! And you don't need to phone me again. I'm absolutely worn out from you bothering me on every date."

"Well, you didn't have to get in the back seat with me."

She glared at him. "You always turn things around. There's nothing wrong with an innocent kiss."

"A kiss is never innocent—especially in the back seat."

"Will you stop harping on that?" she replied with a stammer. "If I didn't like you . . ."

He laughed. "You admit that you do like me then?"

"I'm not in the habit of going out with men I don't like, but you get me so rattled . . ."

He took her hand and his voice was very soft. "Don't you know that I'm in love with you?"

She looked at him, eyes wide and staring. "You've never said . . ."

"I didn't know about it myself, until now," he replied earnestly, and kissed her on the lips.

"Now you go and spoil it!" she exclaimed. "You tell me you love me and then you go ahead and start sparking all over again, as if it's all right."

"Well, isn't it?"

"No. How do you know how I feel about you?"

"You care. I know you do!"

"Talk about egos! My Lord in Heaven! *Caring* and *loving* are two different things altogether."

"Not necessarily. You've got to care before you can love."

"Now you're confusing me." She paused and looked at him out of the corner of her eye. "I think that's what you've been trying to do all along, just so you can have your way with me. Well, I'm not falling for *that*." She paused again and then continued in a small voice. "I bet the other girls fell for your line, didn't they?"

He smiled broadly. "What do you think?"

"I think you are a rat, Clement Story, a big *fat* rat."

"Fat?"

"Well, a big *lean* rat!" She sighed. "Now, take me home, please."

"Very well." He started the car, and drove swiftly down the road. Silence was strained until he turned down a familiar thoroughfare that led by the Sugar Bowl, where he parked.

"Is this home?" she said angrily.

"You wanted to cool off, didn't you?"

"I am as cold as I ever will be!" she said quietly. "If you think that a dish of ice cream is going to . . ."

"Another preposition," he said smugly.

She faced him, eyes flashing. "You are despicable! A very low form of life. I will get out of this car and call a taxicab. I never want to see you again!"

"Even if I said I wanted to marry you?"

"Especially . . ." She looked at him in wonder. "Did you say *marry*?"

"No!" he shouted. "I take that back. Why in the hell would I want to marry you for?"

"Ah, ha!" she cried triumphantly. "*You* ended a sentence with a preposition!"

348

Suddenly he laughed and took her in his arms. In the ensuing silence while he held her close, he murmured. "I do want to marry you. You're the loveliest thing I've ever seen."

"I'll marry you, Clement," she whispered back, then broke from his embrace and looked at him with startled eyes. "Although I don't know why. I've never met anyone like you before, and I don't know how we'll get on in life, because we're so different. But yes, Clement Story, I'll marry you." She paused and waved a finger at him. "But that doesn't mean . . ."

He sighed and looked out the window. "C'mon," he said, "Let's have some ice cream."

Sarah Morton and Clement Story were married in the garden of the Connecticut Avenue house, with Luke as best man and Jeanette as Matron of Honor and Luke III as ring bearer. Sarah's father was dead, so George escorted her down the pebbled garden path. "I don't know if this is proper or not, or what Emily Post would say," he whispered, "but I'm honored to give you away."

"Don't think you're going to get rid of me so easily, sir!" she whispered back. "Seriously, I am pleased to be part of a great family. You've done so much for our cause."

"No," he replied softly. "It wasn't enough, Sarah."

"Maybe there is still time to help our people."

But he did not reply because the strains of the Wedding March, played triumphantly by Clement's band, floated out over the lawn.

Letty, dressed in pale pink organza, did not feel at all like the mother of the groom. She felt exactly twenty-five years old. Looking around at the white, rose-covered arbor that had been erected by the caterer, and watching the guests mill about over the landscaped grounds, it seemed to her that she was lost somewhere in time.

She could not refrain from contrasting this beautiful wedding, that seemed staged like a production at the National Theatre, to her own wedding at the frame church in Angel twenty-six years before. Once again, she saw the sheet-covered tables set on the grass, one displaying the wedding gifts, and the other laden with covered dishes contributed by neighbors. She glanced ever so slyly at the gleaming chafing dishes of beef stroganoff and the two bowls of punch, one a pale lemonade and the other spiked with bootleg gin, and smiled. She stood beside George and smiled. "Can you believe that both of our children are grown and that we are grandparents?"

He took her hand. "No, it doesn't seem possible, does it?" His eyes were very bright and he looked away. She sighed gently. With his illness, sometimes he was overcome with emotion. He must know that he would not live to see his grandson grow into boyhood. He was to be robbed of so much living. Her heart went out to him, yet she must keep under control. It would never do for him to know that she was about to cry.

After Clement and Sarah changed from their wedding finery into traveling apparel, he headed the Stutz in the direction of Baltimore, where they were going to spend their honeymoon. "Are you tired?" he asked.

Her cheeks were still flushed. "Not at all. It was a beautiful wedding, Clem, and sweet of your family to pay for everything."

"It's only right. You have no family."

"But I'm going to." She smiled. "I want many babies."

"Sarah!"

"Well, I do!" She looked at him obliquely. "Don't you?"

"Frankly, I hadn't thought about it, but please, not right away." He grinned. "Let's have *fun* first."

She turned her face to the window. "Knowing how you are, I'm surprised," she replied in a mocking tone, "that you haven't pulled off the road somewhere!"

"Now, Sarah," he chided, "don't start *that* again."

"Well, you're always so—hot and bothered."

"Sarah, after all, we're married now . . ."

"Well, you can just wait until we get to the hotel!"

"Who said anything about not waiting?"

"You're impossible." She set her mouth in a line.

"Well," he said lightly, "you knew that before you married me!"

That night, after a late supper in the wedding suite, they retired to their dressing rooms on opposite sides of the huge bedroom.

Later Sarah, dressed in a high-necked nightgown, and Clement in pajamas, met in the center of the room. "I must say," he said, "our timing is superb! It's like this whole thing had been staged."

"Well," she answered laughing, "wasn't it?"

He turned out the lights and they crawled between the cool white satin sheets. They lay side by side, not touching. Finally she said. "I'm cold. I've never slept between satin sheets before."

"Me, either," he replied, drawing her into his arms and kissing her. "Your lips taste like wild Oklahoma strawberries."

"Is that good?"

"Mmmmmm."

"Your mouth tastes like toothpaste."

"Here I was trying to be romantic . . ."

He kissed her again and drew her body alongside his, luxuriating in the warmth. They continued kissing and he felt heat surround her body like an aura; her breathing was very heavy. "I love you, Clem," she murmured and he began to kiss her neck, then her small pointed breasts. She started to sigh. He was tense with desire and moved over her for a moment and then curled down beside her. "Do you know something?" he asked in a very small voice.

"What, my love?" she murmured.

"I've never been with—I mean I've not . . ." He was thankful she could not see his scarlet face in the darkness.

There was a long pause and then she replied softly. "Are you trying to tell me that I'm your first girl—that way?"

He nodded numbly and then suddenly she hugged him tightly. "I'm glad!" she whispered.

For the rest of the night, they explored the hidden places of each other's bodies; the revelation was exhilarating. Without fear, without shame, they caressed each other, their fingertips lightly discovering new delights until every pore was stimulated; they were consumed with animal heat. Then, as if they had been together many times, he positioned himself over her and she gave a little cry of pain. Her body stiffened and he began to move instinctively within her. Then to a certain staccato refrain that kept repeating in his brain, the first journey was launched. Some time towards morning, when they lay beside each other, still enclosed in wonder, she sighed contentedly. "It was so wonderful," she whispered.

"Was it like you imagined it would be?" he asked quietly.

"Oh, yes, but better somehow—greater . . ."

He nodded. "You're so very special, Sarah." He paused. "You know something?"

"What?"

"I'm awfully glad I waited."

She smiled softly. "I'm glad you waited, too."

"This really is, then, a moment to remember . . . this wonderful sharing . . . " He raised himself up on an elbow. "You know, frankly I was always scared to death that I wouldn't ever find anyone . . . you know, to be with this way. I had visions of myself, playing that damned piano and leading the band on my fiftieth birthday and still—a virgin!"

She giggled. "At least you're honest!" She leaned on her elbow and looked him in the eyes. "I think God protects people like you and me. I think it's all written down somewhere—I mean, how people blessed with talent meet and fall in love and have babies and grow up and die. I think it's all worked out beforehand . . ."

"Oh, I don't think so, Sarah."

"Well, we both have Indian blood. Maybe some brave warrior who has passed on to the other side brought us together."

He smiled. "In that case, if he went to all that trouble, we can't disappoint the old boy, can we?" And with that, he took her in his arms and started a new voyage, a journey that would awaken their new love for each other even more.

* * *

352

Manford Pederson closed his thin alligator brief case with a snap, and called his secretary, Deborah Lindsey. "Let's have dinner at the Golden Calf," he said, "then we can prepare those stock orders for New York."

"I'll have to call Ralph," she replied. "We were supposed to go to the Drexels tonight for dinner."

Manford paused, his hand on the door knob. "Well, if it's inconvenient . . ."

She blinked her blue eyes and opened her scarlet mouth in a wide smile. "I hate the Drexels. It's business. He can go by himself. They will only sit on the back porch after dinner and drink home brew." She patted her sleek blonde head. "Hardly an edifying evening."

They had thick porterhouse steaks at the Golden Calf and then retired to the apartment that Manford kept in the Stanford Arms. The stock letters were checked in fifteen minutes, then Deborah went into the bathroom, and ran a tub. After bathing, she joined him on the couch in the living room. Her body was snow-white, not one freckle marred its utter perfection, and her large, pendulous breasts pressed against his chest.

He took her in his arms and began to kiss her neck. "Did Ralph make love to you last night?"

She giggled. "He's such a beast," she replied between long breaths. "Looks like a gorilla with his hairy body, and then, too, he's so big, he almost splits me in two."

"Yes?" Manford asked. "Was it a wonderful feeling, having that thing . . ."

She shivered. "Yes. Yes. At first he's so brutal that it takes a long time to respond. It hurts so much in the beginning, but then . . ." She paused, waiting for his reaction.

"Yes?" Manford gasped. "Yes?"

She smiled. "Then, as always, my body expands and it's *wonderful* . . ."

"Was it like this?" Manford asked, positioning himself directly over her and sinking down until his stomach was pressing on her. "Was it?"

She sighed. "It was good, but oh, Manford, not like *this*."

In a moment it was all over, and he rolled on his

side, perspiration breaking out in little beads all over his body. He got up with a long sigh and went into the bathroom.

Deborah glanced at her watch and her blue eyes glittered. It was still early. If she could get rid of Manford, she could still meet Ralph at the Drexels. She dressed quickly, ran a comb through her hair, then pocketed the fifty dollar bill that Manford had left on the dresser. She was pleased to see that the piece of furniture was the Heron Hotel Special—veneered birdseye maple.

28

Pastimes

The summer and early fall of 1928 were the most successful in Heron Oil Company history.

Washington society revolved around strict protocol and an after hours array of parties with jazz bands, under-the-table champagne, table-top dancing, and a variety of amusements in which neither George or Letty took part.

"Are you sure you feel well enough to go to the party tonight, George?" Letty asked after luncheon had been served on the terrace of the Connecticut Avenue house.

"Even if they had to carry me on a stretcher, my dear, I would not pass up a party at the White House!" He smiled. "Actually, I feel much better today. The fresh air seems to do me good. I don't feel so bad for a fifty-six-year-old Indian brave."

She was taken aback; he seldom spoke about his heritage any more. It had been years since he had even belonged to an Indian affairs committee. As he gazed out over the lawn to Connecticut Avenue, she knew that he was thinking about the old days in Tahlequah. Since his illness, he seemed more and more introspective. "Shall we take an afternoon nap?" she asked gently. Her joining him was the only way that she could get him to lie down every day.

"No," he replied, "you go on inside. I know there's woman things that you must do before tonight. I'll be in shortly."

Hans called from the drawing room. "Ma'am, Mr. Clement is calling from Indianapolis."

She hurried inside and picked up the receiver. "Mother, what do you think just happened?" her son blurted. "I've signed a contract on the Blue Network for a weekly radio show! Clement and his Cherokee Braves Jazz band is going to be famous!"

Letty exclaimed, "I'm so happy for you, son. Will you be broadcasting from New York?"

"No, Mother, that's the best part. We're returning to Kansas City. The program will beam out from the 'beautiful starlight room high atop the Wyandotte Hotel.' I wish you and Dad could spend a weekend with me." He paused. "How is he feeling?"

"He's still able to go into the office a few hours every morning. Perhaps we can come later in the year."

"I just talked to Luke; he and Jeanette are going to come from D.C. for the first show."

"That's very nice, dear." Letty replied quickly.

"You sound rushed."

"Well, I am a bit. The Hoovers have invited us for a gala tonight."

"You mean at the *White House?*"

"Why, yes . . ."

"Gee, that's swell. Wait 'til the band hears about that! Imagine, my folks being entertained by the president of the United States! Good luck. I'll hang up now, I don't want you to be late. Goodbye."

"Goodbye." Letty replaced the receiver, then rubbed her face with cold cream before lying down for her beauty nap.

The line of cars slowly made their way up the curved drive to the colonial mansion at 1600 Pennsylvania Avenue. Letty wore a new dress for the occasion. "George," she said in the limousine as they reached the portico, "do you think blue organza is too old for me?"

"It's a bit late to be asking my opinion, isn't it?" He smiled and took her hand, "Actually, you look very pretty. Have I told you that I love you today?"

She shook her head. "No, George, not today."

Lou Hoover stood at the head of the reception line

and as she shook hands with each guest, Letty wondered how she kept her elbow length gloves so white . . . "Glad you could come, Letty," she said warmly, and then looked up at George and murmured, "You're health has improved, I see," then more loudly, "It's good to see you again, sir."

"I think I'm the only Democrat here," he whispered.

She smiled and extended her hand to the woman and man next in line, Mr. and Mrs. Henry Ford. Later in the evening, the Fords were once again behind the Herons as the select group went into dinner. George said, "Mr. Ford, you seem to be following me, when actually it should be the other way around."

Henry Ford, a man of little humor, looked at him bemusedly. "I don't know what you mean."

"Your Model T came before *our* production of gasoline!"

Ford smiled wanly. "The Model T, as you may have heard, is no more. The plant is retooling for the Model A, which, we hope won't use as much of your gasoline or oil as the old engine design. But I can tell you one thing, the oil companies will have to come up with a higher-powered gas when we get into higher-compression engines."

George nodded. "We've been doing research in that area for some time. In fact, we're testing a new gasoline with certain additives that should take an automobile up a fairly steep incline without shifting. There will be less carbon flashes in the engine, which should eliminate knocking."

Ford squinted up at him. "And what are you going to call this miracle gasoline?"

"Frankly, I'd like to name it after my wife, but Letty Gasoline doesn't have quite the mellifluous sound needed for selling. Also, it sounds too much like *Getty*!" He smiled. "It should be a feminine name, we think, perhaps Olivia or Ethyl." He sighed. "But engines using it should run with less fuel. I believe in conservation."

Ford looked at him in amazement. "Coming from a man in your position, that statement surprises me."

"We all made mistakes years ago that we're now

trying to rectify. Millions of barrels of oil were wasted. We have a new sophisticated refinery in Tulsa. Along with our conservation methods, we want to develop new by-products that will bring in bigger profits."

Ford smiled thinly. "Then perhaps I'm in the wrong business!"

Letty found herself seated opposite Mary Savor at the beautifully appointed table. The women nodded and once again, the past came flying back and Letty saw the young widow standing over her husband's grave at God's Acre. There was no doubt in her mind that the woman was Mary Darth.

She turned her attention to the roast duck which, although excellent, could not hold a candle to the recipe that Priscilla and she had concocted in the old days at the farm. Actually, she had not cooked in years. Food was now a commodity placed on the table three times a day, which sometimes remained barely touched—especially if she had a great many things on her mind, or was on a slimming diet. It was strange, she mused, how in the first part of the century, what an important part food played in everyday existence, and how unimportant it had become since.

Letty glanced at the group in the Blue Room, but felt no excitement. She was a guest in the most important house in the United States, being entertained by the president and his wife, yet it was, in so many ways, just another dinner party. Was this what growing older meant, being a part of a celebrity world and not enjoying the ambience? Oh, if she could only be the Letty Heron Story that she once was, even for a moment.

After the long dinner, at which she had tried to be amusing and failed, she sought out George, who was seated next to Walter F. Brown, the new postmaster general, who looked extremely bored. Obviously the men had little in common. How pale George looked, even with his naturally dark skin; she noticed that his hand was trembling and knew his point of exhaustion was very near. She found her hostess by the mantel. "Lou, I must ask a personal favor," she whispered. "Is it possible for us to leave early without creating a fuss?"

Lou took her hand. "Of course. Never mind proto-

358

col. I'll have your car brought to the side entrance. You and George slip into the hall; I'll see that a secret service man escorts you." She paused. "I'll explain to the President." Then, "How is George—really?"

Letty sighed. "Not very good, I'm afraid."

"The President was hoping he would head up a committee on foreign trade."

Letty shook her head. "He wouldn't be up to it, Lou. Between you and me, it would disturb him very much to know that he didn't have the strength to do a good job. Like the President, he is a perfectionist. I'm going to try and talk him into taking a long cruise in the Caribbean. Bosley Trenton, our company vice-president, is currently in Venezuela. We would ostensibly be visiting him in the Maracaibo Lake Basin."

On the way back to the house on Connecticut Avenue, George leaned his head against the window and closed his eyes. "Letty," he said softly, "I want to go home."

"We *are* going home," she replied gently, taking his hand.

"No, I mean *home*. I want to go back to Angel."

Her throat constricted. "I thought we might visit Bosley in South America, take a leisurely boat trip . . ."

"There won't be time," he said, his voice barely a whisper. But when he opened his eyes, some of his old spirit returned. "Besides," he quipped, "if tonight turns out to be my last public appearance, I could not have chosen a better stage than the White House, could I?"

Nine years had passed since the Herons had been back to Angel. The train from Enid, which during their absence had grown into a large city, passed prosperous farms—women were hanging out Monday wash, men on tractors were singletoothing recently plowed fields, and hired hands were bringing in the first crop of alfalfa. George opened the window and the smells of early spring swept into the car. "The clover is in bloom, Letty, and there is some sage mixed in with the odor of wild china poppies . . ."

Hans and Clara, the new maid, took charge of the luggage and were the first off the train when they reached Angel. The depot had been expanded, and two new grain elevators reached four stories skyward. "I hardly know the place," Letty exclaimed, surveying the four taxis lined up where carriages used to stop; the watering trough was now a peanut vendor's stand.

A Packard touring car drove up and honked loudly. "Look," Letty waved, "there's John and Fontine!"

John Dice swung easily out of the automobile, waving his ten-gallon hat. He kissed Letty on the cheek and held out his hand to George. "It's been too long, George."

"It has indeed, Senator!"

John Dice laughed. "Never thought I'd see the day that I would be spending so much time in Washington," he replied, "but Angel is my home and always will be."

"Yes," George replied, "my sentiments exactly."

Fontine, a little out of breath, took the stairs slowly to the passenger loading zone. Letty held back a smile. Fontine had gained forty pounds in middle age, and had become as rotund as Bella Chenovick.

"Letty!" Fontine cried, going into her arms. "You're a sight for sore eyes. Sorry I didn't get to see you after our last European trip, but . . ." She looked up at the sky and laughed. "Letty," she continued, squeezing her hand, "isn't fate funny? Here we are, after all these years, back where we started from—back from where we started—oh, to hell with syntax—all that matters is that we're together again!"

John Dice looked at the twenty pieces of luggage that Hans and Clara were assembling. "I don't know how we're all going to fit into the car with all that."

Hans looked up. "We'll take a cab, Senator. I still can't find one valise."

A prairie breeze, carrying spring fragrances mixed with automobile fumes, ruffled the veiling on Letty's hat as Jaundice drove slowly down Main Street, which was now lined with brick and cement block buildings. Baker's Mercantile Store had a new false front, and Doctor Schaeffer's offices were now on the new second floor above the *Angel Wing*.

"What's all this?" George asked, gesturing at the crowd gathered outside the Heron filling station.

"The Saturday drawing."

George exchanged glances with Letty and took her hand. Suddenly the automobiles in the street became horse drawn carriages and Main Street, a country road with fruit and vegetable stands. He saw a stunning woman in a blue dress with matching parasol, and he was asking Sam, Born-Before-Sunrise: "That lady with the blonde hair, who is she?"

George shook the cobwebs out of his mind and looked at Letty, sitting so sedately beside him in the open touring car. He had almost expected to see bright, flushed cheek bones, shaded by the blue parasol; instead he saw a delicately sculptured face, lined with tiny wrinkles under silver gray hair that swept back from her forehead in deep finger waves. He squeezed her hand, realizing that he loved her more than ever.

"You've felt it, too, then," Letty whispered, "this feeling of *deja vu?*"

He nodded, unable to look at her.

"Thought we'd drive by the Chenovicks," John Dice was saying. "The old fruit trees are out early this year. Bella and Torgo went back to Prague to visit relatives, but I expect they're back."

Fontine cried, "Looky there!" The whole hillside was ablush with violent pink. "If there's a peach for every bloom, Bella's roadside stand will do a good business."

"You mean," Letty said incredulously, "that with all their oil money, they still open the stand?"

"Of course," Fontine exclaimed. "Success hasn't turned their heads. They're still bohunks."

"Fourteen!" Jaundice admonished, *"Bohemians.* We don't want to slur our neighbors."

"Well," she replied tartly, "we were slurring them even before we knew we were slurring them!"

Letty saw that George was very pale. "Let's go home," she said, "I hope cook has a good supper prepared." She laughed. "Isn't it strange, I haven't called dinner *supper* in years. Now that I'm back in Angel, I'm going backwards . . ."

"No matter where I go—London or Paris or Amsterdam," John Dice said, "dinner will always be supper to

361

me!" He turned to the right, down a two-lane, paved highway. "Thought you might like to see the new dormitory at the conservatory. There are about nine hundred students this year." The new drive led up by the main house, which had not changed in thirty-six years except that it had been freshly painted white and the gingerbread trim was now deep blue. The new brick building was faced with white granite. The lawn swept up by the road where the mail box had rested in the old days.

"Do you suppose the students know that it used to be called The Widows?" Letty asked.

"Of course!" John Dice replied jubilantly. "I think that's part of the attraction of coming out here in the sticks to go to school."

"Well, I would hardly call this 'the sticks' any more, Jaundice!" Letty exclaimed.

"Aw," he replied, "you're just prejudiced."

As he turned down the red dirt section road, Letty thought about Poppa Dice, that dear man, acting as faro keeper at The Widows.

"It's too bad old Leona's dead," John Dice was saying. "I think she'd approve of her contribution to the cultural life of Angel, except," he added with a gleam in his eye, "I imagine she'd insist on co-educational dormitories!"

It was on the tip of Letty's tongue to protest: But, she's *not* dead! She's living in New York City. But she kept quiet. To the town of Angel and perhaps even to Leona herself, the Widow Barrett had long been dead.

"I'll get you all home in a minute," John Dice said, "but I've got to show you my new house." He turned down the familiar road, which had once been a cow path; as they drove through the line of oak trees, Letty exclaimed, "You've both gone mad!"

The three-story red sandstone and brick mansion was a neo-Greek revival, with two huge white columns on either side of the white-railed porch. A red tiled roof added a complementary finish. "It's just like the Pincheon House in Nathaniel Hawthorn's story." Letty sighed.

"Yes," Fontine cried, "and we've got *seven gables,*

too!" She paused, her eyes sparkling. "Isn't it ostenta-
tious?"

Letty laughed. "Yes, but deliciously so!"

Five minutes later, John Dice drove by the old
Heron clapboard, which was in a state of sad repair.
"Why, it's gone to rack and ruin," Letty said sadly. "I
can't believe Prissy would abandon it. The weeds are
higher than the porch."

"It's too bad," John Dice agreed. "But at least the
farm lands are rented."

Fontine nodded. "She's never come back, you know,
not even after she married Manford Pederson." She
sighed. "How long has it been since you've seen her,
Letty?"

"Three years, I think," she replied slowly. "She's finally got what she wanted, you know. She's one of the
social queens in Dallas. But it makes me very sad every
time I pass by a Heron Furniture Store."

"Yes," George said, "gone are all those traditional
solid woods that last a lifetime. Manford's put everything on a fast production line. Veneer and white glue
and horrible designs. It's all modern and tasteless."

"But, it's *cheap*," Fontine added, "and the kids today
don't know the difference. If it falls apart in three
years, they'll just buy new stuff."

George nodded. "The old days are passing. Everyone
wants to make a million dollars, and Heron Furniture
stock on the market is up to the sky." He paused. "Priscilla and Manford are millionaires many times over."

"Don't say that so regretfully, dear," Letty replied,
"we may not be millionaires in cash money, but we're
still in control of Heron Oil."

George nodded. "Thank God for Luke."

Letty received a mental picture of Luke, seated on
the cow pony with mixed roan blood, riding up ahead
in The Run, glancing back now and then, his eyes filled
with exultation and his brown-blondish hair flying
around his head in the wind. She had not thought about
him in years, and suddenly she turned in the direction
of God's Acre. But of course, George was referring to
Little Luke.

John Dice drew up before the Story clapboard, which

sparkled with a new coat of pale yellow paint. The lush green lawn ran down to the road, and the maple trees that George had planted in 1903 dwarfed the house. "It looks so small," Letty said pensively. "Remember when it seemed as big as the courthouse in Enid?"

Fontine giggled. "My clapboard seemed huge, too. But, after living in that dugout for two years, I remember I jumped up and down when the Poppa Dice nailed the last shingle on the roof." She glanced at Letty in the back seat. "It took so little to please us in those days. Yet, I sometimes think we were happier then, somehow. Life wasn't so complicated . . ."

Letty turned to look at the new church with its cold brick facade. "What's that?" She pointed to a small gazebo near the new sidewalk.

"The old door and frame from the old church," John Dice explained. "I thought you knew that Reverend Haskell had it enshrined when the new church was built. The city council thought that part of the old landmark should be preserved."

"And so it should," Letty agreed, then looked from the new brick building to her old clapboard. Within a thousand yards, one could appreciate the new and revere the old.

George opened the car door with difficulty and then helped her out. She was touched. As ill as he was, he would always remain a gentleman. They thanked John Dice and Fontine and then went up the walk to the porch, arm in arm.

The moment they were out of earshot, John Dice cleared his throat. "Dammit, Fourteen, I wish you'd not keep harping about the old days! The way you talk, one would think that you didn't appreciate what we have now. How'd you like to be back washing diapers and cooking for threshers?"

She looked at him with wonder, and then giggled. "I'm sorry, I do go on, Jaundice. If I get to acting up again, you've got my permission to slap me silly!"

It took George Story a long time to die.

During the first months of summer, he rode horseback every morning for half an hour; when he could no longer keep his balance, even on the sweet-tempered old mare, he would walk over the flat pasture lands—at first unsupported, and then with the aid of a stick. The townspeople whom he had known for over thirty years—the Stevens, the Chenovicks and the Bakers—made regular visits and the house was often merry with high humor. No one let on that the pale, fragile man with snowy white hair seated in the great chair looked ten years older than his fifty-seven years.

Doctor Schaeffer made visits every two weeks, then once a week, and then finally, every other day. Then, when George took to his bed in the newly papered bedroom that overlooked the town of Angel, the doctor showed Letty how to inject the morphine.

As George's appetite waned, Letty gave her box of recipes to the cook, and the smells of the famous old pioneer dishes wafted through the house. She did the baking herself. Taking six fresh, crusty loaves of bread from the oven, she remarked to the cook: "I haven't forgotten how, Tessie!"

Sniffing the air like a beagle, George would say: "Now, don't tell me, that's roast shoat and green tomatoes and cabbage cooked together!" Or: "I'd know that odor anywhere, it's Lavenia Heron's Mulligan stew!" Or: "It's been years since I've eaten reconstituted maize!"

He never complained about his health. But there were days when he looked out of the window, a shrunken version of his former self, with brown, translucent skin and sunken eyes, and he did not see the thriving town of Angel, because his thoughts were back with the tribal leaders in the days when he had fought the cause in the courts of the land. But, somehow, he kept up his spirits. Each Sunday, he and Letty listened to Clement and his Cherokee Braves Jazz Band on the radio, coming all the way from the Rittenhouse Square Hotel in Philadelphia.

Luke, Jeanette and Luke III drove in from Washington. "Have you been reading my reports, Dad?" he asked, and when George nodded, he said, "Well, as you know, we're in good shape. We've opened seventeen new filling stations, mostly in the Southern California area. Standard Oil isn't too pleased about that. Also, several of the smaller oil companies are going public, but I think we should resist the pressure to follow suit. What do you think?"

George nodded, brushing a shock of white hair back from his forehead. "Let the others go public." Then he said up very straight. "We are still a wholly owned corporation. Besides, I don't like the look of the stock market, too much rallying. Are you saying we're low on expansion money?"

Luke sighed. "We are held back. It takes a lot of time, Dad, for the profits to filter down from distribution. I'd like to build another tanker, for instance, and Uncle Bos is barely able to keep the Maracaibo Basin field profitable. We could use a lot of new money there. Then, too, Dad, one of the things I wanted to talk to you about—and Armbuster thinks it's a swell idea—if we're going to have gasoline stations all across the country to compete with Union Oil and the others, I think we should let the station managers buy into their operation."

George raised his eyebrows. "You mean we set them up in business, and they realize the profits?"

"Not exactly." Luke was warming to his subject. "It would work like this, Dad. We build the station for them, put in the tanks and pumps, and deliver the gasoline. They agree to purchase all Heron supplies, we take a percentage of the profits, and they get the rest!"

George nodded. "That's a good plan, son, a damned good idea. It stands to reason that if a man is in business for himself, he's going to rustle up new business. Competition is good, it's democratic."

Luke saw that he was tiring his father. "Well, I think I'll go for a canter. Luke is only six, but it's high time he learned to ride. I got on my first horse when I was two and a half—it's my earliest memory. It seemed then as though I was on top of a ten-story building!" He turned to the door. "I'll look in on you before dinner," he said.

"Just a moment, son." George smiled wanly and held up his hand. "Promise me one thing."

"Sure."

"Don't *ever* go public." His eyes were very dark and some of his old spirit returned.

"I promise, Dad."

Later, as Luke rode over the pasture lands that now covered the places where the oil wells used to be, he was suddenly struck with an idea. He could hardly wait to get home to make an important telephone call.

A week later, as George was resting comfortably after his ten o'clock injection, Luke bounded up the stairs. "Dad, you haven't been out of bed for six weeks. Let's go for a short drive. Okay?"

"I don't know whether I can make the stairs, son."

"Oh, hell, Dad, I'll take you down—no problem." He helped George sit up on the edge of the bed and then dressed him carefully. Very gently, Luke lifted the frail body in his arms and carried him downstairs. He knew his father could weigh no more than ninety pounds. He placed George in the back seat of the Stutz Bearcat, beside Letty and Jeanette.

The air was filled with summer fragrances. George sniffed the prairie breeze appreciatively. "Drive slowly, Luke," he admonished. "I want to enjoy the scenery."

Luke took a roundabout tour over the back roads by the Stevens' farm and pulled out on the newly paved section line road.

"Look," Letty exclaimed, "there's Jaundice and Fontine and Reverend and Thelma Haskell by the side of the road! Wonder what they're doing out here?"

"Well, let's stop and say hello." Luke replied evenly, keeping the excitement out of his voice.

Greetings were exchanged all around, then Jaundice and Fontine stepped aside, revealing a large bronze plaque that had been placed by the side of the road. "Read it, Dad," Luke said.

"Wouldn't you know I don't have my glasses with me?" George laughed. "Letty, will you be my proxy?"

Very quietly, Letty read:

Three hundred feet from this spot

On Easter Sunday
April 3, 1903
Number One Discovery Well was
brought in on the Heron Claim at
10,000 barrels a day

As everyone applauded, Bosley Trenton stepped out from the back of the Dice Packard. Letty looked at him for a long moment, very moved. Bosley kissed her wet cheek and shook George's fragile hand. "You brought her in," George said, glancing at the landmark. "What was it like, Bos?"

Bosley grinned, and his face almost became young again. "Wet!" he replied, and they all laughed. "Wet and very sticky."

Clement, Sarah, and three-year-old Patricia Anne arrived on the train three weeks later. "When the band goes back on the air waves in September, our headquarters will be back at our old stand, the Wyandotte Hotel in Kansas City," Clement announced. "Meantime, I'll have my first real vacation since I got out of the Army." He paused. "Say, has any one heard from Mitch?"

Letty shook her head. "No. Priscilla got a post card from Brussels in 1925. He was working for an importing/exporting company, but when she wrote back, her letter was returned. He's been such a source of grief." She smiled crookedly. "Thank God, I've been blessed with two good sons, two good daughters-in-law, and two bright grandchildren!"

"Well," Clement said, "Mitchell was always kind of strange, even when we were kids. He was always lazy. He told me himself he got kicked out of Stanford because he wouldn't study, and then being dishonorably discharged from the army didn't help matters." He paused. "Imagine Mitch not even knowing or caring about Uncle Edward dying. I'm so glad we can be here with Dad."

Letty nodded numbly and glanced at her watch. "Why don't you go upstairs for a few moments, but don't stay too long. He gets so tired."

Clement found Sarah sitting on his father's bed.

"Come in," George said, "we were just speaking about Indian affairs."

Sarah nodded. "Especially about the allotment issue. President Hoover is at least trying to bring about a reform of the old policies started by the Dawes Act."

"Yes," Clement replied bitterly, "and it's taken forty years to do it!"

"But the president is an honest man," George replied. "I know him well. When he appointed Charlie Rhoads commissioner of Indian affairs, he knew what he was doing. Rhoads is a Quaker banker and is very influential. But I don't know how proper restitution can be made—or even attempted." His voice was very weak, but he went on with a sigh. "The saddest part of the whole question is what is going to happen to all those Cherokees who have been born since the land allotments were handed out? Most of them are illiterate—they live in the hills and timberland, a lost people. The government isn't even aware of their existence in most cases. And what of their parents? They live on their little parcels of restricted land, with a vegetable garden and an old shack. The big acreage has long been snatched away and sold by land grabbers . . ."

George looked out the window to gain composure, then went on, his voice barely a whisper. "I should have done more, children." He shook his head again. "We members of the bar had to stand back while those corrupt men with political influence had educated men and women declared incompetent by the courts. Those men then administered the holdings—selling Indian land right and left for a few dollars an acre, reaping rich rewards themselves . . . Our hands were tied." His jaw began to tremble. "I'm tired now." He looked up. "I think your mother should come up . . ."

Clement exchanged glances with Sarah. They both knew it was a half hour after his usual injection was due. "We'll be up a little later, Dad," Clement replied.

"Oh, son?"

"Yes, Dad?"

"Would you play something for me?" He grinned feebly. "None of that jazz now, maybe something old-fashioned."

Clement went downstairs to the piano and played "In the Gloaming." When he finished, Sarah applauded, then took his hand. "I've been thinking, Clem. We were talking upstairs about people who stick to the old ways. But how about Cherokees who have been reared the American way, like you and me?" She paused, then blurted, "Have you ever regretted that you're a mixed-blood?"

He looked at her with a serious expression, then smiled. "No at least not in a long time. No one has called me 'Breedy' in years!"

Luke III would often curl up on George's bed to be regaled with stories of the old Cherokee days. "Grand-dad," he would say, "please tell me more. I want to know about Redbird Smith . . ."

"You've already worn me out now, Luke Three," he'd reply, "come in tomorrow." Soon Luke III became Luke Three to the family.

With all of the family present, dinnertime became a kind of ritual. The table was extended with extra leaves, and George would be carried down, either by Luke or Clement. Every afternoon, the boys would bathe him in the old-fashioned Japanned plunge that had been bought from Sears & Roebuck in 1903. Twice he was taken for a ride in the touring car, but Letty knew that the resurgence was only temporary, because his injections had been increased to four-hour intervals.

Late one night, there was a flurry of excitement on the drive outside, and Letty rushed breathlessly into George's room. "You have a very special visitor," she said, trying to be calm. "Are you prepared?"

"Am I allowed to guess?" He grinned.

"No. You'll never in the world expect . . ."

The door opened and a woman dressed in mauve came into the room with outstretched hands. Although they had not seen each other in twenty-two years, George recognized the woman immediately. "Hello, partner," he said.

Leona Barrett Elder kissed him on the cheek. "I just

had to see you, George," she said, "but I can only stay a few moments. I'm between trains."

"How good of you to come," he replied softly. He knew she was lying. What would a famous patron of the arts be doing between trains in Angel, Oklahoma?

She sat down beside him on the bed. "You've made me a very wealthy woman," she said quietly, "and up until now, I've never had the opportunity to thank you."

He grinned. "And, Letty and I have you to thank for introducing Clement to Lester Mainwaring."

"Oh, really!" She waved a hand in dismissal. "With that boy's talent, it would have been only a short time before he made it anyway." She leaned forward. "I received your letter about not selling my stock to anyone but a Heron. I wrote your company lawyer that I had no intention of ever selling. Your family will be notified first if I ever do."

Later, Letty stood on the porch and watched the car disappear down the driveway in the bright moonlight. She placed her head on the wooden column of the porch and wept; she had not broken down in a very long time. Then, cleansed and drained of energy, she went up to bed, taking the steps one at a time, holding securely on to the balustrade. At fifty-seven, she felt her life was over.

Late in the afternoon on October 24th, Bosley telephoned Letty. "First of all," he said in a strange voice, "how is George?"

"Very weak," Letty replied, "but he has such spirit! Bella and Torgo Chenovick visited him this morning and . . ."

"Excuse me," Bosley interrupted, "I would like to hear about that later, but for now, is Luke around?"

Letty paused. "Bosley, you sound so strange. Is something the matter?"

He tried to make his voice sound casual. "Just some business affairs . . ."

"Bosley, I know you well enough to know that something has happened. What is it?"

"I don't suppose, by any chance, you've been listening to the old wireless set?"

"No, we haven't had it on all week."

"Well, stocks are going crazy in New York. Prices have dropped alarmingly. In fact, there's been a seller's panic. It appears that some of the bankers in New York, headed by J.P. Morgan, have put together a kind of emergency fund to help steady the ups and downs, but . . ."

"But how can this affect us? Heron's not on the board!"

Despite his efforts to conceal it, Letty could hear the tension in his voice. "That's true. But, if there *is* a stock market crash, and at this point it looks like there might be, it's going to affect every corporation in the country, even the banks . . ." He paused. "My other phone is ringing, just a moment." When he returned to the line, his voice was urgent. "I must speak to Luke!"

"He's out riding, but he should be back any time."

"Have him call me at once," Bosley replied and hung up, leaving Letty holding the receiver in her shaking hand.

An hour later, Luke came down from the upstairs sitting room where he returned Bosley's call. He met his mother in the hall. "It's very bad. We don't know yet how it's going to affect the oil companies . . ." He paused. "Oh, I wish I could talk this over with Dad."

"You can't now, he's very low."

"I know, mother, I know." Luke sighed and looked out of the window at the peaceful countryside. A slight breeze was whispering over the prairie and the sounds of whippoorwills added a pensive note as the bees worked over the blood-red roses climbing over the window trellis. Here in Angel, it was so peaceful, yet in every city in the land, dark clouds were forming over the horizon. "Keep the line free," he said, "I expect a call from Armbuster any time."

George, growing weaker by the day, asked Letty to telephone Sam, Born-Before-Sunrise. "Tell him I need him. He'll understand."

372

Sam arrived two days later, tall and boyish-looking at fifty-eight.

George shook his hand gravely. "How does it feel to be one of the most famous obstetricians in America?"

Sam looked down at his boots and smiled. "Probably," he said in his peculiar high voice, "the same way it feels to be a renowned oil tycoon!" Letty had asked him to say nothing about the stock market crash. Blessfully, George was too listless to read the *Enid Morning News* or the *Angel Wing*.

"Thank you for coming," George said matter-of-factly. "I don't think it will be long now."

The next day, Sunday, he summoned Sam to his bedside early in the afternoon. Although he had just been injected, he was in very great pain, short of breath, and perspiring, but he propped himself up in bed and combed his snow white hair, then asked the family to come in to see him one at a time.

Letty stood in the hallway as George had his private moment with each of them. She marveled at their composure, watching the stern faces emerging from the bedroom. George had taught his children about death, and there were no tears.

Sam came into the room wearing his white turban. George smiled feebly. "I think it's time to begin," he said.

Sam removed from his pocket a small scarlet capsule filled with powdered red mushrooms, and handed it to him with a glass of sweet water.

A few moments later, the room became extremely clear to George. He could see the tiny, intricate designs in the Battenburg lace curtains at the windows. It was as if he were looking through the pattern to the sunlit world outside. He could hear the fluttering wings of the hummingbird working over the trailing roses on the window sill; the wings whispered in his ears. When Letty came to his bedside and took his hand, he could see each strand of her steel gray hair, as if each were magnified a thousand times.

The pain gnawed at his chest and spread outward to every pore, and he thought he could not withstand the exquisite torture. But when he thought that he must cry out in anguish, the pain separated itself into thousands of little pieces of light; each pore opened and released the little prisms, which floated gracefully upward to form a misty cloud over his bed near the ceiling. For the first time in months, he was free of pain.

Then Sam's voice, as high and as soft as the flapping of the hummingbird's wings outside, pierced his consciousness. *"You are going on a journey, my dear friend. Up ahead is a brilliant white light—one source of power that is stronger than any you've known. You must become part of that light . . ."*

George saw the mysterious illumination as if emerging from a long tunnel. He appeared to be suspended in space. He had an intense feeling of belonging to that light and realized that at all costs he had to move toward it.

Letty opened her eyes and spoke, her voice under strict control. "You are loved," she said simply, "You are very much loved."

George opened his eyes drowsily. "And, I love you too, lady . . ."

She continued with the words of encouragement that Sam had taught her: "I can only go part of the way with you now. When it comes time to proceed by yourself, release my hand . . ."

It seemed to George that he was traveling more rapidly now. His body was a free-form mass, as light as the flame of a candle. He knew that he must proceed to the incredibly blue place beyond the light. He felt a joyous new freedom. With great ease and a momentary feeling of regret, he continued to drift outward, spinning toward the new source of blue light that seemed millions of miles distant.

Back in the room, Letty stared at the hand that had withdrawn itself from her grasp, then she tenderly kissed the palm.

PART THREE

The Retribution

29

Breaking the Tides

Luke stood up wearily.

He looked down the conference table, which seemed to stretch into infinity, and addressed the board members of the Heron Oil Company. "I have called this emergency meeting, gentlemen," he said calmly, "because of the obvious problems that we face. We've got to institute immediate measures if our company is to survive as a separate entity." He glanced down at his field reports. "We are producing around eight hundred eighty-seven thousand barrels of oil per day and selling in the neighborhood of six hundred fifty thousand barrels per day. Our tank farms are literally overflowing." He looked up for a moment, his eyes dark. "It's no consolation to know that our competitors are in the same boat.

"Many stations are selling gasoline at lower prices than production costs. Last year, in 1929, the automobile industry manufactured over five million cars, this year considerably less; in the next five years, production may be halved. Our sales analysts predict a new series of price wars among service stations. You can bet Standard Oil will do everything to break us few independents.

"I propose the following drastic measures: that we sell out our interest in the Maracaibo field in Venezuela, cut our drilling rigs from thirty to five, close down the refinery in Tulsa, and initiate a five-day work week." He paused, looking very grave. "Furthermore, I propose that we close the Canadian Wildcat Tool Company and dissolve the Heron Oil Company of Ohio." He swallowed hard; his mouth was dry as dirt. He glanced at Bosley. "It pains me to state that British Heron is also in deep trouble, but Gerald Motley will sell his wife's jewels to buy us out. His offer of one thousand pounds is not generous, but at a time when more money is going out of the company than coming in, I think we should accept it." He paused dramatically, and Bosley had never felt more proud of him than now, at the moment of truth.

"If we can make these changes," Luke continued, "I believe that Heron will survive. Other cuts may be necessary, gentlemen. With the stock market crash, going public is, of course, no longer possible." He sighed and his eyes suddenly looked very old. "I further propose that we suspend all board of director salaries for the years 1930–1931."

There was dead silence; each board member stared straight ahead. Finally, J. C. Armbuster stood up slowly, and supporting his thin frame against the table, raised a withered arm. At eighty-four, he was a shadow of his former self, but his watery blue eyes sparked with fire. "I think this is a remarkable proposal," he said in his high, reedy voice, "one that has obviously caused great personal pain. And I know that if George Story were alive today, he would sanction this proposal. I wish to tender a vote of confidence in our president." He raised his bony hands and started to applaud. To a man, each board member rose and echoed his sentiments.

Luke bowed his head. "Thank you, gentlemen," he said, and the weariness slipped from his shoulders. At the age of thirty-six, Luke had faced his first great crisis—and won.

Letty made a last tour through the empty house on Connecticut Avenue. The servants had been gone for weeks; only the faithful Hans remained. She spent a few moments alone in the bedroom that she had shared with George for ten years, then slowly walked down the stairs, the same stairs that, bedecked in holly and mistletoe, had seen so much activity during each holiday season. She glanced into the ballroom that had been decorated with poinsettias for Clement and Sarah's wedding, and surveyed the side lawn by the terrace where Luke and Jeanette had said their vows under an arbor of red and yellow roses.

She went to the great double front door and turned to the foyer. In her mind's eye, she saw the enfeebled George making his way down the hall, to return to Angel for the last time. It was only then that her eyes scalded with tears.

Hans held out his arm to her. "Never mind, ma'am. Hard times will pass. Conditions will improve."

She pressed his arm; she could not trust her voice. Her new life would start at a small apartment next to the Shoreham Hotel.

On Tuesday morning, August 13th, 1930, Manford Pederson came home for the first time in two days. Weary and haggard, a scraggly beard covering his face, his eyes bloodshot, he staggered upstairs to bed. At first, Priscilla thought that he was drunk, yet one look at his tortured face and she saw that whatever was plaguing him had nothing to do with alcohol. He was drunk with fatigue and he needed sleep . . . .

Mrs. Bellows served dinner on a table in front of the fire, but Priscilla sent the untouched tray back to the kitchen. She knew the servants were listening to the radio, when Mrs. Bellows came in and touched her shoulder. "It's a sad day, ma'am," she said, "The newscaster just told about Heron . . . Can I turn on the set for you?"

She shook her head. "I'll hear the whole story from Mr. Pederson."

"Shall I have your bed turned down early?"

"No, thank you," Priscilla replied wearily. "I'm going to stay up a bit." She poured a glass of sherry and sat before the fire. The wine made her stomach warm. In fact, she was feeling a bit giddy, when she heard Manford's step on the stair. He had shaved, combed his hair, and put on a clean red shirt and blue trousers, but he wore the air of a condemned man. He poured himself a large glass of scotch, took a long pull, and then joined her by the fireplace. "You might as well know," he said dully. "Heron Furniture dropped seventy-eight points on the big board today. Our bankers were on the phone all morning . . . principal stockholders are frantic . . ." His hands were shaking so badly that he could barely light a cigar. He blew the first puff of smoke into the fireplace. "I don't see any way out, Prissy. I won't be able to make payments to the banks or the stockholders . . ." He shook his head and took another gulp of scotch. "I'm not young any more, Prissy, I can't start over . . ."

"What do you mean, 'start over'?" she asked sharply.

He looked at her with wide eyes. "Don't you understand, Prissy, we're broke."

"Obviously, the company's in a bad way, but we can't personally be affected very much. Edward . . ."

"What in the hell are you bringing up Edward for? The man's been dead for four years!" He took a long pull from the glass, then he went on, talking more to himself than to her. "Edward was a fool. He couldn't see his hand in front of his face . . . no imagination . . . plodded along year after year . . ."

Priscilla placed the wine glass on the sideboard. "Now, give me some straight answers, Manford." Her voice rose erratically. "Edward left me a personal fortune. I know he had ninety thousand dollars in life insurance, and this house is free and clear. There's also the farm at Angel, income from crops . . ." She stood up stiffly and stretched her back. "So we are *not* broke. Maybe the company is, but we're not!"

Manford downed the last of the scotch and when he spoke, his speech was slightly slurred. "Dear old Prissy. Edward always said not to bother you with details, that you never had a head for business. His only regret was that you wouldn't let him invest in Heron Oil—that was a big mistake." He looked up and laughed hollowly. "We'd weather this mess if we had a piece of Heron Oil—it'll survive us all. Edward—"

"*Edward, Edward, Edward!*" Priscilla cried, "that's all we can talk about. It's as if he were here in this very room . . ."

". . . and laughing!"

378

"Laughing?"

Manford hugged his shoulders and rocked back and forth in the chair, looking like a mechanical soldier in his red shirt and blue trousers. "The old boy turned out to be right after all. He always said the biggest mistake in the world would be to go public!"

"Manford!" Priscilla screamed, "tell me everything, right now!"

He stopped rocking and looked at her slyly. "You might as well know. When we were first married, you signed a lot of papers . . ."

"Of course!" She retorted hotly, "You had to have permission to go public."

"You also signed a power of attorney." He closed his eyes so that the room would stop swimming, but the sickening motion continued in his head. "The life insurance money is gone, this house is mortgaged up to the hilt . . . John Dice advanced me cold cash and holds the papers on the farm. . . ." He glanced up briefly and the room took shape once more. "They won't be able to take your diamonds." He raised his eyebrows. "Everything else will go under."

She stood over him, looking down at his hunched form in the big chair. "You *bastard!*" she cried, near hysteria. "I can't believe you would do this to me! You said we would be *millionaires.*"

"We were—for a time, but expansion—"

"What happened to the stockholders' money?" She was shaking with fury. "We had a personal fortune, besides."

"I kept buying big blocks of Heron Furniture stock. It was going up and up and there was no end in sight."

"You mean you continued to buy our *own* stock?"

"On margin, in 1928 and 1929 . . ."

"Margin?" she spat out "You *idiot!*"

"Yes, I am an idiot . . ." His voice had fallen to a frantic, drunken whisper. ". . . to have married you! You made Edward's life miserable all those years. Greed—it was pure and simple greed that turned the trick for me. I saw Heron Furniture in the clouds, the sky was the limit . . . now it's gone . . ." He stood up and swayed toward the door, ". . . and so am I."

Then he turned and bowed, almost falling over. "To the lady from Oklahoma, I say 'goodbye'. If I had a hat, I'd take it off to you, but I don't, so as the French would say, *au revoir*."

He staggered down the hall to the front door, Priscilla running after him. She saw the servants huddled in the dining room, watching them, like a family of mice gathered in a cornfield. They had obviously been privy to the beginning of the scene and they might as well see the end. "You can't go anywhere—you're *drunk*!" she cried.

He opened the door with difficulty, then turned and faced her. "I am not only leaving the Heron Furniture Company, and the fair city of Dallas, Texas, but I am leaving you, dear Priscilla White Heron Pederson!" He waved a hand. "Ta, ta!" He slammed the door.

She stood with her back resting against the hard wood of the drawing room door while she heard the Rolls Royce sputter, then roar to life and pull out of the driveway into the street.

Suddenly, she could stand it no longer. She flung the front door open and screamed out into the night: "I hope you die! I hope you get killed! I hope a truck runs into you!"

But Manford Pederson survived the obstacle course through the Dallas traffic, and early the next morning, accompanied by Deborah Lindsey, he chartered an airplane for Mexico City, with fifty thousand dollars in cash stored in his thin alligator brief case.

Clement's itinerary for 1931 included a three-month summer holiday. He liked playing each hotel for two weeks instead of the old six- to eight-month stands at one location. Still, the frequent moves from one city to another was unnerving for Sarah and Patricia Anne, aged five, though they always occupied large suites in the same hotels where the band was playing.

"I think we'll go to Europe this year," he announced one night after the last set. "What do you think, Sarah?"

She looked up from a crossword puzzle, her long swan neck swathed in a filmy chiffon scarf. "I can think of more productive action than traipsing all over England and France with a small child in tow," she replied laconically. "Why don't we wait?"

"Until when?" he said darkly. "This is the first real vacation I've had."

"Yes," she replied tartly, "and it could grow into a permanent one if money gets more scarce. How long do you think that the public can continue to patronize tea dances, let alone go to dinner shows?"

"If prohibition is ever repealed, and people can drink good booze legitimately, it will prolong . . ."

She sighed. "Then you would be playing to a passel of drunks! Oh, I'm so tired of traveling, Clem. Europe would be just another string of fancy hotels that we really can't afford."

"You're so damned practical!" he retorted. "Any other woman would jump up and down with joy at the prospect of traveling abroad." He paused. "You see, what I would like to do is rent a car and just drive, stopping at little villages whenever we get the urge, spending a few days here and there, just enjoying ourselves."

She shook her dark head until her earrings jangled. "No really, Clem, let's just stay home, in one place, and try to lead a normal life—at least for three months."

"You knew what it would be like when you married a musician," he replied quietly.

"Yes, but I had no intention of getting pregnant so soon."

"Do you think I planned it that way?"

"Well, if you hadn't been so naive . . ."

"Well, all I knew about birth control was the rhythm method!"

Suddenly she laughed, all rancour gone in an instant. "That's really marvelous, Clem," eyes twinkling mischievously, "but being a musician, what else could be expected?"

He laughed at his unintentional pun, came up behind her chair and placed his arms around her neck. "I know better now," he whispered, and reached down and kissed her neck.

She nuzzled up against his rough beard. "If you'll

scrape off that beard so your face won't feel like sand-paper when we make love, I'll sleep with you."

"Don't you always?"

She smiled. "You know what I mean!"

He bathed and shaved, then joined her between the cool sheets. "Do you know that you look a lot like Norma Shearer?" he said.

She ran her fingers along his smooth jaw. "You're not unlike Ramon Navarro—except that you don't have a mustache."

"That can be remedied, if it would stimulate you a bit more. If you'd like to pretend I'm Navarro . . ."

"I don't need to pretend you're anyone." She kissed him full on the mouth, ran her little tongue between his lips, then placed her arms around his shoulders and held his chest to her small, firm breasts.

"I'd like to make love to you in a small chalet in Switzerland that was covered with snow," he said softly, "or take you by the water's edge at Saint-Tropez, or chase you down a mountainside covered with flowers. We could take off our clothes and . . ."

She giggled. "Sounds awfully uncomfortable to me. I'd prefer a bed, thank you."

"Everything is so cut and dried with you."

"Not necessarily, but I wouldn't find any fun in run-ning around naked in some meadow, getting stickers in my feet, probably running into poison ivy . . ."

He laughed. "There's no one in the whole world quite like you, Sarah." He kissed her breasts with new fervor, raising himself up slightly. As he moved over her, she responded quickly, which he loved—he never had to wait for her, never had to build an elaborate foreplay, which some members of the band com-plained their wives required. Sarah belonged to him, and he to her—it was this feeling of want and desire that could be fulfilled and renewed in an instant that he loved best of all.

Soon they were gasping, and they rose up to meet each other; finally, in a great rush of feeling, they reached the peak simultaneously, then lay side by side, exhausted. When both regained their breath, they drew together in a lose embrace, then she snuggled down into the warmth of his arms and with his body touching hers, fell asleep.

Toward morning, she awakened, startled to find his eyes open and glazed. "I can't sleep," he admitted reluctantly, "I've been thinking . . ."

"I hope so," she smiled, "I'd hate to think that you've been awake all night just staring at me!"

He laughed and moved his hands across her breasts. "I want to make love to you again."

"Well," she replied pertly, rested from her long sleep, "what's stopping you?"

He pinned her arms back playfully and brought himself over her in one movement until all of his body weight lay upon her. "I want to make love to you under water, with the tides rushing up over our shoulders, and my asparagus—"

She giggled. "Are you still on that tack?" She paused. "Now, that I think about it, that might be fun—if the water's warm."

"Yes," he said, laughing, "else I would shrink up like a pigmy!"

"And I have no desire to be intimate with anyone less of a man than you are." She paused. "I thought I put that rather well, didn't you?"

For an answer he kissed her, pushing his mouth over hers until she fought for breath. Finally she moved away from him slightly. "Whew! Give a girl a chance to breathe!"

"Only if you agree to go to Europe with me. Otherwise . . ."

"All right! I'll go! Now, kiss me again!"

But Clement and Sarah did not go to Europe. Three weeks before the scheduled embarkation on June 5, 1932, she announced that she was pregnant again. "It must have been all that talk about making love on the sand and in the water that did it," she laughed.

"And I suppose I was an innocent bystander?"

"Well," she replied with a twinkle in her eye. "I admit I had some help. Of course, I had my eyes closed. I pretended you were Ramon Navarro in a flowered island skirt singing 'The Pagan Love Song'."

"You're behind the times, my pet," he replied with a

grin. "While I was making love to you, I heard Ginger Rogers singing very clearly quite a different song."

"And, what was that?"

Clement sang in a pleasant baritone the song about going home and getting one's scanties and panties and shuffling off to some place called Buffalo.

Bosley Trenton, Letty at his side, headed the Packard out of Washington, D. C. into Alexandria, Virginia. It was Sunday and the automobile traffic was very heavy. He turned off the main highway and took a country road that ran along the Potomac River. It was a warm day, and the blue river matched the scattered patches of wild lupin on the opposite bank. They did not speak, each appreciating the peaceful journey, but when he turned into the driveway that led up to Mount Vernon, Letty purred with pleasure. "How delightful, Bos."

"I thought we would have luncheon here just for a kick, and soak up some heritage at the same time."

Later, in the tea room, over steaming plates of Welsh rarebit, made from Martha Washington's original recipe (which for the first time in years was made with real ale, the waitress explained, thanks to the repeal of the 18th Amendment), Bosley looked into Letty's eyes "I wanted to bring you here today, because I thought the atmosphere might somehow make it easier for me to make a confession."

"A confession, Bos, now really!" Letty exclaimed with a laugh.

"No, I'm serious. I suppose we really should be back in Angel, because what I've got to relate took place there."

"You're not making any sense at all," she said with a sigh. "Now what is it you're trying to say?"

"It has to do with those early days at the Heron claim." He looked down at his hands. "I was a very ambitious young man then, but I didn't trust my feelings . . ."

"Well, apparently your feelings were right on target, because you discovered oil on the property."

He nodded numbly. "Yes. But I found the oil on my

first visit, only I didn't tell anyone then. Oh no, I was too smart for that!" His voice was bitter with reproach. "I went to a lot of trouble researching oil processing; I wasted months of valuable time. I first met J. C. Armbuster in Beaumont, Texas, and almost got killed, but that's another tale. I wasted so much time that I didn't get around to realizing that I was in love with you . . ." He glanced up at her startled expression.

"Is that your confession, Bos?" she asked quietly.

"Not all of it. At first, I wanted to propose to you, but only because I thought you would come into a lot of money. I was arrogant and short-sighted." It was difficult for him to go on, but he set his jaw and forced the words out of tight lips. "I finally came back to Angel, and when I walked into Edward's cabinet shop and he told me that you and George Story were away on your honeymoon, it hit me that I had really been in love with you all along."

He brought his hands together and closed his eyes tightly. "I was an ignorant fool, a brash and selfish man with the emotions of an adolescent." He paused, then went on softly. "I suppose I grew up that afternoon. When I went to fetch both of you at the depot, and saw how much you loved George, well, it was the most difficult day of my life." He sighed deeply and opened his eyes.

She reached across the table and took his hand. "Well I, too, have a confession, Bos. I was attracted to you. But then you resembled Luke, if you remember, and I was afraid that I was trying to hold on to the past. When you were around, it was as if Luke was not really dead. I'd come into a room and see you standing there, and my heart would do flip-flops. Mother Heron, of course, was enthralled, because when she was with you, she was in a way with her son. But as time passed, and you became a member of the family to all of us, your resemblance to Luke faded." She paused. "I suppose by then none of us remembered what Luke looked like, and anyway, at that point, it didn't matter."

"When George Story came along at the Angel drawing that day, I knew that I loved him. Our love was a very physical thing. . . ." She looked up. "I can say that now," she said with wonder. "All the years we were together . . ."

Bosley smiled. "You know that I'm still in love with you after all these years!"

"Well, Bos, you know that you are loved by all of us . . ."

"What I'm saying is, would you consider marrying me at this stage of the game?"

She took a sip of coffee, then looked up over the rim of the cup. "I'm sixty years old, Bos."

He took a deep breath. "I don't expect that we'll set the world on fire, Letty, but you're alone, and I'm alone . . ."

"I must have time to think, Bos. I wonder what the children would say?"

He smiled wryly. "The boys have always been close to me, of course—Luke more than Clement—still, I don't think they would turn thumbs down."

"I didn't mean it that way, Bos. If I do marry you, I must solve all questions in my mind. Frankly, I had never thought about remarrying."

"George made a much better husband than I would have—in those days. But, one thing that we have going for us, Letty, is maturity. You've been tied down all of your life, and in a way, so have I, because I've been married to my profession. But now that the children have families of their own, there isn't any reason why you can't really start to enjoy life. Travel, for one thing . . ."

She nodded. "But with the Heron austerity program, there isn't much money to do anything."

He nodded. "But no one has money nowadays. We can still make a new life. We certainly didn't have much when we started out."

"That's true, Bos." She looked down at the cold plates of half consumed Welsh rarebit, and glanced around the empty dining room. "Perhaps we'd better leave."

"I want to show you the formal gardens. There are what seems like miles of mazes made out of shrubs." He lowered his voice. "Rumor has it that Martha Washington had them specially designed by a French landscape artist. When George became overly amorous, he'd chase her into the garden and she'd lose him in the maze."

Letty laughed out loud. "I doubt the authenticity of that story!"

"Well," he smiled, "you have to admit that it makes a good anecdote."

"Yes," she agreed, "it does." And as she took his arm, she felt tranquility descend on Mount Vernon, looking out over the huge gardens at the people strolling through Martha's maze. A rosy glow seemed to envelope everything—from the couples arm-in-arm and the little children playing hide and seek, to the flower beds of roses, chrysanthemums, and gladiolus.

Looking up at Bosley Trenton, Letty felt a surge of emotion that while not quite like a young girl's feeling of physical passion, was very much akin to love . . .

30

Deprivation

From November 8, 1932, when Franklin Roosevelt was elected president, until his inauguration on January 20th, was a time of chaos for the American people.

The same day that Letty and Bosley were married, John Dice failed to be reelected as Republican senator from Oklahoma, and came back to the bank in Angel with a heavy heart. He had carried only one county in the entire state—Garfield. Expecting the community to be cold and withdrawn, he was surprised at the warmth of his reception. Bella Chenovick told him, "We're glad to have you back, Jaundice. Maybe you can make some sense out of all this financial mess." She held a barn dance in his honor, even bringing a small cowboy band out from Enid for the occasion. "Torgo can't play all night any more," she said, but when the old man, who had just celebrated his seventieth birthday, stood up on the hastily erected bandstand, he was met with cheers. He played an old sentimental Bohemian folk song with unerring grace, but it was his encore number—"Turkey in the Straw"—that brought down the house.

After the peach ice cream was served, Fontine turned to Bella. "I'm so glad just to be back here permanently," she announced. "Life in Washington, with all those parties, almost did me in. I swear we were on the go all the time, traipsing from one big house to another. I almost wore my legs out."

"Won't you miss it?" Bella asked wistfully.

"My stars, no! I'm going to sit out there on my front porch and just let the world go by, Jaundice is going to look after the bank until he retires, and that's the sum of things. I'm going to bake chocolate pecan cookies and Angel cakes and get up to two hundred pounds. I'm sick and tired of diets."

Bella took her arm, "Remind me before you leave to give you a couple of quarts of spiced peaches." She lowered her voice. "They're especially good, because I put in a shot of cherry wine!" She looked quickly over the barn to be sure that she wasn't overheard and then went on. "Fontine, put in a good word for us with John. Torgo hated to do it, but we took all of our money out of the bank yesterday. This has nothing to do with John, we want him to know that, but it's a small bank and if anything happens . . ."

Fontine wrinkled her forehead. "What do you mean?"

"Well, some banks have closed already in Michigan. Don't you read the papers or listen to the radio?"

Fontine shook her head. "Not much. I don't know anything about politics. I guess that's why I got along so well in Washington. I'd meet all those women, some of whom I liked very much, and I'd just say, 'I don't know whether your husband is a Democrat or a Republican, it doesn't matter to me, but I *like* you'. And I was invited to all the women's parties and we never discussed politics. Jaundice didn't like it very much. He'd say: 'You mean you had lunch with *her*? Her husband is a bitter enemy of mine'," Fontine laughed, "but it made no difference to me . . . I'm a homebody."

The next morning, February 20, 1933, John Dice wrote a most difficult letter: "Dear Priscilla, I do not like to communicate with you under the circumstances of this letter, but I have no alternative. The note on the Heron farm is sixty days past due. As you know from my previous letters, I have personally been paying the premiums for the last year and a half. I am no longer able to render this service for you. I realize your position, and I know how difficult it has been these last three years as a woman alone without income, but the state of emergency that exists in this country is very real. The community of Angel is just now beginning to feel the pinch. If the Heron refinery shuts down (the

389

production of oil hereabouts has dwindled) our citizens will be very bad off indeed. Please bring your payments up to date on the Heron place. I have no wish to fore-close on the property, but unless cash is forthcoming, we will have no alternative. Because of the closeness that has always existed between our families, I have taken no drastic steps before now. Please understand my position. Fontine sends her love." He crossed out 'love' and put in 'regards', then he gave it to the stenog-rapher to retype. He signed the letter simply 'Jaundice'.

Priscilla folded John Dice's letter carefully, then went into the bedroom of the tiny apartment on Young Street in downtown Dallas and knelt in front of the bu-reau. Opening the bottom drawer, she lifted out the tiny jewel case. Five rings remained: a one-carat star sap-phire, an emerald dinner ring, a ruby heart surrounded by diamond chips, a diamond wedding ring, and the plain golden band that Edward had given her when they were married in 1900. She would prefer to sell the band, but the relic was worthless—the gold had worn away in spots. She had been a fool not to have allowed Edward to replace the band with a diamond of suitable size when they'd come into money, but in a weak mo-ment, she had pleaded sentiment and consequently he had given her the emerald ring, far less valuable now than a diamond.

She took the jewel case to the kitchen and cleaned the gems with a toothbrush, soda, and ammonia. Only five pieces remained out of twenty-two! How stupid she had been trying to keep the big house after Man-ford had left and the stores had gone into receivership. What did it matter now if she had been able to keep the payments up on the house for two years, with the sav-ings and loan having foreclosed? As much as she hated the farm, she couldn't let that go, too, especially to a bank owned primarily by that uppity John Dice! It made no difference if he had served one term in the Senate, he was still Texas white trash.

She wrapped the emerald dinner ring in a napkin, which she placed in her pocketbook, then took the bus downtown to see the Jewish pawnbroker.

"President Roosevelt is a sonofabitch!" John Dice cried. "And I'm not saying that just because I'm Republican, either!" His face was mottled red. "Within his first hundred days in office, his meddling has brought about the Agricultural Adjustment Act, which plans to remove forty million acres out of cultivation and reimburse the farmers for crops they would have normally brought in! Paying people for sitting on their ass! I tell you, Luke, it's unconstitutional—Congress has to get money to pay the farmers somewhere. It's going to come from new taxes levied on flour millers, meat packers—all the way down the line. This action has to raise prices to the consumer!"

Luke nodded. "The National Recovery Act limits the amount of oil we can produce, too. Heron can live with it, because we've got our fingers in service stations. We're fighting competition by introducing a higher octane gas and an improved performance motor oil, but you, John, you're stuck here in Angel at the bank . . ."

John Dice nodded glumly. "Yes, I get scared to death every time I look at how many mortgages I've got in the safe. I wouldn't sleep a wink if I went over my holdings. I'm in a bad way." He paused. "Even though I've paid off ten cents on the dollar to all my customers who had money in the bank, I can hardly look anyone in the eyes any more when I walk down Main Street."

"Yet you didn't have to open up after the bank holiday, John. You could've stayed closed like so many other banking institutions."

"I couldn't do that! These people are my *friends*." John rubbed his eyes. "But all these new agencies—the Federal Emergency Relief, the Civilian Conservation Corps—they may sound good on paper, but the national debt's going to hold over for our children's children to pay off! The Works Progress Administration alone cost millions—and for what?—men leaning on a shovel and moving dirt from one area to another!"

Fontine came in from the kitchen, hands on her wide hips. "With this AAA and NRA and RFC and WPA and FER and CCC—why, if my mama was alive, she'd

391

likely say that old Sara Delano Roosevelt was scared by an alphabet while she was carrying Franklin!"

John laughed. "You've got a point, Fourteen, but seriously, with times as bad as they are, I think it would be a good idea if you got rid of the cook and the maid. I've heard some rumblings among the townspeople who apparently don't think it's right for us to have help when they can't even afford food on the table. Also," he paused, "I don't want folks to think that any of their money has filtered down to us."

Fontine sighed. "Well, Jaundice, I've got a sixteen-room house, which you can't expect me to keep clean at my age! I suppose I could go back to cooking, that wouldn't kill me, but I've got to have *one* hired girl! Now, you can't deny me that!"

"All right, Fourteen." He suddenly laughed. "I was just thinking—when we came to the Territory forty years ago, who'd have thought we'd end up like this? With a big mansion—and broke."

She smiled wryly. "Yes," she agreed, "it is kinda funny—and I'm back where I started—in the kitchen."

Mitchell crawled out of the boxcar, stretched his cramped legs and sleepily rubbed his eyes. What town was this? What day was this? He looked down the railroad tracks and saw the sign *Galveston*, and, shifting his knapsack to his left shoulder, joined the parade of men headed toward shanty town.

He joined the other 'bos' around the campfire and listened laconically as a grizzled old man in a frog voice told of his life in Pennsylvania before his wife died and he had taken to the road. It was a tale, with variations, that Mitchell had heard many times in the last several years. He took a small World War canteen out of his knapsack and scooped up water from a nearby stream. As the water heated over the campfire, he placed a small cracked mirror in the fork of a tree and then sharpened his straight-edge razor on a small leather strop. Looking at his haggard reflection, he carefully shaved off four days' growth of beard.

"Heh, heh," the old man cried, "look at the glamour

boy!" And when Mitchell came out from behind the tree, where he had changed into a clean dark blue shirt and pants, the old man pounded his knee. "Goin' out lookin'?" he asked.

"Might as well," Mitchell replied, combing his scraggly hair into a semblance of order. "I'm hungry."

"So are we," the old man replied darkly, "bring somethin' good back."

Mitchell repacked his knapsack, nodded to the men around the fire, and started down the tracks. He fished around in his pocket for a nickel and climbed aboard a bus, and thirty minutes later, disembarked in a more affluent part of town. Sometimes he could tell by the looks of the front yard if a house had no man.

He selected an old Victorian house with waist-high weeds that reminded him vaguely of The Widows. He had not thought about Leona Barrett in years. She had always been nice to him and had not even given much of a lecture when Sam caught him peeking in the parlor when he was nine years old.

He went around to the back of the house and knocked on the rear door, which was opened by a rotund little lady with pink cheeks who reminded him of Bella Chenovick. What was the matter with him? Why was the past closing in? He doffed his cap and smiled. "Your front yard surely looks like it could stand cutting, Ma'am," he said respectfully. "I'd be happy to do a good job for fifty cents."

The pink cheeks faded somewhat. "I don't have any extra cash," she said hesitantly, "but I could provide a meal of bacon and eggs—after you finish."

"I'd be grateful, Ma'am." Some of the bos were arrogant, but he had found through many bitter lessons that it was best to be suppliant.

He mowed the lawn, raked up the leaves and grass, and in twenty minutes reappeared at the back door, expecting to be handed his plate of food to consume on the stoop but instead was invited into the kitchen. He would have preferred to eat outside, away from prying eyes, because he was so hungry. He looked at the table setting for two on the clean oilcloth. "I hope you don't mind joining me," the woman said, "but I get so lonely." She smiled, "And to tell you the truth, it's been a long time since I've cooked breakfast for a man."

After he had washed his hands in the kitchen sink, he sat down at the table. It had been so long since he had eaten civilly, that he had to watch his manners. He carefully unfolded the napkin and slowly began to eat the bacon, eggs, and fried potatoes with her watching him all the time, studying him as if he were a rare find in a curiosity shop.

She was a nice-looking middle-aged lady with a fine complexion, slightly gray hair pushed up under a white house cap and brilliant green eyes that took in every move. She had let him know she was a widow within the first few moments of conversation, yet from her genteel manner, it was obvious that she did not take tramps into her dining room. But she was too old for him; she must be in her late thirties. Then a piece of potato lodged in his throat as he thought, panic-stricken, Why, I'm thirty-eight!

When she looked at him questioningly, he knew what she wanted to know before she asked, but he continued to eat slowly, deciding on which story to tell—the one where his wife had died of tuberculosis and he was left with three toddlers, or the one where he had been shell-shocked in the war, or the one where his whole family had been wiped out in a tornado? Instead he said simply, "My name is Mitchell Heron." Then he went on perversely, knowing that he would never see her again, "and I graduated from Stanford University just before the war . . ." He felt guilty for a moment. Well, he had *gone* to Stanford.

She shook her head sadly. "It's a pity that there's no work for an able-bodied man nowadays."

He smiled wanly. "Believe it or not, Ma'am, I once turned down a big job with my father's company. It was after the war and I couldn't settle down. I got a job with an importing and exporting firm and went to Europe for three years, then held a series of other jobs until the stock market crash."

"Then I take it you've never been back home?"

He shook his head. "I never really got on with my

family. They had a lot of money then, although everything's down the drain now. With my mother it was all show. In Munich, I read in a newspaper that my father had died, and I almost went back then, but she married the vice president of the firm, a man whom I always disliked intensely, so . . ."

"If the newspaper in Europe printed your Dad's obituary, he must have been famous." Her eyes grew large, as round as buttons.

"No, it was only because he was head of a well-known firm."

"Do you mind telling me which one?"

"You've probably never heard the name. It was the Heron Furniture Company."

"Heron?" She smiled softly. "Come in the dining room for a minute."

She opened the door and stood proudly beside the dining set. "This suite was given to me by my daddy. It's as beautiful now as it was then." She removed a leaf from the middle of the table and pointed to the crossbar. "Look!"

Mitchell read: MFG. BY HERON FURNITURE COMPANY, ANGEL, OKLAHOMA, 1910. He smiled. "That's before my father opened so many stores. He probably worked on this himself." He ran his hands along the smooth patina. "He was a master craftsman, Ma'am."

She nodded. "It's my most treasured possession. Oh, I've some chairs that are older and cost a lot more money, but this has class." She smiled softly. "And so do you, young man."

He blushed, unused to compliments, stammered a confused reply, and ambled back into the kitchen, where he picked up his cap. "Much obliged for the breakfast," he said, taking a toothpick from the top of the ice box.

"Wait a moment . . . Mitchell. If you're not due anywhere important, I have a garage and an attic that needs cleaning, and the basement is filled with old papers. I have about a week's work, I guess. If you're a mind to, there's a little room in the back of the garage where you can sleep."

He smiled. "Thank you, ma'am."

"Please stop calling me ma'am. My name is Elizabeth Perkins, but everyone calls me Lizzie."

That night he crawled between cool, homespun sheets for the first time in many months. Not since that night in Los Angeles when he had stayed with a street whore had he slept so comfortably. He was just drifting off when he was conscious of a movement at the door. Although he could doze at the drop of a hat, he had learned to snap awake at the slightest movement—his shoes had been stolen one night on the road while he slept, and he had gone barefoot for two days in the cold of December before pinching the boots off a kid who had passed out on rot gut. He raised up in bed. "Who is it?" he asked, then he saw Lizzie's figure in the moonlight, dressed in a white nightgown.

She sat on the side of the bed. "I thought you might be lonely."

Now that he knew what was expected of him, he smiled. "Not especially." He had no intention of playing hard-to-get at this stage of the game. He hadn't been laid in six months, and with the light from the window shining softly on her hair, the woman was not unattractive. He leaned over and kissed her lightly on the lips; from her response, he knew that her need for him was greater than his for her.

He gathered her in his arms and ran his hands over her plump body. He found the extra layer of flesh exciting; he had never before been to bed with a woman so soft. As he made love to her, extending the foreplay because he knew he would satisfy himself very quickly, small shudders convulsed her body, and he realized that it had been very long indeed since she had accommodated a man. She surprised him with the depth of her passion.

Afterward, she lay contentedly in his arms for a long while, then she brought her fingers down to his groin and began to make little circular motions with her fingertips. When she felt him grow tense again, she swung herself over him until she was looking down into his face. He was not fond of this position; the passive role had always been abhorrent to him, yet lying still, allow-ing her to make love to him was not unpleasant. Sometimes the weight of her body was excruciating, but in a vibrant, thrilling sort of way.

In his mind's eyes, he saw himself being ravished by a beautiful young creature. When he had finished, she did not stop, but went on with her gyrations, which surprisingly enough, made him grow tense again. For a moment, he felt twenty years old!

Still she did not release him. The journey was begun once more, but this time as she approached her zenith, he toppled her over and plunged himself savagely in and out of her body. She sighed and then uttered a little cry and he collapsed against her. They had reached the last climax together.

That first week, even with three good meals a day, Mitchell lost six pounds, which he could not afford to lose. After ten days of nightly love making, he knew that he must leave. Another bo would have handled the situation differently. The woman obviously had some sort of income, yet those nightly sessions were slowly turning into one long nightmare. Finally, one morning while she was at the market, he took twenty dollars from the sugar bowl in the kitchen, rolled up the new suit of work clothes and boots that she had purchased for him, and caught the next freight out of town. On the same box car, he found the old bo from Pennsylvania, who was regaling yet another group of drifters with lies about his former life. When he saw Mitchell, he waved a hand in his direction. "You look well fed. Been in the hoosecow?"

Mitchell shook his head. "No, but I ran into a widow who almost fucked me to death!"

The old man laughed uproariously and pounded his threadbare knee. "You should've stayed with the old broad."

Mitchell shrugged. "I would have, if I'd been ten years younger!" He then rolled himself into a ball in the corner of the box car, and with his head on his clothing package, fell into an exhausted sleep. He dreamed that he was ten years old and attending his first Ringling Brothers and Barnum & Bailey Circus in Enid. In one hand, he held a paper cone of pink cotton candy, and in the other, a quarter. He was fifth in line in front of the loop-de-loop; then he was on the circular ride, being tossed to and fro. He felt a sudden sexual exhilaration.

Mitchell awakened with a start, his head on the cold boards of the box car. He jumped up. The box car was empty. His clothing package was gone, and so was the bo from Pennsylvania . . .

Mitchell walked desolately along Robinson Street in Oklahoma City. The hot June sun beat down unmercifully on the sidewalk, throwing heat waves up into his face. He had managed to pick up two days' work with a threshing crew, until the boss complained of his slowness and fired him.

He had three dollars in his pocket. The city was stifling; he loved the wide open spaces and hated the cooped up feeling of the city. Late that night, he took a freight bound for Wichita, where he hoped to find a few days' work at the stockyards, but in the middle of the night, a light was thrown into the car and three railroad dicks with billy clubs climbed on board, hitting the startled bos on the bottoms of their shoes. Among yelps of pain and curses, the crowd dispersed along the tracks, and Mitchell, running across a field with one of the dicks in pursuit, cursed his lack of youthful speed. The only thing that saved him from being overtaken and hit over the head with the billy club was the fact that his pursuer was a few years older than he was!

Mitchell slept in a haystack that night, the first peaceful sleep that he had enjoyed in many months. He was awakened at sunrise by the familiar sound of a threshing machine nearby and was spotted immediately by the boss, who called out: "Hey, you! Want a job? One of my men just quit."

He got along well with the crew, seventeen young college men who could find work nowhere else. For the next two weeks, working twelve hours a day, seven days a week, going from field to field, and enjoying three "squares" a day, Mitchell pocketed twenty-eight dollars.

One day meshed into the next and incredibly weary,

with aching muscles all over his body, he was barely conscious of time passing. Then one mid-morning as they were riding in the truck down the section road to the next farm, he looked up in surprise to see Leona Barrett's Victorian clapboard. He rubbed his eyes to be certain that he was not daydreaming. But, no, there was the conservatory of music sign. He smiled wryly. "Where's the next stop, boss?" he asked.

The man consulted his breast notebook. "The Dice place."

Mitchell had never considered returning to Angel, but since, by a twist of fate—and he firmly believed in fate—he had been brought back, he became curious at how the community had changed. Once past the conservatory, instead of open prairie, he saw the outskirts of Angel. He looked to the left and sighed with relief. The Story clapboard, freshy painted white, lawn neatly trimmed, looked like a manor house.

A brick church and a new mausoleum graced the grounds of God's Acre. As they passed Main Street, his gaze took in two-story brick buildings that lined either side of the thoroughfare. Then he saw the grain elevator that reached toward the sky, higher even than the new water tower. This was Angel, the town where he had grown up? He shook his head—no, it was a prairie mirage, formed out of the heat waves that always preceded a summer storm.

The thresher, pulled by the tractor, proceeded down an unfamiliar road, and he tried to get his bearings. Was the Heron clapboard located to the right or to the left now? Then he saw a clump of tall trees growing out of an unkempt pasture of weeds, six-feet-tall sunflowers nodding to the sky. He glimpsed a battered grey gabled roof, visible only here and there through the trees that had been small when he was a child. The house was weatherbeaten brown with shuttered windows. The place had gone to rack and ruin, obviously abandoned. He angrily brushed away tears. How ridiculous to be moved by the old homestead that he had hated.

It was ten o'clock as the men moved the threshing machine into a new field of tall golden wheat; at twelve o'clock, the boss blew a whistle and the men stretched their backs and headed toward the section road. Cutting across the creek bridge, they came out into a clearing—the Dices' lower forty. Mitchell stopped in surprise. Instead of the clapboard that he had expected, a huge three-story mansion with tall white columns stood by the side of the road. Lush landscaping rose majestically from the fence bordered by splashes of multicolored flowers in low beds. He shook his head and followed the rest of the men to the back yard, where they washed under the pump. A long table had been set out under the trees in the back yard by the garage where the barn used to be, and two hired girls were placing food on a stand that served as a sideboard. He laughed to himself. Old John Dice must have picked up rarified manners somewhere, serving buffet to threshers!

He had forgotten about the merits of Oklahoma cooking. He helped himself to a mound of fluffy white potatoes and thick milk gravy; fried chicken; short ribs of beef, glazed a warm brown; waldorf salad; fresh peas and onions: buttered turnips and hot two-inch-high biscuits. Pitchers of milk were placed at intervals along the table with hot, steaming cherry cobblers. He ate a breast of chicken with his fingers and then took a spoonful of the mashed potatoes and gravy. With the first taste, childhood memories flooded back: socials at the school, church suppers—and all with Fontine Dice's chicken gravy. There was no doubt in his mind now that she had helped to prepare the meal. He remembered that cobbler was also one of her specialties. After dessert, he took a small plate of chow-chow relish, which was more delicious than ice cream to him—he had not tasted it in eighteen years!

While the other men enjoyed smokes and a short rest, he asked one of the hired girls if Mrs. Dice was about. She nodded and inclined her head toward the house. Mitchell knew that it would never do for the boss to see him go up to the back door, so he sauntered up the driveway, ostensibly stretching his legs. Out of sight behind a privet hedge, he knocked at the side door. A maid answered. "Yes?"

"Would you tell Mrs. Dice," he said politely, "that Mitchell Heron is calling."

A moment later the screen door was flung open and a plump little woman with peroxide curls stood looking down at him. "Mitchell?" a tiny voice said, unbelievingly.

He smiled and doffed his straw hat. "Yes, it's me."

"Well, I do declare! Imagine you turning up after all these years! I suppose you're here seeing your mama."

He looked at her incredulously. "Mother, *here*?"

"Didn't you know? She came back to the claim about four or five months ago. Say now, do come in!"

He shook his head. "No, thank you, Mrs. Dice, I've got to get back to the field."

"The field?"

"Yes, I'm working with the threshing crew."

"Oh, yes . . . of course." Fontine replied. Mitchell Heron working as a field hand? Well, strange things were happening all over the country. Most people thought he was dead. In her mind's eye, she saw the boy Mitchell running over the pasture, looking up at the sky, daydreaming and stumbling over a rock. But here he was in the flesh, a strange wild-looking man with a furrowed face and streaks of gray hair! "You'll be back for dinner, I suppose?" she asked graciously.

He smiled suddenly. "Supper? Yes."

"Come in and see Jaundice. He'll be back from the bank."

"I'll try."

"Maybe you'll go see your mama, then?"

"I should probably telephone first."

Fontine shook her yellow curls. "She doesn't have a phone."

Then the sound of a whistle sliced through the air, and Mitchell took a step backward. "I'd best get back to the field, ma'am." Suddenly he was overcome with uncharacteristic shyness.

Fontine debated all afternoon on whether she should pay a visit to Priscilla, but finally decided against it. On her one and only call, Priscilla had stayed in the shadows of the back porch behind the rusty screen and had answered her questions in a low, distant voice. Humiliated, Fontine had come home and raged to her husband, "Jaundice, that old rip didn't even invite me in. She was rude, *rude!*"

John Dice had taken her arm protectively. "Honey, you'd probably feel the same way if your husband had run away with a lot of money and left you destitute with all your property in receivership. Don't be too hard on Prissy. She's been through hell. Do you know what coming back to Angel has meant to her? Remember, she always hated it here. The state she's in—well, I think Bella Chenovick hit the nail on the head when she said, 'She's in a place we Catholics call purgatory'."

The self-feeder mechanism on the threshing machine developed a cough mid-afternoon. Mitchell and another man who were pitching sheaves of wheat into the quivering mouth of the feeder shrugged and called for the oiler, a squat little man. He ordered the tractor to be stopped and peered into the throat of the monster, then shook his head and shouted for the boss, who grunted and used a colorful hodge podge of oaths that impressed even some of the college men who had thought they had heard all possible combinations. While the boss drove the truck to the blacksmith shop in Angel, the men lounged under the cottonwoods near the creek, smoking, laughing, and telling dirty stories about traveling salesmen and farmer's daughters.

Mitchell ambled down the incline, ostensibly to answer a call of nature, but in reality to head for the Heron clapboard. He easily found the path from the Dice place that he had used as a boy and came up the wide, unkempt pasture in back of the house. Obviously nothing had been done to the place since the family had moved to Dallas in 1913.

He knocked at the back door, but there was no response. The birds chattering in the trees added a bucolic touch to the scene. He went to the front door and knocked lightly. Again, no answer.

He swore softly as his foot went through a rotted step that had been covered by a creeping vine. He was not a sentimental man, but seeing the place in such a deteriorated condition made him very sad. He glanced out

402

over the front yard at the waist-high weeds with seed pods bursting with life.

He shook his head remorsefully and walked around the opposite side of the house. It was then that he spotted the hunched figure at the end of the garden, tending a row of tall string beans. "Mother?" he called, "Mother?"

The kneeling figure got up very slowly; the faded gingham dress clung to the thin frame. Priscilla squinted up and rubbed her back, then came forward. "What do you want?" she rasped, scowling into the sun. She placed a hand protectively over her brow to cut down the glare. "Yes?"

He took a few steps. "Mother? It's Mitchell."

She grasped the wooden garden gate for support. "Mitchell?"

"Yes, Mother, it's me!"

They stood looking at each other. She was very gaunt; the skin seemed to adhere to her bones as if there was no flesh underneath. Her shiny black hair, which he had always remembered swirled on the top of her head, had broken away from the knot at the nape of her neck and hung in pure white strands around her face. This old woman was his mother?

Priscilla gazed at the tall, stocky figure with the broad shoulders and gray streaked hair and thought: This middle-aged man can't be Mitchell! Mitchell was somewhere far away—in Europe, a successful business-man, he couldn't be this odd fellow who looked like a tramp! Then as he drew nearer, she looked into his sunburned face and hollow eyes, and gasped. It *was* Mitchell. Suddenly she was filled with fury. She straightened her backbone and, stood stiffly by the gate, brushing the hair back from her face. "How dare you show your face around here, boy?"

He took a step backward as if he had been hit in the face. "I thought I'd drop by to see you," he said lamely, "since I was in the neighborhood . . ."

Priscilla was surprised at the deadly calm of her voice. "You're just a few years too late." She sighed, then said archly, "Fancy you being in the vicinity!" She examined his dusty work clothes, threadbare and worn shiny in spots. His hair was powdered with wheat chaff and his fingers were grimy. She shook her head. Her Mitchell had always been so elegant, even in his college days. When he was a child, she had always dressed him especially nice. In the closet upstairs hung row after row of little sailor suits and herringbone tweeds. Small caps were stacked twelve high, along with several boxes of Buster Brown shoes . . .

"I'm working on the threshing crew," he explained, "over at the Dices."

"Oh, yes," she said distractedly, "I heard the tractor this morning and wished for a moment that we had planted wheat this year. But there wasn't any money for seed . . ." She looked across the uneven pasture land, her voice a nostalgic whisper. "I used to look over at Letty's Number One rig right from this spot. The steam engine and the sounds of drilling used to drift over the top of the cottonwoods. The noise almost drove me crazy . . ." Her gaze traveled over to his face and she asked plaintively, "Where were you when I needed you?"

He shook his head; all those years in Europe trying to peddle little glass figures that no one wanted; all the years on the road, hungry, lean years. "I don't know, Mother." He made an empty gesture with his big callused hands.

She gazed at him with sudden hated, her voice high and thin. "Where were you," she shouted, "when your father died? Where were you when we needed help to run the business? Where were you when the crash took everything? Where were you when Manford left me?"

He was surprised at her vehemence. "I was on my own . . ." He could think of no logical reply.

"On your own!" she spat out savagely. "And I see, my boy, you're *still* on your own! Well, I hope that you're happy. I hope that you are a success." Her eyes narrowed malevolently. "I assume that the threshing business is very lucrative. As you traipse from field to field, I hope you're proud of your accomplishments." Her eyes were fiery. "Let's see, my boy, you're what— thirty-eight? Imagine, a man of your age and deportment, coming up in the world the way you are! A

thresher, no less? Tell me are you an oiler, or do you drive the wagon loaded with bundles of grain to the machine? Or, holy of holies, do you pitch hay into the feeder? I'm told that's the most difficult task of all." She spat in the sand. "Or are you the boss man?"

"Mother," he cried, "don't . . ."

She raised her chin and looked directly into his eyes, her mouth set in a straight line. "You were always a disappointment to me! We gave you everything—the best education possible, the finest clothes, the best automobiles. You were going to be *different*, you said." She looked at his clothing. "Well, you *are* different. Luke had half your brains, but he worked like hell and graduated from Harvard with honors, while you got kicked out of Stanford because of poor grades. You wouldn't study, you wouldn't use the brains the good Lord gave you. But your father and I thought you could still redeem yourself and become a distinguished officer in the army. What happened? You enlisted as a private and didn't even have the guts to fight! Oh, no, you had to run away to be with some female in Paris. Still, Edward and I hoped that you would pick up the pieces." She paused and looked at him defiantly. "You could have become president of the company. Instead, Manford took over, then when the going got rough, he left with fifty thousand dollars—all the money I had in the world."

She was exhausted, he saw, as she leaned against the garden gate, then with her head down, she murmured plaintively, "Oh, Mitchell what's to become of us?" She glanced up dully at him, all the anger gone. "The world is topsy turvy, and I'm reduced to this . . ." She waved her hand over the pasture land. Tears scalded her pale cheeks. He took her awkwardly in his arms. "I can't make up for what's gone," he said brokenly, "but maybe together we can do something with this old place. The depression can't last forever, Mother. There's got to be a leveling off some time."

She nodded, and clung to him as if she could not believe he was actually there. He heard the boss's whistle wafting faintly over the fields of ripe wheat. "I've got to go now . . ."

"Stay with me, please?" she pleaded.

"I've got to finish out the day or I won't get paid."

"Paid?" She looked up vacantly.

"I've already got a week's wages due—about nine dollars."

"Then we can have meat for dinner?"

He looked down at her head. "Yes, Mother," he replied softly, "we can have meat for dinner."

Mitchell arose at dawn, as was his custom since he had moved back to the farm, and came downstairs. He still received a shock going through the rooms of the old house with the boarded-up windows. Not one piece of furniture had been rearranged; even flower vases long empty of blossoms remained in their original places. The sofa and chairs in the living room were worn threadbare in spots, some of the cushions had rotted with age, and the wallpaper had faded. It was a strange eerie feeling, this stepping back into a faded past.

He made coffee after he had raked up the coals and thrown another log in the cookstove. He reached into the cupboard for a slice of homemade bread, then carrying the coffee mug with him, went out to the barn, hitched the horse to the plow, and started on the upper forty. At ten o'clock, with the sun blazing down in an early heat wave, Priscilla trudged up the incline with a mason jar filled with lemonade. "Drink it down now while it's still cool," she said warily. "If you leave it out in the sun, it'll be so hot you won't be able to get it down."

"Yes, Mother," he replied and took a long swallow. "Are you going into town?"

She shook her head and patted her ten year old blue silk dress with the ridiculously high hem; "I don't feel like walking . . ."

"It's Saturday," he said, to remind her of the drawing.

She shrugged her shoulders. "I never win anything. Besides, I don't have anything to wear. *They'll* all be in town buying groceries."

He knew by "they" she meant the Stevens and the Haskells and the Trunes. He sighed and wiped his forehead before he placed his straw hat back on his head. "What are your plans for today?" he asked.

"What? Oh, bake bread, I guess." She paused. "Oh, what I would give for a piece of store-bought cake!"

"Yours is so much better, Mother," he said, trying to sound cheerful.

She threw him a furious look, and held her hands up, showing her red, callused palms. "If I did go in for the drawing, *they'd* see my hands. I don't have gloves any more." She looked out over the horizon at the rows of plowed earth, meticulous and symmetrical. "I used to have forty pairs, in all the colors of the rainbow, some wrist length, some that came up to the elbows, and two pairs that reached up almost to my shoulder—white kid, they were . . . Now I only have one dress that's proper length. The last time I was walking down Main Street, Bella Chenovick drove by in her new Lincoln." Priscilla imitated her slight accent: " 'Pris-cilla, deah, good to see you. Come over anytime. I'll give you some of my canned peaches!' " Priscilla spat. "The old Bohunk! As if I'd accept a handout."

"Mother," Mitchell said evenly. "Bella always gives away peaches. She didn't mean to sound patronizing."

"The hell she didn't! She and Torgo always put on the dog."

"I wouldn't say that, Mother," he replied casually, "with all their wealth, she still runs the fruit stand in the summer."

"Oh," Priscilla said, grimacing, "that's just to show every one she's a regular person! Don't kid me! Imagine those Bohunks having all that money, while we, who were *born* here in this country . . . It's not fair, Mitch, it's not fair!"

He turned to the plow. Comforting her would only make the situation worse, because she would then try to play on his sympathy. The only time she was quiet was when the radio was blaring from the cabinet. She listened to Kaltenborn and the news every night. Once she turned briefly to a musical program and when he shouted excitedly, "I think that's Clement and his Cherokee Swing Band," she snapped the knob off the set.

"Why would we want to listen to that red Indian! I bet he makes more with a single night's playing than we do in a year. First it was a jazz band, now swing!"

When he got back to the clapboard that night, the breakfast and luncheon dishes remained unwashed in the sink and a wash tub filled with soaking clothes sported a sour green scum. Shaking his head, he went down to Letty's pecan orchard and knocked down a few nuts. If he was especially nice, Priscilla might bake a pecan pie.

Coming back to the house, his overall pockets filled with pecans, he had a sudden yearning to go back on the road. At that moment, he missed the clappity clap-clap of the rails and the vibration under his body as he slept. Then he sighed, and pushed the thoughts out of his head. He had chosen to stay on the farm, and he would abide by that decision. He was, he realized, doing penance for all those years away from home . . .

Late one night, when he was asleep, Priscilla got out of bed slowly so that he old rusty springs would not squeak and tiptoed down the stairs. She knelt by the bottom of the china cabinet and removed a small folded handkerchief from the secret drawer that Edward Heron had designed into the piece of furniture. Then she went to the kitchen and took down a bottle of ammonia and a box of soda from the cabinet. Very slowly and meticulously, she opened the folded square of linen and gave a little gasp of delight. Although the diamond ring was perfectly clean, she took up the toothbrush once more and began to work the paste into the microscopic designs engraved into the platinum setting. Holding the multi-faceted diamond up to the light, she turned it this way and that, a look of indescribable joy on her face. Her private times alone with the ring made up for the drudgery of the days that passed in slow agony. Oh, the jewel was perfectly cut! She sighed, examining the fiery flashes of light. In a way, she reflected, it was as if she were stretched out beside an extremely virile man; tongues of feeling spread out in evanescent waves from her spine. This was the joy that she had missed living alone without the comforts of a male body. Ah, the jewel, the perfect jewel . . .

31

Reprisal

In April of 1935, Bosley received a call from John Dice.

"Has there been much talk in Washington about the dust storms in the Panhandle?" asked John.

"No."

"Well some agency or other should do something for those poor people. I've made a few calls to Oklahoma City, but, hell, Bos, there's no one as uninfluential as a former senator!"

"Well, as you know, most farmers don't qualify for relief other than acreage allowances. The oil companies might provide fuel for tractors and other equipment, but these people mostly use horses to plow and harrow."

"I've loaned some farmers over near Guymon some wheat-seed money, and they put up a forty-acre parcel as collateral. The loan's long overdue and I can't collect. I went over to see them last month. I couldn't believe my eyes, Bos. The dust had been blowing for twenty-eight days straight. There isn't anything left of their land! The crops are gone—blown away or covered up. I even lost all the paint on my car. It's the biggest mess you've ever seen! I don't know what those poor folks are going to do!"

"We've always had some trouble with dust in that area in years of drought," Bosley replied. "I think it's probably because so many of them plowed down too deep on the prairie. Once the buffalo grass is gone, the soil becomes loose. I know there hasn't been any rain in a long time."

"Theorizing is all right," John replied, "but what am I going to do? I can't foreclose, even if I wanted to! What good is that spoiled acreage to the bank?"

Bosley paused. "Send me the note. I'll pay it personally. Any other property out there that you're involved in?"

"No, thank God, but banks in the area must be hard put."

"I'll make a few calls into my government. Some kind of soil conservation program obviously must be set up or that land will never be good again." He hung up the telephone thoughtfully. He knew a great deal about the soil of the area from his trips into the Panhandle—or "no man's land," as some called it. He hoped the drought would break; if not . . .

Luke read over the copy for the stockholder's report and whistled softly. For the sixth year in a row, the dividends had been plowed back into the company, and the board of directors, including Bosley Trenton, who had been appointed to head the executive committee, and himself as president, had turned their salaries back to the Heron Oil Company. In the message to the stockholders, he had written: "With our austerity program in full force, the company is keeping its head above water. All drilling operations have ceased, no new leases have been acquired, and all of our employees enjoy a five day week—all this has been achieved even under the new NRA Code, which restricts our output of oil products. Yet during the last year, we have succeeded in financing fifty-five new service stations, mostly in Southern California. With station managers sharing in the profits and purchasing all supplies from the company, I am happy to report that gasoline sales—especially our new big-performance Ethyl—is up seven percent. The idea of full-service stations with owner-mechanics on duty for automobile repairs is paying off handsomely—particularly since new automobile sales are down and the populace must have older models repaired more frequently."

410

With Bosley's urging, Luke began new promotional activity, personally appearing on the site when new service stations opened amid a fanfare of local publicity in newspapers and on the radio. Attired in the famous blue and white uniform that had been designed by Hattie Carnegie in New York, he would be photographed lever in hand, at the gasoline pumps. The first thirty customers received one gallon of Ethyl gratis, with the president of Heron Oil Company personally pumping gas into their tanks and wiping their windshields. He shook hands with customers and gave away tiny blue brooches of the Heron logo to the ladies, which were far more newsworthy, he felt, than the Sinclair Oil Company's prehistoric animal cards given out to the children. "That's all good and well," he told Bosley, "but kids don't buy gas. With more and more ladies driving cars today, it's important to keep them happy, and considering the brooches cost only three cents each in mass production, it's well worth the effort."

He could not know that ten years later, those depression-day brooches would be considered valuable collectors' items.

From June 10th through November 2nd, 1936, executives of the Heron Oil Company threw their support behind Governor Alfred Landon of Kansas for president, and Colonel Frank Knox, owner of the *Chicago Daily News*, for vice president. "That team can beat Roosevelt," Luke exclaimed during one of the frequent board of directors' meetings. "We've got to save America from socialism. The New Deal must be squelched!"

"I agree," Bosley Trenton said, "I only just wish old Alf had more of a colorful personality. He gives the impression of a fussbudget and he really isn't at all. But, we've got to stand behind him. If Roosevelt is reelected, business will suffer even more. Although Heron Oil is making a slight profit because of our research into by-products, who knows what other bills that spendthrift would push through Congress that sanction even more government interference in business? With around seven hundred codes already in force, we've had to hire a dozen lawyers just to sift through the red tape!

411

The minimum wage law hasn't affected us because we've always paid fair salaries, but this business of unionizing can undermine everything we've set out to do! We've got to maintain an open shop."

Luke nodded vehemently. "I will not have this company run by unions! It's a private corporation."

The officers received a vote of confidence from the twelve men present, each of whom went back to their territories, and climbed aboard the Landon–Knox bandwagon. Even J. C. Armbuster, who was very ill, directed operations from his bed.

Luke told Jeanette: "I believe wholly in Landon—the Kansas Sunflower."

She smiled wryly. "That's fine, sweetheart, but remember, sunflowers wilt in November!"

Her prophecy was correct. On November 3rd, Roosevelt won the election by a landslide.

Bosley came into the small apartment in the Stratford Arms. "Letty," he called, "we've got a problem."

She came in from the kitchen, wiping her hands on a towel. "Yes?"

"We've got to sit down and talk, my sweet."

She smiled. "Whenever you call me 'my sweet', I know you want a favor. What is it now?"

He lighted a cigar and blew the smoke out in one huge puff. "We've lived the last few years very quietly, minding our own business here in Washington. We've not had any publicity, aside from a couple of photographs in *Vanity Fair*." He took another pull on the Havana. "But Luke has been generating a lot of publicity with his public appearances at the service stations all over the country, and it's paid off in increased sales. I'm proud of him for devoting time to this cause, even though it means taking away time from Jeanette and Luke Three."

"Bosley," Letty sighed, "will you get to the point? You do go on and on!"

"It's this," he replied. "*Fortune* magazine is doing a big article on the company and they want photographs of the way we live. Some of our public relations people think that photographing us here in this little apartment will seem constricting."

"I don't know why! With our austerity program . . ."

"It's not that aspect that's troubling them," he countered quickly. "Showing us living frugally is fine and might set an example for some of the other big oil company executives." He paused. "But they think that we should have a more prosaic setting."

"Prosaic setting? I don't know what you mean."

"If we moved back to the farm in Angel . . ."

"Well, Bos, why didn't you say so in the first place!" She smiled. "I wouldn't mind moving back." She tossed her gray hair back from her face. "Washington is dull. I've never cared much for the social life here, not since George died . . . I'm sorry."

"Don't feel that you can't mention his name, Letty."

"But I don't want you to feel—"

"Just because I loved you all those years you were married to him, doesn't mean that he was any less of a friend. You should talk about him. I understand perfectly."

"The clapboard will be far more comfortable than this apartment. In fact, I would have suggested moving back long ago if it hadn't been that so much is taking place here politically."

"Not much any more. Sometimes I feel it would be best not to be privy to so much of what's happening in government. Besides, Luke is here."

"So what about this *Fortune* article?"

"They'll interview us on the farm, take pictures of me riding horseback, you cooking on the old stove. With the harvest around the corner, they might want to show the threshers around the table. You know, homespun activities."

"So we're to return to our roots, so to speak," Letty laughed. "I would like to think that we're doing it for ourselves, not for a magazine."

"We are doing it for ourselves, Letty."

"I wonder," she said, "I wonder."

The two reporters from *Fortune* dogged Letty and Bosley's footsteps for eight days, taking hundreds of pictures. Letty and Bosley went along with most of the suggestions about posing, only drawing the line at such contrived scenes as Letty drawing water from the well and Bosley hitching up a wagon. "Really, gentlemen," she said, "we aren't that backward! The house does have indoor plumbing, you know, and we haven't used horses except for pleasure riding for twenty-five years! We had one of the first motor cars in the Territory!"

At last the men left and peace was restored. One afternoon, Letty strolled down the incline to the Heron clapboard and knocked on the back door twice, but there was no response.

"Is that you, Aunt Letty?" said a voice behind her.

She turned and peered up into the face of a middle-aged man with a dark sunburned face, shadowed by a big straw hat, which he removed, showing a streak of white forehead. "Don't you know me? I'm Mitchell Heron."

She dropped her hands to her side. "Of course, it is you, isn't it?" Tears were very near. "I haven't seen you since you visited us before you enlisted in the service!"

"I've changed a good bit, I guess, Aunt Letty." He paused. "Come on out to the smokehouse, I'm curing some hams. I butchered a sow this morning."

She watched him as he smoothed the mixture of salt, sugar, molasses, and saltpeter over the fat rounds. "I'll help you," she said. "They must be packed tight in the barrel. There. Now add water to cover. That's it. Seal the top and don't even peek for about a month. These hams are big, so it may take two or three weeks beyond that." She looked up and smiled. "My heavens, Mitchell, I haven't done this kind of work in years. I bet I could even make lye soap, too." She shook her head in remembrance, then glanced up. "How long have you been back?"

"Three years in June. I came with the threshers and decided to stay." He looked away, his jaw thrust out, a strange bedeviled look on his face—the same look that he had displayed sometimes as a child when he was caught in the act of doing something wrong. "I guess I'm a pretty sad example of a man, Aunt Letty. I wasted most of my life and didn't know it! I traveled all over Europe, sometimes in style, but mostly not, then I came back here to the States in time for the depression." He looked at her directly in the eyes. "I suppose I've seen almost every city in the country. Sometimes even now I get the itch to just get up and go, but I tell myself that I'm forty-two years old and I'd better settle down somewhere."

"You never married?"

He shook his head. "Never was any place long enough to get permanently interested in a woman." He sighed, and then changed the subject abruptly. "I'd ask you in for a cup of coffee . . ."

"Why, thank you, Mitchell," she replied.

". . . But I hope you understand, Mother doesn't see anyone any more. I think she's taking a nap."

"In the morning?"

He looked away. "She spends a lot of time upstairs. She doesn't come down very often, and frankly, Aunt Letty, the whole place, especially the kitchen, is a mess." He wiped his salty hands on a gunnysack. "I'm not very good at batchin'." He brightened. "Why don't you sit out here under the tree, and I'll heat up some coffee?"

"I'm sure your mother will see me," Letty replied. "After all, we've known each other since we were five years old. And, as far as the house being untidy, that doesn't bother me one whit." She marched to the back steps just as the rusty screen door was thrust open, and she looked up into the face of an incredibly old woman with gray hair hanging down in unkempt ringlets. She drew back. "Prissy?"

"Well, who in the hell did you think it was, Jean Harlow?" came the bitter retort.

Letty ignored the remark. "As you may have heard, Bosley and I have come back to the farm." She paused and then went on gently. "I'm sorry I haven't been over before, but we had some *Fortune* magazine people here, and haven't had a moment's peace."

Priscilla threw back her head and laughed raucously. "Peace is all we have here any more, Letty." She touched her stained calico dress. "Peace and poverty—the two Ps. But I'll tell you one thing, if I had your

415

money, I sure as hell would get out of Angel." She looked at her defiantly. "I suppose you know all about my finances—everybody else does. Manford's somewhere in Mexico, living off his wits, I suppose. He ran off with his stenographer, who came back, I hear, with a suitcase full of money." Her mouth twisted. "He's broke, too, an old man by now, no longer capable of attaching himself to some dumb split-tail . . ."

"Mother!"

"Shut up, Mitch, I'm talking to an old friend, a *dear* old friend." She smiled suddenly, showing stained front teeth. "Roll me a cigarette." She went on, excitement building in her voice. "Isn't it hilarious, Letty—You and I ending up back here where we started? I don't look back any more because if I did I'd go crazy. Do you ever look back?" She squinted at Letty, then took the cigarette from Mitchell, which she licked and lighted.

"No, not much. We're all going through a bad period, but it will get better . . ."

Priscilla laughed hollowly. "Still the incurable optimist, aren't you, Letty? *You're* going through a bad period? Heh, that's a good one. I suppose you're down to your last million dollars."

"Prissy," Letty replied firmly, "we never went public . . ."

"So I suppose you're throwing that up to me, because we did!"

"No! What I'm saying is that we haven't taken any money out of the company for a very long time. This way, we're able to keep Heron Oil fairly solvent—if you'll excuse the pun. At least we're able to meet our bank notes."

"Well, goody for you! I'm not." Priscilla looked skyward. "Let's see, I'm in debt to Baker's Mercantile for sixteen dollars; Mitchell owes the man in the machine shop about twenty dollars for repairing the harrow. There's a bill from young Doctor Schaeffer that I'm afraid to open . . ." She paused and laughed wryly. "Isn't that rich, I still call him *young*, and he's older than we are." She paused. "Now, let's see, I guess we owe, all told, around seventy dollars. That's a lot of money. How much do you owe, Letty?"

"You mean personally?"

"Of course! Since you never had a head for business, I don't suppose that you know how much Heron Oil owes."

"I don't know, Prissy."

She held her cigarette between her two front teeth and puffed energetically. "Pity. Well, I've got to go inside now—it's time for my radio stories." She paused at the threshold. "I can't wait to see what Young Widder Brown does today. She's to meet a rival she hasn't seen in years." She glanced back over her shoulder. "I wonder how she'll handle it?"

Letty drew back as if she had been struck; the implication was obvious.

"Oh, don't mind Mother," Mitchell muttered. "She's just off on a tangent."

Letty looked at him with sad eyes. "She was always rather odd. But you see, Mitchell, you didn't know her when she was young. She was always ambitious, and when the furniture stores were such a success in the beginning, all that money went to her head. She stopped being the Prissy that I knew then. And now, well . . ." She waved her hand. "Be good to her, Mitchell."

"I will," he said with a long, drawn-out sigh. "You see, Aunt Letty, all we have is each other." He turned back to the smokehouse, and Letty walked slowly up the incline, past the cottonwoods and up to the rear door of her house, the same walk that she had taken thousands of times over the years. Only this time, the path seemed forty miles long.

In the summer of 1937, Bosley was called to Oklahoma City and offered the position of head geologist for the State Soil Commission. He stood up before the committee members. "Gentlemen, it is with great sadness that I must decline your offer. I love Oklahoma and I would like nothing better than to take part in instructing the farmers still left in the Dust Bowl about new soil conservation methods, but as you know, I have a sixteen-hour-a-day job with the Heron Oil Company." He paused, and then went on gravely. "What I will do is this: sign me on as an unsalaried consultant and I'll do what I can to help. I'll always be available by telephone and I should be able to arrange a couple of days a month for personal meetings."

"But," Senator Hartsook exclaimed, "we can't expect you to give service without pay!"

Bosley smiled softly. "I'm only returning a favor. Actually, even before it became a state, Oklahoma has been awfully good to me. These farmers are desperate. They must be taught new methods of farming. Fields must be contoured and terraced; cover crops must be planted so that soil cannot blow or wash away. Eventually irrigation will be necessary to stave off drought conditions."

He leaned forward. "We've got to start planning now for the future. I'm not talking about five-year plans, either. I'm thinking about twenty and thirty years from now. You must all personally tour the western and northwestern part of the state. You've got to see what nature has wrought yourselves. Few farmers, I'm afraid, are left. Most of them have taken their families west to California, Oregon, and Washington. Out there now, these poor people are trying to scratch a living by picking fruit and vegetables. Respectable middle-class farmers are now migrant workers. It's a sad state of affairs." He paused and looked down at his veined hands. "They call them 'Okies,' you know."

The first quarter of 1937 was the best in Heron Oil Company history, along with other industries, including steel production. The automobile industry appeared to be pulling out of the slump. At the same time, the national income had risen from forty billion five years before to seventy billion. The second quarter was brilliant, and Luke gleefully announced that dividends would be paid. All members of the board of directors went back on full salary. Luke's exuberance was short-lived. The business index fell from 111.2 in August to 88.9 in November and stocks which had averaged 135.5, fell to 82. Congress was called back for an extra session on

November 15th, but none of Roosevelt's proposed plans were voted upon. Ten million Americans were unemployed by Christmas, and the relief rolls swelled.

In mid-January, 1938, Luke called the board of directors together. J. C. Armbuster arrived in a wheel chair, which seemed to engulf him. His male nurse, a former wrestler, hovered nearby. At ninety-three, huddled in a blanket, his wizened, bald skull emerging only briefly now and then from the coverlet, the old man looked like an ancient turtle. During the middle of the meeting, his head came up and he snapped shrilly, "Luke, you've become a depressing man! With all of the figures that you've thrown us today, one thing is clear—we've survived the Wall Street crash nine years ago to go under now just when we had all hoped to see the light at the end of the tunnel." He paused and ran a dry tongue over drier lips. "I helped form this company, and I'm personally not going to see it dissolve into bankruptcy! I never thought I'd propose what I'm going to suggest now, but I say, go public!" His head darted back under the blanket again. There was dead silence in the board room.

Finally Bosley stood up. "All those in favor of going public raise their right hands."

The directors voted unanimously to go public.

Luke telephoned Letty that night. "It's done, Mother. Stock in the Heron Oil Company will be offered through a brokerage house in New York."

"Well, I'm for it, son," Letty exclaimed, "and if George were alive, he'd agree. I told Bosley yesterday that we've got to grow with the times. Have you called Leona Barrett Elder?"

There was a long pause. "She passed away last week in a convalescent home in upstate New York."

"Oh, no!" Letty sighed, and sat down, resting the receiver in her lap.

"Mother? Mother? Are you all right?"

She paused a moment and lifted the instrument to her ear. "Yes," she replied when she could trust her voice. "I was very fond of her in a strange way. I wish I'd known she was ill, I would have gone to see her."

419

She paused. "She came to visit George when he was dying."

"I didn't know that, and I was there!"

Letty nodded. "None of the family knew. She arrived very late at night. Well, the circle is coming 'round, Luke, coming 'round."

"What do you mean, Mother?"

"Oh, nothing . . ."

"Her lawyer called yesterday. Do you know what? She left all her stock to the conservatory of music, to be held in trust with the dividends going into general expense funds."

There was no answer on the other end of the line.

"Mother?"

"I'm still here, son," Letty finally responded. "If that's all the news, I think I'll hang up. I feel very tired all of a sudden."

"Are you okay?"

"Yes, son, I'm okay." She felt relieved that they could talk about confidential matters on the telephone now. The line was private; she did not have to worry about receivers clicking all the way down the party line. She hung up, walked to the window, and looked out over the prairie land. Her eyes smarted. The tapestry of all of their lives was taking final shape; the pattern was, at last, becoming clear.

Michell came out of the bank with a cashier's check to send with his Sears & Roebuck catalogue order. On the way to the post office, he stopped for a moment to watch the queue lining up in front of the old Heron Service Station to receive the government handouts from the relief truck. Staples handed out this morning included what looked like longhorn cheese, white fish, and five-pound sacks of powdered milk. Mitchell snorted. *Powdered milk*, when townspeople could get fresh milk (if they didn't have a farmer friend who would give them as much as they could drink) for two cents a gallon! He walked past the truck, taking care to look straight ahead so he would not be forced to acknowledge the presence of several old school mates in line. Not that anyone in the town of Angel had money in the bank, but to stand in the hot sun on Main Street behind the relief wagon was an admission that there was not enough food in the house even for breakfast. Indeed, a few of the women with whom he had gone to school were thin and scrawny, obviously undernourished, their dull eyes peering out under wide straw hats.

He mailed the order, and on the way to the blacksmith shop, encountered a group of children walking from the grade school to the Baptist church where the government food program provided a bowl of soup, a piece of white bread, and a dish of boiled raisins cooked by ladies on relief in the church kitchen. He shook his head. After a journey into town, the old farm did not appear to be so run-down. After all, there was meat in the smokehouse and mason jars of vegetables and fruits in the cellar. His mother would never be forced to line up for food.

After supper that night, Mitchell took a sponge bath, then attired in clean clothes, set out for his weekly visit to Belle Trune, who lived in an old shack on the outskirts of Angel a block and a half from the depot. He arrived promptly at seven-thirty. The front door was open and a low voice called: "Mitch? C'min."

Belle was now forty-five, but even with lipstick and mascara, looked much older. They had known each other since the age of seven, when he had given her a penny to peek at her white bloomers. After graduating from high school, he had lain with her for an hour in a haystack, along with two other seventeen-year-olds. Since her latest husband had left her and now that the children were married and had children of their own, she made a few extra dollars a week by accepting the attentions of several men in the community. Holidays excepted, Fridays were reserved for Mitchell. On holidays, Belle Trune went to Mass.

She was dressed as always in a Chinese kimono, brought back, she said often, by her father, who had fought in the Boer War. "Honey," she said, patting her softly dyed black hair, "leave the door open. It's hot in here." She went to the bed, removed the kimono and lay down on the bedspread, her long, lean legs open and inviting. Mitchell took off his clothes, which he folded carefully across the back of a chair, then stood looking down at her. Sex had become a ritual. He could not say in all honesty that she was attractive. Sometimes it took him a very long time to become aroused, but he liked the feel of her soft body. The fact that she liked him *that way* made up for his less than enthusiastic response. Once the journey was launched, the desire rose up in him and the act became enjoyable.

However, this evening he felt more amorous than usual. He lowered himself over her warm body, and she began to move under him with abandon, rubbing her buttocks slowly against the sheet, sending vibrations through his thighs. He became excited at once. "Oh, that's what I want, Mitch," she whispered, and he wondered if she said these same little erotic phrases to other customers. Of course, it didn't matter; she was so practiced in her art, and they had traveled on so many similar journeys together, that he soon felt himself engulfed. She shook her hips and moved under him with graceful maneuvers, gauging his responses. Soon he began to perspire, and their bodies became slick with passion. He made the final plunge and it was over, then he lay on his back, shaken and trembling, while she placed an ashtray on his stomach. "Hey," he cried, "that's *cold*."

She laughed and lighted a cigarette for him.

"You know, Belle, this is the only time I ever smoke. Tobacco tastes good after we've done it."

He took several puffs, snuffed out the cigarette, handed her the ashtray, turned over and started to snore. After an hour, she thought about waking him, then changed her mind. Looking at his callused hands, she knew he worked hard—this man whom she had known as a boy. She would let him stay the night.

Mitchell opened his eyes at dawn, taking a moment to realize where he was, then looked kindly at Belle, curled up in a ring beside him. This was a new experience, awakening with a woman in his bed. Even that widow, Lizzie, had gone back to her room after those exhausting sessions.

He ran his hand over Belle's stomach and she opened one eye. "Mornin', honey." She opened her arms to him. With a night's rest, he was surprised at the immediate reaction. He urgently drew himself over her. Her response was immediate and electrifying. A few moments later it was over for them both. They lay quietly beside each other, exhausted yet filled with a warm glow that made the aftermath of making love a very tender and precious thing.

She cuddled up against him. "We get along well, don't we?"

"Sure. You're swell."

"That's not what I meant," she continued, suddenly serious. "I mean we have a special time in bed, right?"

"Right."

"How about if we do it more often?" She paused. "If I could move in with you . . ."

"What?"

"You need a woman to look after you. I'm a good cook and I keep house well, and I know I could make the farm pay better."

He shook his head. "Belle, I like you a lot, you must know that. But, I'm stuck with Mother for one thing, and then too, I'm an old bachelor, set in my ways."

She smiled and encircled him with her hand. "Still, we could have a lot of *fun*—that would make up for—other things. You must get as lonely as I do . . ." Her eyes were very dark and luminous.

"No," he replied quietly, "I can't say I'm ever lonely. You see, Belle, I don't miss being around people."

"Well, you were always odd, even as a boy. But, I want you to think it over, Mitch. Neither of us are what could be called young. I think marriage would work." She sighed, "I know we could make a success out of farming. You need help. I'm strong . . ."

He stubbed out his cigarette in the tray, then got up quickly and put on his clothes, taking a two-dollar bill out of his pocket.

She shook her head. "Put that back in your pocket, Mitch. If we're kinda engaged, it wouldn't be proper for me to take . . ."

"We're not engaged, Belle," he said flatly, and before she could protest, he placed the bill on the table and was out the door.

He let himself into the back way as quietly as possible. Although it was still early, the house was quiet; evidently his mother was still in bed.

He turned off the old-fashioned gas lights in the living room and had just finished making coffee when he heard a faint mewing sound, as if a cat was imprisoned somewhere. He heard it again and went into the living room. It was then he saw the figure hunched on the staircase. "My God, Mother, what happened?"

Priscilla, dressed in an old blue wrap-around housecoat, lay face down on the stairs. He turned her over slowly and looked down into her blue face. Her lips were purplish-black. He picked her up in his arms. She felt as light as a bird. Her eyes fluttered open for an instant.

"I'll go get Doctor Schaeffer," he murmured, making her comfortable on the settee.

She shook her head. "No . . . time."

"I'll run over to the Storys and telephone." He ran out of the room and raced up the incline, cursing his slow pace; he had left all of his energy at Belle's.

When he returned five minutes later with Letty, she was breathing heavily. He placed a pillow under her head and ran for a blanket. When he returned, Letty was kneeling beside the settee.

Priscilla's eyelids fluttered again, but her breathing became more labored. It seemed an eternity until the doctor's car was heard in the driveway. He arrived with black bag already opened, and taking one look at her mottled blue face, placed a tablet under her tongue. He took her pulse, slid her eyelids back, peered intently into the pupils and barked, "She must not be moved." He prepared an injection. "It's a coronary all right, but I don't know how bad." He paused. "She had a small one, I think last November. She complained of having chest pains one morning, but she was quite recovered by the time that she came into the office." He threw a long glance at Mitchell. "You should have a telephone."

"We—can't afford one."

The doctor's hand was back on Priscilla's wrist, he did not look up as he went on calmly. "I should think that if you saved Belle Trune's fee, you'd have enough to pay for a party line."

Mitchell colored a deep shade of red. A large vein standing out on his forehead, he clenched his fists, then turned to the window.

Priscilla began to moan but did not open her eyes. Mitchell and the doctor carried the limp form laboriously up to her bedroom. "He's giving her a hypo, Aunt Letty. She should be in the hospital in Enid when she can be moved," Mitchell said from the landing.

Letty waited until the doctor came downstairs. "Whatever she needs, send me the bill," she said.

"She must have nurses around the clock if she is going to pull through this time." He shook his gray-orange head and looked around the house, turning up his nose. "A housekeeper is slso sorely needed," he observed, "this place *smells!*"

"I'll see to it, Doctor." Letty replied. It was the first time that she had been in the house since 1916. Each piece of solid oak furniture that Edward had made by hand was extraordinarily beautiful. She rubbed the surface of the buffet and a thick, black, sticky soot came off on her fingers. She shook her head, and started to work. Five hours later the kitchen was spotless. When Mitchell came in from the field, he looked around the room with amazement. "Aunt Letty, you didn't have to do this!"

"Oh yes, I did." She paused. "The nurse is upstairs. Your mother must not be disturbed. She was able to take a bit of soup this afternoon. Now, I want you to go outside and fasten back the shutters on every window downstairs. Tomorrow you should get the ladder and fix the ones upstairs. We've got to have some light in this house." She paused. "Also, you'll be coming over to our house to eat."

"Yes, *Ma'am!*"

Three days later, with the help of a hired girl, the Heron clapboard was spotlessly clean; even the old lace curtains had been washed, stretched on frames to dry, and rehung. True, some of the threads hung loose, and some of the netting had rotted away, but at least, Letty thought, they were *clean.*

* * *

Shortly after midnight, Priscilla opened her eyes. At first she did not know where she was, then her ears became accustomed to the pumping sound of the oil wells. She must think about getting up soon to start the morning chores. The bread would have to be punched down for breakfast rolls, vegetables peeled and sliced for dinner, the kitchen floor swept and mopped. Oh, she was weary, so weary! And her solar plexus ached from those three miscarriages. Then she remembered that the years had betrayed her. She could stay in bed all day if she wanted to; there were no chores to be done . . . There was a movement by the window; someone was lighting the gas lights. "Who is it?" Priscilla asked.

"Just Nurse Balter, Mrs. Pederson," a quiet voice answered.

"What are you doing here? I never have help when I'm sick, why even when I had Mitchell . . . old Doc Burgen . . ."

Nurse Balter looked down into her face. "Go back to sleep, Mrs. Pederson. You've been dreaming, that's all!"

"I'm not dreaming!" Priscilla replied peevishly. "I wish they'd shut the pumps down. They're pounding in my ears." She began to cry.

The nurse left the room and returned with Mitchell.

"What's wrong, Mother?" he asked.

"Have them shut down the wells. The noise is driving me crazy." Silently the tears escaped from her eyelids and ran down her cheeks on either side of the pillow. Then suddenly she hunched forward, clutching at her chest, tearing the nightgown with her ragged nails. Quickly, the nurse admonished, "*Open your mouth!*" and thrust a tablet under her tongue. "Now, be quiet," she said soothingly. "The pain will pass." She threw a frantic look at Mitchell and mouthed the words "Doctor Shaeffer."

He ran down the stairs, two at a time, and used the telephone that Letty had had installed. After he reached the doctor, he called Letty, then retraced his steps to his mother's room.

426

When Letty entered, Priscilla was lying flat on the bed, as stiff as an alabaster statue. Letty looked down into the pinched, pain-filled face. It took all of her strength to smile. "Hello, Prissy," she said softly.

Hate filled Priscilla's eyes. "Get out of my sight!" She brought her hands up to her ears to blot out the sound of the oil wells furiously pumping in the background. The noise was vibrating through her body; there seemed to be a great weight on her chest; breathing was difficult. "You've come to laugh at me . . . because you've struck it rich . . . while I'm here on this goddam claim as poor as a church mouse."

The burning increased in her solar plexus. "I can't have another miscarriage, Letty," she wailed. "Doc Burgen said I'd die." Her face softened, then grew hard again. "There's nothing wrong with *you*, Letty; *you* never had any female complaints . . ." Her lips curled. "I want to be left alone." Her eyes narrowed. "You're not welcome here." She tried to get up and the tablet fell out of her mouth. She clutched at her breast in agony, then went limp and fell back on the pillow. Her face, was a pale, pasty gray. Slowly her lips turned blue. She gasped, and while the nurse hovered over her frantically, a fluttering noise escaped her throat.

Doctor Schaeffer arrived at Priscilla's bedside completely out of breath. His bag was already open and a needle prepared. He made the injection quickly, then placed his hand on her wrist. Her face was now a mottled blue. "I'm too late," he sighed. "She's gone."

Mitchell and Letty sat beside the bed. The doctor had closed Priscilla's eyes, and her face was erased of tiny, interchanging lines of age. Aside from her gray hair, she looked young and almost pretty. Her complexion was waxy now, as if she had never been out in the sun. Letty could not cry.

In the car on the way home, she sighed. "I feel so empty, Bos. I've just lost the best friend I ever had."

He looked at her strangely. "She was a tortured woman."

"Yes and no," Letty replied slowly. "You didn't know her the way that I did. We've been acquainted since 1877. Sixty-three years is a long time. She was, in a way, my counterpart. Now, it's as if part of me is dead."

"The very sad part of all of it," Bosley replied quietly, "is the ring."

"The ring?"

"Oh? Didn't the doctor tell you? One hand was clutched peculiarly, and when he opened the palm, he saw that her huge diamond wedding ring had worn itself down into the flesh. She could have sold that bauble for a fortune any time she wanted to!"

Letty looked off into space. "But she couldn't, of course, because you see, Bos, that's all she had left . . ."

32

Requiem

Bosley drove the new 1941 Lincoln into the barnyard.

He found Letty in the pecan orchard. "Here," he said, "let me knock down some nuts for you. I've been in the mood for pecan pie for months."

"Me, too!" Letty exclaimed, holding out her apron.

He hit the tree with a branch and laughed. "Here we are, Letty, working hard, when we should be back in Washington in the big house with servants to do the work. What are we still doing here in Angel?"

"Living!" she replied. "Just living out our time."

He shook his head. "Let's go back and open up the big place. Our grandchildren and their children should have room to roam about . . ."

"They have that here," Letty answered. "No, Bos, this is really home. I think kids should have the joy of visiting us on the farm. We still have the same values. We've got two hired girls, that's plenty of help. And our friends are here, the Dices and the Stevens and the Chenovicks. We're all growing old together. That's a particular joy. You have the Heron Oil Company, but I know you don't want to retire just yet."

He shook his head. "No, the company's still growing. It's an exciting period, with credit cards and big advertisements in the national magazines. Luke is so good at promotion, and with the new refinery in Enid—"

"Oh," Letty said. "Speaking about Enid, we must run over to Mitchell's store. I need two kitchen chairs rebuilt."

429

"You can't do that, Letty. Mitchell's factory only makes new pieces."

"Of course, but after his dad's original designs. The foreman in the shop can fix my chairs all right." She paused. "Isn't it a stroke of luck that Prissy had kept trunks full of those old drawings in the attic all those years?"

He nodded. "And it's stranger still that the money from Manford's wedding ring started Mitchell in the furniture business? I'm glad that he's amounting to something at last. Edward would be very proud."

Letty smiled. "He would be that." She took his hand and they walked back to the house together, her apron filled with pecans. "You know, Bos, we haven't had the family home for a long time. I was just thinking the other day that Particia Anne will be eighteen in December. We could have a party for her—not really a coming-out party, but a kind of three-generation party."

"That's a good idea," he agreed, "a family reunion. Let's send the invitations out early."

On September 16th, the forty-eighth anniversary of the opening of the Cherokee Strip, Letty in calico with a poke bonnet and Bosley in chaps and ten-gallon hat drove the spring wagon near the head of the parade, just behind the mayor and his family in a covered wagon. The original settlers, some enfeebled and near senility, rode stage coaches, buggies and traps. The parade was very long and the crowds were enormous. Letty looked at the Indians selling their wares in front of the tipis erected on the courthouse lawn, and she was very moved. What would happen to the parade when all the settlers had passed on to greater glory? Would succeeding generations haul out their mothers' cotton dresses and their fathers' chaps and spurs to ride in the procession, or would September 16th fade into a vaguely remembered holiday?

' The telephone was ringing as they came into the house. "Yes?" Bosley said into the mouthpiece. "Oh, I'm so sorry. Yes, Luke, I'll come at once." He hung up the receiver and turned to Letty. "Armbuster passed away this afternoon of a massive stroke. Funeral will be

430

held on Thursday in Washington. He was sharp and bright right up to the end. Just before the last seizure, he looked up at his nurse and remarked: 'Remind me to tell Luke to get a letter out to the board. We've got to get the polymerization plant to produce 100 octane aviation gasoline completed as soon as possible. I don't think they can stop Hitler, and if Roosevelt gets us into the war, it's going to be fought in the air!' He might have something there, my dear. We *will* get that plant finished!"

Letty put her arm around his waist. "Do you want me to go with you to Washington?"

"Would you? Old J.C. meant a lot to me. Our acquaintanceship goes back to Beaumont, Texas in 1901, when I was just an upstart geologist. He was a brilliant man who will be missed." He paused. "Let's drive to Oklahoma City and take a plane to Washington."

He came up behind her and pressed against her buttocks. "Let's go upstairs," he whispered.

She smiled and turned in his arms. "Yes, we must pack for the trip."

"Well, that, too."

"Bosley, are you trying to tell me that you are feeling amorous?"

"What a very nice word for it!"

She laughed and took his hand. "You know, Bos, I love you very much. I sometimes think I don't tell you often enough."

"Well, you're still the apple of my eye."

"Then you're not thinking about trading me in for a newer model?" she quipped.

He shook his head and smiled. "You're quality built. The new models are just thrown together. You might say that they don't have *staying power*!"

Later, he made love to her, slowly and tenderly, and with great affection. Suddenly, her mind went back forty-eight years to that time when the Herons and she had slept in the covered wagon when they had gone into Enid to register their claims.

In her grief and despair, she had never understood why Edward had made love to Priscilla, with Luke buried that very day. It had seemed monstrous and barbaric then. Now, it was perfectly clear—Edward had needed the emotional as well as the physical release. It was the same with Bosley now. His great friend had died, and his emotions could not find release in any other way. She sighed gently, looking up into his care-worn face, and tried to remember what Luke had looked like. If he had lived, would he resemble Bosley now? Then time was swept away as she rose up to meet her husband and lover, and she returned to the present, glowing and alive, every muscle of her body responding to his marvelous lovemaking. Ah, those youngsters who lay together in such passionate embraces, treating their bodies as if time was a fleeting thing—didn't they know that feelings of love went on and on, and never entirely stopped? By 1941 standards, Bosley and she were old, and yet inside, they were young—perhaps not filled with the quickening joy of youth, but young just the same . . .

Luke met them at National Airport in Washington and drove them to the First Baptist Church, which was filled with middle-aged to elderly business men in gray suits, there to pay homage to a business leader of wide and revered reputation. A man like Armbuster had few close friends and his family had long been put to rest. The service was as cut and dried and as acerbic as the old man himself. Letty doubted that the minister even knew him.

Afterwards, there was a luncheon at the National Hotel, a boring affair attended by only half of those who had attended the services. A knot of men in line for the buffet were speaking about the new motion picture, *The Grapes of Wrath*. "It's a devastating film about the migrant workers," one of the men was saying, "and it should be seen by everyone."

"I read the book, but I haven't seen the movie," replied a gray-haired man with a drooping mustache, "but Steinbeck's a genius. I really felt sorry for those Okies."

Letty turned to the men. "You must remember, gentlemen, Steinbeck wrote about a very small segment of farmers from the Panhandle of Oklahoma. However, poor people from Arkansas, Missouri, and Texas were all grouped together and called 'Okies'. The number of

432

actual migrant workers from Oklahoma is quite small."

The man with the mustache smiled. "You seem to be an authority, madame. I'm sorry, I didn't get your full name."

"My full name is Letty Heron Story Trenton, and I'm an *Okie!*"

After a few days in Washington, visiting Luke and Jeanette and seeing a few business people, the Trentons returned to Angel. Then Bosley left for Guymon to conduct another class in new soil conservation techniques. There had been some rain, and the terraced fields were flecked with green. Farmers with government loans were beginning to make a comeback from the earlier days of the depression, and were cultivating their fields with tractors and new equipment to leave more ground cover to prevent further erosion. Dust storms were becoming less and less frequent. Bosley came back with a jubilant air, and was met by an enthusiastic Letty.

While Oklahoma still bathed in the glow of Indian summer, the old clapboard was repainted inside and out and fresh wallpaper hung throughout the house; furniture was reupholstered and a new stove and refrigerator installed in the kitchen, along with new commodes and tubs in the bathrooms. "All of this is so expensive," Letty complained.

"We can afford it," Bosley laughed.

When all was in readiness, Luke, Jeanette, and Luke Three arrived and parked their new cream-colored Rolls Royce in the barnyard. A week later, Sarah and Patricia Anne came in on the afternoon train and Mitchell drove in from Enid. Clement and his band arrived in a large bus, having made the trip in eight hours from Kansas City, where they had finished an engagement at the Wyandotte Hotel. Letty had arranged to accommodate the band members at the Stevens Hotel, which had just added the fifth story.

The house was filled to the rooftops with family members and Clement's 'relatives'—the members of the orchestra. All the leaves had been put into the dining room table, and several borrowed card tables were set

433

up in the living room. Even the kitchen table had been clothed with white for the buffet of fried chicken, mashed potatoes, and all the trimming. And the dessert, as Letty told Fontine when she asked if she could have her hired girls to help wash dishes, of course was Angel cake.

Looking over the table arrangements, she was reminded of the time in London when she had entertained the Hoovers and the Motleys, her first social triumph. After dinner, as Clement played the Grieg Piano Concerto and Letty shivered—the past was very near, and she had the eerie feeling that perhaps Edward Heron and George Story were present in some ethereal form. If it were possible from that great expanse of the "other side," the powers that be would surely let them return to see their children grown up and with children of their own.

The next morning, she telephoned the guests and cautioned, "Please don't show up all at once, because we'll never be able to fit all of you into the house. Come from two to ten." Then she added with a laugh, "I should have had this family reunion in the summer so that we could use the lawn."

The orchestra, crowded like peas and onions in a dish, set up their music stands in the living room, which only left ten feet of space in front of the doors into the hallway. "No one can say that we don't have a full house!" Letty exclaimed as the doorbell rang. John and Fontine Dice were the first to arrive. "Boy," Fontine exclaimed, "this is a regular blowout!" She tugged at her corset, which fitted snugly over her ample frame, and accepted a glass of punch. "My stars, this is delicious!"

John took a long swallow and smacked his lips. "If I didn't know you were temperance, Letty, I'd swear something had been added to the punch.

"It's vodka," she announced with raised brows. "The members of the band smuggled in a whole case."

"You didn't protest?" John asked in wonderment.

"What good would it do? Younger people today like a bit of zip—and why not?" Then she left to greet Reverend Haskell and Thelma, who came in, arm in arm, both of them showing their age.

"I wonder, Jaundice," Fontine whispered, "*who* is holding up *whom*?"

"Fourteen," John Dice admonished quietly. "Hold your tongue."

"Do you suppose," she went on recklessly, "that at their age they're still 'doing it'?"

"No more punch for you, Fourteen—it's obviously gone to your head!" John Dice looked at her sternly, "But to answer your question, I don't think they ever did!"

Fontine hiccuped twice. "All right, Jaundice. If I get to acting up again, you've got my full permission to knock me silly!"

Bella and Torgo Chenovick were next to arrive. Bella was as cheerful as always, and the dimples in her cheeks had only grown deeper with age. She looked ten years younger than her seventy years. Torgo seemed robust and healthy. He handed Letty his violin. "Here, put this away somewhere. With all of these professional musicians, I won't dare play. I didn't know Clement was bringing the whole orchestra!"

Belle Trune and Rochelle Patterson arrived together. Belle, Letty observed, looked quite respectable, with no makeup, but the retired school teacher had taken to darkening her brows and wearing lipstick. Wonders never ceased. The Bakers and the Stevenses were next, and immediately struck up a conversation with Mitchell, who sported a new gray plaid suit and looked very prosperous and distinguished.

The last to arrive was a tall man whom Letty did not immediately recognize in the huge throng that filled the house. Then she opened her mouth with surprise and made her way among the guests to the door. "Oh, Sam!" she cried, kissing his cheek. "I'm so glad that you could come. When we didn't hear from you . . ."

He nodded, and she saw that he had aged well. His dark skin was set off by snowy white hair, but his eyes were piercing and bright—just as she remembered.

"Your invitation finally arrived, having been sent on to my new address. I'm retired now and live in Barbados," he said in his peculiarly high-pitched voice, "I have a house by the sea." He paused. "And lest you think that I am doing nothing with my time, I'm writing a book."

"A medical book?"

He shook his head. "Not really, although medicine does play a part. I'm writing my memoirs."

She flushed with pleasure. "I'm so glad." She paused and looked over the room at the people they both knew so well, and grew worried. "But Sam, will you be able to tell . . . I mean . . ." She stopped in confusion.

He smiled softly. "Yes, lady, I will tell everything as it happened. Your family played such a part in my early life. May I have your permission to speak about those years when Oklahoma was not yet a state? I'll need a lot of information from you."

She nodded numbly. "Tell it," she replied slowly, "tell all of it . . . So many of the original settlers are gone. Leona Barrett left everything to the conservatory of music; Reginald Savor, who married Mary Darth, has been dead for years; and Mary herself has met her reward. Edward Heron and George Story, and those last terrible years that Priscilla endured . . ." She looked at him out of the corner of her eyes. "You're a very brave man, Sam, to go back over those times, but . . . yes, you must tell the truth." She paused. "I suppose it's primarily a story of triumph over adversity."

He opened his eyes wide. "Oh, no, lady, it's a story of courage."

Mitchell lounged with his plate of food near the staircase and talked with Clement. "You know, with all of your classical background, as a kid, I never figured that you'd end up in popular music."

"Neither did I, Mitch. But I'm very happy. The discipline's quite different. Looking back, I don't think I could've cut the concert stage route anyway." He took a forkful of baked beans and smacked his lips. "There is nothing quite like Okie beans, is there?"

Mitchell looked at him sharply. *"Okie?"*

Clement smiled loosely. "It took me twenty years to be able to call myself an 'Okie'. Funny how labels stick, and all because some people in the Dust Bowl migrated to the Pacific Coast in the thirties."

" 'Okie' became a synonym for 'trash'." Clement

nodded. "It's different now. But when I was in the service, they called me 'Breedy'—that hurt for a while until I got used to it. Being a mixed blood never had any significance here in Oklahoma and I didn't feel differently inside, but the army boys sure picked me out. To them I was foreign, even if my people *were* here first!"

"It's strange," Luke put in, pausing with a plate of food near the doorway to the living room, "how our values change when we grow up. We somehow don't get all of the things accomplished that were so important to us as kids. The first thing you learn is *compromise*."

"You both learned your lessons early," Mitchell replied softly. "It took me a long time—middle age."

Luke nodded. "Yet you did what you wanted to do for a long time. Remember, you told me once that you didn't have any ambition and that above all you didn't want to get into the furniture business?"

Mitchell shrugged his shoulders. "Yet I'm really happy for the first time in years. I have some of the best craftsmen in the country working for me. I'm not artistic or very clever with my hands, but I know and appreciate good furniture, and what's more, I can sell it. Then, too, it's making the name of Heron important in the field again." He looked up and smiled. "Of course, your company doesn't hurt a bit, with that blue bird painted all over the country on everything from rubber tires to service stations!"

"I think that would have pleased my Dad more than anything, from what Mother says. Too bad he died before I was born. I guess he didn't even know that I was on the way." Luke smiled crookedly, very much like Letty. "But he picked the ground that contained the anticline. Maybe he was the best one of all, because he set out to do something—make a claim—and did far more than that—he set his family up for generations." He looked from Clement to Mitchell. "And none of us have done that!"

"Uncle Luke must have been a helluva man. But my father made headway, too," Clement replied, "even though he thought he didn't."

"And," Mitchell replied gently, "he fought against great odds."

437

"But the legend that has grown up about George Story among the Indians is far different than what actually occurred. Now he's rated with John Roth, Redbird Smith, and Pleasant Porter."

Luke nodded. "But I think if he imparted anything to us as kids, it was the feeling that what was really important in life was the fighting spirit. You can't win every battle, but he said to take joy in the battles that you *did* win! And then have no regrets. Live and die with a kind of dignity."

"Talking about dignity," Sarah said, looking down from the top of the stairs. "All of you boys are hunched over, with terrible posture, talking a lot of philosophical mish-mash with plates of cold food in your hands. For heaven's sake, go into the kitchen and get some warm food!"

Clement looked up sheepishly. "Go on about your business, squaw!" he exclaimed with a laugh. "You know we boys haven't been together since we've been grown up!"

"I'd say, offhand, my brave husband," she retorted with a grin, "that you are all still behaving like adolescents."

Luke looked up. "You're right, Sarah, you're right. We have regressed to childhood."

Mitchell added, "And, we like it!" A light came into his eyes. "You know, I think we all *like* each other! As kids we were so different, but now that we're in our forties . . ."

". . . And fifties," Luke added.

". . . We see each other differently," Mitchell finished.

Clement nodded. "We've all got to see each other more often in the future. It's ridiculous, each of us going our different ways. We're still a family unit. I think some of our heritage should rub off on our children and, in turn, *their* children."

Luke nodded. "If this family reunion has accomplished nothing else, I think it has shown us that when it's all said and done, all the fame and all the money in the world is just crap unless there is some *feeling* underneath."

At that moment the sound of a lone clarinet wailed from the living room. "Oh, the band is getting restless," Clement laughed. "I'd better get back, they want to get finished here. To them, it's just another play date."

Luke grinned. "Too bad The Widows isn't open, otherwise the boys could all get laid tonight!"

"You know," replied Clement, "I was just thinking the same thing!"

The orchestra began a loud swing tune, then Luke whispered in Clement's ear. "Would you do me a favor? I've always wanted to conduct."

Clement grinned and handed his baton to his brother, then nodded to the members of the band. The moment Luke raised the stick, the orchestra segued into an ear-shattering series of disconnected notes, ending with huge raspberry, to the delight of the guests. Luke laughed loudest of all.

At ten-fifteen, the party still going in full sway, Letty sought out Bosley. "If you don't mind dear, I'm going to steal away upstairs." She smiled crookedly. "It's been a long day and I'm tired. Let the children enjoy themselves a while longer."

"I'll go up, too," he replied, "even watching all this jitterbugging wears me out!"

He took her arm and they went slowly up the stairs.

As they undressed, the swing music stopped. There was a pause, then they heard Clement making an announcement. Then came the unmistakable sound of Torgo tuning up his old violin in the near-stillness of the house. They got into bed and had just turned out the lights when they heard Clement start the old cowboy song that stirred up so many memories . . .

> Come along, boys, and listen to my
>   tale,
> I'll tell you of my troubles on the
>   old Chisholm Trail.
> Coma ti yi youpy, youpa ya,
>   Youpa ya . . .

As the long narrative song continued, Letty was pleased to hear that Clement was singing all the verses.

She took Bosley's hand in hers over his thigh, and thought about all of the trials and tribulations over the last fifty years. "I think you should retire," she said softly, "and let Luke take over." She paused. "Didn't you somehow get the feeling tonight, that we really are not needed the way we used to be?"

After a while, he answered. "You're right, my dear. There are no real challenges left any more—not like the old days. This is a good time for me to get out of the harness and put myself out to pasture, so to speak. No one needs my particular expertise anymore."

She kissed his cheek. "Goodnight."

"Goodnight, my dear."

Letty turned on her side, and the last thing that she saw before falling asleep was the bedside calendar, which was bathed in pale moonlight.

The date was December 6, 1941.